lost ranch
books

XS

www.lostranchbooks.com

WHITE WINTER

To Do Justice

Laurie Marr Wasmund

The White Winter Trilogy, of which this book is a part,
is a work of fiction. Apart from the well-known actual
people, events, and locales that figure in the narrative, all
names, characters, places, and incidents are the products
of the author's imagination or are used fictitiously. Any
resemblance to current events or locales, or to persons
living or dead, is entirely coincidental.

Front cover photograph:
Henry Halgate Storm and John Marr, 1919
Wollaston, Massachusetts
Personal Collection of Author

Back cover photograph:
No Man's Land
Burean of War Photographs

Cover design by Laurie Marr Wasmund

Published in the United States by lost ranch books
www.lostranchbooks.com
ISBN 978-0-9859675-3-6

He has showed you, O man, what is good;
and what does the Lord require of you
but to do justice, and to love kindness,
and to walk humbly with your God?
Micah 6:8

ONE

The sun glittered on the golden dome of the State Capitol, and a cloudless sky carried the promise of spring. The warmth felt luxurious, almost sinful, after the chilly, lightless room where Kathleen spent her days. She tugged at her starched collar and thin tie. Around her, the crowd whistled and cheered in an ear-splitting thunder, and children raced up and down the sidewalks, handing out American flags mounted on sticks. Kathleen took one and twirled it in her fingers. "Thank you!" she called, but her voice was lost in the din.

Along Broadway, the Denver Municipal Band stepped smartly, tootling the songs of John Philip Sousa. They were followed by the aging members of the Grand Army of the Republic, seated in open automobiles, their uniforms as faded and colorless as their hair.

A cadre of Rocky Mountain Rangers, with pennants flying, rode down the street. The horses bore saddles with silver buckles, and the riders wore matching uniforms with scarves of red. The lead horsemen carried the American and Colorado state flags. "We'll go to war for Uncle Sam," one of the riders shouted.

Kathleen stopped, her love of horses overtaking her. She longed to sketch the well-groomed animals with their glistening coats and ornate bridles, but the other girls—recently liberated from the typing pool at Graves Oil—hurried down the street, eager to take full advantage of the two-hour lunch break they had been given.

"We must find a seat up close." Annabel Croft said. "I don't want to miss Mr. Graves!"

"Or his boots!" Mavis Wilson added.

"His boots?" Kathleen asked.

"Yes, his boots," Mary Jane Grayson said impatiently. "He wears the most magnificent cowboy boots—"

"He has them made just for him," Annabel added.

"He must have a pair for each day of the year," Mavis said. "Oh, he has red ones and blue, and one pair has golden toe tips—"

"Made out of real gold?" Kathleen asked.

"Maybe," Mavis said. "Why not?"

"That doesn't sound very practical. Boots get muddy and worse. There's manure—"

"You're such a country mouse!" Mary Jane scoffed. "Mr. Graves doesn't do that. Besides, he's rich. He doesn't have to be practical."

Kathleen turned away. She was the newest, and at eighteen, the youngest of the girls, and they rarely let her forget it. For her benefit, they painted Graves Oil as the best—jobs there were the most highly coveted in Denver, the pay was the highest, and the treatment the fairest. Kathleen knew most of it was true. Even the office building on 17th Street, where the words GRAVES OIL were etched across the imposing stone entrance, was magnificent. The building was of polished granite, with chiseled cornices and the letter "G" prominently engraved over each arching window. A modern revolving door led into a lobby decorated with brocaded couches, silver standing ashtrays, mahogany end tables, and Chinese rugs. The sheen of the marble floor was so unblemished that it looked as if it had never been trod upon by human feet.

And perhaps it hadn't, Kathleen thought, for the main door was not the door through which the employees entered every morning. They checked in at a door in the alley, where a bank of time clocks registered their arrival.

"Sometimes we type letters to the Hyer Boot Company in Kansas when Mr. Graves doesn't like a pair he's received or they don't fit or something," Mary Jane said. "We're all envious of the one who gets to type it."

"His handwriting is so messy!" Annabel complained. "I don't think he had penmanship in school—"

"And once he even came down to the basement!" Mavis said. "We all fell in love. But you know what? Up close he has a scar on his face—"

"From dueling, I bet," Mary Jane said. "Over the love of a beautiful woman."

"Maybe the woman gave it to him herself," Kathleen suggested.

Mary Jane eyed her with disdain. "Just wait until you see him! He's like a hero from a romance novel—tall and blond and as good-looking as Douglas Fairbanks."

"Better even," Mavis said. "Like the Arrow Shirt Collar Man."

"Which one?" Kathleen asked.

"Does it matter?"

"How old is he, anyway?" Kathleen asked. "The Arrow Shirt Collar Men are all young."

Mary Jane barked a sharp laugh. "I'd say he's no more than thirty. You don't think we'd care anything about an old man, do you?"

"To Kathleen, he is an old man!" Mavis screeched. "She's just a baby!"

Annabel pointed to the grassy lawn near the left-hand side of the Capitol steps. "Let's sit over there."

She and Mavis carried a bulging picnic basket between them. Together, they spread a blanket on the ground, and the girls sat, careful to tuck their black skirts neatly beneath them. Just as carefully, they removed their jackets and laid them aside. Their supervisor, Miss Crawley, despised sloppiness.

Mary Jane fished in the basket for a chicken leg. "I've heard that Mr. Graves' parents live in a mansion with twenty-seven rooms, and that he himself lives in a house twice that size. He has two grand pianos in his parlor."

Mavis struggled. "Twenty-seven times two, that's . . .?"

"Fifty-four," Kathleen offered.

"Fifty-four! Why would you need fifty-four rooms?"

"So that his maids and cooks and butlers all have something to do," Mary Jane said. "I bet he even has someone to dress and undress him!"

"What I'd give to be that rich!" Annabel swooned. "All the things I'd buy!"

"What I'd give to undress him!" Mary Jane crowed.

"Mary Jane, you are naughty!" Mavis choked and doubled over. Annabel slapped her back.

There was no escaping the talk about him, Kathleen knew. Jim Graves was famous—at least in Colorado. The headlines of *The Denver Post* and the *Rocky Mountain News* and even the contentious *Denver Express* lauded him on a regular basis: "James A. Graves Gives Another $25,000 to Preparedness Effort," and in smaller print, "Oilman's Generosity Comes on Heels of His First Donation." The business pages quoted him on matters of oil exploration, conservation of fuel and resources, and the military industrialization of America's factories. The society pages reported sightings: on the golf course near Seven Falls in Colorado Springs, at the hot springs vapor caves in Glenwood Springs, at the opera in Central City or a society ball at the Denver Country Club.

She smiled. Seaney—who had no time for pretentiousness— had taken to calling Mr. Graves "His Majesty, The Honorable James A. Graves" when they spoke of him.

"Isn't that Miss Crawley?" Mary Jane asked suddenly.

The girls turned as one. Near the far side of the steps, Miss Crawley stood with a group of women dressed in black. Beside her, two women held a banner that proclaimed, "National Woman's Party." Others posed with signs that read: "PRESIDENT WILSON, HAVE YOU FORGOTTEN THE MOTHERS OF AMERICA?" and "20,000,000 AMERICAN WOMEN ARE NOT SELF-GOVERNED."

Mavis read the last message aloud. "What does that mean?"

"Women can't vote," Annabel supplied.

"We can vote," Mavis argued. "My mom has voted since I can remember."

"We can in Colorado. But not all women in the United States can vote."

"Oh, well, that's just stupid."

As they laughed, Kathleen's attention was caught by a white-haired woman who was speaking with Miss Crawley. The woman's hair was cropped short, as if she had gone to a barber shop, but it framed her handsome face in a simple, commanding curve. Her eyes were light-colored and almond-shaped, giving her an otherworldly beauty. She wore a man's jacket and a pair of trousers that might have belonged to her son. Picking up her pencil, Kathleen started to sketch.

"They look like a sour bunch to me," Mavis said.

"That's why Miss Crawley is over there," Mary Jane said.

The girls laughed again, as Kathleen drew. Miss Crawley demanded dignity, obedience, and absolutely perfect typing from her employees. On Kathleen's first day, a stack of handwritten documents three inches high lay to one side of her machine. Each time the heap began to disappear, Miss Crawley appeared with a ruler and replenished the pile so that it still measured three inches by lunchtime.

"How do you ever get your work done?" Kathleen asked Mary Jane as they walked outside for lunch. Her fingertips felt numb from pounding at the stiff keys all morning, and pain shot up her wrists to her elbows. She could scarcely bend her fingers around the handle of her lunch pail.

"You don't," Mary Jane replied. "You just keep typing until your fingers are so tired you can't uncurl them. The first week I was here, I thought I would turn into a monkey." She cramped her fingers and crossed her eyes. "I look just like old Crawley, don't I?"

"How long have you been working here?"

"Five years, but it's never been so busy!" Mary Jane danced ahead. "Mr. Graves is determined to find every drop of oil in America! And he always gets just what he wants—"

"Five years!" The words slipped from Kathleen's lips. "Believe me, I won't be doing this in five years!"

Mary Jane's spirits had dimmed. "That's what I thought. I was sure I'd be married and a mother by now. But I don't even have a steady beau."

But that wasn't what Kathleen had meant. Not at all.

She finished sketching the head and shoulders of the woman with the light eyes and started a portrait of her supervisor. Miss Crawley's occupation had stripped the far-sightedness from her eyes and the color from her cheeks, yet she had an abundance of reddish-brown hair that she piled in intricate waves on top of her head. In the sunlight of this spring day, it shone a burnished gold.

A chorus of schoolgirls ascended the Capitol steps. Red, white and blue sashes angled from their left shoulders to their right hips, and one young girl was dressed as the Statue of Liberty. Once they were in place, a number of state and local dignitaries—including Mayor Speer of Denver and Governor Gunter of Colorado—gave welcome speeches through a shared megaphone. By the end, the Status of Liberty's arm was shaking as she struggled to hold the torch aloft. Still, she managed to lift it high as the schoolgirls and spectators said the Pledge of Allegiance and joined with the Denver Municipal Band in "The Star Spangled Banner."

Once the audience sat down, Kathleen quickly sketched the girl, trying to capture her expression of physical exhaustion and mental determination. Just as she was about to start a fresh page, Mary Jane said, "Look, there he is! Isn't he swell?"

Kathleen's attention turned to the steps. Megaphone in hand, Jim Graves had moved out from behind the podium, evidently intent on speaking without using notes. His face was well put together, with a generous mouth and strong chin, and his blonde hair waved just enough to please. He stood with an ease that made Kathleen think that he might, indeed, be as marvelous as the Arrow Shirt Collar Man.

"I can't see his boots," Annabel complained. "What do they look like?"

"They're—" Mavis started. "Oh, just have Kathleen draw them for you."

"Would you, Kathleen?"

"Of course." The boots were a voluptuous dove gray, with ribbons of red and blue that twined up the sides and ended at a white star. Mr. Graves had tucked his pant legs inside the boots to show off the beautiful workmanship.

As she sketched, he began to speak into the megaphone.

"Let me tell you a story about why the Preparedness Effort is so important," he said. "In 1914, France was fighting for her life, sacrificing legions of her sons each day. Yet the Germans, with their tanks and flamethrowers and axes that crush bones and skulls, could not be stopped. Nothing stood in their way—not women, or children, or other innocents who were mercilessly slaughtered for the sole reason that they were Belgian or French—and certainly not the modest farms and villages that lay in the green valleys of the Marne. They were knocked down and poisoned by deadly gases, the crops and animals stolen. Everything was destroyed, only the scorched earth left behind."

Kathleen left off sketching, caught up in his words. When he spoke, his lean body solidified, growing wonderfully powerful and lithe, and his words came in a sonorous, easy song.

He lifted the megaphone again. "On the Germans marched toward Paris, pouring down bombs and destruction on the French capital and its noble citizens. The French Army struggled, its reinforcements too distant to save the Eiffel Tower or Notre Dame. But the French people had different plans. The call went out, and the citizens responded. Thousands of French soldiers were rushed to the front in taxicabs and automobiles, enabling the French to turn the tide and save France from desecration and tyranny."

During a dramatic pause, he gauged the crowd with eyes that were as brilliant and blue as the sky behind him.

"Now, you know oil as kerosene and tires and cold cream for your face. But I and others like me know it as one of the most valuable materials that a country or population can have. Think of it this way. Where would the French have been without gasoline? Moreover, what would have happened had the citizens not been prepared? If they hadn't stockpiled fuel or kept the streets in repair? It wasn't the generals and politicians who saved Paris. It wasn't the cavalry or bombs or cannons. It was common people—cab and truck drivers, mechanics, and the petroleum pumpers, *people like you*, doing what they could to save their country from the German scourge. And now, Americans must rise to the challenge in exactly the same way. We must save and conserve and stockpile. We must assist as we can, where we can, to the best of our abilities. In this way—and only this way—we will keep our nation and the world safe for democracy!"

The crowd gave a great roar. Mavis, Annabel and Mary Jane clapped, bumping shoulders as they rose to their feet. Kathleen stood, her sketchbook in her hands. There was so much energy within him. Something so bright, so intense—it was both frightening and exhilarating. What kind of man carried so much grace?

"See?" Mary Jane whispered in her ear. "I knew you'd like him! You should see your face!"

Kathleen watched him as he came down the steps. Donation cup in hand, he moved through the crowd. When he came closer, she could see the fine line of white scar that ran from his right temple to his jaw.

Spectators swarmed around him, pressing their cash on him.

"For the Preparedness Effort," he said. "Thank you, yes, sir, God bless you, ma'am."

As he approached, Mavis stepped into his path, waving her money in the air. "Mr. Graves! Over here! Please!"

His smile widened. "Ah, the lovely ladies of the typing pool."

"You know us?" Annabel's voice trembled.

"Of course."

Mavis and Annabel eagerly placed their dollars in his cup.

"Thank you, Miss Wilson, thank you, Miss Craft—"

"It's Croft." Annabel protested so quietly that he did not hear her.

"Miss Grayson, and—" He came to Kathleen. "I don't believe I know your name."

"I'm Kathleen O'Doherty."

"How long have you been working at Graves Oil?"

"Two months."

"My, I am behind the times." He nodded toward her sketchbook. "What did you sketch?"

"Show him, Kathleen," Mary Jane urged.

Kathleen cradled the sketchbook against her. It was new, bought from the little that remained of her wages after she paid Aunt Maury her rent and handed over the larger share to her mother. She rarely showed her work to anyone but Seaney or her father. Yet a flighty desire to show Jim Graves came over her, and she offered it to him. He glanced at the sketch of the Statue of Liberty.

"You're very good at detail," he said. "But your proportion is off."

"What?" She jerked the sketchbook up, intent on hiding it again.

He reached over and laid his hand on her wrist, staying it. Even though he wore a soft leather glove, Kathleen felt a spark, as if he had touched an electric coil to her skin. She heard Mary Jane gasp, open-mouthed and jealous, and saw Mavis clutch Mary Jane's arm, as if she might topple. Annabel leaned forward, squinting, her mouth open in a surprised "oh."

"Have you ever thought of this?" he asked. "Some of the great artists used grids—something like chess boards—to block out their sketches. The most beautiful cathedrals in Rome were painted grid by grid, after the artist's sketches. You don't think Michelangelo did it from scratch, do you?"

She knew nothing of Michelangelo or great cathedrals or Rome. But Mr. Graves had peeled off the glove of his right hand and was reaching for her sketchbook. Holding out one hand, he asked, "May I? And your pencil, too?"

She hesitated before placing the pencil on his palm. A thick, ropy callus ran up the center. He glanced at her, and she realized her rudeness. Quickly, she gave him the pencil.

He braced it between his index and middle fingers, as if the swollen palm interfered with his ability to hold it properly. Lightly, he scratched a grid over her drawing of the young girl. "Of course, you'd want your squares to be even. You'd need a straight-edged ruler."

But already, she could see. The girl's hand was too short, and her shoulders too broad. Oh, but it would be easy to fix—

He turned the stub of her pencil between his fingers. "Why don't you get yourself a decent pencil?" Then, studying it, he said, "This is from Graves Oil."

She froze, mortified. "I gather pencils from the trash bins at work."

He laughed. "Do you now? That's resourceful."

She could smell the freshness of his clothing and a dash of cologne. He carried with him the physical presence that he'd exhibited on the stage—strength and capability and something like heat. She took a step backward, dizzy. Only then did she realize he might fire her for stealing.

But he was studying the sketch in the opposite corner of the page. "Isn't this your supervisor, Miss Crawley?" he asked.

Kathleen looked at the sketch of Miss Crawley and the light-eyed woman. She had written a slogan from one of the signs along the edge of the paper: "WAR IS A NOT IN A WOMAN'S VOCABULARY."

"I think so," she said, unwilling to point an accusing finger.

"Don't equivocate, Miss O'Doherty," he said. "It's not an attractive habit."

His scolding stung. "Then, yes, sir, it is."

His brilliant blue gaze fell on her. "Were you at the meeting at the Denver Auditorium last Saturday night?"

"I don't go out at night—"

"It was a meeting to discuss our nation's future," he said. "Ten thousand people attended—men and women—from the Governor down to the dog catcher. All the talk was of the 'shining sword of justice' or the folly of being unprepared for attacks from our enemies. There were all sorts of dignitaries present—let's see—an Episcopal bishop, a Jewish rabbi, a Roman Catholic priest, the president of the university in Boulder, a number of lawyers and businessmen. All of them spoke in favor of our going to war." He glanced in the direction of Miss Crawley and the National Woman's Party, then at the slogan on the page. "Does this statement reflect your sentiments?"

Kathleen swallowed. Papa would tell her to speak her mind. So would Seaney.

"I think President Wilson should keep his promise to the voters," she said firmly. "America should stay neutral. We know what's happened to thousands of British, French and German men and yet—"

"German?"

"Yes, German," she said. "Aren't they just the same as our men and boys? Don't they have mothers and sisters, too?"

"It's not particularly popular to sympathize with the Germans just now."

She bridled again. "My father says the war has been manufactured by the munitions and steel barons. Their sons don't have to fight, because they buy their way out. It's a rich man's war and a poor man's army."

"I see," he said. "Well, Miss O'Doherty, it's true that the Germans are men, just as I am, just as your father is, and that their families endure the same heartbreak and sorrow as the French or English. But we've chosen our side, and must live with it, even though America has just as many ties to Germany as she does to France or Britain. We've a large population of German immigrants living in this country, and until Britain objected, we were selling the Germans cotton to make into uniforms. We could just as easily have sided with Germany."

She drew in a breath. "But what about the terrible things the Germans have done? Starving the Belgians, and using women and children as shields, and—"

"So now you've changed your mind?" he asked. "The Germans aren't just innocent boys pressed into service for the benefit of cruel industrial titans and a despotic leader?"

"No, I haven't . . . well, yes." She closed her mouth, willing herself to stop stammering. At last, she admitted, "I don't know."

"You need to know," he said. "I think we'll be at war within ten days."

"Ten days!"

"Perhaps less." He looked out over the crowd, then met her gaze again. "Have you heard of Plattsburg, Miss O'Doherty?"

"No, sir, I haven't."

"It's a town in northern New York, near Lake Champlain, but more importantly, it's the site of a training camp for those who believe—and have believed for some time—that America will enter the war. Men from all over America have paid out of their own pockets to be trained there in marksmanship, the bayonet, surviving in the trenches, and other skills known to the common soldier. Some of those men have names you might recognize—all three of President

Roosevelt's sons attended and he himself gave the opening address—but many were common businessmen such as myself."

Before she could object that he was hardly common, he said, "You can assure your father that it isn't only the poor who will fight. The chance to give one's life in France will fall to us all, I believe."

He spoke the last words quietly, without a hint of correction or contempt, as if he had confided a sorrowful secret in her. Looking down, he flipped the page of the sketchbook and found the boots that she had dashed off for Annabel. With an incredulous laugh, he asked, "You sketched my boots?"

"It's for Annabel," Kathleen said, thrown off by his change of mood. "Miss Croft. She doesn't see well."

"Well, you've done a fine job of it."

His voice held a sly tone that made her think he was teasing. Did he think of sketching as a sinful waste of time, as Mama did, or as a silly quirk of her nature, as Aunt Maury called it? Even Seaney seemed to think of sketching as something she would outgrow, as she had playing with dolls.

Only Papa understood how much she loved to draw.

He had taught her to love the beauty around her on their ranch south of Denver, which he called Redlands. Offering her a blade of grass, he talked of a thousand shades of green. "Hold it up to the sun," he told her. "You'll see them all if you're patient enough. Are you patient enough?"

"Of course I am!"

"Not moving that fast, you're not. Slow down, Caitlin." Papa called her by the old Irish name. "Take your time. Study. Learn."

Now, someone called, "Mr. Graves, over here!"

Mr. Graves glanced in the direction of the voice. "Well, Miss O'Doherty, I must go. Keep up your sketching. You're really quite good." He handed Kathleen her sketchbook and pulled on his glove. Tipping his hat, he addressed the girls, "Another day, then, ladies."

Then, he was gone, swept into the clamoring crowd. Kathleen watched as he moved easily from group to group, thanking those who gave donations and good-naturedly badgering those who hesitated or refused. At last, she had found someone who wanted to see her work, who didn't think it foolish! Almost as soon as the thought went through her head, she realized that she was unlikely to see Jim Graves again.

Annabel, Mary Jane and Mavis surrounded her.

"What did he say to you?"

"It was so hard to hear—!"

The girls talked about it as they sauntered down 17th Street to Graves Oil. In the Ladies' Employee Washroom, they took their time in rinsing their hands, combing their hair, and primping before the mirror, in no hurry to get back to work. Raynelle, the Negro attendant, waited patiently to give them soap and fresh towels.

"I can't believe Mr. Graves wanted to look at your drawings, Kathleen," Mavis said. "I wish I sketched."

"Next time we'll all take along a pad of paper and a pencil," Mary Jane said. "We'll be a whole gaggle of Van Goghs!"

"Jeepers, Kathleen, what if you and Mr. Graves become friends!" Mavis hollered.

Raynelle chuckled, silencing them all. "No woman is just Jim Graves' friend. Everybody knows that."

Mary Jane shot Raynelle a scalding look, while Mavis and Annabel shared a look of mutual contempt. Kathleen took the towel from Raynelle without looking at her. All this talk, all this excitement! She buried her face in the towel, even though she hadn't washed it. She wanted silence, the chance to think.

Mavis whisked the towel away. "Look! I think Kathleen has a love crush on Mr. Graves!"

"No," she insisted. But one look at her reddened face in the mirror betrayed her.

When at last the girls filed back into the typing room, their giggles stifled by Miss Crawley, who was already stationed behind her desk, Kathleen found a narrow box beside her typewriter.

Inside were one dozen newly-sharpened cedarwood pencils, each one emblazoned with the golden words, "Graves Oil."

TWO

Under the bare bulb in the cellar of Sullivan's Grocery, Sean slammed a right hook into a sack of flour. White swirled through the air, mixing with dust from the tamped dirt floor. The yellowish bulb swung back and forth in the haze. Sean jabbed again.

He fought bare-fisted now, putting away the gloves in the same way that he'd put away his boxing trophies from the Parochial League Boxing Tournament and his diploma. High school—meaningless, pointless, worthless. Why had he stayed all those years, hanging on the priests' every word, taking communion with his hair slicked back and his church shoes polished to a sheen, and graduating last May wearing a new suit that had cost Ma a week's worth of wages? It had taken him nowhere, gotten him nothing.

He wiped at the sweat on his face with the back of his wrist. Blood mingled in the hairs on his arm, and his eye throbbed. That thug from Jewtown had given him a shiner earlier. What were those types doing skulking around Berkeley Park? They had no business here.

He socked the flour sack hard enough to rip the cheesecloth. Flour cascaded onto the dirt. He'd be in for it now. He shot a glance over his shoulder, toward the rickety wooden stairs that led up out of the cellar. The store was dark now, deserted, but in the morning, they would all be upstairs—his mother, Maureen, waddling forward on her phlebitis-swollen legs whenever the tinkling bell announced a customer; his father, Seamus, behind the meat counter, hacking away in the dim light.

And himself. Stock boy, delivery boy, errand boy, whipping boy. Saying yes and no like he had no brains of his own. For every blessed minute of every blessed day.

He leaned back against the flour sack, bare chest heaving.

Only this afternoon, he had gotten into another row with Pa. Venturing into the dank corner where his father cut meat, he had picked up a bloody piece from a pile of hacked beef on the butcher board.

"You've chopped it all wrong! You might as well put it in the grinder—"

"Don't you be tellin' me my business," Pa growled.

"You've been drinking this afternoon, haven't you? Where is it?" Sean had searched behind the roll of butcher's paper and spindle of string. "Where's your bottle?"

"Get out of here." Pa shoved him.

Sean's back hit the wall. "No wonder no one comes in here. They're probably afraid they'll find one of your fingers in their Sunday dinner!"

"What's goin' on here?" His mother had stood at the end of the aisle. "What's all this shoutin'? Seaney, you aren't bickerin' with your father again, are you? What have I told you—?"

"He's done the meat so bad it's wasted—!"

"It's none of your worry, now is it?"

Sean had slammed the wall with his fist, then lurched out from behind the meat counter. Unfazed, his mother blocked the aisle, standing squarely before him. "That's enough of that, Seaney," she commanded. "Apologize to your father. I'll not have you actin' the hooligan."

And he was forced to apologize. As always. For the love of his mother.

He flexed his sore fists. What had drawn her to Pa, that dark and sour mix of man? Ma's life was a misery. After Sean's birth, she had filled a family plot with children lost at birth—a couple of babies whose names were given to them only so that they could be buried, little Michael drinking rat poison at age three, Tommy born with one lung, and the twins Fiona and Dorcas lost to pneumonia. Still, his mother remained as true to her faith as she had ever been. Sean knew it was God—not Pa—who had seen her through it all.

Feeling tears in his eyes, he hit the flour sack again.

"Seaney?"

Kathleen stood at the top of the stairs, as if afraid to come down into the murky air. She was dressed in her work clothes, and her hair was a mess, curls going every which way.

"What are you doing?" he asked. "Are you just home now?"

"Yes." She descended four more steps and sat down. Her head was bent, and she cradled something in her lap. In the dim light, he made out a wooden ruler, like the ones they had once used in school. She was busy measuring and marking.

"It's near to dark!" he protested. "What's so important at Graves Oil that you have to type away half the night?"

She set the ruler aside. "I believe I have single-handedly leased the entire western half of America for oil production today. Let me have a swing or two at that flour sack. I'll pretend it's Miss Crawley." In a nasally voice, she said, "It is James A., not James L. I can't believe you do not know that by now—"

"I thought you had that figured out—"

"I thought I had, too, but I couldn't concentrate on anything, and the letters just got jumbled in my head." She stopped and looked at him. "What are you doing down here? What's wrong?"

Sean faltered, embarrassed by his sweaty, naked chest and ripe smell. A true man wouldn't hide in the cellar and pound on a sack. He grabbed his shirt and wrestled his way into it.

"Nothing more than usual." Squinting into the semi-darkness, he asked, "What do you have there?"

"I'm using a grid to make my drawings better. Here, look at this." She handed him her sketchbook. "What do you think? Is it in proportion?"

The drawing was of the Statue of Liberty. "In proportion to what?"

"Seaney!" Kathleen hurried down the last of the stairs and into the cellar. "Your eye! What happened—?"

"It's nothing to worry about—"

Cupping his chin, she tilted his face toward the light. "It's almost swollen shut! Who were you scrapping with this time?"

"Never mind." He pushed her hand away.

"Why do you do it? That's all you do anymore—!"

"Sometimes I win on the streets. I never win one here."

"From the looks of it, you don't win out there either—"

"Don't you start with me!" How could he tell her that the pain of his cuts and aching muscles was the only thing that reminded him he was flesh and blood and nerves? That made him feel alive? He turned the tables on her. "But what about you? Why are you so late?"

"Oh." She retreated to the steps again and picked up her sketchbook. "We were allowed to go to a Preparedness rally today at the Capitol, and after it, all I could do was think about what I wanted to sketch. I made so many mistakes after we went back that Miss Crawley made me retype half my work."

The last word thudded against the dirt floor.

"I wish I didn't have to do this," she said.

"You know as well as I do," Sean said. "You have to help out your folks—"

"I met him today, you know."

"Who?"

"Mr. Graves. He spoke at the rally."

"Oh, His Majesty, The Honorable James A. Graves," Sean sneered. "So, is he as wonderful as the newspapers seem to think he is?"

She gave a shivery laugh. "He's the one who showed me the grid. And he wore the most beautiful cowboy boots."

"Cowboy boots? Who's he trying to be? Hopalong Cassidy?"

She laughed again. "He gave me a box of pencils."

"Why would he give you pencils?"

"So I don't have to take them from the trash. I found the box beside my typewriter when I came back from the rally—"

"This doesn't sound right to me," Sean said firmly. "He shouldn't be giving you anything. He's your employer."

Kathleen snapped. "There was nothing improper—"

"How do you know? Maybe this is just the start—"

"You don't trust anybody, do you, Seaney?"

"Who is there to trust? Nearly every business in Denver has a sign that reads NO IRISH NEED APPLY in its window. He knows you won't find a job anywhere else, and he thinks he can get you to do whatever he wants—"

"You forget that I have some say in things," she said. "You haven't even asked what we talked about—"

"Come on, Kathleen. There's no denying that we're Irish."

She said nothing, and Sean poked at the flour sack, releasing another dusty stream onto the floor. They would never escape their Irish blood. Sean bore the black hair of his father and the china blue eyes of his mother. Every time he opened his mouth, Ireland lilted from it. Kathleen took after her own father, Gerry, whose flaming red hair, freckled skin, and wide green eyes had earned him the nickname of "Irish" O'Doherty. She didn't need to speak to reveal her heritage.

He relented. "So what did you talk about?"

Her lips pursed, and for a moment, he thought she wouldn't answer. "What's going to happen," she said softly.

"And what does he say is going to happen?"

"That we'll be at war soon."

"I could have told you that. But I guess it sounds more important coming from someone who could buy the moon. Just don't let him talk you into anything he shouldn't."

"I won't see him again." She sighed as she twirled a pencil in her fingers. Golden letters near the eraser flashed in the dim light. "These are almost too pretty to use. I think I'll wait until I'm out at Redlands to try them." Her face twitched. "I miss it so much."

"I know," Sean said. "But Ma loves having you here. I do, too."

The last confession made his chest constrict. He, too, missed Redlands, mostly because it was the one place where Maggie and he could be as wild and free as they wanted. There were no customers to report his rudeness or Mag's sullenness, no salesmen who tried to cheat Pa with false weights or to pinch Mag when no one was looking. And Kathleen was always one for mischief, urging Sean to race on horseback—even though he couldn't ride a hobby horse, much less a live one—or to catapult from ropes hung among the willows into the creek, or daring him to walk the narrow ledge of the wooden silo, peering down twenty feet to a sure demise. She ridiculed him for his lack of grace in scurrying over rocks and through scrub oak and up and down ravines as they played pirates or cowboys and Indians or musketeers, but he had loved every minute.

Yet when she spoke again, she reminded him that they were no longer children.

"Do you ever think about who you'll marry?" she asked.

Sean puzzled. How was it that she had come home from work a different person? "The girls in the parish don't give me a second look."

Her face brightened. "It's because you frown during Mass."

"What?"

"They think, if he's such a sourpuss on the day of rest, imagine what he'd be like when he has to work or get up early in the morning."

"So that's it. Well, I'll be sure to grin my way right through the Our Father next Sunday."

She snorted, challenging him. "So who do you want to marry?"

"Well, she has to be strong enough to haul up the tins of beans." He picked at a scab on his index finger. He knew pretty girls from church, but just now he couldn't recall a single face. "I don't know," he said. "I imagine a wife who is so like me, who thinks and talks like me and prays with me, who sees the world as I do. You know that stupid old song, heart of my heart. I want someone who can hear my thoughts before I put them to words, who can figure out what I'm thinking before I do myself. What else could a man want, that and a houseful of children?"

His heart felt strained, as if he had been running or crying. "And she'd have to be Irish."

"Of course." Kathleen chirped in her finest brogue, "'Tis the family's honor what's at stake, young Seaney Murphy Patrick Sullivan, and don't ye be forgettin' it. 'Tis yer duty to ev'ry Irish immigrant who ever left t'e auld sod and ate bread churned of ashes durin' t'e famine, and vomited up bile in Satan's dark hell of steerage itself, all so's we could mine gold from t'e streets of Am—"

"Enough already!" She had never been as proud of their heritage as he was. "Well, so, what about you?"

She put the pencil away in the box. "My plan is to marry a Mormon and become one of his fourteen wives. At least I'd have a few minutes to sketch each day while he's busy with the other thirteen."

"Kathleen!" Sean's throat was raw. Why did it matter that she wouldn't give a straight answer? It was just like her, after all. "Don't tease now. Answer me."

She put a hand on the nape of her neck and ruffled her hair. Sean had seen her do that a hundred—no, a thousand—times. When she was thinking, or plotting, or planning an argument. When she was pondering the mysteries of life. When her mind—which darted anyway—was moving so fast that the rest of the world couldn't keep up with her.

"I'd like to marry someone who'd love me without a single regret," she said.

"Regret? That's a fine way to talk about marriage."

"Well, Papa and Mama—"

She stopped, and Sean filled in what she had left unsaid. Auntie Eileen never seemed to have a kind word for Uncle Irish—and Sean couldn't say that he blamed her. Uncle Irish didn't drink the way Sean's father did, but he didn't seem any better at keeping money in his pocket, either. His crops withered, and his cattle sold poorly at market. Still he dressed and acted like a well-to-do man, while Auntie Eileen remade Kathleen's and her own dresses year after year. Underneath the gussied-up pin stripes and bowler hat, Irish O'Doherty was just a do-nothing gambler.

"It looks like Maggie will be the lucky one," Sean said. "She and Liam have been inseparable since they both learned how to read."

Kathleen laughed.

"Anyway, what's the sense of talking about it?" Sean said. "I'm heir to a grocery that can't even feed its owners."

"You could say that about Redlands."

Sean reached for Kathleen's hand, gave it a squeeze. "You should go to bed. It's late."

She winced.

"What's wrong?" he asked.

"My fingers. They hurt."

THREE

Maggie pricked her finger with a needle. She brought it to her mouth, tasting the dot of blood. Drying her finger on her skirt, she went back to tacking the netting onto Mrs. MacMahon's new hat. It looked like a nest for mice—piles of tattered junk.

Beside her, Kathleen sewed steadily, perfectly comfortable with the hidden tucks and threads of hat-making. The girls sat under the bare rafters of the attic workroom that was known as "Mrs. Sullivan's Millinery." The attic overflowed with its contents—a mirrored vanity and chair, a Singer sewing machine and treadle, and shelves of rough pine that bowed beneath weighty boxes of fabric and trim. Yet in this cramped and inelegant space, Ma designed splendid potpourris of tulle, ribbon, satin and lace for her customers.

Maggie poked her finger again and gave up, tossing the hat on to the vanity. It would never suit Ma, anyway. She caught the reflection of her own eyes in the mirror. She wasn't pretty like Kathleen. Her blue eyes were offset, the right more direct than the left, and her face and nose were long and thin. Her sole claim to beauty was her hair, which was the same tawny color as her mother's. It gleamed with gold and red in the sunlight.

Liam loved her anyway.

She smiled as she thought of him: so straightforward, so determined, so smart. Liam and his older brother, Brendan, had grown up at Mount St. Vincent Orphan Asylum and were beloved by all in the parish. Brendan had taken the vows, but Maggie had won the heart of the brightest and handsomest of the Keohane brothers. One afternoon last July, Liam had kissed her for the first time. It wasn't a real kiss—they were in a rowboat on Berkeley Lake at the time—but since then, more kisses had come. Sometimes, at night, she tried to count them, like sheep, before she went to sleep, but recently, she had lost track.

Now, Kathleen laid down the bonnet of delicately-placed ribbons, springy feathered bluebirds, and false cherries and went to look out the dormered window. Flexing her fingers, she asked, "What happened to Seaney?"

"He didn't get all those bruises from fighting."

Kathleen turned around. "Then how?"

"Pa gave him the one on his chin."

"Uncle Seamus? I wish they wouldn't fight."

Maggie's felt a stab of jealousy. Uncle Irish treated his "Caitlin" as a princess, no need to fear any cuffs on the head from him. He was even kind to Maggie, calling her by the nickname Muffin. But Pa was another matter. Once he started drinking, he took to swinging at whoever happened in his way, his arms thick and muscled, his fists the size of sledgehammers. Although it was usually Seaney who took the brunt of his rages, Maggie had taken her fair share of the blows, too.

"They can't get along at all," she said. "They're at each other night and day."

"Seaney has to quit fighting. Help me persuade him."

Maggie shrugged. "He likes to fight. And you know what? Those boys deserve it, too—"

"What boys?"

"The boys from Jewtown," Maggie said. "They come over here and steal whatever they can, and they carry lead pipes—

"He can't fight them all—"

"Well, maybe you can convince him to invite them home for Catechism, Saint Kathleen."

Kathleen furred out, ready to fight, but Maggie heard voices echoing from the steps below. Ma's rich contralto soared, the brogue she had never lost during her years in America strong and clear. "So, you'll be needin' a hat for the orphanage cake walk, surely?"

"Oh, Maureen," Mrs. MacMahon lilted back. "Danny will fuss if I spend any more. But just show me what you've been makin'.."

"Oh, no, it's not me. It's Kathleen. Aye, that girl has an eye for beauty." Ma appeared at the top of the stairs, huffing to catch her breath. "There she is now!"

Kathleen smiled. "How are you, Mrs. MacMahon?"

"Fine, now, and Maggie, hello to you. The happy day is comin' soon, eh?"

"In June," Maggie said. "After I graduate."

"We'll be lookin' forward to that, then." Mrs. MacMahon's gaze returned to Kathleen. "Look at you! Every time I see you I wish my Elwin was just a few years older."

Mrs. MacMahon's bulk pressed into the room, her heavy vanilla scent overwhelming in the stale air. Unnoticed, Maggie slipped toward the door. Leave Kathleen to simper and sigh, and Ma to wheedle and bargain, and Mrs. MacMahon would walk away with four new hats, rather than the three she'd ordered. Maggie would only get in the way.

Downstairs, she donned a cable-knit sweater and felt hat and went outside. The day was cool and breezy, but the buds on the trees had started to break and tulips poked up through patches of snow. March would soon turn to April and warmth. Someone honked as they drove past on the street. Maggie waved—it had to be someone she knew. Everyone in the parish shopped at Sullivan's Grocery.

She glanced over her shoulder at the blocky brick building. Its plate glass windows were jammed with boxes of Lux detergent and cornmeal and pyramids of tin cans. Handwritten messages on the glass, painted by Ma in egg white and food coloring, advertised fresh tobacco and the week's special, while a netted hat poked up its veil in a bid for attention. "MRS. SULLIVAN'S MILLINERY, UP" read a genteel placard with an elegantly pointed hand.

On the west side of the store, a wrought iron staircase led upward to the rambling apartments where the Sullivan family had lived since Pa's father had started the store for gold prospectors headed for the mountains.

It wasn't such a bad way to grow up, she supposed. When she married, though, she wanted to live in a house that had a porch to sit on in the evenings and a grassy yard for the children to play on. She wanted a husband whose fingernails weren't caked by the blood of the animals he'd carved into steaks, but stained by ink from writing.

A scholar, a wit, a man who wore suit and tie to work.

And that man was Liam.

She walked in the direction of Berkeley Lake. Immediately, the cars along the street vanished, and she imagined herself in a beautiful drawing room, a spectator of a brilliant and hoity-toity soirée. She had started the story last night, working at the vanity in Ma's sewing room, pondering each coy bit of dialogue while gnashing the end of her pencil in her teeth.

Evelyn's heart cavalcaded—how she loved to use words just for their sound!—*in her breast, as she watched George from across the room. His shoulders were square and strong as he stood next to her father, and his words, although she could not hear them, would be sensible and carefully chosen in the way that Father approved. All she wanted, she realized, was to make George understand what a fine wife she would be, and how she would never let anything come between them. She simply had to convince him to ask her to marry him—*

Oh, she loved to write! In her stories, the beautiful, graceful heroine always caught the eye of the strongest, most handsome man, who fell helplessly in love, so taken by her that he would do anything for her. Whatever problems they faced disappeared in a happy ending.

Berkeley Lake spread before her, its deep blue water rippling in the breeze, the snow-capped Rocky Mountains rising up in the distance behind it. Couples strolled along the footpath around the lake, and children played in the tall grass and cattails of the banks. It did not take her long to spot Liam as he sat beneath a cottonwood tree reading a book.

Without glancing up at her, he spoke. *"And for all this, nature is never spent; There lives the dearest freshness deep down things; And though the last lights off the black West went, Oh, morning, at* the brown brink eastward, springs. Because the Holy Ghost over the bent World broods with warm breast and with ah!—"

He stopped and eyed Maggie.

"*Bright wings*," she said. "Gerard Manley Hopkins."

"That's right," he said. "No wonder you skipped a grade in school."

"It was just so I could catch up with you."

Liam laughed. As always, his chestnut hair was parted in the middle and lay tousled and thick on each side, as if he'd run a hand through it. His hazel eyes burned behind round wire-rimmed glasses that were similar to President Wilson's. Maggie's arms felt weak, all the blood draining away. Everything about him was so handsome: the firm mouth, the slightly crooked nose, which had been broken once by a bully, his deeply dimpled chin, the florid color that rose up, as it did in so many of Irish descent, from his neck into his cheeks.

More impressive was his intelligence. He had worked his way through night school to become the youngest bookkeeper ever to work for the Colorado Western Railroad. He was devoted to the Church, too. He raked the lawn at Blessed Savior Catholic Church for Father Devlin and planted pansies in the garden in spring. He shoveled coal into the sooty furnace and cleared the snow from the steps before Mass. Now that Brendan, who worked as hard as Liam did, was the curate there, Blessed Savior had never looked so tidy.

Liam closed the book and reached out a hand to her. "Let's walk."

She took his arm. "Have you been at the Church this morning?"

"Not today," he said. "Brendan and Father Devlin were discussing what the Church will do if there is war. Evidently there's been some sort of communication from the Diocese."

"Oh, the war! Why can't anyone talk about anything else?"

Liam stopped. "Because it's the greatest tragedy of our time, and maybe even in the history of the world. Men fighting one another with great weapons of steel and destruction that are designed for instant death. They don't even know who they're killing. They never even see their enemies' eyes. And for what? For the benefits of commerce and industry!"

Maggie looked away. When he took on a subject, Liam's voice rose, so that it was audible to those around them. Sometimes, his fervor embarrassed her.

"But that's not what you came here to talk about, it is?" he said. "So, what have you been doing this morning?"

"I made a hat for Mrs. MacMahon," she said, relieved by the change of subject. "And last night, I wrote three pages of my story."

"So how is the incomparable Evelyn?" he asked. "It's still Evelyn, isn't it?"

"I love that name," Maggie said. "It's so elegant and musical."

"And Margaret isn't?"

"It sounds like something you would take for a head cold. Maggie is even worse. It rhymes with terrible words—saggy, baggy, haggy, naggy."

"Try Liam sometime," he said. "I've heard it pronounced every way under the sun. Lye-am, Leem, even Laim."

"I think I'll start calling you Lame."

Liam raised his voice again. "There once was a girl named Mar-gar-ET," he declared, rolling his r's in a rich tenor. "Who viewed her name with much re-GRET, But she carried a bright FLAME, For a young fool named LAME—"

Maggie giggled at the pronunciation.

"So never again was she up-SET."

She laughed aloud, and he kissed her temple. "There," he said. "We're equally ridiculous."

"I can hardly wait until June," she said.

"June?" Liam asked. "What happens then?"

Maggie elbowed him. "Nothing if you don't treat me better."

"How should I treat you?" He stopped to ponder. "Should I tell you that I like you? That I'm fond of you? That I am cordially yours?"

"How about 'I love you'?"

"Now, why didn't I think of that?"

"Liam! Liam!"

The voices came from behind them. Maggie glanced over her shoulder. Two boys were running down the bank toward them. She knew them both—Larry Shea and Oren Atkins—from the primary school at Blessed Savior.

"Liam," Larry shouted. "We need your help!"

"What's wrong?" Liam asked.

"Oren kicked the ball too far. It went into the lake."

The boy pointed, and Maggie saw a red rubber ball floating just beyond the tall cattail barrier.

"Now, why'd you do that?" Liam asked.

"I kicked it and it went up into the air," Oren said. "The wind must have caught it. I didn't mean to do it."

Liam looked at the ball, handed Maggie his book of poetry, sat down on the grass, and began unlacing his shoes.

"You're not going to wade in there, are you?" Maggie asked. "The water's ice cold."

"What else?"

"I don't know," she said. "A long stick—"

"We tried it!" Larry insisted. "It didn't do any good."

Liam rolled up his pant legs. "Don't laugh at my fat ankles," he warned, which, of course, made the boys chuckle with glee.

"You'll catch pneumonia," Maggie said.

"No," Liam said. "I'll be in and out before *it* catches *me*."

As Oren and Larry sprinted along the bank, offering advice, Liam waded into the water. The ball floated away, moving about ten feet from the shore. Maggie folded her arms across her chest, afraid Liam might get in over his head, but he called back to Larry. "Bring me your stick!"

Together, Larry and Oren guided the stick forward over the water until Liam could grab it. Liam tapped the ball on the side to try to direct it back toward the shore. The ball floated to the left, out of his reach. He took another step into the lake.

"Be careful!" Maggie called.

This time, when he tapped the ball, it floated backward a few inches. He did it again, bringing it within his arm's reach. Taking a few more steps into the shallows, he dropped the stick, and grabbed the ball. While Larry and Oren called hurray, Maggie shook her head. Liam grinned at her.

As he was rising out of the lake, his feet seemingly slipped out from beneath him, and he teetered. With one quick action, he shot the ball forward toward Oren, who caught it just before it tumbled into the water again. Larry called, "That was close! Good catch, Oren!"

The boys yelled their thanks and ran off, intent on their game, while Liam padded in bare feet up the grass.

"You didn't really lose your footing," Maggie said.

"Every boy should be a hero now and then."

"How are you going to dry your feet?"

"I'm not," he said. "I'm going to stuff them into my shoes, and we'll go back to your place, where you can build me a fire and make some tea."

"Who says I'll do all that for you?"

"I do," he said. "Because you can't resist me, Margaret Mary Sullivan. You've never been able to say no to me."

Maggie held out her hand. "Come on. Let's go warm up."

FOUR

Jim Graves was wrong about the ten days. By the following Friday, which happened to be Good Friday, America was at war. As Kathleen walked with the Sullivan family to Blessed Savior for Easter Mass, she remembered his solemn statement: *The chance to give one's life in France will fall to us all.* She worried about Seaney, who walked beside her, and about Liam, and Brendan, and all the boys she had known in high school and at Church, and about Mr. Graves himself. What would become of them?

At the curb near Blessed Savior, a Model T truck idled, smoke shimmering from its hood, its engine banging. Kathleen's parents, just arrived from Redlands, sat in it. As her mother stepped from the vehicle, her father stayed behind the wheel, a cigarette between his lips.

"Mama!" Kathleen kissed her mother's cheek. "Papa!"

Mama grasped Kathleen's hand and looked at her gloves. "Look at that! Your fingertips are as purple as a plum! What have you been doing?"

Kathleen glanced at the soiled white. Miss Crawley had also upbraided her for the stains. "It's from the carbon paper, Mama. The oil leases have to be typed in triplicate, and the ink just gets everywhere—"

"Well, I'd think you'd have cleaned up for Easter, at least. Did you try bluin'?"

Kathleen felt the familiar twist of her stomach. Mama nagged and chided so much that Kathleen knew that if she hadn't already done something wrong, she would soon. It had always been that way.

"Leave off, Eileen." Papa climbed from the car and looped his arm around Kathleen's shoulders. "Why, look at you, Caitlin, me love. All grown up." Offering his hand, he acknowledged the others. "Maureen. Seamus. Sean. Muffin, how's that lad of yours?"

Maggie laughed. "He's fine, Uncle Irish."

Kathleen leaned into him. She loved her father so—even more than she loved Seaney. He was so handsome and carefree, so strong and lively, so much the opposite of Mama.

"We should be inside." Mama straightened the buttons of the jacket and suit that she had cleverly made over with a new collar and cuffs and shot one last disapproving look at Kathleen.

"I'll see you this afternoon," Papa whispered to Kathleen.

He slipped back into the automobile and gunned the engine, which belched smoke as it trundled down the street. Mama snorted, but Kathleen defiantly waved goodbye.

Papa had never, as far as she could remember, attended Mass. Once, when she asked why, he had replied, "Because the Catholic Church will tell you to do what it says—no argument about it. It'll tell you how to dress"—he plucked at her sleeve—"and how to talk"—he chucked her under the chin—"and how to act and think and breathe!" And with that he had pinched her nose between his knuckles and pretended to steal it from her. She danced around him, laughing and trying to recover her nose, while he held the stolen treasure high in the air, out of her reach.

Once the ruse had run its course, Kathleen said, "The church doesn't tell me how to breathe. I can do that all on my own."

"Not without your nose, you can't," he reminded her.

"But don't you believe in God, Papa?"

"There's no one looking out for us but ourselves," he had said. "Don't you be forgetting that, Caitlin, me love. You have to make your own way. It's all your call and your doing."

"If there's no God, who made the earth so lovely?" she had challenged. "I can't believe that there isn't . . . someone or something. Look around us, Papa. Redlands is the most beautiful place on earth—and it's ours. Shouldn't we be thankful to God for that?"

"Well, aren't you smart," Papa had said, looking out across the land. "Who knows? Maybe that Darwin fellow and I are wrong, but don't tell the apes."

And Kathleen had laughed and laughed at his joke.

During Mass, Kathleen sat next to Seaney, who held himself stiff as a board, his eyes and ears all attentiveness, his heart given over to the Church. Her mind wandered—as it always did. She had not been back to the Capitol since the day she had met Jim Graves, and of course, she had not seen him at work.

It was just as well, she supposed, and yet—

Seaney nudged her. "Pay attention," he whispered. "Think of your soul."

His hand wrapped around hers. Even through her gloves, she could feel his rough calluses and scarred knuckles, and she remembered Mr. Graves' hand. What had caused that tough, uneven ridge that ran up the center of his palm? Surely he hadn't been born with such a malformation. She remembered how his touch had made her arm tingle—

Father Devlin's voice interrupted her thoughts. "Now, Father Keohane will read the Statement of the Archbishops, which we've just now received."

Shuffling a sheaf of papers, Brendan read, "'Standing firmly upon our solid Catholic tradition and history from the very foundation of this nation, we reaffirm in this hour of trial our moral, sacred and sincere loyalty and patriotism toward our country, our Government, and our Flag—'"

Seaney's grip tightened, and Kathleen said a quick prayer asking for forgiveness. What was she doing, thinking of Jim Graves and his touch during Mass? Forgetting that there was a war on? And on this, the holiest of days. Think of her soul, indeed.

After Mass, the parishioners lingered, reluctant to leave for their Easter meals. Up and down the street, cars were parked helter-skelter, along with a few wagons, the heads of the horses hanging in the late morning sun. Along the sidewalk and on the steps, people discussed the European war. Some seemed confused, others overbearing. Leaving the sanctuary, Kathleen found herself pinned by a bantering group against the railing of the stone steps that led to the sidewalk, unable to slip through without seeming rude. Behind her, Seaney, Maggie and Liam were caught in one corner of the porch. Her mother and aunt and uncle were nowhere to be seen.

"President Wilson's callin' for a million men t' join up for t'e fight," Charlie McKenna chirped. "If he don't get that, he' sayin' 'twill be the draft again. And this time, no buyin' yer way out, like before. It'll be all fair and proper-like."

"I won't hold my breath," his brother, Davy, said.

"President Wilson needs to know we've not forgotten our brothers in Ireland," Mr. MacMahon declared. "After last year's Easter Uprising, who's goin' to join up to fight with the Brits? Not my boys, by any means. I'd sooner send them to fight with the Germans!"

"Danny!" Mrs. MacMahon cried. "How can you say that?"

"We could have stayed neutral," he insisted. "There's no need to get involved any further than we are. What say you, Father?"

Kathleen glanced behind her. Brendan stood at the top of the steps beneath the striped white and red brick arched portico, his back against the sanctuary doors, as if he were fending off heathens. Clearing his throat, he said, "Patriotism is part of our belief as Catholics. Our love of our country proceeds from the same eternal principle as our love of God. As Father McMenamin has said, 'Lead on, Our President, lead on.'"

A rumble of approval passed through the crowd.

"God's laws are unconditional and inexorable. The Sixth Commandment states, 'Thou shalt not kill.' We cannot ignore or deviate from His sacred words."

Kathleen looked over her shoulder. It was Liam, who was standing slightly to one side of his brother.

"I'm sorry?" Mrs. MacMahon said.

An uneasy silence fell over the crowd. Kathleen caught Seaney's eye. He gave a shrug, his mouth set in a firm line. One of Maggie's hands was at her throat, as if she were trying to silence Liam by squeezing her own vocal chords.

"President Wilson has said that America should be a 'specific example of peace' for the world." Liam's voice echoed from beneath the portico and into the street. "He said we must devote ourselves to the principles of humanity by staying out of the war. As Catholics, we must do just that. We must follow God's law, not man's sinful willfulness."

"What do you say, Father Keohane?" someone in the crowd called.

Brendan cleared his throat again, and Kathleen saw the sheen of sweat on his forehead. He glanced sidelong at Liam, his glasses in the same round style as his brother's, his eyes the same hazel color.

"Our holy Mother the Church is—" He faltered and began again. "The Catholic Church in America will cooperate in this national endeavor in the highest degree. This war is a contest to determine the supremacy of the spirit of liberty over the materialism of domination. The Church stands for the ideals of democracy, and it will honor the soldier who claims love of God and country as his primary motive for going to war."

"Are you saying we should enlist?"

"I'm saying we should support the war to the best of our abilities," he said. "Now, let us go home, to our own families, and pray for our great nation and the young men who will be its soldiers in this war to save Democracy and Freedom."

A cheer went up, and a wobbly soprano voice began, *"O-oh, say can you see—"*

Everyone snapped to, the men whipping their hats from their heads and the women with ramrod-straight backs. Kathleen joined in, singing the anthem with tears in her eyes.

An eerie silence overtook the family as they walked from the church to the Sullivans' apartments. Maggie had stayed behind with Liam, who had gone inside the church with Brendan. Seaney walked so quickly that Kathleen had to skip now and then to keep up with him. Never one to remain quiet for long, his nerves at last broke free.

"What in the world were you thinking of today?" he asked her. "You couldn't sit still an instant."

She hoped to fend it off. "I was thinking about your black eye."

"You think too much."

"And you don't think enough. If you did, you wouldn't fight."

"Looks like I'll be fighting the Huns from here on."

"Oh, Seaney, don't," she said, an ill feeling creeping into her stomach. "Not on Easter Sunday."

"Why did Liam say that?" he demanded. "We all know the Sixth Commandment."

Sullivan's Grocery came into view. Mama and Aunt Maury swept up the stairs that led to the apartments, while Uncle Seamus went into the store, seeking a bottle after the long dry spell in church. Seaney slipped away to the lot behind the store. Kathleen joined her mother and aunt upstairs in the kitchen.

"Mash the potatoes, Kathleen," Aunt Maury ordered. "Aye, and you should stir the broth when you've a chance, since Mag's not here."

For a time, they worked without speaking. The kitchen was hardly large enough to allow for three grown women in it—much less Maggie—but they moved together in a sort of waltz that had been learned through years of preparing the meal every Sunday.

"What did you think of Liam's speech?" Mama asked at last.

"I'm thinkin' he ought to watch his tongue," Aunt Maury said. "Sentiments are runnin' strong just now. He's like to lose his job or some such thing by goin' against the grain."

Kathleen's anxiety bubbled up. "Oh, I wish President Wilson would have kept his promise to keep America out—"

"Well, there's nothin' to be done there," Aunt Maury said.

"We can vote."

Mama gave a sharp laugh. "Who has time for that? It's a trip to town and standin' in line at that, when there's so much to be done around the place."

"Aye," Aunt Maury agreed. "I haven't the time to figure out if Mr. Whatsit is better than Mr. Whosit, much less anythin' else."

"It isn't only men anymore," Kathleen said. "There's a woman in Congress now. Mrs. Rankin of Montana. And all women should vote when and where they can— "

"That's your father's thinkin'," Mama said.

"No, it's my own," Kathleen snapped. "When I'm old enough, I'm going to—"

The door that led to the inside staircase and the store opened, and Maggie stepped into the kitchen. Her face was haggard and pale, her eyes reddened, as if she had been crying. Afraid she might faint, Kathleen pulled out a chair from the kitchen table, and Maggie stumbled onto it.

"Where's Liam?" Aunt Maury asked. "He's not still tellin' everybody off at the church, is he?"

"No," Maggie said, sniffing back tears. "He's downstairs with Pa and Seaney and Brendan."

"Well, he'd do best to keep his thoughts to himself," Mama said.

Maggie put her face in her hands, her elbows on the table. "I don't see how I'm to make him do that, Auntie Eileen."

"'Tis a wife's job to care for her husband. You'd do well to warn him of his folly."

"He'd just tell me that it's folly that's taking us to war."

Mama and Aunt Maury exchanged a glance before Aunt Maury commanded, "Tell them they're to come up now. Our dinner's ready."

Obediently, Maggie went back down the stairs to the store.

Mama turned a sharp eye on Kathleen. "Carry the serving spoons into the living room," she ordered. "Don't dawdle. Everything's growin' cold."

As Kathleen took her place at the table that she and Seaney had lengthened last night with heavy wooden leaves, the men and Maggie came up from downstairs. Brendan had removed his cassock and wore trousers and Roman collar. Liam looked sullen, and Kathleen hoped that there wouldn't be another set-to at the table.

"Would you please say the grace, Father?" Aunt Maury asked.

Brendan prayed, a long grace on this blessed and troubling day, while the heat steamed from the food. When Kathleen lifted her head after the "Amen," she looked toward Seaney. Since they were children, he had winked at her after grace, but today, his gaze was cast down at his plate.

Mama opened the conversation. "I wish I could see that grand office of yours, Kathleen," she said. "Have you done any special jobs yet? Caught the eye of your superiors?"

The guilt of this week's infractions flamed up in Kathleen's face. "Not yet, Mama."

"I cannot imagine them ignorin' a girl with your skills for so long," Mama said. "Your salary might rise, if you work hard enough."

"It's already ten dollars a week!" Aunt Maury said. "I just wish I could pay such grand wages to have her work for me. My hats are turnin' out poorly just now."

"Your hats are beautiful," Kathleen said. "And I'll help you anytime you need it."

"I'll help you, Ma," Maggie offered.

"Oh, no, 'tis Kathleen I need. But you're gone such long hours—"

Mama glowed. "Workin' you hard, are they? Well, I've no doubt you'll be a secretary to some important man soon. Maybe Mr. Graves himself."

Kathleen's gaze went to Seaney again, as she thought of his new name for Jim Graves: His Grace, The Honorable Hopalong Graves. Again, he did not look at her.

"Didn't you say you were going to the Preparedness rally this week?"

"Yes, Mama."

"Did he speak?"

"Yes, and he's very good." She glanced at Liam, afraid he might object.

"He should be," Mama snorted. "He's been preaching Preparedness for months now in all manner of public places. He's always sayin' we're to be ready for it all. From the sounds of it, he's the one who told President Wilson to declare war."

"He stands to make a fortune from it," Uncle Seamus growled.

"He talks to President Wilson?" Maggie laughed in disbelief. "I didn't think anyone from Colorado was that important."

"He's not the one who'll be fighting," Liam said. "It will be America's workers who'll be called upon to fight. It's their lives that will be sacrificed and for what? Capitalist greed, nothing more."

Without thinking, Kathleen said, "There's a place in the east called Plattsburg where many of America's business leaders are learning military skills. They're going to war just like the rest of us."

Everyone looked at her in surprise, and she stumbled on. "They're willing to leave their companies and fortunes behind to fight. Even President Roosevelt's sons trained there and are planning to go—"

"They're trained to be officers," Liam said. "It's all the same game as they play here. They'll hold the power of life and death over the poor soldiers just as they do over workers—"

"Maybe when the Germans hear that the Americans are coming they'll be so afraid that they'll surrender," Maggie offered.

"More likely, they'll laugh at us," Seaney said. "They think we're weak, useless. I'd like to show them. I'd teach them a lesson or two they'd never forget—"

"Don't be talkin' foolishness in front of your mother," Mama scolded him. "Apologize right now."

"I'm sorry, Ma," Seaney murmured.

"What we must pray for is Peace without Victory, as President Wilson calls it," Brendan interceded. "That is the world's greatest hope."

"What is that?" Kathleen asked.

"It's the idea that the winning side—whether it be Germany or the Allied countries—shouldn't boast of its victory and inflict misery on the people who have lost, as a conqueror might. The end of the conflict should be greeted with compassion and aid. It should bring the unification of Europe, not more division."

"That isn't likely to happen," Liam said. "Six million men have been deliberately killed! British, French, German—it doesn't matter! Six million—an entire generation! And now, without being asked to give sanction or consent, the people of America have been ordered to join in as well!"

"Liam," Brendan warned gently.

Liam rose. "I'm very sorry. Mrs. Sullivan, Mrs. O'Doherty, Mr. Sullivan. Sean, Kathleen, Maggie, I'm sorry."

He turned and left the room. At once, Maggie jumped to her feet, her cloth napkin dropping to the floor. "Liam!" She ran from the room. "Liam!"

Brendan stood. "You must forgive him. He's taken this very hard." Graciously, he added, "I need to see if there is anything I can do."

"Aye, we'll keep the food warm," Aunt Maury said.

Mama watched with a sour expression as Brendan left the room. After the door closed behind him, she said, "Quite an Easter this is, with everyone runnin' mad and upset. You'd think President Wilson would have waited to make his grand announcement until next week."

No one replied, and silence settled over the room. Utensils scraped against plates, and the clock on the mantel ticked its regular rhythm. Food stuck in Kathleen's throat, but she didn't want to swallow, afraid she might choke. Then, as if it were all Kathleen's fault, Mama attacked. "I hope you've not been sketching again," she said. "You should be thinkin' of your work, not of drawin' and wild things and such. Such a waste of time. Such a foolish pastime."

Kathleen's stomach twisted. "I don't draw 'wild things,' Mama. The last things I drew were the Statue of Liberty and"—she faltered as she remembered the sketch of Jim Graves' boots—"and that sort of thing."

"This kind of talk makes me think that you're doin' exactly what you shouldn't be. Your fascination with sketchin' makes you disrespectful to your elders."

"Mr. Graves doesn't think it's disrespectful."

The instant she said it, Kathleen regretted it. She had had no intention of telling her mother that she had met her employer.

"What's this?" Mama asked. "When did you see him?"

"At the rally. I sketched a few things, and I showed them to him."

"Did he ask to see them? You didn't think he'd want to look at them, did you? Because I doubt a man of his importance would have time for—"

"He asked me to show him."

As Mama pondered that bit of news, Aunt Maury came to Kathleen's rescue. "Calm down, Eileen," she said. "She's a good girl, and I'm sure she did nothing wrong. She helps me in the kitchen and pays her rent on time. I've no quarrels with her sketching some, if she wants. It's a harmless hobby."

Mama gave Kathleen one last glare, then abruptly changed the subject. Kathleen studied her plate, while Seaney etched an ugly gash through his mashed potatoes, and Uncle Seamus dozed in his chair. Outside, they could hear Brendan and Liam quarreling.

Late in the afternoon, Kathleen heard Papa's car pull up in front of the store and ran outside to meet him. He was just coming up the steps to the outside landing. The sky had started to dim with the approach of evening, but noise still echoed from the park beyond. He leaned against the railing and lit a cigarette, gazing toward the mountains. Gray, snow-filled clouds floated above them. "Look at that," he said. "The weather's going to change."

"What do you think about it all, Papa?" she asked.

"About what?"

"Don't tease!" she cried. "The—"

"Come, Caitlin, I know. The United States of America is officially a nation at war."

She breathed in the cool air. To her left, the stairs ran down to the street. Below, to her right, was the garden, where Maggie was sitting on a barrel, clutching a sweater around her. Liam stood near the garden shed, his face hidden.

"They're bragging about it over in the park." Papa inhaled from his cigarette. "All afternoon, they've been at it, talk of saving the world by killing Germans. We have so many wonders in this world. Automobiles and trains and man can fly—think of it, Caitlin, we can fly!—and what do we use it for? To destroy our fellows. To make the world a stinking bog of carnage. And now America has gone and set herself on the fool's errand just because Morgan and Carnegie are unhappy that they can't sell to both the Germans and the Brits."

"Seaney said he would go and teach the Germans a lesson."

"He may have to live up to that," Papa said. "Although I've heard that conscription won't start until age twenty-one."

"Oh, that's only two and a half years from now, and it's already lasted three! Liam was so upset that he couldn't even eat." She told her father of Liam's speech at the church and the row at the table.

Papa glanced toward the garden. "So that's what's going on. He's wiser than I thought." He turned back to her. "So, what about you? Have you any new sketches to show me?"

"Oh, no! I mean, I'm working on a new way of drawing, and I haven't quite—"

"A new way of drawing? Well, that's something. Where did you learn it?"

Just as she hadn't wanted to tell her mother of Jim Graves, she discovered that she didn't want to tell her father. What made her feel that way? For as long as she could remember, she hadn't kept any secrets from Papa.

Yet, much too often this week, she had found herself thinking of Jim Graves and rehearsing conversations that would never take place. *See, I have tried using a grid to draw this child playing with a hoop. It makes it so much easier, so much better.* Every time she opened her sketchbook, she thought of showing him—not Papa or Seaney—her sketches.

She had sent Mr. Graves a note of thanks for the pencils—something that she did not want anyone to know. During her lunch break, she had walked it up to the fifth floor of the grand office building, where everything was marble and polished wood and brushed silk on the walls. In the outer room of Mr. Graves' office, she had handed the note to a male secretary, who had taken it in two fingers, as if it were written in poisoned ink. She had no idea if he had passed it on to Mr. Graves.

"Someone showed me," she said at last. "But Mama and I had another row at lunch."

"Over sketching, I suppose."

"She doesn't want me to—"

"Now, now, she wants the best for you. Don't forget that."

Kathleen nodded, although her stomach knotted. It was Mama who had scraped together enough money for her to take a six-month course at Barnes Commercial School in typing, bookkeeping, and stenography. It was she who had encouraged her to apply at Graves Oil, instead of a local bank or doctor's office. Perhaps it was true—she wanted the best for her daughter.

"Look, there's Venus," Papa said.

Kathleen smiled. This was an old game, one they had played nearly every evening since she could remember as they walked along the creek or sat on a red-rocked knoll high above the prairie at Redlands.

Papa continued. "The same sky that hangs over us hangs over China and Australia—"

"And Antarctica and Brazil." Kathleen played along.

"And Siam." He tried to trump her with an obscure place.

"And Tierra del Fuego."

"Whoa, girl! What was that? Tee-ahr—?"

"Tierra del Fuego," Kathleen said smugly. "It's near Chile."

"Where did you come up with that?"

"At work, there are maps pinned up on one wall that show where silver and gold and those kinds of things have been found. Miss Crawley uses them to find where Mr. Graves is drilling for oil so we can spell it right." She did not mention that when Miss Crawley found Kathleen studying the maps and neglecting her typing, the pile at her elbow had increased by yet another inch. "Most are just maps of America or the western states, but one shows the whole world."

"Well, I'll just have to come up with something better than County Cork or Ballingeary from now on." He kissed the top of her head. "I suppose we'll be naming French towns soon. Thank God this is the War to End All Wars. It has to be, with so many young men sent to their graves for it."

Kathleen's heart twisted. "I want to come home," she said. "I don't want to work there anymore—"

"Caitlin, me love," Papa soothed. "It's helping us out, your bringing in wages. And you know there's nothing at Redlands for you.

Two hundred acres of dry land that doesn't grow a blessed thing, and if I miss one more payment, the bank'll take it back anyway."

"No, Papa, it's so beautiful—"

"You can't fill your stomach on beauty."

"But I could help you in the fields, and we'd make it better. I'd help Mama with the chores, too. I'll take a job mucking out the livery in town—anything! As long as I'm out of Graves Oil—"

"No, Caitlin, no." His voice hardened. "You've done well to take this job. Your mother says you're one of the best typists they have—"

"Mama says what she wants to think, not what's true—"

"No dragging it out, now. You hear me?"

What had happened to making her own way? But she didn't want to argue with him. Not on Easter Sunday, as dismal as it might have been. Not tonight. Not ever.

"Yes, Papa," she said.

He put his arm around her, and she nestled against him. Together, they watched darkness fall.

FIVE

Overnight, banners printed with KILL KAISER BILL were hung across streets, and signs in storefronts read, NO PERSONS OF GERMAN HERITAGE ALLOWED. Posters of Uncle Sam urged America's men to make the ultimate sacrifice for freedom, and the newspapers printed photos of grinning men jamming into recruiting offices. Anything that smacked of Germany was banned. Frankfurters transformed into Liberty sausages, and sauerkraut was renamed Liberty cabbage. Patriotic festivals—bonfires, picnics, baseball games, shooting contests, boxing tournaments—were planned for every weekend, all to raise money for the troops. From the staff that angled from the brick wall of Sullivan's Grocery, Sean hung an American flag that proudly flapped and fluttered in the breeze.

On Wednesday, he arrived home just in time for dinner. As always, his mother was in the kitchen, cooking. Kathleen was setting the table, while Maggie poured water into the teakettle to brew. Entering the kitchen, he kissed his mother's temple. "Good afternoon, miladies," he said cheerfully.

Instead of smile and swoon as she usually did at his charm, his mother snapped, "Where have you been this afternoon? Your father's been lookin' for you. He had to make the deliveries himself."

"Sorry. I was busy."

Kathleen glanced a question at him. She gingerly sorted knives and spoons, as if her fingers were aching again. With a wink, he plucked the silverware from her and spun it toward the plates.

"Busy!" Ma dumped a pot and potatoes thudded into a colander. "With so much to do here, you think you can just go off without tellin' a soul, and—"

"It won't happen again."

It seemed to take forever for the potatoes to mash and the steak to fry. Forever for his father to come up from the store after Maggie had been sent to fetch him. Forever for Pa to stop raging about the fresh carcass from Irish that hung in the cool room, uncut and useless, because of Sean's irresponsibility. Even grace seemed to take longer than usual tonight. Sean waited until everyone's plate was filled, and the first bites were taken.

"I've an announcement to make," he said.

Kathleen shifted, wary. Maggie squinted, ready to mock. Sean waited until Pa left off wolfing down his food for a minute, and Ma quit fussing over the gravy boat.

"Aye, what is it?" she asked. "Eat up, Kathleen, everything's all right, is it?"

"It's fine, Aunt Maury," Kathleen said.

"I went out to the Armory today." Sean's words tumbled over one another. "I've enlisted in the American Expeditionary Force. In a few weeks, I'm joining the rest for a trip to France."

With a rabbit-like cry, Ma half-rose from her chair, then fell back, her hands over her face. The gravy boat clattered to the floor, brown sauce splattering the worn linoleum. Sean jerked out of his chair, catching her before she fell.

"Ma," he pleaded. "Ma, don't cry! It's all right! Maggie, help me!"

"You're only eighteen!" she sobbed. "Too young—!"

Maggie steadied her mother. "Ma, don't cry, please, don't—"

Sean rose, tears in his own eyes. "I've done what I had to do, Ma. Try to understand." He met his father's gaze. "President Wilson's begging for a million good men."

Pa fumbled with the cup of tea in his hands.

His mother started to keen. "Oh, Seaney, Seaney, you're my only baby boy! My only! Little Tommy and Michael both in their graves! My only one, my only—"

She had not wailed like this in years, since the last lost baby. Jolted, Sean looked around the kitchen for help. Kathleen had disappeared.

"Maureen," Pa said. "Maureen. Enough now. Stop it now—"

Sean ran from the kitchen as Maggie and Pa helped Ma from her chair and down the hall into the bedroom. Bursting onto the outdoor landing, he breathed in ragged gulps. What had he expected? For his mother to bless his decision? For his father to salute him? Why did he always imagine something different from what he got? His eyes filled again with tears, and the black line of mountains blurred into dark night sky.

Kathleen leaned against the railing a few feet away.

"Why didn't you tell me?" she demanded. "Why didn't you talk to me first?"

He swallowed. "Because you would have tried to talk me out of it."

"Of course I would have! What were you thinking? It's so stupid, all those men dead—"

"I've made myself proud," Sean interrupted. "Be proud of me, too." When she did not answer, he added, "I need to see if I can make good. And if I 'go west,' as they call it, well, no one can ask more of me, and if I come through, I'll be better for it."

He stopped, his breath catching in his throat. He had not yet stated his reasons for enlisting—perhaps he hadn't even thought of them until now—and he found himself feeling both uncertain and even more determined.

"You see that, don't you?" he said. "I had to do something. I couldn't stand working for Pa forever. You know that."

"But we'll have to live here day after day knowing . . . I can't stand it here without you!"

"You love Ma, and she loves you. I know it's not Redlands, but it's almost as good as living at home, isn't it?"

"It's not that. I just . . . oh, Seaney, you're so lucky you can leave!" She crumbled again. "But you're not lucky—of course not, going to war! I don't know what I'm saying. I'm just—"

But he was lucky. Today, as the men stood in line, waiting to add their names to the list, they had talked of whipping the Germans and making them crawl under the rock of shame. Never again would they threaten anyone's freedom. The words traveled up and down the ranks, catching fire in the spring sunshine. Beat the Heines! Stop the Huns! Bash the Boche!

There were no uniforms to be had and only one Springfield rifle, which passed through eager hands again and again. Yet there were plenty of doctors to do physical examinations—eye and hearing tests, reflexes, muscle strength—and worse, the vaccinations for typhoid and smallpox that had left Sean's arm stinging. After the men had been mustered in, they lined up in military formation and learned "right-face" and "about-face." At the end of the day, after they were dismissed, they'd all shaken hands with one another—factory workers in ragged undershirts, farm boys in denim overalls, students in narrow ties and white shirts, bankers in business suits—all pledged to the great cause. For the first time, Sean felt as if he belonged.

He thought of confiding in Kathleen, but he feared the lump in his throat would dissolve into tears. Instead, he chose to joke. "I suppose Liam will have a conniption fit over this."

Kathleen didn't laugh, and Sean's courage failed. "You'll look after Ma for me? I feel so bad for her—"

"I will. Of course, I will." Kathleen choked, and suddenly, she was sobbing as uncontrollably as his mother.

"Come on." He hugged her. "Don't cry so. It'll be all right."

A whirlwind month followed. Every morning, the newly-minted soldiers of the 137th Division marched in uneven lines up 16th and down 17th Street on their way to training. There, they learned about military drill and rules and regulations in the mornings, classes that Sean found dull after the demanding Jesuit curriculum at Blessed Savior. Still, many of the volunteers struggled, too poorly educated to understand the manuals and read the tests. Once the basics were covered, the officers in charge seemed as uncertain about what happened next as the enlistees themselves, so the men spent the afternoons sitting in the spring sunshine, smoking and talking, and receiving the well wishes of passers-by on the street.

In the evenings, in a most unsoldierly manner, Sean went home to eat and sleep. His mother still greeted him tight-lipped and sorrowful, so he took it upon himself to teach Mag to drive the truck. At the very least, he could see that Sullivan's Grocery wasn't deprived of a delivery wagon. After dinner, he and Mag tootled along the empty dirt roads west of Denver, more bent on getting out of the house than on the lessons. They talked of everything and nothing— Mag's teachers at school, who had once been Sean's, the men that Sean had met since he'd enlisted, and, always, the folks at church.

"Give it more throttle," Sean directed her as the truck sputtered up a hill.

Maggie moved the throttle, and the Model T lurched forward.

"Not that much."

"Gads," she groused. "This thing is touchy."

"At least they've got it now so you don't have to back it up the hill. The gas used to drain away when the front end went up a slope."

"Oh, if I had to do that, I'd just give it up."

Sean hung one arm out the window and splayed his fingers so that the warm air rushed through them. The pastures were starting to green, and the foothills had taken on the appearance of a greenish-blue patchwork quilt. He waved at farmers who were plowing their fields behind teams of heavy-footed draft horses, women pulling dried laundry from clotheslines, and children playing in the ditches, wishing that he was in uniform so they would know he was going to serve his country. At once, he chided himself. Who had he joined for? Himself or America?

"Now, turn it around," he told Mag.

She shoved the throttle back and forth, plying the pedals on the floor, and made the turn after six attempts.

"You'll never make it up the alley near the church," Sean warned.

"I'll never try," she said. "I intend to get very strong so I can carry stuff in from wide, flat, open spaces."

He bent his head out the window, letting the wind blow through his hair. Contentment surged through him, but he knew it wouldn't last. Sometimes at night, he woke up in a sweat, terrified of what waited for him in France. Other times, the enforced idleness of his days grated on him, and he wished that he had just stayed at Sullivan's Grocery, where, at least, he was always busy.

They arrived at the store, and Maggie inched the truck into its spot next to the back door. As she shut off the engine, she asked, "How did I do, Private Sullivan, sir?"

"Not bad at all, Miss-soon-to-be-Mrs.-Keohane."

Neither of them moved from the cab, basking in the golden light and fresh air of spring. On the street in front of the store, Danny MacMahon passed by, his silver-headed cane in his hand.

"Do you have any pepper?" Sean asked.

Mag laughed. "That was a silly game."

As children, they had hidden behind the cracker barrels in the store and blown pepper from the palms of their hands toward the customers. It was ten points per sneeze.

"You're just mad because I always won," Sean said.

"You always won because you're such a blowhard."

Sean laughed. "No, I won because you were too chicken to get close enough."

"I wasn't about to let Pa take my hide off for that."

Her words sobered him. He wouldn't miss that at all. "I'm sorry I'm going to miss your graduation," he said. "If you hadn't skipped eighth grade, you might still be in school when I come home."

"Heaven forbid," she said, then quickly added, "My being in school, that is, not you coming home."

He tried to stifle the ache that was rising in him. "I'm sorry I'm going to miss your wedding."

She looked down at her hands. "I'm worried about Liam."

"He's not going to back out, is he?"

"Not in a million years!"

Sean laughed. "The war, huh?"

"He used to read so that he would know more than anybody else." She attempted a laugh. "Now he reads so that he can argue with Brendan or me or whoever is convenient."

"Surely he'll get over it. It's just the shock of it all, don't you think?"

"I don't know," she said. "I hope so."

"Mag." Sean's throat tightened up again. "You can write to me as often as you want. I'll write back as soon as I can. I can't guarantee anything, but—"

"No one can, can they?"

The call to report to Fort Riley in Kansas came in June, and the city of Denver responded with the greatest send-off ever staged. Sean plucked at the sleeves of his graduation suit as he marched from the State Capitol to Union Station. Confetti showered him, loosed by workers who leaned from the windows of office buildings on 17th Street. It clung to his hair and caught up in the laces of his shoes. Piles of it, slippery as snow, collected on the street. The Denver Municipal Band wound down the pavement, playing "The Battle Cry of Freedom" and "Dixie," and a mounted detachment of the Colorado National Guard rode in formation, also on its way to war. On both sides of the street, hundreds of spectators see-sawed in a blur of red, white, and blue.

Sean grinned and waved, deafened by the cheers and whistles.

At Union Station, the band forced itself onto the platform. Sean twisted through the mob until he spotted Pa, Liam, Maggie and Kathleen. Ma had stayed home, too distraught to leave her bed.

Pushing forward, he worked his way to his family. Maggie rushed to him and wrapped her arms around his neck. He held her, feeling the tremors shaking her ribs. She carried some of Ma's heavy, rose fragrance with her. Sean closed his eyes, breathing deeply.

"I'm proud of you, me brother," she said. "I'll miss you."

"I hope you and Liam are happy," he said. "He's being a good sport about this. At least, he's not giving me an earful."

"Don't worry, he already gave me one about it." She pressed something into his hand. "This is for you."

It was a red, satin ribbon decorated with sequins. Across the top, "Sean" was clumsily sewn with black beads. A picture of Jesus had been glued toward the bottom.

"It's a bookmark," she said. "Will you use it?"

He stroked it with one finger. "I don't know how much reading I'll be doing."

"Look at it when you write to me, then."

"Mag"—there was so much he hadn't yet said—"be good and listen to Ma."

"Be safe—please—and come home."

They hugged again, then Sean moved to Liam. "Take care of my squirt of a sister."

Maggie protested with a tearful laugh. "Seaney—"

"I wish you well." Liam shook Sean's hand. "I'll pray for you, Brother."

His father came forward as the train whistle blasted the first boarding call. He grasped Sean's hand. "Goodbye, son. 'Tis a fine thing, you know. Servin' your country."

"Thank you, Pa." Sean clasped his father's hand between both of his. His father stepped back, unsteady.

Then, there was Kathleen. She tried to smile, to act brave. Sean tried to do the same, to ignore the red rims of her eyes and the dark circles below. He kissed her cheek. "Don't forget about me in the romantic darkness of the Graves Oil typing pool."

"Don't forget that we're all waiting for you to come home." She faltered, then hugged him. "Oh, Seaney—"

The train whistle shrieked again. A cheer split the crowd as the men hurried on board. Sean kissed the top of Kathleen's head, hugged Maggie again, and ran. He swung his valise up the train steps and worked his way inside, stalled behind men who shouldered trunks and enormous bags of food. What did they need all that for? They were starting new lives. He leaned out the open window to call goodbye. The train jerked forward as the band burst into *The Battle Hymn of the Republic*. "Glory, glory hallelujah," the men on the train sang. Sean caught sight of the girls, who were waving wildly and blowing kisses.

He craned his neck out the window until they disappeared from sight.

SIX

In a pasture in eastern Colorado, Jim Graves squatted and crushed sandy soil between his fingers. Squinting upward into blue sky, he listened to the deafening throb of machinery. The engine hissed, and the cables whined as the drill bit chewed its way through sand and rock. Realizing that he had been holding his breath in anticipation, he exhaled. He loved the chase—man against nature, who never gave up her treasures easily, though his wits and intelligence were pitted against her. Brushing dust from the toes and vamps of his cowboy boots, he rose.

The foreman crossed the field, his face in a scowl. "I don't know, Mr. Graves. We been drilling a long time now. You'd think the gusher woulda come in by now."

"It's there." Only last night, Jim had studied another core sample from the well. Laid out on a newspaper in his hotel room, the cylindrical clump of dirt was the golden tan of brown sugar. "Keep going."

He left the site as darkness fell, retiring to the clapboard hotel on Main Street, which was the only hotel in town. As he ate in the dining room, he noticed the proprietor's daughter, a woman in her mid-twenties, whose dark hair drooped with moisture from the kitchen cooking pot and whose lips were unusually red. Her shoulders were broad from years of hard work, but her waist was still slim. She served Jim and the one other patron of the hotel, an elderly man who did not hear well enough to converse, then wiped her hands on her apron as she returned to the kitchen.

When the woman brought him a slice of pie, Jim asked, "What excitement is there in town tonight?"

She gave a crooked smile. "The circus comes through every year. You just missed it."

"It's a long wait until the next."

"What are you doin' in town?"

"I'm drilling for oil."

"My husband got blowed off a well fourteen months ago down in Oklahoma." She nodded toward a little boy playing in the corner. "Left me with Jesse not even two years old."

"What's your name?"

"Daisy Ellington."

"That's pretty."

She shrugged, not as malleable as he had hoped. "Will you be here long?"

"A few more days."

"I'll cook somethin' special, then."

She left for the kitchen. Jim went to his room, which was neat and clean, the sheets starched and ironed. He removed his jacket, twisted on the kerosene lamp, and sat at the round, claw-footed table that had been placed in one corner of the room. Gathering papers from his briefcase, he studied the results of the test wells, the dip of the sand, and the pay limits of the pool one more time. He was sure that this well would come in; it was simply a matter of nerve—of which he had plenty.

As he rose from the table to dress for bed, he looked around the shabby, spartan room. This was how he had lived since Henry Ford decided every American should own an automobile: alone and away from the luxuries of his life in Denver. It seemed ironic— during his early childhood, he was ensconced in beauty and riches. His mother, Victoria, had filled the Graves' mansion with nattily-dressed, perfumed women, and pampered children. Delicate pastries were served by bustling maids, while someone's untalented daughter played the piano. His mother presided over these gatherings with practiced smile and beautifully coiffed hair. "Mr. Graves will be so pleased to see us tonight," she said. "He so likes it when we are happy."

Sometimes Jim would protest, more in rebellion than truth, "I am unhappy." Given to dark moods and inexplicable sadness, he confounded his mother. She set out to placate him: *Look, Jimmy, I have brought you a new wind-up soldier, a new bicycle, a new puppy. Look, Jimmy, your father has brought you a pony from the Indian chiefs in southern Colorado. It is named Ouray. Let us see your smile.*

The next evening, when Jim came in dusty and hungry from the field, Daisy was waiting for him at the door of the hotel dining room. Her face was flushed, and she breathed as if she'd been running.

"I'm sorry I didn't recognize you before now, Mr. Graves," she said. "I was tired, I think. Jesse'd been fussin' the past few days with a runny nose, and—"

Jim laughed, surprised by her fervor. "That's quite all right."

She thrust her hand forward. "But you're the one who's always talkin' up the war. I read all the newspaper reports about it, and now, I'm so glad to meet you—"

He shook her hand. "The pleasure is mutual, Daisy."

Once again, he dined with the elderly gentleman before retiring to his room. Shortly after nine, there was a knock at his door. Jim rolled down the sleeves of his shirt and reattached his collar. After caching his papers in his case, he went to the door.

Daisy stood in the shadowy hallway. "I thought you might want somethin' to drink." She carried a tray that held a decanter of whiskey. "This is Dad's best."

"Well, thank you, Daisy," he said. "You'll have a glass with me?"

She set the tray on the table, then turned toward him, the color high in her cheeks and her lips nearly apple red. Jim could see a small mole near her bottom lip and a triangle of dark spots near her right temple. He wondered why she had come to his room at such a late hour and with the distinct smell of lilac. Nervously, she wiped her hands on her skirt.

He offered her a chair before sitting across the table from her. "Please sit down."

She poured the whiskey into two tumblers. Raising one, she said, "To our great country."

"To our great country," Jim repeated.

She took a deep pull, obviously accustomed to drinking. Setting down her glass, she said, "I wanted to talk to you about something since you're so important in the war and all."

He leaned back and pulled at his collar, wishing he hadn't refastened it. "I'm hardly important, Daisy, but what is it?"

She glanced toward the window as if she expected someone to be peering into the room. "There's some Germans who live around here, there's lots of them, really, and they say they come from Russia, but they're really just Germans. They're all farmers, or they work in the sugar beet fields up north of here. They've got properties all the way to the state line, I think."

Jim tried to parse the breathless, tangled statements.

"I don't think they support the war," Daisy said. "I think they're hopin' America loses."

"What have you heard them say?"

"Nothin'," she said. "But they talk German, not American."

"You mean English," he corrected.

"They come into town in groups—lots of 'em all at once. They go to all the stores, and there's no way to watch 'em all."

"Do they steal?"

"I never heard that." Her voice dropped to a whisper. "I don't think they've surrendered their guns, like they was supposed to when President Wilson called for war. I think they still have 'em and are gettin' more besides."

"Why are you talking so quietly?"

"You don't know who's listenin'," she said. "They could take over the whole town and hold it for the Kaiser."

Jim swallowed his doubts that the Kaiser would want such a forlorn place. "Daisy," he said gently. "I think you might be taking gossip as truth—"

"But it's in the newspapers all the time," she protested. "About Hun plots to poison our fields and ruin our food. Who was it that was gonna blow up the Erie Canal or somethin', that Von Pope—?"

"Von Papen," Jim said. "And it was the Welland Canal in Canada—"

"And just last week, four steers was found slaughtered on the Cook farm, just east of town. They didn't even take the meat, they just killed 'em and left 'em to rot. It's the Germans trying to scare us, I know it is."

"Surely you have a county sheriff or town marshal here."

"Well, sure we do," she said. "Henry Waring's our sheriff, and he's real nice and all, but—"

"Have you talked to him about this?"

"Oh, he knows," she said smugly. "Him and a bunch of others have sworn to be Nathan Hale Volunteers—"

"What's that?"

"You mean you ain't heard of it?" She scoffed. "The Nathan Hale Volunteers keep the Germans under their thumbs, watchin' every move, makin' sure that the Huns don't do anything that ain't American. They drive by the Hun places at night to see if there's anything goin' on and keep a watch on them at the post office. You know, they say that that Adolph Coors fellow who used to make the beer up in Denver was puttin' arsenic in it. Not enough to kill, but enough to make anybody who drinks it sick as a dog."

At that, Jim laughed. "I can assure you that Mr. Coors was doing no such thing. I know the gentleman."

She stood. "You don't believe me? Now, he's makin' malted milk for kiddies since there's Prohibition. He could kill them!"

"Sit down, Daisy," Jim said. "Have another drink." He poured from the decanter, and she sat once more. "It's not that I don't believe you. It's just that, sometimes, perfectly innocent actions are misconstrued or interpreted as something else."

"The Germans ain't never been innocent. They're beasts come out of hell."

Jim pondered that. "The next time you hear or see something that you don't think is right, call your local sheriff and he can sort it out. President Wilson has asked us all to be vigilant. You'll be doing your patriotic duty."

"Then you think I'm right?"

"I think you're a good American citizen keeping a sharp eye out for the good of our country."

She played with her glass, turning it around and around. "Do you have a wife at home waitin' for you?" Quickly she added, "Roy, he'd go out on the road for weeks. I never could tell when I'd see him."

Jim stifled his amusement at the question. "No, I don't have a wife."

"That's good. It ain't no life for a woman, seein' her husband now and then, and never really knowin'. They had to send somebody to tell me he was gone."

"I'm sorry."

She looked up at him, her dark eyes tearing and her red lips damp. Jim had the feeling that this wasn't the first time she had brought a bottle to a man's room and stayed for more than conversation. He leaned back, waiting.

She lost her nerve. "I should go," she said. "Dad doesn't always hear when Jesse wakes up—"

"You don't have to go. Finish your drink."

He watched as she downed the rest of the whiskey. She stood, swayed a bit, and touched the top of the table to balance herself. Then she walked over to him, bent down, and took his face between her hands to kiss him.

Jim reached for her.

Later, as the night deepened into silence, he lay awake, listening to Daisy's heavy breathing. The metal springs of the bed pushed through the battered ticking of the mattress under the weight of two, causing a sharp poke in his back. After a while, he rose to have a cigarette. The window looked down on the intersection of Main Street with the dirt highway that led out of town. Both were deserted, although a tinkling sound could be heard from a tavern halfway down the block. That was probably about as much of the night as this town ever witnessed.

He exhaled. It seemed the Russian Germans were guilty of nothing more than speaking their native tongue and travelling in groups. How easy it was to find an enemy in this world.

Daisy stirred in the bed, and Jim turned toward her. She ran a hand through the dark hair that cascaded at her shoulder. "I should be going," she said.

"Of course," he said, glad to be rid of her.

"You'll think about what I said?" she asked as she pulled on her stockings. "You'll tell them up in Denver about how much danger we're in out here from all them Germans."

"I will if there's a need for it."

"There's gotta be some way to send 'em back to their own country or somethin', right?"

"Some of them are probably American citizens by now."

"But if they ain't actin' like Americans and supportin' the war—"

"We'll see."

He found a twenty-dollar bill in his money clip. After she had pulled on her dress, he held it out toward her.

She merely looked at it.

"I can't take that," she said. "It don't seem right—"

"Buy something for Jesse with it."

"I didn't do this because I need money," she said heatedly. "I got plenty of money from the settlement after Roy died and from workin' for Dad—"

"Think of it as an early Christmas or birthday gift. Money you can use for what you want, not what you need."

She reached for the money, but withdrew her hand. "I'm not that kind of woman."

She was out the door before he could speak. Jim folded the bill and slipped in under the lamp, where she would be sure to find it when she cleaned the room.

The next day, the drilling ground on at the site of the well. The foreman wiped his forehead. "You sure it ain't a dry hole?"

"I'm sure," Jim said. "I'll be back in a few weeks, when it's farther along."

He left town on the evening train without saying good-bye to Daisy. By midnight, he was in Denver.

****

The home of Arthur and Victoria Graves in Denver's Cheesman Park could not be described by any other word but ostentatious. Built in Romanesque style, its predominant feature was arches—side by side along the covered porch, at either end of the grand parlor, and cascading in mirror image down magnificent hallways. The walls were papered in Italian damask, and from the ceilings hung crystal chandeliers. The furniture in the parlor was upholstered in rich brocade, with golden threads tracing lines through the fabric. Tiffany lamps stood on solid mahogany tables, and paintings the size of murals hung along one paneled wall. They were mostly landscapes and hunting scenes, done by artists of the West—Bierstadt's Long's Peak, Max Cornelius, Remington, Russell. A family portrait, commissioned nearly two decades ago, hung above the fireplace, showing proud parents and four children.

Jim stood by the window, looking out at the garden, his back to the elegance. Seated on the lush divans and chairs were the regular Friday evening guests: his mother, father, and sister, Eleanora Brently, and his aunt and uncle, Minerva and Donald Davis, Samuel Fallows—a second cousin or something—and his wife Gladys, and the Crawfords, his parents' best friends. The talk was turning, as it always did, to war.

"Germany should have been stopped when the *Lusitania* went down," Samuel blustered. "A hundred Americans dead, and not a thing done about it. The Sussex pledge has long been a joke."

"But now it seems that America is giving all her energies to the business of war and forsaking all other occupations," Uncle Donald inserted. "The factories are setting up to make planes or weapons. What will become of the necessities of life?"

"As long as we can still shop in New York," Mrs. Crawford said, and Jim's mother laughed with her.

Uncle Donald continued. "The United States has promised France alone twelve thousand planes and five thousand pilots within a year. That sort of production will require the dedication of every industry in the land."

"How does that affect you, Jim?" his mother asked.

Leave it to her to direct the conversation back to him. Blonde and blue-eyed, his mother exuded such energy that everyone else vanished in her presence. Although she stood little more than five feet tall, Jim could not help but think of her as towering over the others in the room.

"The European war effort runs on oil," he said. "And America's army will, too, once it is organized and at full strength."

"I've heard that President Wilson is talking of lowering the conscription age down to seventeen and extending it to forty," Uncle Donald said. "Not enough men have come forward to enlist."

"Maybe they should let women enlist," Eleanora said. "That should please Mrs. Anthony's followers."

Laughter rounded the room. Jim moved away from the window and passed through the sumptuous arch that separated the parlor from the library. Ensconcing himself in a thickly upholstered leather armchair, he lit a cigarette. He could still hear the conversation, but he did not have to answer in here, amid the bookshelves. The room was drenched in shadow; only a single lamp burned on a corner table.

"Have you heard that Governor Gunter has ordered the Colorado National Guard to protect Cheesman Dam?" Samuel asked. "He's afraid that German conspirators will dynamite it."

"I've heard that the Denver Union Water Company and the Colorado Power Company are both under military protection," Mr. Crawford added.

"And we're not to buy from German shopkeepers because they have put ground glass into their sausages," Mrs. Crawford said.

Eleanora laughed. "Ground glass?"

"That's what I've heard, anyway," Mrs. Crawford snipped.

Samuel changed the subject. "I think America has more to fear from the empire of Japan than it does the Germans. If we are attacked on America soil, it will be by the Japanese."

"The Japanese!" Mrs. Crawford exclaimed. "Why in the world would they attack America?"

"Those who are living here have already threatened war in California because they've been denied ownership of land. I say we're lucky to have the Immigration Act that was just put in place. All sorts of undesirables are kept out—not only the Asiatics, but degenerates and criminals and the illiterate, too."

Jim closed his eyes. The whole country, it seemed, was bent on a witch hunt to find the most egregious enemy.

"Jim."

He sat up a bit straighter. Eleanora stood in the archway, her blue eyes—so like his mother's and his own—brilliant even in the dim light. She wore a filmy turquoise drape, which was overlaid with a gold bodice that sparkled with a fringe of silver bugle beads. A wide, beaded belt encircled her waist, ending in a gold oval-shaped buckle. In her fair hair, she wore a gold and silver brocade braid. On her feet were the barest of golden slippers. She looked like a Roman goddess come to earth.

"Are you quite certain that your sausages are free of ground glass?" he asked.

Eleanora laughed again, a light trill. "I don't believe even our best novel writers could invent some of the things that are being said just now."

"I heard something similar during my trip to the eastern plains last week. A concern over malted milk."

"It all seems rather hysterical, doesn't it?" She moved into the shadow of the library, her dress still sparkling in the dim lamp light. "What are you doing? Have you come in here to pout?"

"It's impossible," he said.

"Oh, you are pouting." She took a cigarette from a jeweled case. "I didn't think anything was impossible for you. So what is?"

Jim leaned forward to light the cigarette. "America has made promises to the French and British that it can never keep, but they're so exhausted that they haven't thought to question how we plan to accomplish our goals."

"Oh, that." She puffed once. "It's all so tiring, isn't it?"

"You heard them—twelve thousand airplanes and five thousand pilots. How can that happen? We have almost no pilots or aircraft capable of war. And a complete navy—when we have only a handful of ships that would stand the test of battle."

Eleanora sat across from him in another plush armchair. "You're doubting our sage president, then?"

"I'm doubting the entire expedition."

"My, my, the great Preparedness man comes clean."

"That's the problem. We are not prepared. For years, Wilson has dragged his feet, giving into popular panic and refusing to militarize, and now, we are far from being ready for this." He smashed the butt of his cigarette into a silver ashtray. "Our soldiers will be babes in the woods."

She exhaled a long, steady stream of smoke. One of her most alluring habits was her ability to coax the world to hold its breath while waiting for her to speak. She never hurried, never grew anxious or nervy, as Jim so often did. "Why don't you join up?" she asked. "Then you would be cannon fodder with eight seconds—isn't that the number?—to live on the battlefield. You'd have no worries."

"You forget I went to Plattsburg. I'm officer material."

"Summer camp for the brave and true and ridiculously wealthy." She laughed. "I'm sure officers don't last long on the battlefield either."

"In any case, President Wilson won't let me join. I'm 'temporarily exempted due to my employment in an industrial enterprise essential to the war effort.'"

"Ah, yes." She exhaled again. "Essential personnel. Does our president expect you to find enough oil to fuel the entire war machine?"

"America is already producing seventy percent of it."

"Then there is room for improvement."

Jim said nothing. The honor of being indispensable rankled him. He had been named First Lieutenant at Plattsburg after completing the required courses and tests. Yet that was now a useless achievement, as he had been stripped of the responsibilities of the rank. The war would grind away in Flanders Field while he spent his time in the oil fields of Wyoming and Oklahoma.

"Since so many of our charming young men have already gone, it seems almost pointless to declare war," Ellie said. "Half of the boys from Yale and Harvard are in France as Lafayette fliers, and the yachting competitions have come to naught—pun intended—for the past two seasons."

"I doubt they're doing much besides seeing out the war in the music halls of Paris."

"Still, they are there, and fully involved in the matter."

She waited, gauging his reaction, trying to assess the damage. She knew she could drive him into self-loathing and despair by pointing out his weaknesses and failings. Dear Ellie—it might hurt if he were not capable of inflicting the same on her. They had grown up knowing that each was equally disappointing to their parents— something they were never allowed to forget. To prove it, Ellie had married at twenty to a young mining engineer with the suitably upper-crust name of Anderson Brently. By the time she was twenty-five, she had left him. At twenty-seven, she sued for divorce in a scandal that had cost the Graves' family much of its standing in the stranglehold of Denver's social register. Now at thirty-five, she vowed to remain unmarried for the rest of her life.

For his part, Jim had managed to shame his parents while he was still at Princeton. The embarrassment, although not nearly as public as Ellie's fracas, had—of course—involved a woman.

"Well, if you can't join them, beat them," Eleanora said. "With all your abilities and money, you should be able to find a way to do something heroic." She waved her cigarette toward the parlor. "After all, Mother and Father's ambitions are focused on you. I am already spoken of in the past tense."

He stopped himself from squirming, which would have delighted her. His thoughts went back to the portrait of the Graves family above the fireplace in the parlor. It had been painted before the accident, when all four Graves children were alive. When he looked at it, he saw only Stephen. The eldest, the golden boy, the one who was first in his class, who excelled at math as much as he did football, who possessed an overabundance of the Graves charm and intelligence. He had been the one upon whom all hopes hung: a sterling college record, a political career, marriage into the rarified realm of Denver's Sacred 36, which the Graves family had never been able to crack. But he had died at fifteen, long before any of it could be realized.

"I'm not sending any more men to France," Jim declared. "The halls at work are already devoid of men, and I can't even find boomers anymore. Only drunk and down-on-their-luck fools who are as likely to be killed through stupidity as to earn a day's wage."

"Boomers?"

"Men to work the oil rigs."

"You and your utterly un-endearing oil talk. Has anyone ever told you that it's boring?"

"They wouldn't dare. I'm too rich."

She laughed, inhaled, blew out, then leaned forward, as if a great epiphany had come to her. "So don't send more men to France. Send women."

"I beg your pardon?"

At once, her facade vanished. "They're clamoring for nurses' assistants and the like in France. Women who can fix cars, women who can write letters, women who can type—just about anything. The Red Cross and the YMCA have already sent legions of women across the pond. Why don't you create your own Relief Society?"

"That's as much a folly as Ford's Peace Ship."

"No, it isn't," she said. "Why shouldn't we have a share in it? We're expected to sit out every major event in history while men fumble their way through it—"

"We? You're starting to sound like those awful suffragists of the National Woman's Party. Have you considered chaining yourself to the Capitol until you are recognized as a fully equal member of society?"

She leaned back into her chair. "Snideness doesn't suit you the way it does me," she remarked. "But, yes, I think you should send me. And a group of women volunteers. Only a few to start with, others to follow. We'll go where we're needed—"

"You intend to wander around France looking for things to do? You've been reading too much about the Angels of the Battlefield."

"We could be a social service organization—"

"Careful, Ellie. The Red Cross demands chastity and moral purity."

"You find this funny, don't you?"

"I find it cock-eyed."

"No more cock-eyed than promising twelve thousand planes when America hasn't a single military pilot to its name. No more idiotic than fighting a war on a foreign continent in the first place." She thought for a moment. "The suffragists will love you for it. They'll vote for you when you find the time to run for governor."

"And the National Peace Party—which is made up of the same women—will hate me." He reconsidered. "It is dangerous, you know. The Germans have raped and pillaged their way through Belgium and France."

"It's dangerous to walk down the street," she countered. "Or to eat sausage, or wash with soap that the German peddlers have supposedly tainted with poison." She paused, then added, "And if you won't agree, I'll speak to Mother."

Jim laughed, but his chest tightened. If their mother thought that there was any advantage in it, she would endorse it whole-heartedly and harangue him until it happened. He was, after all, the only son now.

"Come now, Ellie," he chided. "You've seen the photos of men in France and England who no longer have limbs or noses. I've always thought you preferred your men with all their parts."

"Yes, but I'm at the age when a woman is considered hopeless if she doesn't have a husband. I have to dedicate myself to charity and good works instead."

"I doubt that."

"It's brilliant, Jim. It would be a spectacular publicity stunt for you, and it would allow me to escape from Mother's disapproval for a while."

"By leaving the country?"

She waved a hand in mock dismissal. "We do what we must."

He mulled it over. She was right, it would make for ample publicity, and Ellie was as smart and capable as he was. He needn't expend much energy on it.

"You'll plan it all?" he asked. "I won't have to do anything but finance it?"

"You won't have to do anything but sign the checks, darling. I won't bother you with a single detail."

She came to him and kissed his forehead. Turning away, she glided—the Roman goddess of Succor now—toward the parlor. As she rounded the corner, Jim heard her say, "Mother, Jim has agreed to the most marvelous idea!"

Late that night, Jim returns to his own house in Cheesman Park, only three blocks from his parents' home, after dropping Eleanora off at her apartment near the Capitol. He stands for a moment in the foyer, the echoing silence of the three-story work of art folding around him. Everything is brilliant here—the marble floor, the grand staircase with a fifteen-foot tall stained glass window crowning the landing, the glittering chandeliers overhead. The house is rich in color—woods of dark mahogany, marble of pinks and gray and dove white, high ceilings with murals of blue, burgundy and gold.

No one is waiting for him—he had driven the Mercer Raceabout himself tonight—so he removes his greatcoat and lays it on the credenza. Harris, his valet, emerges from the hallway that leads to the back of the house. "Good evening, sir," he says. "There is brandy in the study."

"Good," Jim says. "Nothing more tonight."

"Goodnight, sir."

As Harris gathers up the coat, Jim goes into his study and closes the door. The room is swathed in dark, heavy furnishings and décor—a polished walnut desk that required the effort of four men to move it; bookshelves filled with tomes on history and economics, which he had studied in college; and crimson floor-to-ceiling drapes over the vast window at the far end of the room. He clicks on the desk lamp and pours the brandy, then sits in a cowhide-covered armchair near the fireplace. As he crosses his legs, the light reflects on his boots—tonight, black with an emerald green twine up the side welt.

His mother had seen Ellie's grand plan differently. "This must be seen as your action," she had told Jim, blithely dismissing Ellie. "A plan to involve all Americans, regardless of gender or lowly birth."

"How very democratic of you, Mother," Eleanora said.

His mother had cast a steely look in her direction. "My Ladies National Service Organization has been given a list of classes by the Red Cross for the education of the population. It's very possible that the young ladies would benefit from taking them."

Jim had looked over the list before handing it to Ellie: Elementary Hygiene, Home Care of the Sick, First Aid to the Injured, Good Citizenship, National Preparedness, and the Americanization of the Foreign Born, among others.

Ellie had balked. "If we take all these, we won't make it to France for years."

"I am Brigadier General of the organization," his mother huffed. "It would seem rather negligent if my own daughter's charges failed to take them."

"Brigadier General?" Jim asked.

"It was decided that our organization would follow the same pattern as a military unit. So, yes, as the leader, I am referred to as the Brigadier General."

So even his mother had earned a military title.

After much back-and forth, it was decided—not necessarily by him—that the first cadre of four young women bound for France would come from within the ranks of the secretaries and stenographers at his own company, with Eleanora as their chaperone and sponsor. The young women would be paid whatever salary they currently made, plus a benefit sent directly to their families. Their transportation, training, uniforms, and all other needs or requirements would be financed by Graves Oil.

He goes to the desk to pour another drink. A crumpled piece of paper lies on the ink blotter. He picks it up and smooths out the wrinkles. Written in perfectly even Catholic script, it reads: "Thank you for the pencils. I will use them wisely to make them last as long as possible. I am sorry that I've been collecting stubs from the trash, but there are times when a good amount of lead is left. It seems a sin to waste it."

It was signed in with flourish: Kathleen Maura Bridget O'Doherty.

He'd forgotten about it, delivered to him long ago at work by his secretary and left here after he pulled it from his coat pocket. He reads it again. It is so naïvely prim, so school-girlishly righteous, so undeniably Catholic. And so Irish. Did she realize as she wrote it that she was sloughing off her culpability for taking company property by pointing the finger at those who threw away perfectly good lead? Did she even think twice about using the word "sin"? And such a mouthful of unwieldy names for such a petite girl.

He laughs aloud before he tosses the note in the trash. Leaving the study, he climbs the sweeping oak stairs, passing beneath the stained glass window of a beautiful maiden carrying a lute. On either side, colorful peacocks strutted in full fanfare. His bedroom, behind the fourth and final door along the left-hand hallway, is another room of deep maroon flourishes, ornate cornices, and dark, polished wood. A hand-woven Chinese rug of red and gold lies on the floor, and two velvet-upholstered chairs sit before the fireplace.

In the bathroom, he washes up and dons the smoking jacket that Harris has laid out for him in the dressing room. Yet, instead of going to the bed, he opens the door into an adjoining room that is decorated in a pristine cream color, so light and pure that it is tinged a faint pinkish-orange by the light of the electric lamp. A canopy of filmy cloth arches over the wide bed and falls in gentle, soft drapes. Plush pillows bedeck the satin coverlet, so many that nearly half the bed disappears beneath them. A chair and fainting couch occupy one corner. In the other stands an armoire of dark, glimmering wood. On the vanity lies a silver-backed brush and comb. A mirror arches over the vanity, its edges scrolled with delicate, floral designs.

He doesn't often come into this room. It was designed for a woman, with closets that span the full length of the wall and its own bath and dressing room. His bachelorhood is a mystery, not only to his parents, who are eager to see him make a marriage into Denver's society circles, but to the gossipy Denver newspapers. How can a man who is so successful, who was a millionaire by his own hand by the time he was twenty-five and now, at thirty, a leader in the state, still be single?

Ellie claims it is his penchant for lower-class women that keeps him from choosing a presentable wife. Perhaps it is; certainly Daisy Ellington fits the bill. He thinks again of Kathleen. What would it be like to possess such an unspoiled, untamed creature? A woman he could teach to love and think—she's already displayed a pleasing curiosity and boldness—and to share his wealth and worth.

He feels the darkness coming on again. Is it loneliness—he, who never lacks for a woman on his arm, who is considered the premier guest at any function he attends, who is expected to accomplish great things in his lifetime? Is it unhappiness, the child of his past crying out again, missing his dead brother and sister? Or is it that, after aligning himself with the titans of business in New York and Philadelphia and pushing America into war, he is now stuck here, left out, forgotten while the butcher, the baker, and the candlestick maker march off to glory?

He curses himself for leaving the brandy below in the study. It is the one thing that soothes him when he finds himself in this mood. Closing the door to the cream-colored room, he makes his way downstairs.

SEVEN

Maggie stood in front of the full-length mirror in Ma's attic, looking at her own reflection. She was dressed in her wedding dress, the one that had been worn by Grandmother Murphy, long before the voyage to America, when she still lived in County Cork. The lace of the collar came all the way up to her chin, and the dress weighed on her shoulders, its yards and yards of fabric made heavier by hundreds of tiny seed pearls sewn to the bodice. The leg of mutton sleeves were a confection of lace and beading that covered her arms all the way to her fingertips. A full-length lace veil cascaded from the top of her head to the floor, lying over her shoulders like a cape. All she could see of herself was the tiny oval of her face and a few strands of hair near her forehead. The rest of her was swallowed in faille and lace.

Ma fussed with the veil, while Auntie Eileen tugged at the hem, her lips clenched around a passel of straight pins. Sometimes it was hard to remember that the two were twins. Auntie Eileen's mouth was a colorless button, and her blue eyes were drained of color, while Ma's cheeks glowed with a rosy fullness and her hair shone golden red. It wasn't that life had dealt Maggie's mother a better hand than Auntie Eileen's. After their double wedding ceremony, Ma had lost babies one after another, while Auntie Eileen had only been able to have the one.

"And we're to keep our peach pits for some reason," Ma was saying. "What do they use those for?"

Maggie answered. "They extract the charcoal from them to put in the gas masks for the soldiers—"

"Oh, none of that now, it's too ugly."

Silenced, Maggie gazed into her own eyes again. Not a single American soldier had set foot in France, yet the war seemed to run everyone's life. No one could talk about anything else just now, and Liam's voice was the loudest of them all.

She studied the lace on her wrists, afraid of what she might read in her own eyes. He had been talking not only to the people he knew, but to anyone who would listen. The war, he had concluded, was not a "just war," as the Church had deemed it, but a travesty of greed and waste. "Morality is universal," he said. "It can't be shaped and distorted to fit the situation at hand."

She looked up again. Surely, he would forget about it once they were married. What man didn't want a loving wife and—she mentally crossed herself—plenty of children? The brick house that Liam had rented provided ample room for a family. It had three bedrooms upstairs and a kitchen and parlor with fireplace on the main floor. Even better, a bath had been squeezed into a pantry next to the kitchen, with running water in the tub—a luxury that Ma and Auntie Eileen didn't even have. Maggie thrilled as she thought of it all: her clothes hanging in the closet, her shoes on the floor next to Liam's, her pillow on the bed beside his, the two of them lying side by side—

"Charlie McKenna has been turned down," Ma said. "One leg's longer than t'other, so the army won't take him. He's become a Four Minute Man."

"Well, he's a lucky fellow, isn't he?" Auntie Eileen said.

"I thought we should buy a Liberty Loan from him, but Seamus said the McKennas never fail to buy the cheapest, and Roddy won't part with a dime more than he has to. So we'll not be supportin' Charlie."

"It's for America, Ma," Maggie interceded. "It's for the troops. Maybe even for Seaney."

"Aye, but Charlie gets five dollars a week for sellin' them, don't think he doesn't."

Maggie heaved a sigh; those two lived by their own logic. Fingering the seed beads on the bodice of her gown, she asked, "Who wore the dress when you were married?"

"Your auntie did," Ma said. "I wore a white confirmation dress."

"I wish now that you'd have worn it, Maureen," Auntie Eileen said. "I don't think my marriage has lived up to it."

"Ah, Eileen, 'tis a shame, 'tis a shame."

Maggie picked at a loose bead on the sleeve. It seemed odd that Uncle Irish was considered a worse catch than her own father. He was always jovial—as far as she knew, at least—and had a kind word for everyone. She smiled as she thought of his pet name for her: Muffin.

Ma cleared her throat. "There is somethin' we need to talk about, Mag," she said stiffly. "'Tis your duty as a wife."

"My duty?" Maggie asked.

Auntie Eileen took over. "It's somethin' you must abide, now, hard as it may be. Somethin' you must put out of your mind, except when you must endure it, and you must endure it because you must have children. That's a wife's secret burden, you know."

Ma nodded her head in sage agreement, but Maggie laughed.

"Are you talking about sex?" she asked. "I know all about that."

Ma winced at the rawness of the word, but Auntie Eileen asked, "How do you know? Who told you?"

"The girls at school talk," Maggie said. "It's just a natural act, like breathing or eating. I don't know of anyone who doesn't know that."

Both Ma and Auntie Eileen looked as if they had been slapped.

"Who's tellin' you all of this?" Auntie Eileen demanded. "It isn't Kathleen, is it?"

"No, it isn't Kathleen." Maggie laughed at the thought of talking about sex with her prissy cousin. "Jenny Winslow had a pamphlet called, 'When You Marry,' and we read all the interesting parts."

"Surely that's a sin," Ma said.

"Reading isn't a sin, Ma." Maggie shifted, the dress barely budging around her. "Are you finished yet?"

"Well, I hope if you have any questions, this Jenny girl is around with her fine pamphlet," Auntie Eileen said tartly. "Now, stand still."

Maggie let her mother and Auntie Eileen undress her. They lifted away the veil, and then carefully undid the dozens of pearl buttons that ran down the back to Maggie's waist and up her wrists to her elbows. She stood with her arms slightly bent and hands hanging, a manikin with no will of her own, as the dress slid from her shoulders and pooled on the floor. Once she stepped carefully around it, she shook her entire body, which felt as if it had just lost twenty pounds of weight.

"How many hours do you think it took to make it?" she asked her mother.

"'Tis not the hours, but the love that matters."

"And the love it stands for," Auntie Eileen added.

Maggie raised her eyebrows. She'd never known her aunt to say anything tender or sweet. Affection rushed through her as the two busied themselves in securing the buttons again on the dress before hanging it. She knew they loved her. Why, then, was she so critical of them? Why did she find it so hard to love them as they were in return?

"Ma," she said. "Thank you."

"For what?"

"For the dress and"—she gestured at her stick-like body, clad only in a slip—"fixing it to fit me."

"Well, I don't know who else would wear it," Ma said. "Kathleen, someday, of course. Then we'll redo it for her."

Auntie Eileen nodded sagely, and Maggie kissed her aunt's cheek, then her mother's.

Donning a skirt and blouse, she went outside. The warm May breeze blew against her arms and legs, and she realized how much heat the wedding dress had trapped against her body.

She found Liam, as she'd expected, at Blessed Savior, standing on the steps and talking with Frank MacMahon. Both Liam and Frank were dressed in their work clothes—Liam in tie and business jacket and Frank in his coveralls.

"Well, it's done," Frank said.

"Yes," Liam said. "It's done."

"What's done?" Maggie asked.

"We registered for the Selective Service today."

"Oh." A jolt rose up from Maggie's belly. "It doesn't mean you'll have to go. And anyway, Seaney says it's not so bad."

"I don't know what my dad will say," Frank said. "He's hell-bent that none of us join with the British, and Donnell and Pat aren't about to cross him. But I've no wish to come up against the Selective Service Act."

"The yoke of the tyrant, you mean," Liam scoffed. "They should have let Teddy Roosevelt take his minions and go."

"What do you mean?" Maggie asked.

"He wanted to raise an all-volunteer militia to take to Europe. President Wilson wouldn't see it."

"I'll let you know what my dad says tomorrow, Liam." Frank tipped his hat toward Maggie. "Evening, Maggie."

"Goodnight," Maggie called gaily. Turning to Liam, she asked, "Do you want to walk for a while?"

"Let's do."

Maggie linked her arm through his. He struck out at a brisk pace, as if he were trying to run away and leave his skin behind.

Maggie laughed. "Slow down a little. We have all evening."

He stopped walking. "I think I've done something wrong."

"At work?" Maggie's heart thumped. Liam worked with ledgers and accounts; he was highly trusted, and any mistake would be critical. "Was something out of balance?"

"It isn't that," he said. "I signed up today because I was told to do so, not because I believed it was the right thing to do. It wasn't my free and conscious choice, directed by my beliefs. I did it just because the other men were."

"You had to do it. You shouldn't feel bad. As you said earlier, it's done, and that's that."

"I suppose it is," he said. "But I can't help but think that if this war were truly just and honorable and everything else they say it is, then we could have raised a volunteer army, and conscription wouldn't be necessary."

Maggie stepped away from him. His voice had taken on its rich timbre, as if he were making a speech. "Liam, please," she said. "I don't want to talk about the war. I . . . want to, well, I want to talk about other things."

"I'm sorry," he said. "I just . . . I shouldn't have signed up."

"Yes, you should have," she protested. "You should have because you are a good man and a good American."

He opened his mouth as if to argue, then swallowed it. "So, what did you do today?"

"I tried on my dress." She danced ahead, her excitement washing away his dark words. "Oh, Liam, it's so beautiful! But thank heavens the wedding is in two weeks and not in July. I'd die of heat exhaustion, it's so heavy."

"Well, we wouldn't want that."

He said it lightly, but his pace had picked up again, and Maggie knew he was thinking beyond her, beyond the wedding, beyond the war and the world even. She wished he were not so smart, that he didn't think all the time. The moment she thought it, she scolded herself. She loved him as he was.

She tried to think of things to talk about. Certainly, she couldn't bring up Charlie McKenna and his role as a Four Minute Man—that would take them back to the draft. She didn't want to mention that the Knights of Columbus were calling for all available ladies to come to the Church every Thursday afternoon to sew and pack bandages—even though he probably knew that—or that she had been asked to join once she was married.

And, certainly, Seaney's adventures would stir up trouble. She thought of the letter that she'd received from him:

Dear Little Sister,

Well, here I am in Kansas. Over Colorado's border for the first time in my life. It's nothing like home here, only flat prairie and a sky that's too pale to be blue. It's sweltering hot, too, and the flies and mosquitoes are the size of birds. Don't laugh—it's true. Although you should see the fireflies. They are God's most delightful creatures, like little angels with wings aglow.

We're mixed in now with a bunch of other fellows from the states around here—Nebraska, Kansas, Missouri, South Dakota, Arizona and New Mexico. All in all, we are a sorry lot. When the sergeant calls right-face, half of us go right, the other half left, and the other half just stand there and look stupid. And don't think I've forgotten my math, either. When there are that many men threatening to stomp on your toes, it seems like there are three halves.

Our first job was to build the barracks where we sleep—there was nothing here but a few leaky tents when I arrived. Now we have leaky barracks, with doors that don't close and windows that might as well not be there. It's called Camp FUNston, but FUN it most certainly is not . . .

Maggie smiled to herself. Scaney always could make her laugh.

Continuing through the neighborhood, she and Liam passed the neat brick houses that Maggie had always loved. Berkeley Park wasn't yet part of the city, but it wasn't entirely country, either. Many of the houses still had plots of open land behind them. Where the measured urban blocks ended, a large red brick building appeared. It consumed two full city blocks, and a full-scale farm, with dairy barns, pens for livestock and plots of crops stretched behind it. Both Maggie and Liam stopped and looked toward Mount St. Vincent Orphan Asylum. A group of boys played on the lawns, watched over by a nun, who waved when she saw Liam.

He waved back. "Good evening, Sister Francis Xavier."

"How are you, Liam?" the nun called. "Maggie, dear?

"We're fine, thank you, and you?"

She did not hear them, her attention trained instead on a boy who was brandishing a stick. "Herbert, put that down—"

Maggie shivered. "I'm so glad our children will never know that place."

"It wasn't so bad."

"Billy McArdle broke your nose there!"

"I started it."

She hugged his arm. "Of course, you did, hothead."

"It was justice, my darling," he said. "He stole Martin Winters' apples, which Martin had picked himself. It didn't seem fair to me."

They turned away, continuing to walk until the sun had nearly set. By then, they had returned to Sullivan's Grocery. As Maggie started up the wrought iron steps to the apartments, Liam grabbed her arm and swung her around, so that they were concealed beneath the steps. She giggled—more than once they had hidden from Seaney or Pa there. At one time, it was because they didn't want to give up their game of hide and seek or whatever they were playing. Lately, though, it was for another reason.

Liam kissed her on the lips.

She locked her hands behind his neck. "Soon enough, we won't have to do this."

"Not soon enough for my liking."

A thrill went through her as his tongue touched the sensitive inner skin of her lips. At the same moment, she felt the need to speak.

"It will be all right," she said. The words sounded fearful in her ears, nearly desperate.

He stroked her hair. "Of course it will."

A month later, Maggie sat in front of the mirror once again, a sheet of paper before her, a pen in hand. This time, the vanity was in Liam's house, in the bedroom that they called their own. On the page, she had written, *Evelyn's first week as George's wife was nothing like she'd expected,* but nothing more. How could she write about married life? There was so much she couldn't say.

The wedding had been beautiful. Some of the parishioners had decorated the church with flowers from their own gardens, and the day was bright and sunny, casting a rich bluish light through the stained glass windows. Kathleen had been bridesmaid, wearing the dusty rose-colored dress from her high school graduation one year earlier and carrying a bouquet of daisies and iris. Liam stood at the front of the church in a new suit and thin tie, his collar so stiffly starched that, in the evening, Maggie would discover a line where it had pressed into his chin. Frank stood up with Liam, while Brendan presided over the wedding Mass. After a reception in the church basement, Liam and she had borrowed a car from the Erwins, their landlords, and had driven into the mountains for their honeymoon.

And that was when Maggie had learned that sex was not at all akin to breathing or eating. Even now, she remembered the wonder of that first night. She loved the caress of Liam's fingers, his lips against the skin of her arms and breasts, the weight of his body on hers, flesh to flesh. She thought of the taste of his tongue, and the powerful thrust of his hips.

That was not something she could write into Evelyn's story.

She bit at the end of the pen, then wrote: *George's house was a fine bungalow, and Evelyn worked hard to keep it spotless and prettily decorated. She sewed new curtains for the bedroom and put a patterned chenille spread on their bed. The living room was still in need of "feminization," but a few throw pillows and a candlestick here and there, and Evelyn was sure it would turn out nicely. What a lot there was to do now that the honeymoon was over!*

She stopped writing again, memory pulling her once more away from the story. The newlywed Keohanes had spent their honeymoon at the hot springs in Glenwood Springs. Every morning, Liam would go for a swim. He swam the way he spoke—with a ferocity that cut through the water. His arms and legs were muscled and smooth, and his hair glistened in the sunlight when it was wet. Sorry that she had never learned to swim, Maggie sat on the edge of the pool and held his glasses for him. His near-sighted eyes seemed directed inward as he rose out of the water and came toward her. It was only when he was quite close to her that vibrant expression flooded his face. Once, he had pulled her into the water with him, and she had felt the heat of her husband all the way through her limbs, breasts, and stomach. Liam had danced her around a few times, their legs entwined, his arms around her, keeping her safe from the tug of the deep water.

The screen door downstairs opened with a creak of its springs, and Maggie tucked the pages of the story into the drawer of her vanity. With a primp of her hair, she scampered down the stairs and into the narrow hallway. She wore an apron that Ma had sewn for her over the cotton shift that she had donned this morning.

Liam was just dipping his fingers into the basin of holy water that they kept on a pedestal by the door. Once he had said a prayer and crossed himself, he said, "Hello, Mrs. Keohane. What did you do today?"

Rising up on her tiptoes, she kissed his cheek. "I wrote part of a story, about Evelyn's first week as George's wife—"

"I hope he doesn't come off as a baboon."

"Not at all." She snuggled in his embrace. "And I made a roast, and—"

"I can smell it," he said. "Is it time to eat?"

She laughed. "That's one thing that will never change—your appetite. Go wash up."

After dinner, they sat in the living room. Liam leaned back in the armchair, his glasses folded neatly on the table beside him. As he rested his eyes after the long day of squinting at numbers, Maggie read the evening newspaper to him. She started with "What's New in Washington."

"The Espionage Act will soon arrive on President Wilson's desk for signing," she read. "It is intended to prevent insubordination in the military and to stem the tide of public dissension directed toward America's entry into the European war."

Liam opened his eyes and sat forward. Maggie glanced up at him, then kept reading.

"President Wilson has long encouraged Congress to take action toward those who spread 'the poison of disloyalty' in our nation. 'Such creatures of passion, disloyalty, and anarchy must be crushed out,' he said. 'They are not many, but they are infinitely malignant, and the hand of our power should close over them at once.'"

"Keep reading," Liam urged her.

"The Act makes it illegal to spread disloyal or mutinous information with the intention of interfering with the operation of the Armed Forces of the U.S., which is punishable by death or by not more than 30 years imprisonment."

She stopped, her heart beating hard in her breast. She felt as if her lungs were being pummeled, all the air draining from them. Even reading these words frightened her, as if she had unleashed ideas that should never be considered.

"Is there more?" Liam asked.

"No," Maggie lied. She jumped to the next article. "State News: Local Lambs Sold for Top Market Price—"

"Soon it will be a crime to have any free thoughts at all."

She stopped reading. "Laws are made to catch criminals, not to trip up common, hard-working citizens. They're talking about spies and Germans, not ordinary Americans like you and me."

"Aren't we all the same in the eyes of the law?"

Maggie looked back to the newspaper, stumbling through the state and local news, her mind rushing ahead of her mouth. *Poison of disloyalty. Must be crushed out. Infinitely malignant.* By the time she had finished, Liam had leaned back in his chair and closed his eyes again. The natural light in the house had nearly failed, but Maggie made no move to click on the electric lamp on the table. Liam exhaled a rasp of snore, and Maggie resisted the urge to go to him and touch him, kiss the top of his head, or take his face in her hands. *Oh, Liam, Liam, my love,* she thought.

He came to with a twitch. "I dozed off—"

Maggie held out her hand. "It must be time for bed, then."

They moved together toward the altar that stood in a corner of the room. Kneeling, Maggie folded her hands. On the altar—a small table covered with a clean linen cloth—was a statue of the Virgin Mary, a rosary and Bible, and a votive candle that Liam lit. Above it hung a silver crucifix that had come from her mother's family in Ireland. Looking at it, she tried to rid her mind of her worries and to focus on the prayer.

"Before the closing of the day," Liam recited, *"Creator, we Thee humbly pray, That, for Thy wonted mercy's sake, Thou us under protection take. May nothing in our minds excite Vain dreams and phantoms of the night—"*

Maggie shuddered inwardly. As a girl, she had imagined the phantoms of the night near her, just waiting for God to look away so that they could swarm in and steal her from her parents and brother. She knew they had stolen her mother's other children, the babies buried in the cemetery, and she doubted a simple prayer would keep them away. Even now, she wasn't sure it could.

"Amen." Liam crossed himself, and Maggie did the same. "Amen."

She fell asleep that night with Liam's arm resting across her, just beneath her breasts. Early in the morning, though, she woke and found herself alone in bed. Rising, she wrapped her robe around her and went downstairs.

Liam was not in the parlor, but Maggie found a neat pile of papers on the dining table. Picking up a sheet that lay catty-corner in the stack, she was greeted by his rolling handwriting:

Dear President Wilson,

Please allow me to introduce myself. My name is Liam Keohane, and I am a parishioner at Blessed Savior Catholic Church in Denver, Colorado. I am writing to you, sir, because I feel I must speak. I am strongly opposed to the war, and I am appalled that the United States has entered into it. I have been brought up in the belief that I should follow the path of Jesus, who preached the doctrine of non-resistance and who proved that belief by dying on the cross. When human law conflicts with Divine law, it is my duty to uphold the laws of God. Guided by conscience, I must tell you that prison or death would be the path I would choose over joining any branch of the military—

Maggie half-crushed the paper in her hands.

Liam came in from the kitchen, carrying a glass of water. "Did I wake you?"

"What are you doing?" she demanded. "Why are you writing to President Wilson?"

He sat down, took the paper from her, and calmly smoothed out the wrinkles. "You've always known I speak my mind."

"You only wrote this because of that article in the newspaper! Prison and death were mentioned there—"

"I wrote it because the article showed me what I need to do," he said. "I hadn't realized until now that taking any part in this war—even something as simple as registering for the draft—is a violation of God's law. This cruelty, this brutality—pitting one man against another, against his own neighbor—denies Christ's sacrifice."

"You don't intend to send this, do you?" She knelt down on the floor next to him. "Oh, Liam, let's burn it!"

"I have every intention of sending it."

"But why? You can't change what's happening—"

"Perhaps I can't. But I can't let what's happening change me."

"It's all my fault!" Maggie cried. "I shouldn't have read that to you—!"

"Maggie, stop." He ran a hand down her face. "Don't apologize. If I hadn't written it now, I would have written it tomorrow, or the next day, or the next. It has nothing to do with you."

"But . . ." Her voice sounded weak and child-like. "But, if you just wait, maybe the war will end, and it won't matter anyway. They say it's almost over now, because the Germans are afraid to face the Americans."

"They say a good many things, but there is only one truth, and that is God's law."

"But, but—" Maggie sputtered, no other arguments coming to her.

He smiled at her. "You know I've loved you all my life, since the first day I saw you after I came to Mount St. Vincent's and . . ."

His voice trailed off, leaving her to pick up the story. She clenched her jaw, fighting the urge to wail in anger. Oh, why had she read that newspaper article to him? Why hadn't she just skipped over it and read about sheep and crops and railroads? She drew in a ragged breath, then said, "And my second grade class was there singing Christmas carols and giving gifts that we'd made to the orphans—"

"And there you were," he said. "Your mother had wrapped your hair in rags the night before to make ringlets of golden-red and you wore a green velvet dress and wee lace-up black boots. And when you opened your mouth to sing, you had no front teeth."

"Don't remind me."

"I fell in love with you all the same, although I'm glad your teeth have come in."

She did not laugh. "Come back to bed. Forget all this."

"I can't, my dearest love," he said. "I won't."

EIGHT

When the second Liberty Loan drive began in July, the female employees of Graves Oil were asked to attend a meeting before the rally at the State Capitol. As Kathleen and the other girls in the typing pool swung happily down 17th Street, Mavis asked, "What do you think he wants?"

"Who cares, as long as we get to look at him?" Mary Jane said. "Look, a parade!"

The girls skipped toward Colfax, where young men passed by in the street, while the Denver Municipal Band played *When Johnny Comes Marching Home*. The crowd chimed its approval as the troops made for the Capitol.

"Another 10,000 of our boys will head for France today!" a young soldier shouted. "The war can't last long with us comin' at 'em!"

"Isn't this the grandest?" Mary Jane asked. "Yoo-hoo!" she shrilled. "Bash the Boche!"

One of the men blew her a kiss. "Will you be waiting for me, darlin'?"

"You bet," Mary Jane shouted. "My friend, too!"

"Now there's one worth coming back for!"

"Come on, Kathleen, wave!" Mary Jane grabbed her arm and pumped it back and forth. "Why are you so stiff?"

Kathleen could not stop thinking of Seaney. She had helped Aunt Maury clean his room. As Kathleen tucked lavender sachets into the drawers that held his clothes, Aunt Maury sat on the bed, exhausted. "I'm so glad you're here," she said. "With you breathin' this air and walkin' these floors, I can almost believe that my Seaney is here, and close my eyes for some rest."

Kathleen had kissed her aunt's forehead. "I miss him, too, Aunt Maury." She had tried to pray for her cousin, yet her prayers took on one unending chant, one ragged plea: *Please don't let Seaney die, please, please.* Even though he was only at Fort Riley, she already imagined him in France, behind razor wire and sandbags.

"Come on, let's go!" Mavis yelled.

The girls followed the parade to the lawns in front of the Capitol, which were swarming with people. Along Colfax, every vehicle—from bicycles to trolleys—had come to a halt. Store clerks, milkmaids, factory workers, girls in school uniforms, and society mavens in brooches had all turned out for the rally. Denver was rapidly becoming a city of women and children.

Mr. Graves had already taken up his position on the steps of the Capitol. His boots were of a cocoa-colored leather that looked expensive even from afar. His head was slightly bent as he conferred with two women. One was older, with silvery blond hair under a stylish, ostrich-plumed hat. The other was as beautiful as a calendar girl.

Through the megaphone, Mr. Graves called, "I've asked the ladies of Graves Oil to come early today for a very special reason. I'll only be a moment—any longer and the Four Minute Man will make me buy another Liberty bond. I already have a desk full."

He waited for the laughter to abate.

"We all know families who have sent their young men to the war in France. Some of you have already said goodbye to the men you love. They will be far from home there, and far from America. To assist our men overseas, I am proposing to send a troop of women to France to aid with the war effort. The Graves Family Foundation Relief Society will join with the Red Cross to bring comfort and succor to your sons, brothers, neighbors and friends who are serving in the American Expeditionary Force. The young women who are chosen for the Relief Society will remind our troops of the women who are waiting here at home in America for their return; they will help them to remember how dear and perfect the women of our country are. To further explain our mission, may I introduce my sister, Mrs. Eleanora Brently, to the stage?"

"What's this?" Mavis demanded. "What did he say?"

"Shh," Kathleen snapped. "Listen!"

Elegant and graceful, Mrs. Brently, accepted the megaphone from her brother. She wore a light gray dress beneath a cape of cobalt blue, and only her delicately-curled golden bangs were visible under an austere white wimple. When she shrugged her shoulders, Kathleen saw that the cape was lined with red, creating an angelic vision of red, white and blue. Speaking into the megaphone, Mrs. Brently outlined the program: the women of the Relief Society would undergo interviews and physical exams in order to be chosen; they would be trained by taking approved Red Cross classes to offer social aid to the troops; all costs of the expedition would be covered; and any woman employed at Graves Oil who was at least twenty-one years of age could apply, if she secured consent from her nearest male relative of legal age.

Kathleen breathed out in disappointment. Twenty-one! Yet Seaney had joined the army at eighteen, and he hadn't needed Uncle Seamus' permission.

Mrs. Brently surrendered the megaphone, and Mr. Graves took the stage once more. "Any female employee of Graves Oil who is interested should contact her supervisor for the application form. Those of you who are thinking of this—whether at this time or with regards to a future selection—I want you to know: If chosen, you will be serving America in a way that is as significant as any of the soldiers who are bound for France. You will be true patriots, like Betsy Ross and Clara Barton. You and your families can take great pride in your devotion and sacrifice for a free and democratic world!"

As applause burst out among the women in the crowd, Kathleen clapped half-heartedly. France! A whole world away, a place where everything was new and exciting and bold! She had to figure out a way to go.

A short, balding Four Minute Man nudged Mr. Graves aside. "How many of you have purchased Liberty Bonds?" He shouted into another megaphone. "Remember, a bond slacker is a Kaiser backer! Support the troops!"

"I'm doing it," Mary Jane declared. "I'm going to ask Miss Crawley for an application as soon as we're back at work!"

"I don't have a male relative of legal age," Mavis lamented. "Billy is only sixteen. Besides, I can't leave Ma. Her pleurisy has gotten worse."

"I can't go," Annabel said. "My eyes—"

"And Kathleen is too young!" Mavis crowed.

Kathleen eyed Mr. Graves, who had come off the stage to speak to a number of eager women. Without planning it, she drifted toward him, moving closer and closer until she could hear his words. Before she thought of what she was doing, she heard herself saying, "Mr. Graves."

He directed a warm gaze toward her. "Yes, Miss O'Doherty?"

"My cousin is going to France although he is only eighteen," she said, more heatedly than she intended. "And his father did not have to sign a permission statement. Yet he'll be in more danger than women in a Relief Society would ever be—"

"I see," he said. "How old are you, Miss O'Doherty?"

"I'll be nineteen in three weeks."

"Eighteen, then," he corrected. "I believe that common sense dictates that a woman of such a delicate age should not be subjected to the horrors of war—"

"What about the young women of France and Belgium? They've been subjected for three years now—"

"I doubt they've had much choice in the matter." He gave her an appraising look. "You have a distinct disregard for rules, don't you?"

She stammered. "I don't . . . when they're unfair, yes."

"An age limit is to be expected. Your cousin wouldn't have been able to enlist if he had been younger." He paused. "But if you're so determined, why don't you apply?"

"I . . . what?"

"You'll still need your father's permission."

He turned away to answer the question of another employee. Kathleen was left behind, unsure whether he had just suggested that she could to go to France or whether he was—as she always suspected—teasing. Already, though, she was scheming: Papa would never deny her.

On Saturday, she talked Aunt Maury into going to Redlands. Maggie drove, the delivery truck jolting over the rough dirt roads southwest of Louviers. Sitting between Maggie and Aunt Maury, Kathleen raised her shoulders and squeezed her arms against her sides, trying to keep out of the way. All the same, whenever Maggie worked the throttle, she elbowed Kathleen.

"How am I doing, Ma?" Maggie asked.

"You're quite the driver, Mrs. Keohane."

"Seaney taught me well. Although it doesn't help that I don't have room to move."

"Sorry," Kathleen said insincerely.

It was hard for her to be patient. In her satchel, she carried with her the application to the Graves Family Foundation Relief Society, neatly filled out and ready for her father's signature.

She was rewarded at last by her first glimpse of Redlands—the little house and barn and windmill tucked down into a draw that protected it from wind and snow. A rugged ridge of red sandstone jutted upward into blue sky just beyond the house, and Ponderosa pine dotted the green rolling hills nearby.

Maggie guided the truck to a stop in front of the farmhouse, and Kathleen climbed out as quickly as she could. While Maggie and Aunt Maury headed for the kitchen door, she slipped around and went in the seldom-used front door. A yellow collie dog came at the sound, at first wary, then wagging his tail in delight.

"Scamp." She patted his head. "How are you, old boy?"

Running up the stairs, she went to her bedroom and changed into her bib overalls. As she clattered back down the steps, she came face to face with her mother.

"Where are you goin'?" Mama asked.

"To ride Napoli," Kathleen said.

Mama snorted. "You come in here and sit down."

"Where's Papa?"

"He's out in the field. Now, come on, the least you can do is talk to your mother for a few minutes."

Resigned, Kathleen went to the parlor and sat on the couch next to Mama. She said nothing—she wasn't expected to speak until spoken to. Instead of addressing Kathleen, Mama asked Maggie how she liked married life.

"It's fine," Maggie said a bit vaguely.

"Well, of course, it's fine, but tell me what you're doin' with your days."

Kathleen stopped listening. The application for the Graves Family Foundation Relief Society had appeared in an envelope next to her typewriter in the same mysterious way that the pencils had. She wondered if the male secretary had carried it down to the typing room, most likely holding his nose the entire way.

"When I'm done with my housework, I write," Maggie was saying. "That's if Ma and Pa don't need me at the store."

"Write?" Mama asked. "You're a grown woman now. It's time to give all that up."

"She will when she has a baby," Aunt Maury assured her.

Kathleen glanced at Maggie in commiseration. Obviously, her writing was considered just as silly as Kathleen's art. Maggie's face was set, a smile frozen on her lips, as if she had turned herself into a statue.

"Seaney says they must learn French, for some reason," Aunt Maury said.

"Maybe because they are going to France," Kathleen suggested.

"Seems the French would learn English, seein' as how we're comin' to help them," Mama said.

Kathleen stood and went to the window. Why were they so backward, so blind? Why did they think only of themselves, when the entire world was in turmoil? How she wished she were somewhere else, with people who talked about important things. Immediately, she felt guilty—how could she think so poorly of someone she loved?

"How's your work goin', Kathleen?"

Mama's voice cut into her reverie and doubled her heartbeat—here was her chance. "There's a competition that I want to enter, Mama."

"A competition? What's it for? A secretarial position? A raise in your pay?"

"No, it's for a Relief Society." She left the window and sat down next to Aunt Maury, facing her mother. "Mr. Graves and his sister are looking for four young women to go to France with the Red Cross."

Mama's face closed with belligerence, while Maggie's expression transformed to one of curiosity.

Aunt Maury spoke. "To go to France?"

Kathleen turned toward her, hoping for an ally. "There's a call for women to go to France because so many of the men are gone. They need women to keep records and type—I'd be typing, Mama. I'd be helping the American army, and even helping Seaney in a way."

The words echoed once, then were stanched by the couch and curtains. The clock on the mantle ticked, and Scamp's wagging tail beat a lazy rhythm against the floorboards.

At last, Mama spoke. "You can do your typin' here. You're not goin' to France."

"But Mama—"

"Aye, it's a godless country, that one, with the Frenchmen chasin' after every woman ever to set foot on their soil—"

"They're fighting the Germans. They're not chasing after girls—"

"What do you know about it, now?" her mother challenged. "You've not been there."

"The Germans are worse," Aunt Maury said. "There are such stories—"

"I want to help with the war." Kathleen boiled over. "After all, it's my patriotic duty to do something besides sit in a basement typing documents that don't even mean anything to me!" She stopped and took a breath. "Seaney's already joined—he's already on his way to France. I'm just as mature and responsible as he is, and Mr. Graves' sister, Mrs. Brently, will be there to make sure we're safe—"

"'We're safe?' We? Who are you talkin' about?"

"I mean the girls in the Relief Society—and me, if I'm chosen. She'll see that we—that they—are safe. She's very sure of herself—"

"What is her name again?" Mama asked.

"Mrs. Eleanora Brently. She's old, at least thirty—"

"That name rings a bell." Mama eyed Aunt Maury. "Does it sound familiar to you, Maureen?"

"Not as I can say—"

"I believe there was some sort of scandal in the newspapers a few years ago about her. In fact, I believe she might be divorced."

"Divorced?" Aunt Maury exclaimed. "Surely not—"

"Yes, I do believe so." Mama's certainty made it true. "It explains why she has the time to go off gallivantin' around France."

"Surely a man as God-fearin' as Mr. Graves wouldn't allow a woman of her kind to chaperone young girls," Aunt Maury said. "Especially in a country as dangerous as France."

Kathleen's temper snapped. "How do you know that Mr. Graves is God-fearing? And how do you know Mrs. Brently isn't?"

"Kathleen!" Aunt Maury said in surprise.

"Apologize to your aunt," Mama demanded. "You'll not be disrespectful because you think yourself better than you are. Your Mr. Graves must be pretty taken with himself to come up with this. Sendin' young women to France—that's a sinful idea, and Father Devlin would tell you the same, sinful and prideful—and you'll not be thinkin' on it any longer."

"I'm sorry, Aunt Maury," Kathleen said. "But Mama, the Knights of Columbus are setting up canteens run by girls in train stations all over America for the soldiers—"

"The Knights of Columbus aren't sendin' them to France, now, are they? Those girls go home at night and go to Mass whenever they're told." She shook her head. "This is all your father's fault, talkin' to you about Darwin and China."

"This is my idea, Mama," Kathleen lashed. "I haven't talked to Papa about it—"

"Nor will you, because this discussion has ended."

Kathleen stood and ran from the house, ignoring her mother's call, "Kathleen! Come back here right now!" At the corral, her horse,

Napoli, neighed impatiently. She went into the barn, the horse at her heels, and found her blanket, saddle and bridle.

Darwin and China, indeed! Why did her mother think she was such a simpleton? Why did she think that she couldn't take care of herself? She was doing so in Denver. She was doing everything that Mama wanted her to do—pay rent, go to Mass, work for the KC packing relief kits for the soldiers. She had proven herself completely capable.

She slipped the bridle over Napoli's head and stroked his soft, sorrel neck. "Oh, Napoli, I miss you so."

Someone laughed behind her. Maggie had followed her out of the house. "You left smoke as thick as a battlefield in France in there. Auntie Eileen is still going on about it."

"Go away," Kathleen said, leading the horse out of the corral. "Leave me alone."

"I don't think you'll be going to France soon."

Kathleen heaved the saddle over Napoli's back and cinched it around his girth.

"I hear Charlie McKenna's looking to settle down, since the Army won't have him," Maggie said. "What about it? His five dollars a week added to your ten would make the two of you pretty well off."

Mounting Napoli, Kathleen flung back, "At least he's a patriot. He isn't going around telling everyone the war is wrong."

She clucked her tongue, and the horse whipped his head up and down before he shot forward. She rode wildly, letting the wind blow the tears from her eyes into streams that ran into her ears. She shouldn't have said that to Maggie; she shouldn't have disobeyed her mother and run out of the house. But she wanted this so much! She urged Napoli up a steep hill to the rocky ridge that rose behind the house, a perch that overlooked the valley below. Near a trio of Ponderosa pines, she reined him in, both of them breathless.

From here, she could see the farmyard in the valley floor, and the fields beyond. Breathing in the fresh, cool air, she tried to calm herself by taking in the beauty below. Deep draws dipped here and there, flanked by cool stands of Ponderosa pine and scrub oak. A few wildflowers dotted the fields, the sentinels of a full and lush summer. The creek meandered through the bottom of the valley. The sky was dotted with magnificent, snow-white thunderheads above the lofting peaks of the distant Rocky Mountains.

How she loved this land!

She spied her father's run-down truck parked near the creek. She urged Napoli down the hill and into a gallop across the grassy field below, racing toward the vehicle.

Papa looked up, a startled expression on his face, a post-hole digger in his hands. Kathleen pulled back on the reins. Napoli neighed and whipped his head a couple of times, coming to a side-stepping halt next to the truck.

"I thought I was being attacked by wild Apaches," Papa called. "You've raised a cloud of dust from here to the mountains."

Kathleen easily managed the prancing horse. "Surrender, cowboy!"

"Whoa, boy, whoa." He grabbed Napoli's reins, and the horse began to calm down. "I surrender. I always do. I surrender my heart to you."

Kathleen rubbed Napoli's neck. "It's so much fun to ride again."

"The only thing missing is poor Sean hanging on to your waist, trying to keep from falling off and breaking his neck."

"He never has liked horses."

"He might like horses if they were ridden in a reasonable manner." He waved toward the overalls and old flannel shirt that she wore. "You don't much look like the foremost stenographer of Graves Oil today. Did you take the day off?"

"We finished most of the leases yesterday." Dismounting, she blurted, "Papa, there's something I want to ask you."

"Then ask away." He wiped his hands on his overalls and began walking toward the creek. Kathleen walked with him, leading Napoli and explaining the Relief Society.

"Slow down," he said. "I'm not sure what you're talking about."

Kathleen launched into the explanation again, this time ending with the complaint: "Seaney went to war, and he's not twenty-one, and—"

"Sean is a man," Papa said. "There's a difference."

"You're always telling me that women are as smart as men, and that I'm as smart as—!"

"And so you are."

They reached the banks of the creek, and Kathleen let go of Napoli's reins so he could drink. Papa sat down, patting the grass next to him. Reluctantly, Kathleen took a seat.

"Then, why shouldn't I go to France?" she asked. "Why can Seaney go and I can't?"

Papa took his time in answering. "Sean needs to grow up and see that he's not the grand rooster he thinks he is, but only a little bantam cock in this world."

"But that doesn't have anything to do with me!"

"It does." He cupped his hands to light a cigarette. "You're already growing up in the way you should. Look at you—living in Denver, working a good job, and bringing home money. And soon enough, you'll have a husband and a couple of babies of your own. That's where your life will be—in your husband's home."

"That's not what I want!" she said. "I don't want to—!"

Papa exhaled. "You probably wouldn't see him, anyway."

"What? Who?"

"Sean," he said. "France is a big country, and it's not likely your paths would cross."

"I know that. And I don't care. At least, I'd be doing something useful there."

He turned to look at her. "You don't care about Sean?"

"I mean, I do care," she stammered. "Of course, I do. But—"

"You're looking at this as a way out of your job, aren't you? Isn't that the real reason you want to go?" He tossed the spent match toward the creek. "That's no way to end your troubles. They're just as bad or worse when you come back."

She sulked. She had never dreamed that her father would stand in her way.

"Papa, please," she said. "I could see the places we talk about, that we read about. You know, Paris and Marseilles and all the other places. I could sketch them for you. I'll never have a chance like this again!"

"Most people wouldn't want a chance to see a war."

"It's a chance to do something for others," she said, then admitted sheepishly, "I can't go without your permission."

"Aye, so that's the rub." He put his arm around her and hugged her to him. "All right, let me think about it."

"Oh, Papa! Thank you, I won't disappoint you—"

"I haven't agreed," he warned. "We both know that your mother will have my head if I do."

"I could make you so proud of me—both Mama and you."

"Go on with you now. Take Napoli for another run. He's been bored to death since you've been gone."

Kathleen jumped to her feet and mounted the horse, swinging easily into the saddle. After a wild wave to her father, she galloped away, positive that she had won the day.

NINE

The American Expeditionary Force is the Army of Imagination.

Standing beneath the Kansas sun, squinting across a prairie where nothing stands out above the grass—not a tree, not a rock, not even a yucca—Sean broils.

"I never knew I could sweat so hard," he says to his bunkmate, Kevin Neal.

"And we ain't even to France yet," Kevin replies.

Sean and Kevin found one another at Fort Riley almost immediately, recognizing the Irish and the Catholic in each other even before they exchanged names. At twenty, Kevin still carries the raw-boned gangliness of the teenager. His hair is sun-bleached strawberry blond, and his face is plastered with freckles. He has a broad, white-toothed grin, and a tuneful tenor voice. He comes from South Dakota, from prairie that is not so different from where they are now.

Their lieutenant, William Morgan, flips through a sheaf of mimeographed orders. Beside him, Sergeant Hicks studies a compass.

"According to the diagram, we should march southeast one and a half miles at one-hundred nineteen degrees," Lieutenant Morgan says.

"Right Shoulder Arms!" Sergeant Hicks bellows.

The men hoist their honed wooden sticks—their "guns"—and wait for the next command.

"Company! Forward March!"

The troops move out, dressed in blue denim bibbed overalls that are their "uniforms." Not even General Wood, who is in command of Fort Riley, knows whether uniforms will arrive from the federal government before the men leave for France. So here they are, an Army of Farmers.

Their military objective attained—after only one more stop to consult the orders and the compass—they stand at ease, waiting for Lieutenant Morgan to issue another order. Silently, Sean scoffs. As if the Germans in France will wait while the Americans figure out what they're to do next.

Lieutenant Morgan confers with Sergeant Hicks, and it is decided that the unit hasn't marched far enough. Once again, the men shoulder their "guns" and strike out to the southeast, moving farther from Camp Funston and food and rest.

And lo and behold, in another half-mile, they come across a set of barrels perched horizontally on wooden legs that have well-worn McClellan saddles cinched around the fullest part.

Lieutenant Morgan wipes his face with a handkerchief. "We need volunteers to get on the barrels so that we can conduct mounted drill," he calls.

"What's that?" Kevin whispers.

As if he heard him, Lieutenant Morgan says, "Mounted drill is designed to train military men not only how to process and ride as soldiers—which, as you can see, we can't do—but to aim at and apprehend a soldier on horseback."

Still, no one speaks.

Lieutenant Morgan flips to another page. "I'll call the names of volunteers," he says. "Private Anderson, Private Carrington—"

Sean prays that his name is not called.

"Private Neal, Private Rogers, Private White."

"Damn," Kevin breathes.

The men move forward and loiter around the saddled barrels. At last, Lieutenant Morgan says, "Go ahead, get on them. Umm, Boots and Saddles!"

Kevin puts his left foot in the stirrup and grabs the pommel of his saddle, which shifts under his weight. The pommel is now perpendicular to the earth.

"Ride 'em, cowboy!" someone shouts, while others jeer and catcall. Kevin struggles to put the saddle aright.

"Don't use the stirrups," Lieutenant Morgan huffs. "Just hoist yourself up. The rest of you, quiet!"

"Atten-TION!" Sergeant Hicks barks.

The "volunteers" settle onto their mounts, their faces a testament to how foolish they look. After the troops listen to the explanation—read in a stultifying monotone by the sergeant—as to where to aim, they queue up into lines to practice shooting at the figures straddling the barrels. Holding up their whittled sticks and peering down the length of the wood, they pretend to fire their weapons. One of the mounted soldiers viciously kicks his barrel with his heels, mimicking an escape from the armed troops. One of the armed men yells "Bang!" when he shoots his quarry. They all laugh, and Lieutenant Morgan, who seems disgusted by the situation, does nothing to stop them. When Sean's turn comes, he aims at Kevin, who clasps a hand over his heart and calls, "I'm dead!"

As Sean takes his place at the end of the line, he fumes. This isn't what he signed up for, this little boy's game of cowboys and Indians, this stumbling around in the heat, this stupidity. They're supposed to be engaged in the War to End All Wars, in the War to Save Democracy, in the Fight for the Free World.

The travesty of Fort Riley doesn't end after the long marches, either. The few available guns that the enlistees use to disassemble, clean and reassemble are muzzle-loaders that were captured from peasants during the Spanish-American war. They aren't even American-issue. For artillery training, machine gun nests are marked on the ground, and the men squat next to them and "shoot" at enemy positions denoted by red flags stuck in the Kansas prairie. Trench warfare is practiced in a drafty barn. On a terrain that is supposedly on an unfathomable one-one-thousandth scale of a French trench, the men gather behind a pile of dirt hauled in off the plain and peer through binoculars to the other end of the barn, where a mechanism in the ceiling drops white wooden balls that are supposed to be the "bursts" of a bombardment. One man is supposed to report how many bursts he sees, while another records the timing and positions of the bursts. At the end of the exercise, no one's tallies are the same.

The American Expeditionary Force is the Army of Protestants, too.

On the first Sunday after they arrive, Kevin and Sean show up for church services only to find at the pulpit a Methodist minister who preaches about cleanliness, obedience, and abstinence and never mentions Christ. Not a single priest has been assigned to Fort Riley.

"No Mass! No confession!" Kevin cheers. "We're free!"

But Sean feels lost, not liberated. He misses the words, the Latin, so mysterious, so infused with holiness. He speaks them when he is alone, delighting in the cadences: *"Pater noster, qui es in caelis, sanctificétur Nomen Tuum . . ."*

The only thing that feels real at Camp Funston is the lack of amenities. The train that carried Sean from Denver to Kansas arrived in the darkness after midnight—an intentional ploy by the government and the railroads to prevent troop movement from disrupting normal passenger and freight travel. From the depot, he followed his fellows to the showers. Running water has been installed at Fort Riley, but it has yet to be heated. After the freezing shower, a doctor inspected the incoming enlistees and gave whatever vaccinations were necessary—all of this before the poor boys were issued new underclothing and their blue denim overalls. For those who made it through, a meal of hot coffee and sandwiches awaited. After that, they bunked down on straw-filled bed sacks thrown across steel-spring cots for a short night's rest.

To Kathleen, Sean writes: *Next week, we'll be learning the bayonet by stabbing it into sacks filled with sand that we've been working for two days to fill. Some of the boys have painted ugly faces on the canvas and named their creations "Fritz." It's a huge joke, but once we've stabbed all our Fritzes to bitzes (ha ha!), then we'll have to shovel all that sand up and start over again. I just hope they give us something sharper than kitchen knives for it all.*

It seems that it's been years since I saw you, but the calendar says it's only been a few weeks. Time is the enemy here in Fort Riley.

Time and the terrible boredom of obedience. He is faceless in this army, indistinguishable from any other greenhorn. He marches, studies the Field Manual, which is a mimeographed document clumsily translated from the French, and polishes his boots like a mindless machine. There's no glory, no honor, no pride, or sense of accomplishment.

"Hey, Sullivan," a soldier named Danhour calls. "Was that you or some other clod who dropped his stick during drill today? Too bad it wasn't loaded."

"Maybe it was Neal," Sean teases.

"Not me," Kevin says. "I thought it was you, Danhour."

"Ha!" Danhour says. "The whole shame of it is that they'd think you two will sarv yoor coontry."

Sean's muscles tense. "What's that supposed to mean?"

"Listen to you." The men around Danhour quiet, expecting trouble. "You Papists would sooner fight for your fellow church-goers than for America. All them German Cat-olics don't have a thing to fear from you."

"What the hell?" Kevin says.

"I heard that the Irish want to side up with Germany," Danhour continues. "They don't want to fight with the British."

"I'm fighting for America," Sean says. "As much as you or anybody else. The Church has said, 'We are all Americans—'"

"Don't quote your damned mick slop at me."

At once, Sean is on his feet, dragging Danhour from the bunk. He lands a right on Danhour's cheekbone, the pain of the blow resonating up through his knuckles into his shoulder. Danhour pulls himself up off the floor and comes at Sean, stabbing at his shoulders with his fists. He's larger than Sean, heavier, just the sort of opponent Sean used to seek out in the alleys of Berkeley Park. The blood pounds in Sean's head, in his clenched hands, through his dancing legs. "What did you call me?" he shouts. "What did you say?"

He thrusts again, dodges Danhour's fist, and delivers a punch to Danhour's stomach. Danhour wraps his arms around Sean and squeezes. Sean breaks free with an elbow in Danhour's gut and jabs with his right, not aiming, hitting the air as often as he connects with Danhour's face. Danhour comes back, catching Sean in the left shoulder. Socking him in the gut, Sean gains the advantage. He throws Danhour on the floor and straddles him, ready to pound the stuffing from his face.

"Stop it!" Lieutenant Morgan has come into the aisle. "Let him up!"

Someone drags Sean off Danhour, pinning his arms between them. Sean shrugs away with a "Get off me!" His head rings with the loud, satisfying buzz that he remembers from the streets. No matter how much the pain, there's always that surge of adrenaline, that thrill of something won.

"Attention!" Lieutenant Morgan commands. "What's going on here?"

The men around Sean snap to attention, their hands at their foreheads. Sean rubs his knuckles, cracked and bloodied by the fight, before he joins them. He feels blood trickling from his nose. Lieutenant Morgan glares at him, then asks Kevin, who stands at Sean's shoulder, "What happened, Private Neal?"

Kevin does not answer.

"You'll answer me or you'll be written up as well," Lieutenant Morgan threatens. "What happened?"

"It was a misunderstanding, sir," Kevin says. "Over heritage, sir."

Someone snickers, and Lieutenant Morgan's eyes search for the culprit. Once the laughter stops, he asks, "Heritage? What's that supposed to mean? Private Sullivan?"

Sean says nothing. Lieutenant Morgan stays silent long enough for Sean's body to start aching from the effort of holding himself rigid and still. He's sweating again in the ninety-degree heat, the perspiration pouring from his temples. But he's no tattletale, even though anger runs through his mind as if a dam has broken.

"We'll try this another way," Lieutenant Morgan says. "And if I don't get an answer, then you'll all do two hours drill. Exactly what is your heritage, Private Sullivan?"

Sean swallows. "I'm Irish, sir."

"Where were you born?"

"Denver, Colorado."

"I wasn't aware that Colorado was in Ireland," Lieutenant Morgan drawls. "Tell me, exactly where is County Colorado? Anywhere near Blarney?"

He makes no effort to stop the men from laughing. Instead, he fixes his eyes on Sean, as if waiting for Sean to crack or wither under the humiliation.

"I was born in America, sir," Sean says fiercely. "But I am a member of the Catholic Church, and my parents are first-generation Americans with family in Ireland, who fight for Ireland's freedom against the British, and—"

"Well, bravo for them," Lieutenant Morgan says. "But I'm only asking about you. Your family history is none of my concern. And your religious beliefs are of no importance to anyone. You could believe in a two-headed elephant, for all I care. Do you understand?"

The men guffaw as Lieutenant Morgan waits for Sean's response.

"Yes, sir," Sean says at last.

"Now, how did Private Danhour misunderstand your heritage? Is he as confused about geography as you seem to be?"

"Ask him," Sean says, adding a belated, "Sir."

"What about it, Private Danhour?" Lieutenant Morgan says.

"I didn't do anything, sir," Danhour lies.

"That's not what Private Sullivan seems to think."

Someone laughs again, and Lieutenant Morgan tires of the ruse. Wheeling, he orders, "Sergeant Hicks, one hour of drill. Full company. Now. Move."

"Yes, sir!"

"Except you, Danhour, Sullivan. Attention!" Sean and Danhour snap upright again. It isn't until the last man has left, and the echo of the marching ranks has died, that Lieutenant Morgan addresses Sean again.

"No matter what you believe yourself to be, Private Sullivan, you are an American. And you'll be fighting in France as an American soldier. When that day comes, I don't think you'll care if your parents are Irish or Polish or Swede. But you might want Private Danhour next to you."

"That's what I—"

"Do you understand, Private Sullivan?" Lieutenant Morgan's eyes bore into him. "We're in this together."

Sean swallows hard. "Yes, sir."

"What about you, Private Danhour? Are you willing to put aside this petty squabbling and act like an American man should?"

"Yes, sir!"

"The two of you will be doing two extra hours of drill each day for the next two weeks to see if you can't kiss and make up. Do you understand?"

Both men chime, "Yes, sir."

"You're dismissed. Now, clean yourselves up."

Danhour whips around and runs for his bunk. Sean wipes the back of his hand over his messy nose, then goes to the metal troughs at the end of the barracks, where a pump brings in water for washing and drinking. In the blotchy shaving mirror that hangs above the trough, he sees his face. Bloody nose, cut lip, a bruise on one cheek. He's grown slow, loose, careless, in the time he's been off the streets.

His face scrubbed clean, he goes outside into the Kansas night. He gulps at the air, but it is so wet and heavy that it refuses to enter his lungs. The trills of the cicadas and chiggers and the hum of the mosquitoes around his ears soar through in his head. His eyes sting with tears.

The company marches past him. "Hey, Sullivan," someone shouts. "How's your two-headed elephant?"

Sergeant Hicks growls a command for quiet, but laughter snakes through the men as they chant, "Right, left, right—"

Lieutenant Morgan is right. Sean is as much of a man as Camp Funston is a military base.

TEN

Seated at a mahogany table in the Board Room of Graves Oil, Jim watched as the others sifted through the applications for the Graves Family Foundation Relief Society. He had been talked into helping with the selection process by Ellie—who sat next to him—and their mother. The others on the selection committee were Mr. Hobart, the senior accountant at the firm, and Miss Crawley from the typing pool. Nine women from Graves Oil had applied to go on the mercy mission.

Ellie pushed an application in his direction. "Read this one," she said. "She seems to be patriotic enough."

Jim skimmed the application, reading nothing. "So she does."

"Oh, dear," Mr. Hobart, who had expressly stated his disapproval of the project, mourned. "This one wants to go to France to meet a husband."

"I was afraid of that," Miss Crawley sniffed. "Romance."

Jim felt Ellie subdue a snicker. She picked up another application and began to read diligently to hide the curve of her smile.

"Odd," she remarked. "This one is barely nineteen. Why in the world would she think to apply?" She flipped to the final page. "She has her father's permission."

"Let me see that," Jim said.

The name on the application offered no surprise: Kathleen Maura Bridget O'Doherty. The little minx. She had managed to secure her father's signature, although Jim had been certain when he issued the challenge that she would not. After all, what prayerful, protective, priest-loving Catholic father would allow his innocent daughter to go to war?

"What is the girl's name?" Miss Crawley asked. "She should be warned that she cannot waste the time of her superiors—"

"Kathleen O'Doherty," Ellie said, with some pleasure. "From the typing pool."

"Oh, my." Miss Crawley sat back, her face draining of color. "I'm so sorry, Mr. Graves, sir. I didn't give her the application, and I've no idea how she could have—"

"I wonder if she convinced a friend to ask for one," Mr. Hobart suggested.

"Only Mary Jane Grayson approached me, and her application is right here—"

"I gave it to her." Jim paged through the application. Kathleen's prose was as ambitious as her sketches. "And I think we should offer her an interview. Her response to the question of why she wants to go is well-written. She seems to have altruistic reasons."

Mr. Hobart gaped, and Eleanora eyed him with suspicion. Only Miss Crawley had the nerve—or the gall—to speak. "She is one of our worst typists," she declared. "She is messy and slow, and she doesn't pay proper respect to instructions—"

Mr. Hobart followed. "Did she mislead you about her age by claiming to be twenty-one? If so, she should be relieved of her position—"

"She informed me she was—at the time—eighteen," Jim said.

Mr. Hobart cast an outraged look toward Miss Crawley. Beside Jim, Eleanora observed it all, cool and unruffled.

Mr. Hobart sputtered, "There's something more to be considered, sir. With such a name, Miss O'Doherty is undoubtedly Roman Catholic."

"Is that a concern?" Jim asked.

"I think there is always a question of whether a Roman Catholic is a true American." Mr. Hobart's voice rose. "They have their own schools, and they pledge allegiance to the pope. Their lives are filled with backwardness and superstitions. And the Irish are the worst—"

Jim interrupted, directing his question to Miss Crawley. "Does she try to indoctrinate the other girls in the typing pool? Does she flaunt her belief or force trinkets of her faith on them?"

"No, sir."

He tossed Kathleen's application onto the pile and rose from his chair. "That's it, then? We'll interview the"—he shuffled the applications—"six we have chosen tomorrow. Miss Crawley, would you and Mr. Hobart please make arrangements with the girls for the interviews and notify those who were not chosen?"

"Yes, sir." Both spoke at once.

"And, Mrs. Brently, I will see you tomorrow as well?"

"Of course." Ellie stood on tiptoe to kiss his cheek. Into his ear, she whispered, "What does she look like?"

He patted her hand. "Tomorrow, then."

The women were all the same. Driven, dedicated, and solemnly aware of the gravity of the cause for which they were applying. It was not until Kathleen O'Doherty entered the room that Jim sat up and took notice. Her hair was stripped of its glorious unruliness and bundled in a severe bun, and she was dressed in a plain white blouse and black skirt, with the mandatory men's tie. She stood before them—the committee had declined to offer the candidates chairs—with her face flushed and a trace of breathlessness around her lips.

"Please, relax, Miss O'Doherty," Ellie said. "We only want to become acquainted with you."

Kathleen's eyes slid sideways to Miss Crawley, who sat forward, hands clenched in a knot on the table, her mouth drawn up in distaste. "Yes, ma'am, Mrs. Brently," she said, despite a quiver.

"Tell us about yourself."

Kathleen told of growing up on her family's ranch, which she called Redlands, and of coming to work in Denver to help with her parents' financial situation. She spoke of an aunt and uncle with whom she lived and of cousins.

"My cousin, Maggie, married recently, and my cousin, Sean"—her gaze slid to Jim—"is with the AEF at Camp Funston." She paused, then added, "He's only nineteen, too."

Jim swallowed a laugh. He could imagine how she must have reacted when she was corrected or scolded as a girl. Most likely, she had never done what she was told to do in her life.

"Why do you believe you should be chosen for the Graves Family Foundation Relief Society?" Mr. Hobart asked.

"The Catholic Church teaches a strong belief in service to others," she said. "I have been helping with the war effort every Saturday, after my shift ends here"—she hastened to add—"in packing kits and rolling bandages for the soldiers who are going overseas. I would like to be able to do more for them—"

"Such as?"

"It's said the conditions are very hard in France, sir," she said. "And that the soldiers need a kind word or a comforting gesture as much as they need food or water. When I think of it, I imagine my cousin in France, far from his family, with only his faith to guide him. I hope someone offers him kindness while he's so far away from home. I wish I could do the same for others."

Silence ticked through the room. At last, Ellie said, "That's very well-stated."

"If I may ask, Miss O'Doherty," Mr. Hobart inserted. "How would you characterize your loyalty to your church? Is it your foremost concern?"

"What?" Kathleen blurted, then corrected, "I'm sorry, I don't understand the question."

"Would you call yourself an American first or would you say you are Irish and a Roman Catholic first?"

She glanced at Jim, obviously flummoxed. "I was born in America, so of course, I am American," she said slowly. "But I'm of Irish descent and my family is Catholic . . . I still don't understand the question."

"The Irish in America have spoken out against supporting the French and British, siding instead with the Germans—"

"Oh, that." She looked toward Jim, evidently thinking of their conversation at the rally. "I really didn't mean—"

"I believe we have our answer." Jim shot Mr. Hobart an annoyed look. "Let's move on."

Miss Crawley spoke. "Do you have any nurses' training?"

"No, ma'am."

"Can you speak French?"

"No, ma'am."

"What clerical skills do you possess?" Mr. Hobart asked. "Other than, um"—he looked at the page in front of him—"typing."

"I took a six-week secretarial course at Barnes Commercial School."

"What special talents would you say you have?" Eleanora asked.

"I sketch." Her face brightened. "I draw what I see."

She looked at Jim again, and he smiled in acknowledgment.

"I believe I could capture what is happening in France in my sketches," she said. "Much as the Nash brothers have done."

"Would you sell your prints?" Ellie asked. "We could not condone anyone making a profit or gaining recognition from this mission."

"No, oh, no!" Kathleen said. "But I would want to show them to as many as I could so that they might understand the situation. Would that be allowed?"

"You're speaking of showing them to friends and family? Not the public?"

"Yes, ma'am. To my father and . . . I think of it as a duty, somehow, something that I should do"—she faltered, then resumed—"If I were to go to France, I would want everyone within my acquaintance to share in that experience with me." She tipped her head, as another thought came to her. "I would never draw anything that I couldn't show to the priests at my church, if that's what worries you."

Ellie snorted aloud, and Kathleen's face reddened. She glanced at Jim, as if begging for help. Stifling a laugh, he said, "Thank you, Miss O'Doherty. We will be making the final selection in the next two days."

"Thank you." She moved toward the table and stuck out her hand to him. With a laugh, he shook it. He suspected someone—most likely her father—had coached her to end the interview this way.

Kathleen went down the table, shaking everyone's hand, including Miss Crawley's, who nearly growled when Kathleen thanked her. Then, with an awkward little curtsey, she left the room.

Jim waited until the door had closed behind her to face Mr. Hobart and Miss Crawley.

"I think our youthful candidate presented herself quite well, don't you?" he asked. "I recommend that we include Miss O'Doherty in the group."

"Yes, sir." Mr. Hobart's face blanched.

Miss Crawley did not acquiesce as easily. "I believe that there are more promising candidates. And the age limit is still set at twenty-one—"

"There are three other spots to fill," Jim said, sufficiently imperious to ward off any objections. "That's it, then? Thank you all."

No one spoke as he exited the room, but Ellie flew out into the hallway after him.

"I won't have you making this into a farce, Jim," she said.

"Shh." He guided her into his office, which was just across the hall. Going to his desk, he sat in the plush, leather-upholstered chair and reached for his cigarettes. He motioned one toward Ellie, but she shook her head.

"You can't choose the girls on your own," she said. "It's a committee decision—"

"Then let the committee choose the others."

"This isn't a contest to find the next girl for your harem," she exploded. "It is a serious effort to do our part in—"

"I do my part," he returned. "Damn it, Ellie, I've been supporting this war for three years now, giving to the French orphans, the Czech displaced persons, Canadians who've lost their limbs, and on and on—"

"But this is mine!" She banged her hands flat against his desk. "It's my idea, and I've put all the work into it! I begged the Red Cross into making us an auxiliary—"

"You forget I donated enough so the Red Cross wouldn't dare refuse—"

"I designed the uniforms and I'm making all the transportation plans! I want it to succeed! I want it to mean something, to show Mother that I can do something that matters—"

"So it isn't for our Brave Boys Overseas?"

She twisted away and paced across the deep-piled Oriental rug to the window. "You may live in Stephen's shadow, but I live under the curse of what Elizabeth might have been. If they'd grown up, they would have made mistakes just as we have, and we'd all be equal. But they didn't, Jim. They *didn't*."

She turned toward him, tears in her eyes. He could not remember the last time he had seen Eleanora cry. It must have been when they were children.

"Ellie." He went to the window and took her in his arms. She leaned into him, a rare admission of weakness. "I promise, I won't jeopardize it. I know what Kathleen O'Doherty is, and God forbid that I sully anything so perfect and pure."

"Why did you give her the application?"

"Because she asked," he said simply. "And you have to admit, she's the only one who showed any gumption." Seeing the skepticism in her face, he added, "I like her, Ellie. She has something the others don't."

"I suppose if she went to France, she would be safe from your charms."

"Possibly." Jim laughed. "But if she stays here, I may be forced to break my promise."

Two days later, as Jim returned from a meeting with the Director of the Colorado Western Railroad, he chanced upon Kathleen. She sat in one of the leather-upholstered chairs outside of the Board Room, alone and nervously clutching her satchel in both hands. She wore her work costume and white gloves that showed quite a bit of wear. Individual strands of hair had escaped from her tight bun to create a halo of gold-red around her head, and one wavy lock played havoc on her forehead.

"Miss O'Doherty," he said. "What are you doing here?"

She started as if she had been caught committing a crime. "I'm waiting to speak to Mrs. Brently. I was called up here along with the other girls. They've all gone in, one at a time. I'm last, I guess."

Jim glanced toward the closed door of the Board Room. "So she's inside with one of the young ladies?"

"Yes, sir. With Mary Jane Grayson."

"Well, there's no point in your sitting here alone. Why don't you come into my office while you wait?"

Kathleen looked longingly toward the Board Room, then said, "Yes, sir."

As they passed Jim's secretary, Joel Spratt, in the anteroom to his office, Jim said, "When Mrs. Brently comes from the Board Room, would you ask her to come in? Miss O'Doherty will be with me."

Joel exchanged a dark look with Kathleen and nodded. Jim opened the door to his office and watched as Kathleen looked around the palatial setting, taking in the dark wooden wainscoting, the floor-to-ceiling windows, and the fine paintings on the wall. Her gaze then skimmed over the gold-framed diplomas and awards that hung on one wall and the bookcase filled with the annals and texts of the oil industry.

"So what do you think of this place?" Jim asked.

"I've never been anywhere so fancy. It's all so beautiful."

"As is the company I'm keeping."

Her face flushed in a gratifying way. Motioning to a couch in one corner of the room, he said, "Please sit down, Miss O'Doherty. Would you like something to drink? Water? Coffee?"

"No, thank you." She smoothed her black skirt down carefully before she sat. "Thank you for giving me this chance to join the Relief Society. I never expected—"

"Nor did I."

Jim poured himself a tumbler of water over a finger of whiskey, then sat in an armchair opposite her. As he crossed one leg over the other, he saw Kathleen eye his boots. Today, they had toe wrinkles stitched in turquoise and uppers inlaid with triangles of royal blue.

He twisted so that the boots were plainly in view. "Do you intend to sketch my feet again, Miss O'Doherty?"

"No, sir." She laughed—or hiccuped, it was hard to tell which—at the suggestion. "But I will have to tell Annabel—Miss Croft—about them. She talks about them all the time."

"I'm glad to be the object of such fervent interest," he said. "They add a little mystery, I think."

"Mystery?"

"My life is so public. Everyone knows my cars, they know where I live, they know where I am and what I'm doing most of the time—the newspapers make sure of that. But they never know what's on my feet until they see me."

She laughed again, this time in a manner that he recognized.

"So, do the ladies of the typing pool talk about me?" he asked.

Her eyes swept downward, away from his face, while her lips curved upward. "They say you have a different pair of boots for every day of the year," she said.

Jim recognized the challenge of the flirt. With a sly smile, he said, "I'm hardly a man of such means, Miss O'Doherty. What else do they say?"

"That you have a house with fifty-four rooms and two grand pianos."

He laughed. "Truthfully, I would have to count the number of rooms, but I'm afraid it would fall far short of fifty-four. As for the pianos, I have one, as most American households do, but I'm not musically inclined. Are you?"

"Not at all!"

"Well, then, we'll have to avoid musical soirees together, won't we?" She blushed again, and he nodded toward her satchel. "Of course, you have other talents. May I see your sketches?"

Eagerly, she pulled her sketchbook from her satchel and handed it to him. He thumbed through it, studying each picture. Kathleen had a flare for detail and artistic framing, but her sketches were often cloudy and unbalanced—almost messy—as if she had hurried through them in order to sketch something else. As he looked at the drawings, he became aware that she was sitting statue-still on the couch, her hands clasped so tightly that her knuckles were white.

"Does this make you nervous?" he asked.

"When someone looks at them, I see them as he—as you—would," she admitted.

"How do you imagine that I see them?"

"I know they aren't that good and that they probably look childish—"

"Did you know that you have an Irish lilt to your voice when your dander is up?"

She winced. "I don't mean to—"

"Don't fret, it's charming." He looked again at the sketch book. "But never apologize for your faults unless you can't avoid it. And never try to guess what someone else is thinking. You'll always be wrong."

Flipping another page, he came across a sketch of a solemn, steel-jawed young man whose eyes were light and whose hair was portrayed as thick and black. He wore the newly-designed uniform of the American Expeditionary Force.

Jim held up the picture. "Now, who's this tough-looking laddie here? Not a beau, is he? You've drawn him with a tender hand."

Kathleen's voice grew misty. "My cousin. I drew that from a photograph he sent to his mother, my aunt Maureen."

"So this is the fabled cousin. Well, with the likes of him abroad, we should see the Germans stopped in no time."

She said nothing, and Jim glanced up at her. "Did I offend you?"

"No, sir." She looked up, her eyes wet. "It's just that I miss Seaney, and I worry about him. I pray every night that he comes home to us."

"Rest assured that he is engaged in a worthy cause," Jim said. "Seaney. Or Sean, I assume. So, your entire family is Irish."

"Yes, my mother and her sister came to America when they were just four years old. My father was born here, but his family is from Ireland, too."

"And how did you come to Graves Oil?"

Kathleen faltered. "My mother, well, she felt it was a respectable company."

"Be honest, Miss O'Doherty," Jim scolded. "The Barnes Commercial School sent you to Graves Oil because they know that I have no qualms about hiring Catholics. Isn't that so?" When she nodded, he added, "I find it absurd that so many businessmen do."

"Thank you. It's so hard to find jobs—"

"Oil is a democratic business, Miss O'Doherty," he said. "In the fields, I work with black men who haven't yet forgotten the yoke of slavery and Cherokees who won't even speak to a white man. I see no difference in their work. I would rather they see no difference in me."

She drew in a breath. "Yesterday, at the interview—"

"Yes?"

"What was Mr. Hobart asking me? It seemed that he wanted me to choose between being American and being Catholic."

"I believe that's exactly what he was asking you to do," Jim said. "It was nonsense—his prejudice brought to light, nothing more."

"Oh." She leaned back, obviously still puzzled. "What should I have answered?"

"I think you should have popped him in the jaw."

Laughter burst from her. "That's what Seaney would have done."

"So the legends of the Irish temper are true, are they?" he teased. "I'll have to remember that, if we're to be in this together. Tell me, how did you convince your father to sign the permission statement for you?"

"Oh, that." Kathleen looked down at her hands again. "My father would do anything for me."

"There's more to that story," Jim said. "What is it?"

She bit her lip. "My mother wasn't in favor of my applying for this, and they had a terrible fight. Mama still isn't speaking to Papa."

"Well, I hope it turns out well." Jim laughed. "Having a father that one likes is a rare thing. I must admit, however, that my father is responsible for my success."

"How so?"

"Seven years ago, when I had only just graduated from college, he signed over to me his interest in a failing oil exploration company that he had acquired through his dealings in coal properties. He wanted nothing to do with it, thought it was essentially worthless. I found there were a number of oil companies in the same straits— out of money to drill or lay pipe, but with some tangible assets and desirable leases. I bought a couple, then a couple more, and so on, and formed Graves Oil. I did it the same way that Rockefeller formed his Standard Oil Company or Sinclair his—although on a much smaller scale. Last month, I picked up a refinery in Tulsa."

"I don't understand. Picked up a refinery?"

"I bought it. Acquired it. What did you think? That I lifted it from the ground? I'm no Hercules."

She missed the joke. "I . . . I don't know. I'm not sure what a refinery is. The oil business—"

"Makes for a very dull conversation," he interrupted. "Tell me what you want from life, Kathleen O'Doherty. What is your deepest ambition?"

She met his gaze squarely. "I want to go to France."

"On one condition."

"Anything!"

"Don't ever agree to that," he warned. "The condition is this. Your sketches come to me first. I will see that your family has them after I've looked at them, and I promise, I won't keep any for myself, unless you allow me to."

"But . . . why? I mean, why would you want to see them first? You know that I don't always have the right sense of proportion, and that I'm just learning—"

He reached for her hand, which twitched as if he had pinched her. "Calm yourself, Kathleen," he soothed. "I just want to see what you see. You said in the interview that you felt it was your duty to show others what you see in France. I plan to hold you to that promise."

"So—" She stopped, then started again. "Are you saying I've been chosen to go to France?"

"Yes, my sweet," he said. "You have been chosen to go to France."

"Oh!" Kathleen put both hands over her mouth. "I don't believe it! I'm so—!"

The door opened, and Ellie came into the room.

"I'm afraid I've let the cat out of the bag," Jim said.

Ellie took it in stride. Coming to Kathleen, she offered her hand. "Congratulations, Kathleen," she said. "Come with me and we will discuss the details."

Kathleen hastily stuffed her sketches into her satchel. Jumping up from the couch, she grabbed Jim's hand. "Thank you, oh, thank you so much!"

She shook it until Jim laughingly removed it. As Ellie escorted Kathleen from the room, she gave Jim an eyebrows-raised look of warning. He smiled roguishly at her in return.

Yet, after the two had gone, he became aware of something he hadn't felt in some time. It was a sense of lightness, a flurry of warmth in the heart, a heightened state of interest and intellect.

The mood carried him through the remainder of the day.

ELEVEN

Once the members of the Graves Family Foundation Relief Society are named, there are rules of etiquette and French phrases to memorize, taught by the eloquent Mrs. Brently. The girls sit through a host of Red Cross classes, which are organized by Mr. Graves' mother. Each girl signs an oath that Mrs. Brently has devised, based on the strict rules set forth by the Red Cross: There will be no smoking, drinking, swearing, or other immoral activity at any time. Uniforms will be worn at all times while on duty and never off duty, and no accessories, such as brooches or lace, may be added to the uniforms. There will be no fraternization with soldiers of any army, whether American, British or French. The girls are to remember that they embody the virtue, piety, and unblemished moral exceptionalism of the women of the United States of America in all ways and at all times.

Kathleen is relieved that Mary Jane Grayson has also been named to the Relief Society. The others are Helen Parsons from bookkeeping and Harriet Mills, who is a secretary for a vice president of the company. Helen, who is twenty-four, stands no higher than Kathleen's shoulder and has dark hair and black eyes. She says little, but she always seems to be the first to answer questions or to accomplish an activity. Harriet is twenty-five, with a ringing laugh that no one can resist. She calls herself "Hank."

The girls are given uniforms identical to the one Mrs. Brently wore at the Liberty Loan rally. When Kathleen first tries on her uniform, in front of a triple mirror in the dressmaker's shop where the garments are to be altered, she shrugs her shoulders back, as

Mrs. Brently had done, so that the cape's red lining shows against its outer blue. She, too, is a portrait of America's womanhood in red, white and blue.

"These capes alone cost forty-five dollars," Mary Jane whispers to her. "And we're to have two of everything! Wimples, dresses, capes, gloves, stockings and shoes. And winter boots, too. They say the winters are much colder in France than they are here."

Hank fingers the wide white collar of her dress as she looks at herself in the mirror. "If I have to surrender to the Germans, I'll just do this." She flaps the collar back and forth with her fingertips. "No white flag for me, I *am* a white flag!"

The three of them laugh—Helen doesn't do much of that, either. Despite the overly large collars, the uniforms are eye-catching, much like Mrs. Brently herself. Whenever Kathleen sees her, she straightens up and tries to hold her shoulders back and her chin up in the same stately position. But Eleanora Brently is not easily imitated; she moves, breathes, and speaks with an innate grace that Kathleen, with her country upbringing, cannot match.

The girls pose for a formal portrait that is released to newspapers throughout the United States. Mrs. Brently and Mr. Graves sit in chairs while the four women stand behind them. In the photograph, Mr. Graves wears an expression of great ease and elegance, while his sister gives the photographer a haughty once-over. His boots are sepia in the picture, although they are made of carefully worked Moroccan leather with red stitching on the toe wrinkles.

Always, the girls are aware of him, just as enamored of him as the typing pool was. When he comes into a room, the mood lifts with his electric energy. When he speaks, all eyes settle on him, all ears listen. He asks Kathleen about her family: "How are your parents getting along?"

She laughs, embarrassed that she revealed the family spat to him. "Fine, sir," she says.

"Come now, Miss O'Doherty," he says. "We have no secrets."

"Mama is still mad," Kathleen admits. "But Papa says she can go jump in a well."

He laughs—a sound that she has learned to treasure.

"How do you think you'll do, being so far from home?" he asks. "It's your first time, isn't it?"

"I think I'll be fine. My cousin will be there soon, and even if I don't see him, I'll know he's near. But I will miss Redlands and the mountains."

"There is no more beautiful place to live than Colorado," he says. "My family has land in the mountains near Evergreen. My grandfather built a summer home there patterned after a Tudor castle—"

"A castle!"

"He called it Inglesfield, after our ancestral home in England. It has stone steps that lead up to the door and a great hall with a stone floor." He laughs deprecatingly. "It's a foolish endeavor—and cold, too. It has eight or so bedrooms and a dozen fireplaces."

"Do you go there often?"

"No." His expression tightens. "I haven't been there in many years."

"If I had a castle, I'd be there every chance I had." She catches herself. "I'm sorry, I didn't mean to—"

"That's quite all right," he says. "I'm sure you'll see any number of castles during your time in France. It's a lovely country."

"You've been there?"

"Years ago, on a Grand Tour of sorts, when I was twenty-one." Sobering, he adds, "I hope the war hasn't changed it too much."

No matter where the Graves Family Foundation Relief Society goes, photographers follow. The girls appear at Liberty Loan rallies, parades, troop send-offs at Union Station, and dances, salons, and tea receptions for Denver's high society. Photographs are taken of them in the marbled corridors of the State Capitol as they meet with various state legislators and Governor Julius Gunter of Colorado. They pose amid the columns of the pavilion at Cheesman Park and are rowed by strapping Marine recruits across the lake at City Park, all smiling for the cameras. To show their fitness, the four girls are tasked with running around the track at Denver East High School in the blazing August sun, while photographers snap their photos. To prove their pluckiness, they smile for the camera as they bare their arms for vaccinations against smallpox and typhoid. There is no time for work, or friends, or family, although Kathleen continues to be paid.

The excitement is contagious. Aunt Maury clips out articles about the Relief Society that she sees in the *Denver Post, Rocky Mountain News* and *Denver Express*, nearly filling a scrapbook even before Kathleen leaves for France. She keeps it side by side with a scrapbook that she is making for Seaney. Papa is delighted by Kathleen's luck. "I've always known you are the best, Caitlin, me love," he says. Only Mama holds out, complaining, "I think Mr. Graves has done this just so he can get more pictures of himself in the newspaper. Look at this!" She points to a montage of photographs from a musical evening, where the girls, led by Mrs. Brently, each presented a patriotic poem. Mr. Graves is there, smiling beatifically from a seat on the stage. There is even a photo of Kathleen at a dais, in wimple and wide-collared dress, with a caption that reads: "Miss Kathleen O'Doherty of the Graves Family Foundation Relief Society recites Tennyson's 'Ring in the Larger Heart.'"

Soon enough, though, it is time to leave for New York. Kathleen writes to Seaney, *We are taking the train to New York, where we will spend three days before boarding the ocean liner to France. I am on my way!*

Seaney is still at Fort Riley.

TWELVE

The suite at the Biltmore Hotel in New York City glittered—the flowers touched with gold dust, the silver service sparkling on the table, the gilt-edged china, the gold-embossed humidors, the silver ashtray stands. Around Jim, who was dressed in white tie, a dazzling array of friends gathered. They were mostly acquaintances from college, a fast-living, carefree set who never missed a party thrown by one of the Graves siblings. Ellie herself sat in the middle of the room on one of the silk-upholstered couches, primly drinking punch and speaking in a too-too cultured voice. Her dress tonight was rose and gold, beads and spangles turning her into a glittering jewel.

Across the room, seated on another couch, were the four girls of the Graves Family Foundation Relief Society. They had shed their uniforms now and were dressed much as girls from the provinces might be. The clothes they wore were home-sewn—neat enough, but unfashionable. Kathleen had paired her high-collared, shapeless garb with a hat that seemed both excessively ornate and startlingly dull.

They had arrived in New York that afternoon, only to be greeted by a bevy of photographers at Grand Central Station. Decked out in their uniforms, the girls had smiled and posed as the photographers snapped their pictures.

"Did you invite every newspaperman in New York?" Jim had asked Ellie.

"I tried, my dear brother. Now, smile as the future governor of Colorado would."

On the train, Jim and Eleanora had traveled in style in a richly upholstered drawing room with its own bath and dining arrangements.

The girls of the Graves Family Foundation Relief Society had traveled less splendidly in two sleeping cars with two berths each, with the lower berth folding up into a seat during the day. Jim had spent most of the time working, letting Ellie lecture, instruct, and shepherd the girls. In the evenings, she returned weary and wan.

"Is your flock tucked in?" Jim asked her one evening, when she appeared especially haggard.

"They are like girls at a Campfire Girl cook-out. They never tire of telling stories of pet dogs, and riding horses, and falling into lakes from tire swings and the like." She traced a path down the rain-streaked window with one finger. "In some ways, I envy them."

"Surely you wouldn't want to be poor and daft."

"No, but their lives are still ahead of them. They were given nothing at birth, and still have nothing, but it doesn't seem to bother them. They have no delusions or expectations, no preconception of how the events in their lives might unfold."

Ellie's comment had stayed with him. He had noticed the girls' spirit, too, but even more so, he noticed Kathleen. In the evenings, he grew impatient as he waited for the girls to join them in the drawing room for the evening meal, the only meal they took together. As they dined, he positioned himself so that he could watch her. She struggled mightily to imitate Eleanora's graceful ways, and to be the recognition-worthy young woman she wanted to be, and to act older and more sophisticated than nineteen. Mostly, though, she tried to avoid his gaze.

Yet, at times, she would meet it, with curiosity and frankness in her eyes. And something more. As much attraction as he felt for her, certainly, but challenge, too. As if she were waiting for him to speak his mind. Or—more likely—as if she were dying to speak hers.

The lobby of the Biltmore Hotel connected directly to the train terminal. As the girls had come up the staircase to the marble-tiled foyer that led to the elevator, Jim had found himself next to Kathleen. "This is the Kissing Room, Miss O'Doherty," he whispered in her ear. "So named because many passengers meet their lovers here."

She had given him a sidelong glance that made him wish he could be alone with her, free of this folly. But a sharp look from Ellie and a puzzled glance from Mary Jane Grayson had spoiled the moment.

He had raised his voice so that it was no longer intimate. "A businessman can arrive on the train, secure a room in the Biltmore or one of the other two hotels here, conduct his business in one of the meeting rooms, eat at the fine hotel restaurants, and catch his train home without ever having to step out onto the sidewalks of New York."

Mary Jane had squeaked out, "My word! I've never heard of such a thing!" as she stared at the richness of the décor, but Kathleen had asked, "Why would he want to do that?"

"I beg your pardon?" Jim said.

"If he has traveled for days to arrive in a city—especially a city as grand as New York—why would he want to leave without seeing it?"

Perhaps Ellie's envy was warranted: the whole world was still ahead of these young women. Just now, however, they looked miserable. Earlier, the reception had included New York's dignitaries and society notables—even the mayor had shown for a few minutes—but at this late hour, only a few friends were still hanging on, drinking whatever was left of the punch and eating what remained of the food. The girls huddled together, speechless, their faces showing dismay and exhaustion.

"Jim!" Evan Lockridge, a friend of Jim's from his days at Princeton, called. "Where is your rye?"

Jim looked toward Ellie for permission to bring out the liquor, but she shook her head.

"Have more punch," she suggested to Evan.

Jim motioned, and one of the waiters, hired for this affair, dipped a fresh glass of punch from the bowl and carried it to Evan.

He looked at it with distaste. "Where have you gone, Jimmy boy?"

"West, with the buffalo and Indian," Marie Grissom said. "And where Prohibition has been passed."

"So it has." Jim gestured for his glass to be filled with punch. "But I was able to purchase the liquor from many a fine restaurant before the law went into effect. I have a private stock that will last for years."

"Only you would think to do that, darling," Marie said.

"Only he would have the money to do that!" Evan said. Turning toward the girls, he added, "You have to understand, Jim was our leader in all things wicked. He disregarded the fraternity house rules, the grand laws of the university, the finite rules of the universe even! There was one time in Mexico—"

"We don't need to go into that," Jim cautioned.

"Without you, sir, we would have nothing." Evan lifted his glass of pinkish punch in a toast. Paraphrasing a popular Irving Berlin song, he said, "And now, we're all out of step but Jim!"

Everyone joined in the chorus, mock-toasting Jim every time his name was sung.

"I've heard," Evan continued, "that there is nothing like the adrenaline surge one feels in battle. It's said to be a sensation far greater than any other, including"—his naughty wink was greeted by giggles and whistles—"and that some men long for it and throw themselves into the fray at every opportunity. They become as mechanized and brutal as the machinery on the battlefield."

"Ah, man is nothing but a savage!"

Another toast was proposed. "*Dulce et decorum est pro patria mori!*"

"Oh, give it up with the Latin. What is that? Sweet and . . .? "

"Sweet and honorable it is to die for one's country," Kathleen said, flicking Evan a look of disdain.

"Look, we're upsetting the guests of honor!" Marie went toward the girls. "Aren't you just the sweetest things? Shut up, you beasts! You're making her cry!" She jostled her way onto the couch and cuddled Kathleen against her. "Don't worry, honey. Usually we're regular cut-ups, but this war's just made us all so ghoulish and dull."

Jim watched as Kathleen struggled to move away from Marie on the crowded couch, but she was blocked by Miss Mills, who sat next to her.

"I'll tell you what, Jim," Marie simpered. "Maybe I'll don a nun's wimple and join up with your girls. I'd make a wonderful

Salvation Sister." Leaning her head against Kathleen's, she added, "We'd be good do-gooders, don't you think?"

"You wouldn't make much of a nun," Evan sneered.

Angling away from Marie, Kathleen stood. "Excuse me," she said as she went outside to the balcony.

Ellie shot Jim a scalding look, then started to trail Kathleen out the door.

He caught her arm. "I'll go."

"See that she doesn't jump," Ellie hissed.

As he walked out the door, Evan's voice echoed behind him. "Now we're becoming downright maudlin. Are you sure there's no booze?"

"Miss O'Doherty." Jim joined her at the railing. "What's wrong? Are you ill?"

"I needed fresh air," she said tightly.

Jim breathed in the muggy haze. Beyond the Biltmore and over the roofs of other buildings, the canopy of trees in Central Park was visible. "Well, you won't find it here. It makes one appreciate our thin, dry air, doesn't it?"

She did not reply, but leaned against the stone railing and looked toward the park. Ellie's warning skiffed through Jim's head. "You don't intend to jump, do you?"

"What? No, I—"

"Just teasing."

She cast a look behind her, her face tightening into a frown, as laughter echoed from the suite.

"What is it?" he asked again.

"The way they talk," she steamed. "As if it's all a game."

Jim took his time before replying. "You have to understand, the wealthy of America have been supporting this war for three years now. Who do you think has been providing money for the relief efforts in Britain and France? You've read about it—Rockefeller's plan to feed all of Belgium and such. He isn't the only businessmen who has taken up the cause. We all have. Perhaps we are a bit jaded at this point."

Her anger flared. "So I should just laugh with those people about the dangers of the battlefield? Are they so important to this country that they don't even have to worry about being called up? That they don't even consider enlisting?"

"I can't speak to that," Jim said. "But right now, 'those people' are my guests and, I might add, are helping to finance our Relief Society. They came to meet you and the other girls. For that reason, I'm not inclined to call on them out about their patriotism. I don't believe you should, either."

She bridled. "My cousin may give his life for this country, and they . . ."

She cast another glare toward the suite. Jim used the opportunity to light a cigarette. "That's true," he acknowledged. "Your cousin may die. But don't be so naïve as to think that his great sacrifice—if it comes to that—is so very extraordinary. He's a man without position or wealth, and he's giving what he has to give."

Kathleen's breath rasped. "You mean his life instead of money?"

"If you want to put it that way."

"How else can I put it?" she fumed. "You said you'd gone to that place, the military school—"

"Plattsburg?"

"—to learn to be a soldier. Yet you haven't gone to France. You're not even in the army."

Jim blew out a calming mouthful of smoke before answering. "Consider this," he said at last. "What worth would I have in No Man's Land?"

She eyed him as if she were sizing up his qualities. "You'd be an officer, wouldn't you? You wouldn't be a soldier like my cousin is. My friend Liam says that the men who went to Plattsburg will be officers who will tell the poor what to do, just as they do here at home."

"And who would do my work here—which not every man can do?" Suddenly, Jim's superb poise melted away. "You have no idea what's happening to businessmen such as myself. The government wants more development, more production, more exploration. Jesus, it's like I'm owned—"

She winced at the language, and Jim retreated.

"I'm sorry, Miss O'Doherty," he said. "I shouldn't have spoken so crudely."

She, however, didn't retreat. "So you're not going to France?"

"No, I'm not. It's President Wilson's decision, not mine. He has designated certain industrial endeavors as essential to the nation's welfare. Oil production is one of them. Patriotic duty requires me to remain here."

She pondered that. "But you're making money from it, aren't you?"

"Yes, I am," he said coolly. "Does that make it wrong? Am I a bad man? Sinful or evil? Tell me, Kathleen. What am I, according to your Catholic schoolgirl's opinion? Or your opinionated father's? Or your cousin's or friend's? You seem to have a host of advisors for your thoughts—none of whom seem to know much about the world."

"They know about the world," she protested. "They're smart and they read."

"And what about you? Do your opinions come only from them, or can you think for yourself?"

"I can think for myself!" She swung around, so they no longer stood side by side, but face to face. "And I don't believe that one man's life is worth more than another's. My cousin is a fine person. He's generous and smart, and he will someday be a good father—"

"Are you implying that my guests don't have those qualities? Or that I don't?"

"I'm not implying any of that, sir—"

"For God's sake, don't call me sir," Jim snapped. "I believe it was your St. Matthew who first said, 'Every man according to his ability,' long before Karl Marx appropriated the phrase."

When she didn't reply, he continued, "Your father would be considered, as I am, essential personnel, since he is contributing to America's food supply. How old is he?"

"He's over forty, too old to—"

"President Wilson has already announced that he will change the age of conscription to available men between eighteen and forty-five. Your father will soon be the right age to be conscripted. Won't you be glad that he is able to do his duty to America at . . . what is it you call it? Redfield?"

"Redlands," she said softly.

"Isn't that true?" he asked, unwilling to let her slip away from this question. "Wouldn't you rather see your father safe in the United States than on a battlefield in France?"

She turned on him. "You twist things, you make them so confusing that they are impossible! You want me to choose, but you never ask fairly! My father, Seaney, whether I am a Catholic or an American—"

"You forget, I didn't ask you that—"

"—you take a question and add all sorts of extra things to it, so that it becomes an argument, not a discussion at all!"

"That's because most of the situations we face in our lives are difficult and fraught with untenable conditions," he retorted. "Maybe going to France will open your eyes to—"

"Kathleen?"

Mary Jane Grayson stood at the door of the suite. She glanced at Jim, then at Kathleen, a look of shock on her face. Jim turned away, flicking his cigarette butt over the railing. He was breathing hard, as if he had been running.

"We're going to our rooms," Mary Jane said. "Mrs. Brently says we have a busy day tomorrow."

Most likely Ellie wanted the girls out of the way so she could bring out the liquor that was stashed in the sideboard. But Kathleen rushed toward Mary Jane, as if she had offered her salvation.

"Goodnight, Mr. Graves," the girl who called herself Hank said, while the other two, Mary Jane and Helen, echoed, "Goodnight, Mr. Graves."

He composed himself. "Goodnight, Miss Mills, Miss Parsons, Miss Grayson," he said, then added coolly, "Goodnight, Miss O'Doherty."

She countered with a scathing look. "Goodnight," she said evenly. "Sir."

****

Later that evening, after the party in the suite had ground into bleariness, Eleanora knocked on the door of Jim's bedroom.

"You don't think we made a bad impression on them, do you?" she asked.

"They're probably all writing home about the decadent rich. Watch out, Ellie, you might have some angry parents to deal with."

"Any affair that Evan and Marie attend is bound to get out of hand." She shrugged. "What happened between you and Kathleen on the balcony?"

He hedged, uncertain of what she knew. "She didn't jump."

Ellie gestured in annoyance. "Why did you make that remark about the Kissing Room to her?"

"Oh, that," he said. "Why? Is her face still red?"

Ellie scowled at him. "This is a girl who has probably never truly spoken to a man other than her father or her priest, Jim, and you promised me you wouldn't—"

"I wouldn't sell Miss O'Doherty short, if I were you."

"She's asked if she can go to Mass on Sunday, while I take the other girls to Fifth Avenue Presbyterian."

"Oh, good Lord."

"That seems an appropriate reply. I'm beginning to think Mr. Hobart was right about dragging a Roman Catholic along."

Nothing about Kathleen would be easy—Jim saw that now. His heart felt twisted—as twisted as she had accused him of being—unresolved anger still roiling inside. It was sheer stupidity on his part. She was a country girl, little more than a child, a silly office girl. She was hopelessly naïve, irrefutably caught up in some sort of idealist vision of the world that had no resemblance to reality. She could offer nothing that he wanted.

"The concierge has confirmed the times for Mass at St. Patrick's," Ellie was saying. "They are comparable to the services at Fifth Avenue. But I can hardly put her in a taxi and send her off by herself."

"I'll see she gets there," Jim said. "But I'm not going with you tomorrow. You'll have to handle the sightseeing alone—"

"But I've asked half of New York to come with us. The publicity would be—"

"And that is why I would rather not go," he said, unwilling to admit that he had no desire to spend the day dodging Kathleen's censure.

She arched her eyebrows, but did not question him. "All right," she agreed. "But you will keep your promise about Sunday, won't you?"

"Yes, don't worry about that."

"Goodnight, then." She rose. "I have to go see that Evan doesn't spill any more on the carpets. I'm afraid you already owe the Biltmore for one."

After she left, Jim stood by the window, smoking. Soon enough, Kathleen would be gone and he would be out of this tangle. Soon enough, he would be back to being the master of his world.

THIRTEEN

There is so much to do in New York City. The girls spend Saturday sightseeing in their Relief Society uniforms, Mrs. Brently and a guide named Mr. Andrews always at their sides. They gawk among the massive monuments of the financial district, taking photos with a camera that Helen has brought along, a gift from her uncle. The buildings are too large to be caught in a single photograph, so Helen patiently takes a photo of the bottom floors and then the tops, far above her head. At last, one of the newspaper reporters who accompanies them tells Helen he will send her photographs of each building, complete and uncut.

The Municipal Building, Civic Center, the Woolworth Tower.

Across the street from the Equitable Building, the girls are photographed standing on the sidewalk in single file, from the shortest, Helen, to the tallest, which is Hank. The photographer coaches each girl to lean out so that all of their faces are visible, one above the other. Then he directs them to point with their right arms toward the fortieth floor of the building. The photo will appear in the New York newspapers with the headline: "Wild West Girls Meet the Big City." In the photo, Mrs. Brently stands to one side, cool and elegant.

The Brooklyn Bridge, the Statue of Liberty, Coney Island.

The ocean.

Kathleen stands at the stone railing at Battery Park and wishes that her father was there. More so, she wishes she had a camera like Helen's instead of her sketchbook. With that, she could capture the scene exactly as it appears. *Oh, Papa. I wish that I had the talent to draw it as it is. I can only catch so little of it.*

But even as she revels in the sights, her stomach bobs into her throat. Mr. Graves is not with them, and Mrs. Brently has said little about his absence today. Surprisingly, Kathleen is disappointed. Last night, when she went to bed, she had cried herself to sleep, overcome by fatigue, homesickness, and an urge to throw her pillow or the lovely vase on the table or *something* at something. Or someone. Most likely, at him.

Yet, now, she peers down sidewalks with the hope that he will stroll around the corner, his cowboy boots a splash of color against the gray, a half-arrogant, half-charming smile on his face. What had she been thinking, to challenge him as she did? Why did she become so angry? Why is she still angry? It is foolish—everything, her whole life, is in his hands just now. She cannot throw it away simply because he is a . . . because he is . . . well, because he is who he is.

And who is that? Is he wrong to be making a fortune from war? He is truly a champion of the military, a hard worker, a model of the Protestant ethic, just like President Wilson. He is respected and admired. He is above reproach, and his work for the United States of America is necessary and noble.

Isn't that enough?

"We're going to the Presbyterian Church tomorrow where President Roosevelt's son was married," Mary Jane says to Kathleen as the sea breeze blows fresh on their faces. "Where are you going to church?"

"St. Patrick's Cathedral, I think," Kathleen says.

"Mrs. Brently," Mary Jane calls. "Is St. Patrick's Cathedral a famous church, too?"

Mrs. Brently gives a silvery laugh, something that she does quite often. "Yes," she says. "I believe it has quite a prestigious history."

That evening, Mr. Andrews and Mrs. Brently escort the girls to the appropriately named Liberty Theater where they take in a musical revue called "Hitchy Koo." The women in the show wear clinging, spangled costumes and huge headdresses with flowers and feathers, and the jokes presented by handsome, rail-thin men in tuxedos cause the audience to erupt with laughter. The highlight of the production—for the girls, at least—is a song sung by Frances White called "I'd Like to Be a Monkey in the Zoo."

Back at the Biltmore, free of Mr. Andrews and Mrs. Brently and too excited to sleep, the four girls dance and sing as they dress for bed. They occupy two rooms, with an adjoining door between them. Mary Jane and Hank sport shawls as feather fans, while Kathleen and Helen do a frantic tap dance that ends with both girls on one knee in a pose worthy of Al Jolson.

The evening concludes with Hank and Helen, in one room, singing on one side of the closed adjoining door, *"Gee, I'd like to be a monkey in the zoo,"* while Kathleen and Mary Jane, in the other room, reply with the second line: *"Why, you'll never find a monkey feeling blue!"*

Suddenly, Helen—the most reserved of them all—throws open the door and bursts into Kathleen's and Mary Jane's room, warbling newly-remembered lyrics: *"Gee, I'd like to be a monkey in the zoo, You wouldn't have a bit of work to do, You've got no one to please, All you do is look for fleas, Oh, I'd like to be a monkey in the zoo."* At that point, all four are holding their aching stomachs and gasping for breath. Hank rolls on Kathleen's and Mary Jane's bed, laughing until she chokes and has to sip from a glass of water that Mary Jane fetches for her.

Early in the morning, they settle into bed and sleep.

All except Kathleen, who wonders yet why Mr. Graves did not join them.

Dressed in their best, the girls met Mrs. Brently and Mr. Graves in the lobby of the Biltmore Hotel on Sunday morning. Mrs. Brently looked resplendent in a navy velvet suit with gold buttons and a low-slung hat with a red bow on its brim. "Kathleen," she said. "My brother is going to escort you to St. Patrick's today while we attend Fifth Avenue Presbyterian. I trust you don't mind?"

It wasn't a question, but a command. Kathleen glanced at Mr. Graves, who nearly outshone his sister in his tailored morning coat and pin-striped trousers. He tipped his hat and smiled graciously. "I hope that doesn't displease you, Miss O'Doherty."

His words carried a bite in them. Unable to meet the fire in his blue eyes, Kathleen looked away. "Thank you," she said.

Two chauffeured Pierce-Arrows awaited them at the curb of the Biltmore. Hank, Mary Jane and Helen waved to Kathleen as they climbed into one of the cars with Mrs. Brently. The chauffeur of the second car held open the door for Kathleen and Mr. Graves. Kathleen slid across the seat, putting as much space between them as she could.

As the car rolled away from the curb, Mr. Graves asked, "Did you enjoy sightseeing yesterday?"

"Yes, very much, thank you."

"And the performance last night? My sister told me that one song seems to be a favorite among you young ladies."

"It was a song called 'I'd Like to Be a Monkey in the Zoo.'" Despite herself, she laughed at the memory of the night's revelry. "We all thought it was funny."

The car ride took almost no time at all. The chauffeur parked in front of an imposing stone church with two spires. It was the largest church Kathleen had ever seen. She craned her neck to take it in, but she could not see the entire building.

Mr. Graves climbed out and offered her a hand. "Here we are, Miss O'Doherty."

She stepped onto the sidewalk. "Are you coming with me?"

He glanced upward to where the bells tolled. "No, I don't believe so."

"Are you joining the others at the Presbyterian church?"

"I don't think I'll do that, either. But I will be right here when you come out from the service." When she opened her mouth to speak, he said, "Better hurry, I believe it's very near time."

She mounted the steps and moved into the vestibule. After dipping her fingers in the holy water and crossing herself, she walked into the inner sanctuary.

All at once, she could not breathe. Her throat closed, as if she might sob. Looking upward, she traced the massive columns to where they spread outward into perfectly joined latticework, as if they were lilies. Everywhere she looked, she saw color and light. She tried to remember every detail so that she could tell her father and Seaney. She turned around and smiled at a couple who had entered behind her, hoping they would share her joy. The man nodded politely, but they continued up the aisle without comment.

She genuflected and entered the row of chairs to kneel in prayer. The organ, its pipes spanning an entire wall, began to play, and she bowed her head, tears in her eyes, and thanked God for the beauty of the world.

As promised, Mr. Graves was waiting for her when she came from Mass.

"How was the service?" he asked.

"Wonderful!" She no longer cared that he was angry with her or she with him—she had to tell someone. "The cathedral was so beautiful—far more than I ever could have imagined. Every inch has some detail. I could have stayed all day."

"Did you remember to pray? Or did you spend your time admiring the architecture?"

"The Mass was beautiful, too—"

"I'm glad you found it meaningful." He placed a guiding hand on the small of her back. "Let's walk a bit."

"Aren't we to meet the others for lunch at the hotel?"

"I don't think so today," he said. "I think we'll find our own."

"But—"

"Am I twisting the issue too much for you, Miss O'Doherty?"

Nerves, excitement, and fear all bubbled up in her, and she laughed. Then she realized that she should apologize. "I'm so sorry I said what I did," she said. "I shouldn't have spoken out so. It was impolite and disrespectful. I have always been told I think too much."

"Do you?" he asked.

"Do I . . . what?"

"Think too much."

With a sting, she recalled his accusation that she could not think for herself. Defiantly, she said, "I believe I think in the way I should."

"Bravo, Miss O'Doherty." He glanced up as the breeze blew a whirlwind around their heads. "I don't see any flaw in thinking too much. If more of us did, there might not be a war and you might not be going to France."

"Oh, no, I wouldn't want that," she reacted. "I mean . . . I should want—"

He laughed. "I believe you twist things up enough all by yourself, without my help."

Central Park appeared before them, its Mall shaded by graceful elms. The sun shone through the branches of the trees, warm where it struck the pavement, cooler as the shade stole over Kathleen's face.

"Look at this!" she exclaimed. "It's lovely."

"Let's find a spot to eat. I have a picnic lunch for us."

He turned and signaled, and Kathleen saw that the chauffeur who had driven them to St. Patrick's had been following at a discreet distance. In his arms, he carried a wicker basket. The man found a patch of grass near a large elm. From the basket, he took a thick blanket and spread it on the ground.

"That's fine, Curtis," Mr. Graves said.

The chauffeur tipped his hat and left.

"I didn't even know he was there," Kathleen said.

"A good servant should be discreet."

"But—"

"Let's leave that discussion for another day," he said. "I believe you might be a bit of a socialist, my sweet."

She straightened her skirt beneath her as she sat, uncertain how to respond.

"It's muggy today." Mr. Graves removed his hat and coat and rolled up the sleeves of his shirt, then loosened the tie around his neck. Stretching out his legs, he crossed his ankles so that his boots—reddish with white triangles—tapped together. "Are you going to open the basket or shall I?"

Kathleen lifted the lid. Inside, she found roast beef, apples, salads, breads and cakes, all in genteel silver containers and wrapped in linen. The signature of the Biltmore could be found on every bowl. The silverware, with a trademark "B" molded upon it, was wrapped in individual napkins. A small nosegay of pansies and bachelor's buttons stood inside a silver vase in one corner of the basket. Kathleen gently removed it, and Mr. Graves set it between them on the blanket.

"This isn't lunch," she exclaimed. "It's a feast!"

He peered into the basket. "We could survive for two to three weeks on it. We'll join the Central Park squatters and live in a tarpaper shack. What do you say? Are you game?"

She did not reply—confused, again, by his teasing. At once, she was aware that almost no one could see them here, hidden as they were behind the elm. She could hear the voices of the other Sunday strollers on the Mall, but could catch only a glimpse of brightly colored clothing as they passed. What if Mrs. Brently and the others happened upon them here, so intimately concealed?

"Let's eat," Mr. Graves said, letting the question go.

"May I say grace?" Kathleen asked.

"Of course," he said, although he did not bow his head.

As they shared the meal, he asked her more about the excursion of the day before and about the Mass at St. Patrick's. After they finished the dainty offerings of Charlotte Russe that had been packed in the lunch and put away the silver service, he lifted the basket to reveal an oblong packet beneath it. "Open it," he said.

Kathleen tore open the brown wrapping paper. Inside was a new sketchpad, its pages much sturdier and thicker than any she had ever owned. "Thank you," she said. "Oh, it's lovely."

"And it will be even lovelier once it is filled with sketches that you draw in France."

She studied a blank sheet in the pad. She had been wrong about him. He was generous and kind; he wasn't flawed or deceitful. When she looked up, he was watching her in a way that made her wonder if he had read her thoughts. "Thank you," she said again, her face flushing with heat.

"Why don't you start your artistic journey by sketching me?" he asked.

"You?"

He laughed. "You needn't look as if you're going to lose your lunch over it."

"I'm sorry." Kathleen swallowed hard. "I don't know if I can."

"I thought you were intending to sketch all of France," he protested. "Besides, I know you can draw people. You sketched your cousin."

"He didn't know about it. I drew it from a photograph that he sent Aunt Maury from Fort Riley. I don't think I can draw anyone if they're looking me in the eye."

"Then I'll turn away."

"I'm not always good at this," she said. "I just draw what I see—"

"That's all I'm asking." With one finger, he lifted her chin, and she felt the electric pulse of his touch. "You've managed my boots quite well in the past. Just draw those, and then plant the rest of me in them. Like a potted fern."

She laughed, but she felt a surge of panic. How could she sketch him? His magazine-illustration face, the muscles in his neck, his Adam's apple, the curve of shoulder and arm and chest—

"Well?" he asked. "What do you say? Do I merit your artistic attention?"

"If you don't watch me," she said. "If you don't ask to see it until it's done, and if you don't expect too much from it."

"Too many ifs," he grumbled. Rising, he went to stand next to the elm tree, leaning back against the thick trunk. The sunlight filtered through the leaves, dancing on the ground with the soft breeze. A few leaves drifted past him to the ground.

Kathleen balanced the sketchbook on her lap, choosing a view that afforded her only the right half of his face. He had never tightened the tie, and his wrists hung from his sleeves. He lit a cigarette, then rested his left hand in the pocket of his trousers. His right hand moved between his lips and his waist.

"Did you know there is a castle at the other end of the Park?" he asked. "It's called Belvedere, and it sits on the edge of a lake. The name means 'beautiful view.'"

"Another castle!" she said. "I didn't even know there were castles in America, and now I've heard about two—yours and this one."

"Inglesfield—our property—probably has the most beautiful setting I've ever seen. It sits about three quarters of the way up one mountain and overlooks the valley below. Everywhere you look is pristine and wild." He paused, then said, "We used to spend every Christmas there, a full house, all of us tumbling down the stairs in the morning to open presents, and Mother and Father waiting for us—"

"All of you? Do you have brothers and sisters other than Mrs. Brently?"

He glanced at her, then remembered his promise and turned away. "We did. We had a sister and a brother. Elizabeth and Stephen."

"Where are they now?"

"They died when I was eight. At Inglesfield, in fact."

"What?" Kathleen breathed. "How?"

He blew out smoke in a deep, steady sigh. "There's a lake in the valley, not large, but deep near the center. One Christmas, we were given a new sleigh and horse for a gift. Stephen was fifteen, then, and bold—always carving sledding tracks through the trees or skating with dangerous speed over the ice. He was not to drive the sleigh without my father's permission, but my sisters and I convinced him to take us for a ride while our parents were visiting neighbors."

He resettled himself against the tree trunk. "So, away we went, singing and shouting and ringing bells. When we came to the lake, Stephen didn't think twice about taking the sleigh across. We didn't consider the weight or remember that the weather had been warm the previous week. A little short of the middle, the ice cracked, and the sleigh overturned. The horse broke free and ran, but the sleigh sank halfway beneath the surface—in a heartbeat, it seemed. Elizabeth, who was only ten, went in first, then Ellie—Mrs. Brently— who was twelve. They were wearing heavy skirts, petticoats, woolen coats that weighted them down like stones. I grabbed the runner and held on, my head just above water."

He looked out across the sun-dappled lawn. Kathleen held her breath, waiting for his words.

"Stephen dove in to find the girls," he said. "He was able to drag Eleanora to the surface. He went in again after Elizabeth and never reappeared." He quieted for a moment. "My parents found us around nightfall."

He exhaled roughly. "My father crawled across the ice—at least, that's what I've been told—and dragged Ellie, who was barely breathing, back to shore. Then he came back for me. When he pulled my hands from the runner, the skin peeled away—"

Kathleen's eyes watered. "Your palms—"

"Ah, yes. Of course you would have noticed." He opened his hand and studied it. "They were frozen to the runner. I don't recall whether it was painful—I don't remember being taken from the ice at all. But to this day, I have no feeling in my hands, only enough in the tips of my fingers to feel extreme heat or cold." He reached up and touched his cheek. "I cut my face that day, too. I have no idea how."

He plunged his hand back into the pocket of his trousers. "The top floor of my parents' house was turned into a hospital. Every reputable doctor and nurse in the city was called in to help us. Ellie had pneumonia, but she survived."

"Thank God!" Kathleen said.

"I've never had reason to thank Him," he said bitterly. "After that day, I quit believing in God, and I've seen nothing as I've aged that has made me reconsider. This war, in fact, has convinced me that there is nothing . . ." His voice trailed away. "Have you finished that sketch?"

"No. No, I was listening—"

"Then I'll seal my lips. Finish it, please."

But it was no good; all was ruined. Kathleen could not still the images in her head. The young child gripping the steel bar, while the strong, brilliant boy fought before sinking into the freezing waters. The girl—Mrs. Brently!—motionless on the ice. The more she drew, the more she recognized what Jim and Eleanora were—the ones who had been left behind, who felt they had received a gift of which they weren't deserving, or who had stolen something from the others. She laid down her pencil.

"Let's see it," he said.

"It's not very good—"

"It doesn't matter." He came to her and studied the sketch. She stood, uncertain as to what she should do. For one moment, his face grayed, and she knew he had recognized in the sketch what she now knew: under all his grace and lightness was insurmountable despair.

"I've never talked about that day to anyone before," he said. "Ellie and I rarely mention it, and if we do, it is only in the . . . abstract, I might say. I trust you won't spread this to the other girls. For Mrs. Brently's sake, at least."

"No, I wouldn't do that."

"Thank you." He rolled the sketch and tucked it beneath one arm. Then he took her face in his hands. "Come back to Denver with me, Kathleen. Marry me."

"What?" The word came out as a gasp, not a question at all.

"You should marry me." She saw the idea taking form in his eyes. "It's that simple."

"I don't understand," she said. "Are you teasing me?"

"Not in the least. I'm as sincere as I've ever been."

"But you were so angry with me the other night—"

"Don't you think that's part of it? I don't want a woman who isn't my equal."

"I'm not your—"

"Perhaps not yet, but you will be," he said. "I'd see to it. I'd teach you what you want to know and show you what you don't yet know. I could give you everything, Kathleen. You would never need to ask."

She breathed deeply, trying to clear the jumble in her head.

He spoke again, with difficulty. "There's a time, a moment, when a man thinks . . . There's a chill in the air just now."

She could not deny that. The streams of khaki-clad men at Union Station or Grand Central. The terrible headlines in the morning paper, more and more French and British dead. The machines that spread flame and gas and death to hundreds in an instant. And Seaney, so far away in Kansas, stabbing bayonets into sandbags named Fritz.

"What are you thinking?" Jim asked.

"You can't just marry on a whim," she offered stiffly. "Marriage is for eternity."

"Yet a man can join up and march away to die in Flanders on a whim. Isn't that what your cousin did? Isn't that what most of them are doing, what's actually expected of our young men? And a young woman can join a Relief Society and escape from her dreary job and overly officious supervisor. You can't deny that one, my sweet."

She said nothing. Could marriage be entered into so lightly? Could it be chance, an afternoon's sudden decision, a wink and a nod? Could it shore up the dread, compensate for shortcomings and things that have been lost?

"Put your arms around my neck," he said.

She stepped away, but he caught her around the waist with one hand and pulled her close. "Don't be afraid," he said. "Just do as I ask."

She lifted her arms and placed her hands on his shoulders. His hands moved over her shoulders, down her sides, coming to rest in the small of her back. She brought her hands together on his neck, but the springy curls at the nape of his neck tickled, and her fingers strayed into the softness of his hair. Without willing it, she rose onto her tiptoes, moving closer to him. He kissed her lips, his mouth warm and supple on hers, demanding more and more, until she pulled away, some kind of sound—an objection? a cry? a moan?—issuing from deep in her throat.

"It feels good, doesn't it?" He whispered near her ear. "You, with me, at this moment of our lives. We could be so happy." Tenderly, he added, "Say yes."

"But, I want to go to France. I want to do something good—"

"You don't have to go to France to do good," he said. "I want children. A son to inherit the company and a daughter to spoil, and more, to fill up the house. Isn't raising a family doing something good? Isn't being the wife of a man who loves you?"

A husband, a home, children. Everything that every woman should want. What had Papa said? *That's where your life will be— in your husband's home.*

"Didn't it feel good to kiss me?" he asked.

He trailed his finger along her lower lip, and she pulled away as sensation ran through her entire body, every vein surging with heat.

"Ah," he said. "So you felt it as strongly as I did."

She would be safe with him; she would be free of cares. She thought of Redlands, of the worn-out buildings and back-breaking work. *There is nothing here for you, Caitlin,* her father had said again and again. *You can love it as much as you want, but you can't make it pay.*

Yet she had come so far—more than a thousand miles from home and Mama and Papa—and couldn't stop now. But—

"You said you love me." Speaking the words hurt, as if she were opening herself to ridicule or blame. "How could you . . . when did you, how do you know?"

He pushed back a lock of her hair. "Because when I look at you, I don't want to look away. When I talk to you, I wish we were somewhere alone, where no one could disturb us. When I kiss you, I want what every man desires from a woman, and what he hopes she desires from him. When I'm angry with you, as I must admit I was the other night"—he laughed—"I want to have it out with you so we can talk like this again." He looked directly into her eyes. "I don't believe my feelings will change, either. They haven't since the first day I met you. Don't you feel the same?"

Did she? Was that why she was so disappointed that he did not join them yesterday? Was that why she reacted as she did when he touched her? How would she know that she loved him?

"But—" She swallowed again. "If I don't go to France, I will never know whether I am . . . "

"Whether you are what?"

"Whether I can do what the Church says I should, be a good servant of God, and whether I can see what my father wants me to see, and whether I can be what, well, what you're asking me to be, someone who knows enough about the world to talk about it and who doesn't just repeat what others think." She took a jagged breath. "This is my chance—the only one I'll ever have—to go somewhere and do something new." She paused, then admitted sheepishly, "I'm not much of a typist."

He laughed. "So I've heard. It's what you really want, then?"

"Yes, it is," she said with newfound confidence.

"Well, I am man enough to know when I've been skunked, Miss O'Doherty."

Her nerves broke, and she laughed at his choice of words.

He kissed her forehead. "So you will send me your sketches, as you've promised? And you'll write to me as well?"

"All of them, I promise, yes, and I'll write."

"Do you have enough pencils?" he asked. "I'm afraid it might not be as easy to find chewed up, discarded pencils in France as it was at Graves Oil."

"I still have those you gave me—"

"I will send more, then." He ran a yearning finger down her cheek. "When you come home from France, you'll be a woman. You will never be this innocent and free, this unpolished and uneducated—yes, don't argue, you are naïve—again. I'm sorry I won't be there to see you grow up."

He held her against him, and she closed her eyes, smelling his cologne and the warmth of his skin. Her heart pounded yet—from excitement, surprise, the sense that this was all too much, or not real at all. He kissed her again, softly this time, although it made no difference to her body. She felt herself drawing nearer, wanting more.

"Gee, I'd like to be a monkey in the zoo, Why, you'll never find a monkey feeling blue!"

The song echoed down the long row of elms.

"I believe our friends are here." He kissed her one last time. "Well, Kathleen, it seems that you're off to make your way in the world, while I am left here alone. I don't think you realize how cruel this is."

"I'm sorry."

"Never apologize for knowing what you want, my sweet."

She said nothing, not entirely sure she did know what she wanted. A proposal from a man who carried with him such power, such energy, was more than she would ever have again. But going to France was also more than she would ever have again.

He stepped away from her to straighten his collar, tie, and sleeves. As he slipped his coat on, Hank, Mary Jane and Helen appeared on the Mall, followed by Mrs. Brently.

Jim offered Kathleen his arm. "We should join them, don't you think?"

They walked out together—a sight that managed to stop the girls in their tracks. Mrs. Brently raised her eyebrows in a question.

"Kathleen!" Hank called, and the other girls gathered around her, all talking at once.

"You should have been with us—"

"The church was so big! I bet your church wasn't half the size—"

"Where were you at lunch?"

After she'd answered all the questions and insisted that St. Patrick's Cathedral was larger than any church in New York— whether or not it truly was—she sought out Jim. But he'd slipped away, leaving Mrs. Brently to take the girls to the Central Park Zoo.

He is there the next morning at the docks. After the Graves Family Foundation Relief Society poses for one more round of photographs, and after their matching trunks, all embossed with the information of the Society and their own names on them, are consigned for loading onto the ocean liner, the *New York*, he gives a solemn speech, reminding the girls of their patriotic duty, their humanitarian purpose, and of their roles as representatives of the grace, honor, and perfection of American women. He then presents each of the girls with a brooch of the American flag detailed in glittering stones. The brooches are to be worn on their capes—never on their uniforms.

Having spent a sleepless night in wondering if she has made the right decision, Kathleen waits for some word in the message that might be meant for her. When he hands her the velvet-lined box holding the brooch, he asks, "May I pin this on your cape, Miss O'Doherty?"

The other girls gawk as Jim pins the brooch on the cape's collar. Kathleen wonders if they see the way his knuckles brush against the tender skin of her throat and the way her face colors at the touch. He steps back and sizes up his work.

"*Bon voyage, mademoiselles,*" he says. "*Au revoir.*"

The girls laugh, delighted by his French. Then, the members of the Graves Family Foundation Relief Society board the ocean liner and the horns blow, and the great ship is underway, her smokestacks leaving a black trail in the sky. She is bound for Bordeaux in a convoy of more than three hundred ships. As Kathleen, Helen, Mary Jane and Hank wave from the railing, Mrs. Brently close behind them, Kathleen sees Jim standing on the dock, leaning against the Pierce Arrow. He doesn't wave, but neither does he take his gaze from her. At last, she loses sight of him.

They sail past the Statue of Liberty, heading toward open sea. As the shoreline recedes, Mrs. Brently appears at Kathleen's shoulder.

"Did you enjoy your time in New York?" she asks.

"Yes, oh, yes, thank you."

"I want to tell you—" She pauses as the horn blows. "My brother is, at times, impulsive, which, as you may guess, has served him well in his business ventures. He's also easily swayed by a pretty face and figure, and you have managed to capture his full attention."

Does she know of the marriage proposal? Kathleen stammers, "I, I—"

"Whatever he said to you," Mrs. Brently continues. "Whatever he may have asked of you, I hope you won't think of it from here on. He sometimes speaks too freely and doesn't always mean what he says."

She does know, Kathleen thinks, and she feels her face flush with heat.

"I thought he was teasing at first," she says. "But—"

"Ah, yes, he enjoys that, too." Mrs. Brently touches Kathleen's shoulder. "I'm glad you saw it for what it was. We needn't speak of it again."

She ebbs back into the crowd. Mary Jane, Hank and Helen are watching the swells in the ocean with glee. Kathleen joins them, but something aches now. She wishes she had spoken honestly to Mrs. Brently. It didn't feel like teasing, she would tell her, and his kisses certainly weren't contrived. Why would a man of his stature ask someone in her position to marry him if he were not serious? She could have whispered it to any of the dozen newspaper reporters who dogged their trail; she could have told the other girls. She could have threatened to ruin him if he did not keep his word; at the very least, she could have caused enough scandal to imperil the Relief Society.

No, he must have meant it—at least when he spoke of it. But perhaps it was just that—a moment's impulse—and Mrs. Brently is right.

Yet somewhere deep within, Kathleen knows that isn't true. She remembers his words: *Don't you want to be the wife of a man who loves you?*

She glances back toward New York. The Statue of Liberty is growing smaller, and more and more ships are joining in the wake of the *New York*. A troop ship appears to one side, so close that she can hear the whistles and calls of the khaki-clad soldiers on deck. Mary Jane and Hank laugh when they spy a young soldier viewing them through binoculars.

"Look, Kathleen," Hank says. "He's blowing a kiss to you!"

Kathleen reaches up and adjusts her wimple, then gathers her beautiful cape about her.

She is leaving America, she is leaving home.

She is leaving him.

FOURTEEN

Maggie pushed another barrel across the end of the truck, then hopped from the bed and pulled it down beside her. Rolling it over the ground, she left it at the back door of Sullivan's Grocery. When she straightened up, her spine gave a spasm, and she put both hands on her hips, rubbing the muscles of the small of her back. No wonder Seaney was so eager to join up with the Army. Fighting Germans had to be easier than this.

She leaned back against the wall of the store, seeking shade. Pa didn't expect nearly as much from her as he had from Seaney. For once, she was blessed to be a girl. And a married woman. She'd gained a new respect from both Ma and Pa now that she wore Liam's ring. She touched the plain band of gold. She had never before been as happy as she was now.

She adjusted the scarf that covered her hair and went back to the truck. Sitting on the bed, she swung her legs, which were sheathed in a pair of Seaney's old britches, around and stood up. She had just rolled another barrel forward when Ma came out of the back door of the store, Brendan at her side.

"Mag," she called. "Brendan's come to talk to you."

"Thank you, Mrs. Sullivan," he said.

As Ma went inside, Maggie dropped onto the bed of the truck, her legs hanging free over the edge. Brendan wore his Roman collar and black coat and trousers. On his head was a fedora.

"Hello, Father." She swung her legs back and forth like a naughty child. "What brings you here? Not official business, I hope?"

"Maggie, you need to come with me now. It's Liam—"

Maggie jumped off the bed, landing awkwardly. Brendan caught her arm to keep her from stumbling. "What's wrong?" she cried. "Is he hurt?"

"No, but he's in trouble. Can we use the truck?"

"What?" she asked, before realizing that he meant the delivery truck. "Where are we going?"

"Downtown. Go inside and wash your face and hands, but don't take time to change. And don't tell your parents. We need to leave immediately."

Maggie ran up the outside steps to the Sullivans' apartments. At the kitchen sink, she scrubbed the dirt from her hands and dashed water on her face. Pulling off the headscarf, she ran her fingers through her curls. When she got back to the truck, Brendan was sitting in the passenger's seat, smoking a cigarette.

"Tell me what's going on," she said, as she pulled away from the store. "What is he doing downtown?"

"He's giving a speech at the Capitol building, right now."

"But he's at work."

"No, he's not. Avery Deets called me. Liam never went to work today." Brendan exhaled. "Maggie, this isn't the first time—"

"The first time for what?"

"That he's spoken in public. He's been doing it in the evenings, after work, too. He's already been warned by the police to stop."

She pressed on the gas, urgency ricocheting through her body. She tried to understand Brendan's statement—*this isn't the first time*—but nothing seemed clear. Liam came home late, sometimes, but his job was demanding and important. He had also been attending meetings with some of the men from the railroad to talk about conditions and pay, but that was to be expected. One thing was certain: he had said nothing to her about public speeches or missing work.

There could be no mistake about where Liam was speaking. A crowd had gathered around him as he stood on the Capitol steps, the white stone sizzling in the bright sun. With him was a band of grim-faced protesters, who stood in morbid silence, holding banners and signs. WILSON PROMISED TO KEEP US OUT! REMEMBER THE SOMME! A squat woman dressed in black wore a gold star—the symbol of a dead loved one—on her arm. A bearded man raised a placard that read, SOCIALISTS FOR PEACE.

"You're breakin' the law!" someone shouted. "Call the police! Haul these traitors away!"

"Please listen to me," Liam called. "Most of the men being drafted today are kind, peace-loving men who are working for their families. They're supporting their parents or wives and children. They aren't the well-to-do men who went to Plattsburg—they aren't from the leisure class that can buy an officer's rank—but from the millions of the workers who willingly—no, gladly—carry on their backs the weight of America's greatness and through whose efforts the rich have become so powerful. What interest do such men have in this war, this squabble between foreign nations?"

"Coward! Slacker! Benedict Arnold!"

"But they are now being forced to serve," he continued. "They are being driven into the trenches—boys who are too young to vote or live independently, but who are presumed by our government to be old enough to decide the terrible questions of life and death—"

A chorus of catcalls and booing drowned out his words. "Hang him!" someone shouted. "Death to traitors and cowards!"

Maggie staggered, thrust back by the hatred of the assault. She could not breathe above the rising urge to scream. "Brendan," she gasped. "You have to make him stop!"

When Brendan made no move, Maggie started forward. Brendan caught her arm.

"Conscription not only forces men's bodies to do what they do not want, but their minds as well." Liam shouted above the racket. "It makes them the slaves of venal authority. It takes away their power to think their own individual thoughts, it makes them expert with guns and weapons of death that no mother or father would want their child to touch. It engenders contempt for human lives—"

"I'm not like you!" a woman shrieked. "I'm a patriot!"

Liam turned toward her. "I, too, am a patriot. But I am also a believer in the Word of God. I am not a coward or a slacker or any of the other names that have been so readily attached to men who speak from their conscience. God has said, 'Thou shalt not kill,' and God's law is superior to any human dictate in any case. And for that reason"—Liam held up a sheaf of papers—"I will not fill out the Questionnaire that was sent to me by the United States government in order to assess my fitness for conscription. I will not participate in any activity that furthers the cause of this heinous and unjust war!"

He began to tear the Questionnaire in half, dropping each scrap on the ground. Maggie heard a number of gasps, as if the audience was too shocked to respond to what it was witnessing. The pile at Liam's feet began to shift in the warm breeze, portions of the Questionnaire blowing away onto the lawns. Here and there, people picked them up, their outrage growing.

"That's a government document!" a man shouted. "You're destroying the government's property!"

"What's going on here? What are you doing?" A uniformed police officer stepped through the crowd and confiscated the papers from Liam's hand. "This is a Draft Questionnaire—"

"I am a soldier of peace," Liam proclaimed. "And as a soldier of peace, I will live and die!"

"It's you again, huh?" The policeman signaled his partner. "Help me take these folks in!"

"Let him be!" Maggie cried. "This is a free country!"

Brendan stepped forward. "Please, my name is Father Brendan Keohane, and I serve at Blessed Savior Catholic Church. This man is my brother—"

"I'm his wife," Maggie said. "Let me take him home —"

A wad of paper—part of the destroyed Questionnaire—struck her left arm. The blow stung, and as the missile landed at her feet, she saw that the paper was wrapped around a cherry-sized rock. The crowd jeered as another wad hit Brendan, who raised a protective arm against the attack: "Look at the sissy priest!" "Why aren't you at war, Father?" "Go back to the Vatican and stay there!"

"Maggie, stand behind me," Brendan ordered.

"I'm staying with him." Maggie pointed to Liam, whose arms were pinned behind his back as if he were a common thief. "He's my husband—"

"Maggie, no," Liam said. "Go home—"

"You're a little young to be a wife, aren't you?" the policeman asked. "How old are you?"

"Eighteen."

He eyed her clothing. "And where do you work, Missus? At a pig farm? Soo-ey!"

The spectators laughed, and the police officer addressed Brendan. "Your brother was told last week to stay away—"

Suddenly, a man rushed from the crowd and spat into Liam's face. Maggie screamed as the white glob fell from his cheek to his shirt, just over his heart. Liam made no response, as if he didn't feel it.

"Go home!" the policeman shouted at the spectators. "Get away before you all end up in the pokey!"

The crowd dispersed, cursing and calling names as the police dragged Liam and the protesters toward a paddy wagon on Lincoln Street. Maggie started to follow, but Brendan caught her arm.

"We have the truck," he said.

She drove, obeying the directions that Brendan gave her without hearing them. She had never been this frightened in her life—not even when Pa slapped her or Seaney around, or when Ma cried for days after another child was lost. This was something new—a fear that she couldn't find a way to solve the problem, a certainty that the world might never be right again.

The Denver County Jail was constructed of majestic stone, with tall arched windows extending for two floors and a generous round window set into its great front facade.

"It looks like a church," Maggie said.

"Don't be fooled," Brendan replied.

He was right. Inside, the sun that shone through the rose window became brittle light that blinded but did not warm. Maggie shivered as Brendan asked the officer at the front desk if they could see Liam. The officer told them to take a seat on hard benches that stood against the walls of the foyer.

"You should have told me he was doing this," Maggie accused Brendan, once they were seated. "You should have stopped him."

The question echoed up against the high ceiling of the anteroom. "Shh," Brendan cautioned. "I have a responsibility to my parishioners—"

"You have a greater one to Liam," Maggie hissed. "Look at all the times he fought for you when you were in the orphanage. Think about how he stood up for you when—"

An officer approached. "My name is Sergeant Lavin," he said. "You're looking for Liam Keohane?"

"Yes," Maggie said. "He's my husband. This is his brother."

Sergeant Lavin led them through a locked, barred door into the interior of the jail. The sunlight from the immense window did not reach this far, and Maggie gagged at the smell that wafted through the corridor. Vomit and urine and more—the stench brewed around her. She swallowed, covering her mouth with her hand, afraid she might faint. Her shoes stuck to the floor, and something damp crept up one stocking. A brown haze hung in air.

Sergeant Lavin unlocked the door of a small room at the end of a hall. Inside, Liam sat at a table, a sheaf of papers in front of him.

"Liam!" Maggie rushed forward to embrace him.

"No touching," Sergeant Lavin said. "Sit over here. You, too, Father. Don't move or you'll have to leave."

Meekly, Maggie sat across the table from Liam. Brendan took the seat beside her.

"I'll come back in two minutes. Use them wisely." Sergeant Lavin eyed Liam. "Tell your friends here the deal you've been offered. They might help you to change your mind."

An officer slipped inside the room as Sergeant Lavin closed the door, and Maggie heard the key turn in the lock. She glanced at the officer, who remained near the door, but his face was expressionless.

"What deal?" she asked. "What do they want?"

"You shouldn't have come," Liam said. "I don't want you to be part of this—"

"Brendan told me—"

Liam cast a furious gaze at his brother. "You knew my wishes, and yet you chose to disrespect them—"

"I had to," Brendan said. "She has to know."

"What is the deal?" Maggie asked again.

Liam fingered the papers on the table. "If I fill out the Questionnaire, all charges will be dropped."

"And you can come home?" Maggie asked. "Oh, Liam, do it! Do it so you can come home."

He twisted a pen in his fingers.

"You must think of Maggie," Brendan said. "You must think of your wife, of your promise and commitment to her. You must think of the Holy Church—"

"So should you," Liam said. "You're a priest, Brendan, a man of God. You should be beside me, speaking out as loudly—no, more loudly—than I am against the killing of men."

Maggie picked up the Questionnaire. Sixteen pages long, it started with basic questions about citizenship, race and occupation, and moved to details about income, property owned, and taxes paid. A long section was devoted to dependents and whether the wife was able to work.

"These are simple questions," she said. "Why can't you just fill it out? It isn't killing, it's just answering." She reached for Liam's hand, then withdrew, afraid that the officer would end the visit. "You registered in June, now you're just finishing that up."

"I did," he acknowledged. "I registered, and it has been on my mind that I have already broken the Sixth Commandment. I have already participated in the war. But no more. I can't betray my conscience nor the principles that guide it, which are those found in God's word—"

Brendan broke in. "To care for your wife and children is just as—"

"Our government cares nothing for wives and children. There would be no war if it did."

"You'll never be drafted by the Army," Brendan argued. "Your eyesight will keep you from ever serving—"

"So I should hide behind my physical defects? I'm not a coward."

Maggie responded. "Then why weren't you brave enough to tell me what you're doing? Why have you been hiding this from me?"

The door rattled, and Sergeant Lavin came into the room. "Time's up," he said. "What have you decided?"

Without speaking, Liam offered the Questionnaire to him. Sergeant Lavin took it and paged through it. "I see," he said. "The arraignment will be tomorrow. Officer Davis."

The officer came forward, grabbed Liam by the right arm, and jerked him out of the chair, as if he had refused to move.

"Stop it!" Maggie cried. "Liam, please, do as they say! Please, for me!"

She lurched forward, fear biting at her heart. Brendan restrained her, his hand on her shoulder, as Officer Davis pulled Liam from the room.

"Remember the Sixth Commandment, Father!" Liam called as he disappeared into the darkness.

As the door closed behind Liam, fury rose in Maggie—at Liam, at Brendan, at Sergeant Lavin, at the war and its stupidity. With a rough shrug, she pulled away from Brendan, whose hand still rested on her shoulder.

Sergeant Lavin opened the door to the hallway. "You see, Mrs. Keohane, your husband is unwilling to abide by the laws of this country. He is a traitor."

"He is not," Maggie protested. "He's standing up for what he believes in—"

"We need to leave now," Brendan interrupted. "There's nothing more we can do."

They drove back to Maggie and Liam's house in silence, but when they arrived, cars were parked along the street, and a number of people had gathered on the lawn in front. Maggie knew most of them—Frank MacMahon and his parents and brothers and others from the church. Pa was there, too, his face dark and dour.

"Evidently the news has spread," Brendan said quietly.

She made no effort to crawl from the truck. "What is the name of the group whose meetings Liam attends?" she asked. "Where they talk about better pay for the railroad workers?"

"It's called the People's Council of America for Democracy and Peace. It's an organization that seeks to defend the rights of freedom of speech and assembly during the war. We're all afraid they will disappear."

"We?" Maggie asked. "Do you belong to it, too?"

"Yes, and Frank and Donnell." He looked at the group on the lawn. "We're also asking for the repeal of the Conscription Act and for the government to stop forcing working men to give up their livelihoods and go to a manufactured war." He paused. "It's a noble cause, Maggie."

"Not if it takes Liam from me!"

She climbed from the truck and slammed the door as hard as she could. Pushing her way through the crowd to the kitchen, she found her mother making coffee. Black, gravelly grounds spilled from the grinder, and the counter was flooded with water.

Maggie touched her mother's shoulder. "Ma, don't cry."

"So you're home? Where's Liam?"

"He's in jail. He'll be charged tomorrow."

"What's he thinkin', shamin' us this way? With Seaney on his way to France and all—"

"I don't know," Maggie wept. "I don't know."

"Seaney could be killed! And Liam, sittin' there, sayin' he won't go—!"

"He's doing what he believes," she said, but the words sounded even weaker here than they had at the jail.

"'Tis one thing not to like the war," Ma said. "But to be standin' in public and hollerin' about it is a sin against those who are sacrificin' their lives for it—"

"I know, Ma."

Conversation drifted into the kitchen from the other room. Maggie went to the doorway and leaned against the jamb. A crowd had gathered inside, now, and Dr. Thorp and Ed Barry, both members of the Draft Board, were standing near the fireplace, Brendan at their side.

"If he would just fill out the Questionnaire, we could see if there is a deferment possible for him," Ed said.

"That's not likely," Dr. Thorp said. "Because the Church has vowed to support the war, Catholics cannot be considered as conscientious objectors by the military—"

"But he has a wife to support—"

"A wife who is already working and earning wages at her parents' store," Dr. Thorp reminded him. "I believe there would have to be a baby or children to feed."

"Liam's right," Danny MacMahon blustered. "No Irishman should join to fight with the British—"

"They send C.O.s to the mines and factories," Pa rumbled. "Teach them a few things about lovin' this country by makin' them work at hard labor."

Brendan turned away and moved toward the window, where he lit a cigarette.

Tears in her eyes, Maggie slipped from the kitchen and through the parlor. Upstairs, the bedroom she shared with Liam was shrouded by drawn shades against the Indian summer heat. Without removing her shoes, she dropped onto the bed and let the tears drip on the pillow shams and into her hair. How could Liam do this to her? She had always loved him, since they were children, and she had always known that he was outspoken. In fact, she had always been proud of it.

She rolled to her side. *But I haven't been. More than once, I've wished he wouldn't talk so loud or so much or . . .*

Furious again, she sat up, pulled off her shoes, and lobbed them against the wall of the bedroom. "All I wanted was to be your wife," she rasped. "All my life, all I've ever wanted is to love you and be loved by you and—"

"Maggie?" She heard Brendan's voice at the bottom of the stairs. "Are you all right?"

Ma's voice followed. "Did you hurt yourself?"

Maggie went to the door and called into the hallway. "I'm all right. I dropped my shoes."

"Are you going to bed?" Ma asked.

"Yes."

She changed into her nightdress, the voice raging in her head: *I would give my life for you. Why won't you do the same for me?* She could not silence it, even when she lay down and closed her eyes, and even when she put her pillow over her head to drown out the voices of the men downstairs. *I'm so angry, I'm so angry, I'm so—*

Unable to stand it any longer, she sat up and went to her vanity. Looking at her reflection in the mirror, she let a new voice overtake her, one that could silence all the others and make her forget the sorrows of the day: *Evelyn knew that George had a secret, and she was sure it had to do with her birthday* . . .

At the arraignment, Liam's bail is set at $2500. When Maggie hears the amount, she sobs. No one she knows has ever had that kind of money; she doubts most people make that much money in their lifetimes.

Yet, a few days later, as she is sitting in the parlor, darning socks and shirts—Ma has told her to stay busy and keep her mind off her troubles—Liam walks through the door, with Brendan close behind him.

"Liam!" Maggie jumps up and runs to him, but he steps away when she tries to wrap her arms around him. When she lifts her face for a kiss, she sees that he has a black eye and cut lip, still crusted with dried blood. "What did they do to you?" she cries. "Did the police do this?"

Without answering, he walks to a chair and gingerly sits down, holding his left side.

"How did you get out?" Maggie asks. "Who paid the bail?"

Brendan answers. "Some of the folks in the parish felt that the judgment was unfair. They offered the money on the condition that Liam leave off his speech-making."

"Who did this to him? Why?"

"Evidently the Denver Police do not care for conscientious objectors," Brendan replies.

Together, they guide Liam into the kitchen, where Brendan helps him out of his filthy clothes while Maggie fills a bath for him in the tiny bathroom closet. Once Liam has bathed—stepping in and out of the tub with the help of Brendan—the two help him upstairs to bed. After Liam is settled, Brendan takes his leave.

Maggie rubs liniment on Liam's ribs. She is certain that one on the left side is broken. "You need a doctor," she says. "Should I call Dr. Thorp?"

"Brendan told me he spoke out against me. I don't need to hear more."

"But . . ." She falters. "I'll make you tea, then. What do you want to eat?"

He lies back and closes his eyes. "I've had nothing but bread and water for five days. I don't know that I can eat anything solid just yet."

Maggie thinks of all the angry things she had planned to say: the accusations that he does not love her, that he is selfish and heartless, the demand that he become a proper husband or else, or else . . . But there are bruises up and down his back, stomach and legs. Her own body aches, her heart feeling squeezed and tight, as if the damage has been done to her as well.

"What did they do to you?" she asks weakly.

"I don't want to talk about it."

"I've missed you. I've been so scared."

He opens his eyes. "Maggie." He strokes her face with scabbed knuckles as his eyes fill with tears. "Maggie, oh, Maggie, I wish you did not have to bear this—"

"Then, don't make me, Liam," she whispers. "Don't do this."

He closes his eyes. "I need to sleep right now. We'll talk later."

Maggie goes to the door, but she doesn't leave. She watches as Liam gingerly rolls to his side. He seems to fall asleep immediately, but his breath is harsh, exhaled with a whistle and grunt from his lungs. The sound repeats rhythmically in her head as she goes downstairs. Why would he allow this to happen to him? Why wouldn't he do what he must to end it?

In the parlor, she kneels at the altar and prays, *"Thank you for bringing him home. Please let him see that he needs to be here, with those who love him so—"*

God is my enemy, a voice within her head replies. He is taking Liam from me.

At once repentant, she prays for forgiveness and crosses herself. Yet the words lodge in the back of her head, still virulently alive.

Rising, she goes to the door and finds the afternoon newspaper. On the front page is an article entitled: "Blow to Patriotism of Real Americans." The text reads, "Mr. Liam Keohane of Denver claims he is a Soldier of Peace, and that his faith, which is Roman Catholicism, will not allow him to participate in any activity that is related to the war. Yet the people of Colorado will soon recognize that Mr. Keohane is a member of the Army of Cowards and Slackers that refuses to do its duty. Recently, while imprisoned in the Denver County Jail, Mr. Keohane wrote a treatise called, 'The Soldiers of Peace Are Being Punished,' which he sent to the *Denver Post*. In it, he claimed: 'Those responsible for this war—those presidents and kings who have cast this hardship upon their own nations—should stand trial for compelling millions of innocent young men to do their slaughter for them . . .'"

There is more, but Maggie cannot read it. Covering her mouth, she sobs.

FIFTEEN

Five days out of Halifax, there were no more lights. Only ocean. All day and all night, the ship pitched and plunged in the relentless North Atlantic, burying its prow up to the anchor chains. Sean was thankful that his prairie-boy stomach could bear it. The men who couldn't had to brave the bitter temperatures, hanging over rails that could freeze their skin.

Tonight, he sat at one of the long, splintery tables in the mess hall, sipping at his coffee from a tin mug. It sloshed—everything on board sloshed along with this ship. Men packed the mess hall, filling the benches that were nailed to the floor, and smoking cigarettes until the acrid haze made Sean's eyes burn. Some of the crew sat by the stove in the corner, drawn in by song and warmth. They were Brits—the ships in the convoy were mostly British registry, escorted by French submarine hunters, transporting American troops in true allied cooperation.

In another corner, an American sergeant read aloud the poems of Robert Service. Near the door, a concertina wheezed out chords, played by a boy from Iowa. He sang a rich tenor: "*Shine on, shine on, harvest moon, up in the sky, I ain't had no lovin'—*"

Sean was trying to write to Kathleen, but to grip a pen while the paper swam beneath his eyes was excruciating: *Imagine it— hundreds of us crammed into tiny bunks, faces within inches of each other, our blood (and dinners) slopping back and forth with the waves! Our mattresses are stuffed with straw packed hard from too many bodies, and whatever we can find becomes a pillow. Some of the boys have started sleeping on the deck, where at least there's some air to breathe, even if it is cold enough to freeze your lungs. But sometimes, the ocean is rolling so hard that we're just as likely to fall off as to fall asleep.*

Our food is pretty poor, with hard tack being about the only thing worthy of eating. There's a canteen on board, where we can buy fresh buns and even some fruit for a small fortune. Apples are two for five cents, and chocolates are $1.75 a pound! If we charged those kinds of prices back in Denver, we'd be out of business in a week. As it is, we soldiers are the ones going out of business because we run the risk of starving to death if we don't partake at the canteen. It's good old-fashioned American capitalism at its best: take 'em for all they're worth.

We've only seawater to bathe in, for the fresh water is for drinking only. I feel like a hunk of salt pork after every shower—

Sean glanced up, resting his eyes. Kathleen had already left America on board a luxury ocean liner. No itch-inducing straw or salt water-filled eyes and ears for her. According to Ma, who had sent him the information, everything connected with the Graves Family Foundation Relief Society was first-class, top-tier, and fancy-dancy.

Don't you worry about me, he wrote. *We are required to wear our life belts all the time, so that we bump around like whales. We keep a full cartridge belt and canteen, too, just so that if we go into the drink, we'll have something to drink. And speaking of whales— I've not only seen those, but sea gulls and dolphins, too. I never thought I'd see those kinds of creatures in my lifetime . . .*

One of the British soldiers had attracted a crowd of young Americans to his side with his stories, and Sean bent forward to hear. The Brit—he was no more than twenty—was talking about the trenches, about the terrible noise of bombardment.

"You can't think," he said. "And there comes a time when you can't hear anymore—"

"How come you're on this ship, now?" asked a boy from Georgia.

The Brit's voice grew ragged. "Last March, I was shot. Right in the nape of the neck. Shot and gassed, too. The whole trench, everybody in it, shot, and only a few of us still alive. We had to lie there for hours, waiting for the medics—they couldn't get in because of the shells—and we just lay there, bleeding and crying for help. My head was hanging by only a single cord, half my neck shot—"

"If you was hurt that bad"—the Georgian turned skeptic— "you'd be dead with the rest of 'em."

The Brit jumped to his feet. "I am dying! I've been dying since that day! And yet they're sending me back! That's how it is, Yank! That's the way it is! I don't have much time to live, and here you are, calling me a liar—!"

"I'm not—!"

"Hey!" one of his shipmates called. "Settle down, Port!"

"Here!" Port ripped off his stocking hat. "Feel this! Run your hand over my head and you'll feel the scars—"

In the opposite corner, the concertina fell silent. The poetry reading stuttered to a close. The Georgian lifted a timid hand. He had almost touched Port's head when the man gave a godawful scream and fell, flailing on the floor. "Oh, my God, it hurts! It hurts! Don't let them do it! Don't let them cut—!"

Sean leaped to his feet. Port was shivering like a dying dog, his eyes rolled up in his head, his hands beating against his own chest. Sean flattened himself against Port's shoulders, while the boy from Georgia lay across his hips, trying to keep him from crashing into the unforgiving legs of the nailed-down tables and benches. A couple of the sailors piled on top, wrestling the Americans. Port's jolting head slammed again and again into the wooden planks until a thin stream of blood ran down his temples. The ship heaved, and steins, cigarette lighters, books, and tin spoons cascaded from the table. The men rolled with the waves, crashing as a heap into the wall.

"Stop it!" Sean commanded. "Stop!"

Port grabbed onto the front of Sean's shirt. "You have to go over the top," he croaked. "You have to kill them. They're coming, can't you see? God, they're here! My God! My God!"

The last screams mimicked the bleat of the veal calves Pa used to butcher in the corrals behind the store. Sean slapped at Port. "Let go of me!" he roared. "Let go!" Port clenched tighter to his shirt, both hands now. The others tried to drag him away from Sean.

"Please, kill me." Port thrust his face into Sean's ear. His hot breath stank, and his saliva and tears pooled on Sean's neck. "Don't make me go back! They'll send me back to the trenches, so, kill me, please, kill me—"

"Let me go!" Sean punched at him. "Get away!"

"Please, please, kill me, kill me, now, please—"

"Leave me alone!"

"Move out of the way!" The voice came from behind Sean. "Surgeon! Move!"

Sean tried to scramble away, but Port's fingers dug into his chest, his fingernails ripping through fabric and flesh.

"Watch out, son." The surgeon squatted and slapped a cloth over Port's face. "Turn your head away," he told Sean. "Don't breathe."

Sean looked away. After a moment, he felt Port's fingers loosen. But the Brit still breathed, "Kill me, kill me, kill me—"

The others tugged on him, and he fell away from Sean, landing in a lump halfway under a table. Sean squirmed out of reach.

"Kill me, kill me—"

The surgeon doused the cloth with fresh chloroform and pressed it over Port's nose and mouth. Sean could still hear the grim chant, the words seeming to come from Port's lungs with each breath.

He pulled himself up, wobbling to his feet. Port's body went limp, knocked out by the drug, and the surgeon stood. "Good Lord, he took almost a pint." He dried his hands on a clean towel. "Are you all right, Yank?"

Sean nodded and wiped his nose on the back of his hand. Blood. Somehow he'd been kicked or hit in the nose in the scuffle. He felt bruised all over, and filthy, poisoned by the Brit's sour saliva. The scratches on his chest stung and itched. Swaying like a drunkard, he climbed up the ladder to the deck, stumbling out into the frigid air. He could see nothing. It was dangerous to be out on deck at night, more dangerous to be careening about, without a handhold. Still, he pressed forward until he butted up against the ship's railing.

Kill me, kill me—

His stomach rumbled once, and he vomited, hard and painfully, over the side of the ship. He laid his head against the railing, his hands holding tight to the icy metal. The warmth of tears ran down his cold skin. "*God in heaven!*" he prayed. "*God in heaven, please . . .*" But nothing more came.

Where was God when that poor fellow fell in the trenches? When he went berserk?

After a while, he became aware of the roll of the ship beneath him, of the smell of burning coal and the salty tang of the ocean. Somewhere down the deck, to his right, someone else was vomiting his own dinner. The engines thrummed their low, monotonous song.

"Private Sullivan."

Oh, Jesus, Lieutenant Morgan. Sean snapped upward, nearly losing his balance. Lieutenant Morgan reached out a hand and steadied him. Sean wiped his sleeve across his face, leaving a smear of blood and snot on his shirt. With effort, he saluted, his hand seeming to weigh as much as lead. He was in for it now. Lieutenant Morgan would probably accuse him of starting the whole melee.

"Are you all right, Private?" the Lieutenant asked in a low voice.

"Yes, sir."

"You'll have to make a report—"

"I know." Dizzy, Sean reached for the railing with one hand. For a moment, he thought he might vomit again. "What happened to him?"

"He's been taken to sick bay." Lieutenant Morgan looked out over the water. "Strapped down for his own safety. You should be checked out by the doctor as well."

"I've only a few scratches—"

"He has his hands full tonight, but tomorrow morning, you're ordered to report to sick bay."

"Yes, sir."

Sean expected Lieutenant Morgan to leave, but he lingered at the railing. Diaphanous trails of phosphorus, split and swirled by the convoy's prows, glowed bright green in the light of the full moon, like a bride's veil. Sean thought of his mother, making hats of tulle and lace so rich and colorful that they looked like portraits, and homesickness swelled up in him. He turned to the railing and leaned on it with both arms, his hands hanging over the inky toss of the sea.

He could still hear the refrain: *Kill me, kill me—*

Suddenly, he could stand it no more, blurting, "Do you think, sir—"

He stopped, ashamed.

"Yes?"

He swallowed to rid his voice of its tremor. "Do you think it would have been better if that Brit had died in the trenches?" Tears crowded in his eyes again. "Rather than live on in such a miserable state?"

"Who knows?" Lieutenant Morgan's voice cracked. "If he can't determine what's real—"

He said no more, but Sean heard it anyway: Any one of us on this ship could face the same fate. Any one of us could be driven mad, could fall victim to what the newspapers call "shell shock" or "trench madness" and lose himself.

A tear slipped from Sean's eye. He should go downstairs, before he revealed himself again to Lieutenant Morgan as a weakling. He did not want to be thought of as a coward. He kept his gaze on the brilliant phosphorus path behind them.

"You'd better go down to your bunk, Private," Lieutenant Morgan said, as if he, too, wanted to be alone. "There's a lifeboat drill at o-six hours."

"I'd like to sleep out here tonight, I think, sir," Sean said.

"All right. I'll allow it."

Sean went down to the lower deck to retrieve his mattress, sleeping bag, and his duffel for a pillow. When he returned, most of his compatriots were already on deck, having staked out a corner near the bow of the ship. They were singing in soft, soulful voices: *"I dream of Jeannie with the light brown hair—"*

"Come join us, Sean," Kevin called.

As Sean threw down his bedding, he heard another voice, "Hey, Sullivan, why don't you offer that Englander one of your plastic saints to pray with?"

It was Danhour, of course. Without waiting for Sean's reply, he called, "Maybe he could use your two-headed elephant."

The remark—made so long ago by Lieutenant Morgan at Fort Riley—had followed Sean all the way across the country.

"Shut up," he said, unable to manage much more.

"That Port is one crazy fellow." A man named Arnold shook his head. "Think we'll all end up that barmy?"

Nauseated again, Sean went to the railing, leaving behind the talk and the fear. In front of the ship were four others, steaming along through the night. The phosphorus rode the waves left in the wakes, like gleaming balls floating in a tub of water.

Kathleen had always said that God could be found in nature. Tonight, however, Sean couldn't find Him anywhere.

SIXTEEN

In France, the Graves Family Foundation Relief Society was to report to Montdidier for service. After a week of sightseeing in Paris—the Eiffel Tower, the Arc de Triomphe, the Place de la Concorde—and two weeks training at the Red Cross, the girls boarded a *camion*, or covered truck, bound for the north.

"How far is Mount Did-y-er?" Hank asked Mrs. Brently.

"That's Mone-dee-dee-AY," she corrected airily. "It's some sixty miles from Paris, I believe."

"How far is it from where they are fighting?" Mary Jane asked.

"That I can't tell you," Mrs. Brently replied.

The trip took longer than expected. The roads were muddy, pitted, traveled by convoys of *camions* and teams of horses and legions of marching men. Every time a military vehicle or a column of soldiers appeared on the road, the driver of the *camion* would pull to the side and wait for the traffic to pass. The girls peered out from behind the canvas tarp of the bed, gawking at the soldiers, as if the Frenchmen would look different from the boys of America. And in many ways they did. Their tattered sky blue uniforms seemed all too light and frolicsome for the task of war, and their faces were ashen or gray, not at all the healthy, sun-kissed complexions that the girls knew from living in Colorado.

Toward the end of the day, when Mrs. Brently asked, in her flowing French, how much longer before they arrived at Montdidier, the driver shrugged.

"*Nous verrons*," he said.

"I don't need to speak French to know that means never!" Mary Jane whispered in Kathleen's ear.

Trying to avoid being jounced off the bench-like seats in the tarped back of the *camion* took most of the girls' attention and energy. Kathleen fretted as she tried to keep her uniform from being stained by oil, mud or whatever else moiled on the floor. Mrs. Brently worried about the trunks, which slid back and forth across the flat bed, and about the boxes of supplies that the Red Cross had given them for the canteen. The girls ended up taking turns at bracing the trunks and boxes by sitting with their backs to them or holding them on their laps.

By the time the driver announced Montdidier, the sun had set. He braked the *camion* in the middle of the road and turned off the ignition, leaving the girls in near darkness. Peeking around the tarp, Kathleen saw that other vehicles and wagons were parked along the road as well. An eerie deadness lay over the scene, as drivers smoked without speaking beside their *camions*. The wagon masters stood beside their teams of horses, the cheek pieces tight in their hands.

"*Pourquoi arrêtons-nous ici?*" Mrs. Brently whispered to the driver through the canvas portal that divided cab from bed.

"*Un détour militaire.*"

As they bandied back and forth in French, Kathleen became aware of a deep roar in the distance, like a rushing river that had overflowed its banks. Suddenly, the sky to the northeast exploded in color. Two red flares shot straight upward, breaking into stars that illuminated the road and then showered back to the earth in glittering tendrils.

Mary Jane screamed, while Helen grabbed Kathleen's hand. Hank squatted on the floor of the *camion* and covered her head.

"*Silence!*" the driver snapped. "*Vous ferai descendre sur nous!*"

Mrs. Brently turned back to the girls. "You must be very quiet," she said. "Evidently, there is something happening at the Front."

"Are we that close?" Mary Jane asked.

Mrs. Brently did not answer. "There's a roadblock up ahead," she said. "So we shall have to walk into town. The driver believes it is safe enough. He will wait with the trunks."

The girls climbed from the back of the *camion* into the night air. Free of the smell of wet canvas, Kathleen breathed in deeply, but the air carried with it a smell of burned hair and a spicy tang, as if someone had spilled pepper or turmeric. The road was soupy with yellow clay-like mud. She could feel her shoes growing heavier with each step, caked with ooze. A chill was descending on the night, and fog was rolling in. She drew her cape around her, but the cold pierced through her clothing.

"Please stay as close as you can to me," Mrs. Brently said.

Kathleen clutched Mary Jane's hand. On the main road through the town, the tall, mansard-roofed houses were dark and asleep. Yet, ahead, at what looked to be the train station, lights blazed. As the girls neared the station, Kathleen could hear a buzzing, like a crowd of people humming in different keys, and above it, the terse, brisk orders called out in French. Long shapes lay on the train platform. There were hundreds, placed as closely together as they could be. She watched as two men hefted one up by poles attached to either end, and she understood.

These were not baggage. They were stretchers of wounded men.

Mrs. Brently glanced to her left, taking in the desperate scene, then said, "We shall have to see how we can help." She crossed the platform and went into the building. The girls followed.

A gray-haired man waved his hands at them. "*Sortez! Sortez!*"

"We are the Graves Family Foundation Relief Society," Mrs. Brently said. "We are here to provide social support—"

"*Sortez! Tout suite! Il y a du travail à faire!*"

"What does that mean?" Hank asked Helen, who was the only one of the girls with a true command of French.

"He wants us to go outside. He says there's work to do."

"Maybe we should leave."

"Mrs. Brently told us to stay here."

Soldiers rushed past them to the dispatch center, and the girls backed into a corner, attempting to stay out of the way, until they were nearly stepping on each other's toes. Mrs. Brently continued to argue in French with the gray-haired man. The more she spoke, the more agitated he grew.

"Maybe we should go outside," Kathleen said. "Maybe this is for military only."

Hank and Mary Jane nodded, and she led them out the door, hoping to slip around the corner and away from the frenzy. But someone called to her just as she was about to round the building. She turned toward a woman who wore a white wimple similar to her own.

"*Mademoiselle, s'il vous plaît, pouvez-vous m'aider?*"

The woman spoke so quickly that Kathleen's rudimentary knowledge of French escaped her. "I'm sorry," she said. "I only know a bit of French—"

From the darkness beyond the building, a voice asked, "Are you American?"

"Yes," Kathleen said.

A man in military dress stepped out of the shadows, his face obscured by a chauffeur's cap. Quickly, he translated the French woman's words. "She's asking you to help with eye-washing."

"I'm not a nurse." Kathleen glanced at the bodies that jammed the platform. A locomotive puffed noisily on the rails. "We aren't trained—"

"You can learn," he said. "I'll teach you." He spoke in rapid French to the nurse, who nodded her head and waved toward the first line of stretchers on the ground. "Some of these boys are Brits or colonials. You won't have any trouble communicating with them."

"I'll come, too!" Helen called. "I speak French!"

Kathleen and Helen followed him to the front of the station. The nurse handed him an oilskin bag, which he gave to Kathleen, and a jug of water, which he handed to Helen. All the while, he spoke in English to the girls.

"They've been in a gas attack," he said. "Some were caught face-on and others in the blow-back—"

"Blow-back?" Kathleen asked.

"When the wind shifts directions." He watched as the nurse squatted next to a soldier who was writhing in pain and began to unwind the dirty bandage that circled his head. "Mustard gas attacks the moist parts of the body first, usually the eyes."

"Are you a doctor?"

"I'm an *ambulancier*, an ambulance driver."

"*S'il vous plaît!*" groaned the soldier.

"*Oui, restez, restez,*" the nurse said. "*Ouvrez vos yeux autant que vous le pouvez.*"

"*Je ne peux pas.*"

"What are they saying?" Kathleen asked.

"She's asked him to open his eyes as much as he can, but he says he can't."

Kathleen leaned forward for a better look as the nurse tossed the used bandage aside. The skin on the soldier's face was mottled by angry, raw blisters, his eyelids swollen to the size of orange rinds. The skin was discolored, even in the white wash of flood lights from the station. Kathleen's stomach rebelled in a wave of nausea, and faintness filled her head. Her feet wobbled beneath her.

"Are you all right?" the ambulance driver asked.

"I don't know—"

"You have to be," he said. "You have a choice. These men don't."

The nurse took from her kit a tool that looked like a protractor that a child would use in math class. With it, she spread and pulled back the soldier's eyelids, exposing the white of the eye. Then she signaled to Helen to hand her the jug of water. Kathleen stepped back, as if she could escape, and the ambulance driver caught her by the arm. "*Calmez, calmez,*" he said. With her free hand, the nurse poured water from a narrow opening into the right eye of the soldier. Water streamed down his face onto the ground beneath him.

"*L'autre,*" she said, just as quietly, and repeated the procedure on the other side.

The ambulance driver spoke again. "They think they're blind, because their eyelids are swollen shut. It's terrifying for them—they don't know where they are or who is helping them. Some think they've fallen into the hands of the Germans."

When the nurse was finished, she nodded at the driver, then gestured at Kathleen.

The ambulance driver knelt down next to the soldier and motioned for Kathleen to hand him the oilskin bag. Taking a roll of damp gauze from it, he said, "What she wants you to do is to lay a bandage over his eyes. These have been soaked in alkaline water—"

"What's that?" Kathleen asked.

"Purified water and baking soda. It eases the burn. When you lay the cloth over the eyes, do it as gently and lightly as possible. Whatever you do, don't let him rub his eyes or it will start all over."

He gently laid a piece of gauze across the soldier's face. Leaning down, he said, "*Dieu vous protège.*"

Kathleen caught a familiar word: God. "What does that mean?"

"God bless you." He glanced up at both girls. "Where are your gas masks?"

Kathleen stumbled. "I don't—"

"Our luggage is still outside of town," Helen said.

"The gas could be coming this direction," he said. "If you hear the sirens, lay these strips over the mouths and noses of as many of the soldiers as you can. Be sure to protect yourselves, too. It's primitive—it's what they did when the gas attacks first started, when they didn't have masks."

"Why didn't these men have gas masks?" Kathleen asked.

"The masks are only good when they can find them and have time to strap them on."

"Where's yours?"

"Sorry?"

"Where's your gas mask?"

"It's in my Packard, which is just over there." He gestured into the darkness, then looked up at her with eyes that were clear and light-colored. "It's kind of you to ask."

The nurse signaled to Helen to bring the water, and Helen hurried off. Kathleen knelt to help another soldier, while the *ambulancier* watched. "*Oh, God, please don't let the gas come this way,"* she prayed. She could not bear to think of her own skin blistered and raw, her eyelids sewn shut.

"*Merci,*" the soldier said as Kathleen gently laid the gauze over his eyes. "*Merci.*"

Scolding herself for her selfish thoughts, she said, "*Dieu vous protège.*"

She moved on to a third soldier—the nurse was now two men ahead of her—and gently draped his face with the gauze. "Thank you, Miss," he said.

"You're British," Kathleen said.

"I'm a Colonial," he said. "From Brisbane."

She reached down and patted his arm. "You'll feel better soon."

The Aussie screamed. Kathleen jerked her hand away, losing her balance and sitting down hard on the mud. She clamped her hand over her mouth, afraid she would vomit or cry out herself.

"What happened?" the *ambulancier* asked as he bent over another man.

The Aussie caught his breath. "She touched me. Sorry, mate—"

Kathleen spoke through tears. "All I did was pat his arm—"

"Mustard gas gets caught up in clothes," the *ambulancier* explained. "And it doesn't wear off. When the cloth makes contact with the skin, it feels like fire. Don't touch anyone more than you need to. You could be burned, too." He looked at her hands. "Don't you have gloves?"

"In my trunk," she said weakly. "Still—"

"Still on the *camion.*" Peeling off his gloves, he handed them to her. "I have more in my rucksack." When she made no reply, he added, "Think of the good you're doing. Don't think about what's happened here."

She looked up into his clear eyes.

"You can't stop that," he said. "But you can make it better, at least for these men."

She closed her eyes to quell the tears. When she opened them again, the *ambulancier* had disappeared.

Kathleen slid on the leather gloves, warm from his hands. They were too big, and she had to remove them to cut the bandages. She was falling far behind the nurse, and she was starting to feel dizzy and ill. The flesh of the men smelled of meat that had dropped into the fire, and the rawness of their blisters reminded her of how badly it hurt to burn her finger on a cast iron skillet. *Don't think about what's happened here,* she told herself, but she could not help but realize that the men seared by gas were the least wounded of the lot. All around her were those who were suffering from much worse. Without the ambulance driver there to keep her focus, she felt herself being drawn under—there were too many who needed her, she could not keep up, she didn't even know if what she was doing helped.

"Kathleen!" It was Hank, who carried a steaming pitcher and tin cups on a tray. In the lights from the station, her face was yellowish, her eyes showing shock. "What are you doing?"

"I'm bandaging eyes for—" She looked around, but the nurse had disappeared. "They've been caught in a gas attack—"

"Where's Helen?"

Kathleen pointed to the right with her chin. "Over there. Where's Mary Jane?"

"She and Mrs. Brently are making coffee and cocoa. That man she was talking to is the *médecin en chef,* I guess, which is the head doctor. He told Mrs. Brently that he didn't care what we had come for, we were to do as he said."

Kathleen leaned over her patient. *"Dieu vous protège,"* she said, trying to imitate the calm voice of the *ambulancier.* "God bless you."

The soldier made no reply.

She stood, ready to move to the next, but Hank said, "Mary Jane is crying. This has really frightened her."

Kathleen looked across the platform. More and more soldiers were being moved to the ambulance train, but hundreds still lay on the ground, unattended. Kathleen's eyes watered in the damp air of the night, and her feet were wet and cold. The platform swarmed with soldiers, nurses, doctors, and aid workers—anyone who could help.

A voice rang out. *"Vite! Vite! Médecin!"*

Kathleen went back to work. She needed no translation to know what that meant.

****

It was after midnight before the platform was cleared. Kathleen had not seen the *ambulancier* again and had been recruited for other duties—spooning soup into the mouth of a soldier whose hands were bandaged; taking the names of a number of Tommies; running back and forth to fetch rolls of bandages for the nurses. Around ten, the fog had grown dense, and cold rain had started to fall on the men who still lay on the ground. A few tarps were found and laid over them, but most of the wounded were left unprotected and untreated. Some were carried into a tent behind the railroad station. It didn't take Kathleen long to figure out that they were those who had died—or were soon to die—while waiting for help.

Mrs. Brently found her as she was holding the hand of a soldier whose jaw had been dislocated. He had a lopsided, skeleton's grin, the skin missing, his lips skewed. Already, Kathleen felt numb—how many wounds had she seen tonight? Thank God for the garish station lights that rendered everything in black and white. A French nurse was cleaning the wound. Kathleen's job was to hand her bandages.

"Kathleen," Mrs. Brently said, quickly looking away from the carnage. "When you are finished here, come inside."

Once the man was bandaged, Kathleen dragged herself to her feet and went into the station, where she found Mrs. Brently inside, alone, writing a telegram at the dispatch station.

"Ah, there you are," Mrs. Brently said. "The others have gone to our rooms. We're being billeted in the hotel, about two blocks away." She folded the paper and gathered up her cloak. "This can wait until tomorrow."

They walked into the night. The main thoroughfare through town was crammed with *camions* and horses pulling wagons, all stalled, while men streamed down the center of the street in both directions. No one spoke, it seemed, or even breathed, but the equipment of the marching men sounded a rhythmic clank, clank, clank. Kathleen shuddered.

"Are you all right?" Mrs. Brently asked.

"Why are they so quiet? Why aren't they talking? They seem as if they're dead." Kathleen covered her mouth as something like a sob burst forth. "I'm so sorry. I shouldn't have said—"

Mrs. Brently embraced her. "Shh," she said. "Don't think on it now. We'll talk more about it tomorrow."

"All right," Kathleen said in a voice that was too small to be hers.

As Mrs. Brently opened the door of the hotel, the sky split with two red flares that burst into stars. The rumble started once again, deep and ominous.

A voice sounded behind them. "Good evening, ladies. Are you enjoying our nightly entertainment?"

A British officer on horseback had stopped in the street beside them.

"I'm sorry?" Mrs. Brently said.

"The show from the Front." Leaning forward in the saddle, he pointed. "The star shells light up the sky long enough so that the Heines can catch the stragglers in No Man's Land. Or so they think. We're ready for them, though. You hear the cannons? Those are ours. We're blasting them as hard as they're blasting us. Any German on the field is as good as dead."

"So, they're fighting now?"

"Not seriously." He shrugged. "You're American, aren't you?"

"Yes," Mrs. Brently said. "We're from Colorado in the Western United States and attached to the Red Cross in Paris."

"Leave it to the Yanks to send their women into battle before they bother to come themselves," he said bitterly. "We've yet to see one of your soldiers."

"We have come of our own volition," Mrs. Brently snipped. "And we are proud to be here."

She turned abruptly and passed through the door, with Kathleen following. After signaling to the proprietor, she led Kathleen through the lobby and up four flights of winding, narrow stairs to a corridor that was little more than shoulder-width.

"The bath is that way," Mrs. Brently said, waving a hand. Pausing at the door of a room, she said, "The others are asleep—or, at least, they were—so enter quietly. Your bed is at the back of the room, to the right. No lights are allowed, so you'll have to find your way in the dark."

"Thank you. Goodnight."

"Goodnight."

Kathleen took a step or two before she stopped. "So, what we just saw wasn't a real battle?"

"I'm not sure," Mrs. Brently said. "I think that's what the officer said."

"Then what does a real battle look like?"

Mrs. Brently smiled, wrinkles of exhaustion around her eyes. "I'm afraid we'll find out soon. But for now, we must get some sleep. We don't know what tomorrow will bring."

Kathleen repeated her goodnight. She crept into the room, trying to discern shapes and distance by the thin moonlight. Suddenly, the sky lit up again, and she saw it all—the four beds, each in a corner of the room. Sitting on the one near the back, she took off her heavy, mud-crusted shoes and cape. Reaching up to smooth back her hair, she found that she had lost her wimple somewhere. Her head was unprotected, her hair soaked from the rain.

"Kathleen?" someone—she thought it was Mary Jane— whispered.

"Yes, it's me."

"What's going on out there?"

"It's some sort of attack at the Front," she whispered back. "We were told it wasn't serious."

"What does that mean?"

"I'm not sure. But Mrs. Brently said we'd better try to sleep, just in case we have to"—she could not think of words to describe what they had just been through—"tomorrow."

She slid off her dress, and the cold of the room struck her. She did not know where her trunk was. Had it arrived or was it still on the *camion*? She had nothing to sleep in but her camisole and bloomers, and she had no woolen sleeping bag to wrap around her. As she hung her wet, filthy stockings over the rail at the end of the bed, her hand chanced upon a warm spot beneath the sheets and the thin blanket. Someone had thought to put a hot water bottle in the bed for her.

She slid beneath the sheet and pulled the bedding up to her shoulders, savoring the feel of the heat against the soles of her feet. Clasping the hot water bottle against her breast, she wondered if she would ever be warm again.

The murmur of the war continued for another hour. It isn't serious, Kathleen told herself. Hadn't the British officer called it nightly entertainment, as if it were a fireworks show on the Fourth of July? Yet, if it was only fanfare, where had all the desperate wounded come from?

She remembered Mrs. Brently's words: *Don't think on it now.*

Yet the tears kept coming.

Just as the *camions* and wagons in the street outside began revving and creaking again, Kathleen finally fell asleep.

In the morning, she awoke full of memories of the night before. The blistered faces, the blood-stained ground, the soldier with the skeletal grin, another who had grabbed her skirt with a hand that was shredded into strips of flesh. Worse, the men who marched in the darkness, their faces blanched of emotion. And the terrible commotion of the night. She lay as still as she could, trying to will her stomach not to rise up into her throat. Soon, she became aware of the sound of sobbing.

She sat up and looked around the room. It was rectangular, with armoires separating the two beds on the longer walls, and an elaborate desk and chair that sat beneath the window at the back of the room, directly opposite the door.

"Mary Jane?" Kathleen whispered. "Hank? Helen?"

Mary Jane sat up in her bed, sobbing. "It was horrible, all those men—"

Kathleen threw back her covers and went to take Mary Jane in her arms. "Shhh," she said. "It's all right."

By now, Hank was awake, and Helen was stirring.

"I want to go home! I wish I had never come—!"

Kathleen looked to Hank and Helen for help, but neither answered, either too sleepy or too upset to reply. "I felt that way, too, last night," Kathleen confided. "But they need us, they—"

"I can't do this! Handing out soup to men who are bleeding on the floor! Watching them die right in front of us!" Mary Jane sought out Kathleen's eyes. "One of them did! He just fell over, and they came, and carried him away like he was a hunk of meat!"

"But you helped him," Hank offered, awake now. "He was hungry and cold and—"

"I didn't! I didn't! I ran away and hid in the back of the canteen!"

At that confession, Helen, Hank and Kathleen looked blankly at one another.

"Next time, you won't," Kathleen said. "Next time, we'll be ready."

A light knock sounded on the door, and Mrs. Brently entered the room. She was dressed in a fresh dress and wimple. Evidently, their trunks had arrived.

"What is wrong?" she asked.

"Mary Jane is upset," Helen said.

"What's the matter?"

Mary Jane spoke through sobs. "Oh, Mrs. Brently, can I go home? Do I have to stay? Do I have to do this—?"

"Oh, my dear," Mrs. Brently sat on the bed beside her, and Kathleen moved out of the way. "We came into a difficult situation last night, but it won't always be that way."

"I can't stand it," Mary Jane said.

Mrs. Brently put an arm around her, then addressed all the girls. "I want to say how proud I am of the way that you handled last night. We did what we needed to do—we offered whatever useful, kind action we could. We came to help, and we kept our honor and our word last night. Don't you think so?"

"Yes, ma'am," the girls—except for Mary Jane—echoed.

"Mary Jane," Mrs. Brently said. "You'll come with me this morning. The rest of you can go to the kitchen for breakfast. Then

I want you to go to the canteen—it's in a terrible state after last night—and clean it until it is the most welcoming canteen in France. I'll be along later."

"Yes, Mrs. Brently."

"Are our trunks here?" Kathleen asked. "I'd like my other dress—"

"Why don't you wear what you had on last night? When we open the canteen, when it's clean and bright, you can change into something fresh."

"I—I . . ." Kathleen said.

"What is it?"

Kathleen glanced at Mary Jane, whose haggard face was stained with tears. "It has blood on it," she said.

Mrs. Brently's enormous poise ruptured. "Of course," she said. "First, you need to take care of yourselves and your clothes, and then you can . . ."

She trailed off, as if she, too, might sob with Mary Jane.

"Then we'll go to the canteen," Helen supplied.

"Yes, then you will go."

Bringing their trunks up to their rooms is no easy task. Because the stairwell is so narrow, the three girls—Helen, Hank and Kathleen—have to shoulder the trunks like dock workers. At the landings, they pass the trunks up and over the banister to the next level.

"Well, we've had our exercise for today," Hank says as they unpack the trunks and hang their clothes in the armoires.

Once they are settled into the hotel, they leave for the canteen, which is a billowing, white tent with a packed dirt floor that stands to one side of the train station. Evidently abandoned in a hurry in the past, the forty gallon metal cans that are used to mix coffee and cocoa are encrusted with dried scum, and the deep fryer is filled with rancid grease. The three of them—Hank, Helen and Kathleen—divvy up the jobs. To Hank falls the scrubbing of the shelves and café-like tables and chairs; to Helen, the task of cleaning the deep fryer and primitive stove; and to Kathleen the scouring of the metal G.I. cans, as they're called.

Her thighs ache, and she can barely stand to squat as she had last night. Her shoulders sting, too, from hunching over to lay the damp cloths on the soldiers' faces. She works harder, reaching far into the can, swiping at every particle—if she stops, she will start to think. She will remember last night.

At regular intervals, the girls hear the march of boots in the street outside. The trains come and go, more troops climbing from or boarding throughout the day. French soldiers peek inside the tent. By early afternoon, Kathleen has the cans scrubbed and Helen is tentatively making her first batch of doughnuts from a recipe that she finds in the Red Cross handbook. It isn't long before one of the G.I. cans steams with hot coffee, and the doughnuts mound in a basket on the makeshift counter of the canteen.

They open the canteen at five-thirty in the afternoon, which is the time marked on a small, hand-printed sign near the door. It will remain open until eight o'clock. When Helen finally lifts the flaps of the tent, the soldiers crowd in, and the girls call out, "Welcome! How are you?" or *"Bien venue! Comment allez vous?"* It doesn't seem to matter that they don't speak enough French to understand the reply or to carry on a conversation.

Hank and Kathleen ladle coffee into tin cups, while Helen sells packages of cigarettes and chocolate. She gathers a crowd around her, most of them teasing her about her clumsy pronunciation. One dashing French soldier comes behind the counter and finds a long piece of doweling that is stashed beneath the counter. He threads the doughnuts on the dowel, then urges Hank in fairly good English, "Now you hold them out"—he demonstrates—"and we reach and take them. You do it for the trains that come by, too."

"So that's what it's for," Hank says. "I thought it was for our protection."

"Were you planning on hitting them with it?" Kathleen asks.

"Sur la tête." The soldier knocks his knuckles against his own skull.

"Why not?" Hank says, and both Kathleen and the soldier laugh.

By six, when the news of the canteen's operation has evidently spread, Kathleen has cocoa ready for the soldiers who flock into the tent, and Hank is brewing a soup that strongly smells of fish.

"Guaranteed to clean the rust off their teeth," she says, tasting a spoonful.

The girls suggest adding more water, but Hank defends herself, claiming that she followed the recipe in the Red Cross book to the letter. The men who take cups of it don't seem to mind it at all.

The funniest moment comes late in the evening when Helen claps her hand over her mouth as a gang of French soldiers laughs.

"What happened?" Hank asks. "What did you say?"

Helen whispers in her ear.

Hank erupts in laughter. "What were you trying to say?"

"*Vous êtes une bonne âme,*" Helen says. "You are a good soul."

"What is it?" Kathleen asks.

Hank whispers to Kathleen. "She said, '*Vous êtes un bon âne,*' which means 'You are a good A-S-S.'"

Kathleen lets out a snort, and they all laugh.

Late that evening, after the girls clean up and close the canteen and go to the hotel for dinner, Kathleen realizes how tired she is. Hank and Helen must feel it, too, for no one speaks as they eat the hot food served to them, barely noticing its taste. Worried, Kathleen finds herself watching the door. She notices Hank and Helen watching it as well.

Mary Jane does not join them.

SEVENTEEN

Maggie sat on a straight-backed wooden chair in a classroom at Blessed Savior Catholic School. She wore a white wimple on her head and an apron with a large, square red cross on it. Her scalp itched under the heavy cloth, and she could feel sweat pricking her back and armpits. On the table in front of her, a pile of cotton was accumulating, carefully cut into four by five squares by Mrs. MacMahon and Mrs. McKenna. Maggie's job was to insert a bundle of gauze between two squares and to pass them to Mrs. Crane and Mrs. Davis, who would neatly sew the edges together. At the end of the assembly line, Ma bundled them in red, white and blue ribbon and packed them in a box marked on each side by a red cross and labeled "Bandages, Knights of Columbus Red Cross Auxiliary, Blessed Savior Catholic Church, Denver, Colorado."

Mrs. Corwin, whose fingers swelled with arthritis, had the job of reading the newspaper to the ladies. "The Army's censorship isn't usually given a kind word by the Sammy who falls afoul of it," she read. "But now there is way for the common soldier to get the better of the censor. Letters of a personal or family nature can be placed in a blue regulation envelope that is supplied at the rate of one per man per week. The 'Lady in Blue,' as it is called, is then sent to the base censor rather than to the soldier's officer, who knows him well. Used by the English and French for some time, the Lady in Blue allows the soldier to have his personal news read by someone he is unlikely to meet during his military service. More than one letter can be forwarded, but all must come from the same soldier—"

"Oh, the regulations they have to follow," Mrs. MacMahon interrupted. "Donnell says the Landing Force Manual for the Navy has more rules to learn than the Catechism—"

"What a thing to say!" Mrs. McKenna laughed.

Mrs. Davis vied for attention. "My nephew, Robby, has sailed for France, and he says—"

Mrs. Corwin, who was also hard of hearing, continued: "The doughboys have greeted the Lady in Blue with enthusiasm. 'It's a great deal,' said one. 'If me and the missus are havin' a bit of a tiff, I don't want the captain knowin' it. I don't want him gettin' into our makin' up, neither, by gosh and by golly, when, maybe I've sprung a little poetry on her, and her picture is lookin' down from the wall and the moon is shinin' outside, and I'm feelin' lonely all by myself here. It's a powerful relief to sit down and tell her about it all. What do I care if some fellow in another part of France, who I'll never see, reads it? It just might seem like a touch of home sweet home to him, too.'"

The ladies laughed. "Oh, our boys!" Mrs. McKenna gushed. "They are the sweetest in the world!"

Maggie hid her smirk. She could have written something that sounded more believable than that. She tried to imagine Seaney using "by gosh and by golly." He would probably rather eat dirt.

"How is Seaney getting along, Maureen?" Mrs. Crane asked, as if she had heard Maggie's thoughts. "You've heard from him by now, surely."

Maggie glanced toward her mother. Ma's face showed little expression—her eyebrows slightly lifted, her lips curled in a close-lipped smile, her chin higher and jutting out just a bit. Since Liam's troubles began, her mother had adopted this mask whenever she waited on customers or spoke with anyone from the Church.

"He landed in England a month ago and spent ten days marchin' with the troops from one coast to t'other to catch the boat to France," she said.

"Ten days?" Mrs. McKenna wondered. "I don't remember England being that big."

"Anyway, as he writes it, the crossin' of the ocean was uneventful," Ma continued. "He says he spent most of it tryin' to keep warm when they did their drills on the deck of the ship. Most days, icebergs were floatin' by."

"Icebergs?" Mrs. Crane said. "Puts me in mind of the Titanic—"

"It's a fine feeling to have a son on the way to war," Mrs. MacMahon said. "My Donnell—"

Maggie focused on placing the cotton between the layers of fabric. No one had asked her about what it was like to be a married woman or how her husband was faring at his job. In fact, no one asked about her husband at all, and she offered no information. Even though both Liam and Brendan encouraged her to keep up her work for the Red Cross, it was impossible to ignore the gazes that slid away from her face and the stony silence that followed.

"What about your lovely niece?" Mrs. Crane asked. "I saw the picture of her Relief Society that was published in the newspaper the other day. They've been in France for some time now, haven't they?"

"Aye, her first letter from France came to us just yesterday," Ma said. "She says if one of the girls doesn't run the gramophone in the canteen, the Frenchies fight over which record is to be played. They want the girls to hear all the French songs, and Kathleen says, they want them to sing with them, too. She said that if she could only sing in French, she'd be able to say whatever she needed. It's the speakin' of it that leaves her cold."

"I bet they don't have the likes of John McCormack over there," Mrs. McKenna said, as another round of laughter circled the room.

Maggie bent over her work. News of the Graves Family Foundation Relief Society's exploits irked her even more than sappy stories about the American Expeditionary Force. The *Denver Post* had recently printed letters written by each of the three girls— one had already returned home—under the glowing headline: "Colorado Ladies Do Patriotic Duty in France." A grainy photograph accompanied the letters, the girls posed near a white tent, with Kathleen smiling happily under a wimple similar to the one Maggie wore now. One of her sketches, a steamship near a dock, had been published with the caption: "The port of Bordeaux, France, just one of the sights seen by the Graves Family Foundation Relief Society on their way to the European War."

More and more, Maggie had taken to comforting herself by repeating stories in her head. No obstacles or snubs or jealousies stood in the way of Evelyn and George:

Evelyn was prettier and sweeter than George had fancied she could be. He watched his wife secretly: her creamy white skin where not a blemish could be found and her auburn hair that curled around her shoulders. All this appealed to him, but it was her green eyes, round and heavily lashed, that brought his feelings to a boiling intensity. The world's finest artist himself could not have painted such undeniable beauty—

"Good afternoon, ladies."

Brendan had come into the hive of woman's activity. The women greeted him politely—after all, he was their priest—but Maggie could hear the coolness in their voices. Anyone connected to Liam was jinxed. After acknowledging them, he asked, "Maggie, Mrs. Sullivan, may I speak with you for a minute?"

Maggie laid aside the bandages she was sewing and shed her wimple and apron to follow Brendan. Ma did the same, hefting herself out of the chair and puffing down the hall to the office. Just as the three were about to enter, Father Devlin hailed Brendan from the office across the hall. "Go in," Brendan said to Maggie and her mother. "I'll be along as soon as I can."

The two women went into the office. As Ma settled into an upholstered chair in front of the desk, Maggie poked around. Brendan's office made her think of a grand, old library in a Victorian novel. An ornate brass fan hung from the high ceiling, and the curtains were drawn against the brilliant western sun. The walls were grayed with age, the corners shadowy, and the carpets matted from wear. The heavy wooden desk sat near the door, and four chairs waited expectantly for some poor parishioners who needed advice.

The bookshelves were filled with heavy, leather-bound books, and on Brendan's desk was a hodgepodge of erudite texts and his own writings. Maggie swept a hand over a book that lay on the desk, then squinted at a printed pamphlet that was half-covered by it, trying to decipher the writing upside down.

She went around the desk to take a closer look. The pamphlet was called, "The Case Against Conscription." Trembling, she opened it and read:

"Young Men of America,

"You have been convinced that it is your patriotic duty to fight in this war, but what voice did you have in this decision? None, for in all the history of the world, every nation that has gone to war has done so without the acquiescence of its people. Moreover, it is the ruling class of capitalists and exploiters that declares both war and peace—"

Maggie's heart shuddered. She would recognize Liam's writing anywhere. She knew what words he loved and how he phrased them. Oh, God, what had he done now?

Brendan stepped into the office. "Thank you for waiting." Spying the pamphlet in Maggie's hands, he added, "I see you've found what I wanted to talk to you about."

Maggie closed the pamphlet. "What is this?"

"Liam had them printed and mailed to all the members of the Knights of Columbus."

Quickly, Maggie turned to her mother. "Did Pa get one?"

"Yes, he did," Ma said, her voice cold and tight. "And he went to the meeting last night, too."

"What meeting?" Maggie asked.

Brendan spoke. "Last night, the Knights resolved at a special meeting to expel Liam from membership."

"That's ridiculous!" Maggie protested. "He's always here, doing something for them—"

"He's betrayed their trust by continuing his resistance to the war."

Brendan's voice carried a harshness that she had never heard before. A wave of dizziness struck her, and she plopped down in a chair. Liam loved the Knights, who worked to better conditions for the orphans at Mount St. Vincent, as much as he loved the Church itself.

"How could you let them do this to him?" she asked Brendan. "It will kill him to be forced out—"

"I had no say in the matter, and I couldn't jeopardize—"

"Your own position?"

Brendan sat at his desk. "My office is to 'offer, bless, rule, preach, and baptize,' according to the promise I made to the Church. I can't forfeit it for one man, even if he is my brother."

Furious, she asked her mother, "Did Pa vote against Liam? Did he want to see his own son-in-law expelled from the Church?"

"He voted what he thought best," Ma said stonily. "Liam promised he'd show some sense, and all the good folks put up the money to see him out of jail, and now . . ." She flipped her hand toward the pamphlet that Maggie held.

"Why didn't you show it to me when Pa got it?" Maggie demanded. "You should have let me know—"

"'Twas too late by then, wasn't it?" Ma said. "The damage had been done."

Maggie covered her mouth with her hand.

"Liam hasn't been expelled from the Church," Brendan said. "I've looked into it. An expulsion from the Knights of Columbus doesn't affect Liam's or your communion with the church. The two of you can still celebrate the Mass."

"Why would we?" Maggie asked. "When everyone has turned against us because he doesn't see things the way they do—"

"Maggie, be fair—"

"No!" she said. "I'm tired of this, I want it to stop!"

She stood, but a rush of blood to her head made the room spin. Her arms and legs felt heavy and numb, as if weighted down by stones. She grabbed the back of the chair for support.

"What's wrong?" Brendan asked as Ma stood and took Maggie's arm.

"I'm just dizzy. I'll be all right in a minute."

"I'll fetch a glass of water."

"No, I just want to go home."

"I'll take you home," Brendan offered. "Do you want to go with her, Mrs. Sullivan?"

"Aye, I do," Ma said.

"And, Maggie, I'll talk to Liam once he's off work. Let me take care of it."

She nodded, too ill to speak. While Brendan went to fetch the parish car, she tried to stop the swirling of her head. Why would they do such a thing to Liam? She wanted to claw out the eyes of every woman who had been sewing bandages earlier, each one knowing that her husband had voted to shun Liam. Hypocrites!

Ma and Brendan escorted her to the car, holding her up by the elbows. At home, Maggie went directly upstairs and lay down on the bed. Almost as soon as her head touched the pillow, her stomach gurgled, and she jerked upward. Pulling the chamber pot out from beneath the bed, she vomited the lunch that she had eaten a lifetime ago. Lying back again, she folded her hands on her breast, as if she might pray. All she had ever wanted was a home, like this one, and a husband who adored her, a husband like Liam. All she wanted was the joy of a family that—

A family. A child. Liam's child.

She counted backward. The wedding had been in June, and it was now October.

No wonder the heat aggravated her so. No wonder hauling for Pa had become a punishment. No wonder every smell caused her to gag.

She sat on the bed, hugging her knees. Soon, she heard her mother laboring up the steps, balancing with both feet on each stair before attempting the next. Breathless and cross, Ma came into the room, a tray with tea and toast in her hands. Casting a sniff in the direction of the chamber pot, she said, "You've made a mess here."

"I'm sorry," Maggie said. "But, Ma, I think—"

"How long has it been since your monthly?" Ma asked starkly. "That's what's goin' on here, isn't it? You're goin' to have a baby?"

Undaunted, Maggie giggled. "Isn't it wonderful?"

With a doctor's precision, her mother asked her about the signs. Once Ma was satisfied, she said, "Maybe this'll settle Liam down and make him come to his senses."

"I know it will," Maggie said wildly. "What do I do?"

"What do you mean?"

"To take care of the baby so he's healthy and strong. What do I do?"

"I thought you knew all about that," her mother sniped.

"What?"

"Before you married, you informed me you'd read all about it."

Tears welled into Maggie's eyes. "I don't, though," she admitted. "Ma, I need you."

"Well, that's somethin' at least." Ma relented. "Come now, it will be all right. I'll tell your father you need to stop doin' the heavy work, and you tell Liam to stop his antics and be a man."

At once, Maggie was sobbing. "Oh, Ma," she cried. "I don't understand what he's doing. Why is he doing this to me? And to you and Pa? Why doesn't he love me enough to stop?"

The last words came out in a shrill cry. Her mother bundled Maggie in her arms and rocked her back and forth. "Come now, we must trust in God. He will see you both through this."

Maggie drew in a shaky breath, but said nothing. Why would she trust in a God who didn't even take care of one of His most faithful servants?

"Ma," she said tentatively. "You don't think . . . well, so many of your babies . . ." She could not finish the sentence. "You don't think the same thing will happen to me?"

"Not if you pray over it," Ma said. "We'll say a Hail Mary now."

Ma painfully lowered herself down to kneel beside the bed, and Maggie joined her. Yet, even though she spoke the words with her mother, she couldn't keep her mind on the prayer. Oh, this baby had to be healthy, it had to be perfect. She could not bear to go through what her mother had as a younger woman. And it had to be sweet and beautiful enough so that Liam would . . .

"Amen," her mother said, and she crossed herself and echoed, "Amen."

After she helped her mother to stand again, Maggie said, "Please don't tell Seaney. I mean, you can tell him about the baby, but not about Liam. And Kathleen—oh, please don't tell her. She'll gloat."

"She will not," Ma scolded. "But she doesn't need to know. The two of them are far enough away that bad news is likely to strike a hard blow. Now, come on, let's put you to bed."

As if Maggie were still a child, her mother helped her to take off her shoes, skirt, and blouse, leaving Maggie in camisole and drawers. She smoothed back Maggie's hair, kissed her forehead, then brought the blankets up tight around Maggie's chin, despite the heat of the afternoon.

"There now," she said. "It will be all right. Surely Liam will see what he needs to do."

When Liam came home that night, Maggie was waiting. After her nap, she had gone downstairs to sit on the couch in the parlor, her feet propped up on a pillow, just as her mother told her to do. Meanwhile, Ma had worked on dinner in the kitchen, leaving the house with the smell of a hearty stew and fresh baked bread. Late in the afternoon, she had gone home.

As soon as Liam had taken off his hat, hung up his coat, and crossed himself with holy water, Maggie called to him. He rounded the corner, his face pale and drawn for only an instant before it lit up with a smile. "So this is what my beautiful wife does all day while I'm at work," he said. "It smells pretty good in here, though."

Maggie bounced up from the couch to kiss his cheek. "I have a surprise."

"All right."

Sitting side by side on the couch, his hands in hers, she said, "We're going to have a baby."

He did not smile at once, but sat silently, preoccupied.

"Aren't you happy?" Maggie asked. "Isn't this what you wanted? What we wanted?"

He kissed her forehead. "Oh, my darling, yes."

Maggie laughed, relieved. "It's wonderful, isn't it? We'll be so happy now. We can put this all behind us. And the people at the church will forget about it in a while, and I'm sure they'll let you back into the Knights."

Liam let go of her hands. "Brendan told you about the Knights, then?"

"Yes, but it doesn't matter now. We have what we want, and—"

"It does matter," Liam protested. "It matters to me, to us, to this child—"

"Our child? Why does it matter to him?"

"The Church is where Brendan and I have been best loved," Liam said. "And we have loved it in return. For it to turn its back on me, when I am following the word of God—"

Maggie's joy evaporated. "I have loved you best! And I am here, right here! I haven't turned my back on you—"

"It isn't the same—"

"Why did you write that pamphlet?" she demanded. "You promised everyone that you wouldn't speak out—"

"I promised I would give no more speeches. I didn't promise to stop expressing my thoughts."

"It's the same thing! The people of the parish paid so you could be out on bail, and you gave them your word. And what about me? You didn't even tell me you had written it—"

"The fight isn't yours."

"No, but I am. And this baby"—she folded her hands over her stomach—"this baby is yours, and it will need you—"

As he rose, the haunted look returned to his face. "I won't argue over this, Maggie. It has nothing to do with my love for you. It isn't between the two of us. I want you to take care of yourself. Being upset isn't good for you or for the baby."

Maggie's head spun, just as it had in Brendan's office. "You don't care about the baby! You don't care about me! All you think about is your fight with President Wilson. He probably doesn't even read the letters you send him—he probably doesn't even get them—and all you're doing is making a fool of—!"

"You're calling me a fool?"

"What you're doing is wrong, Liam. It's against the law, it's not patriotic or even worth it!"

"So I should die in a ditch in France, just to be patriotic? To show everyone that my life is worth it? I should abandon my faith and what I believe just so I can follow a law made by men?"

"No, no, of course not, but, Liam—"

"What you're talking about—laws, patriotism—has nothing to do with our duty to God."

"But it has to do with our duty to each other and to America—"

His jaw set. "I'm going for a walk."

"Don't leave me—!"

Maggie followed him to the entryway, where he grabbed his coat from the peg on the wall and slammed out the door. With a fist, she hit the door as the latch clicked. To argue on this day, of all days! It should be the happiest day of her life! Leaning against the door, she sobbed until her throat ached.

In the kitchen, she covered the food that Ma had left with cheesecloth and set it to cool on the counter. Then she sat down at the kitchen table to wait. After an hour, she could stand it no longer. She retrieved her sweater and went out into the golden light of the evening.

She knew exactly where to find him. He was bent over the newly-named "Liberty Garden" at Blessed Savior, digging up weeds with a trowel from between the pumpkins and tossing them into a pile behind him. Without speaking, Maggie knelt down and pulled up a few dandelions that hid beneath the wider leaves of the vines.

"You're only pulling the tops off doing that," Liam said. "The root's still there."

She pulled a few more weeds, the sap leaving brown spots on her hands. At last she asked, "Isn't this helping the war effort? The garden was never this big until the war started. Isn't sewing bandages for the Red Cross helping the war effort? That's what I was doing this afternoon."

"I'm weeding the garden for Father Devlin," Liam said shortly. "And you're free to do whatever you feel is right."

Maggie tossed a dandelion toward the pile. "Then I'll join you. I'll protest with you, and carry a sign, and be arrested, too." When he did not reply, she prodded further, "Is that what you want?"

"Do you believe the war is wrong?" he asked. "Do you think it is the most heinous and monstrous thing to happen in our lives?"

"Yes, I think it's terrible," she said. "I wish Seaney wouldn't have gone—"

"Would you risk your life to try to stop the war and save him?"

"He joined on his own. He wanted to go, to get away from Pa."

"But you wouldn't put yourself in peril to keep him from fighting?"

She said nothing, suspecting that either answer she gave would be wrong. At last, she said, "I don't know what you want from me. I don't understand how to make you happy. I don't want to be on the opposite side from you. I don't want to be your enemy."

"No one is my enemy."

"Then, your adversary or whatever you want to call it."

She attempted to stand, but nausea swirled through her head. She fell back, one hand on the ground to keep her upright, her legs folded beneath her.

Liam rushed to her side. "Let's go home. Here, let me help you up."

They walked back to the house, Liam's arm around Maggie's waist, supporting her. At home, she went directly to bed.

Liam came up to the bedroom late in the night. Without opening her eyes, Maggie listened as he took off his shoes, his trousers, and his shirt and folded them carefully over the chair. She did not ask whether he had been writing another treatise or letter. She did not want to know. After he had slid into bed, she lifted her head.

"I'm sorry," she said.

He did not reply at once, and Maggie held her breath in the darkness.

"You may not always think it," he said. "But I love you more than I love myself. I love both of you. This baby, it is what I have always wanted. You, my darling, and it."

"It?" she asked. "It's 'him.'"

"Are you sure? It could be a girl. We could name her Alice, after my mother."

He laid his hand on her shoulder, and she rolled into his arms. He kissed her, and she put her hands on either side of his face, drawing his mouth to hers, wanting more and more. Throwing her leg over his waist, she urged him closer and closer, and inside of her. She ran her hand down the muscles of his shoulder and back, over his hip, to his thigh. Seeking his mouth, she opened her lips and tasted the warmth of his tongue. He made a sound in his throat, a moan or rumble of pleasure, that sent coils of sensation through her. She rolled on to her back, carrying him with her, so that she could feel the full power of his body. Closing her eyes, she lost herself in his strength and desire.

After, Maggie ventured in a whisper, "With this baby, you can get a deferment. Dr. Thorp said that if there was a baby—"

"No, Maggie," he said aloud. "There won't be a deferment."

He fell asleep almost immediately, as if his soul was at peace.

Maggie lay awake until the sky lightened with the dawn.

EIGHTEEN

Late in October, winter came to Montdidier. The wind blew, bitterly. Rather than snow, it rained in icy sheets that slickened the muddy streets and frosted the shell of the canteen. The coffee and cocoa froze in the enormous cans, and the girls had to stoke the wood stove from noon until the canteen closed. Mrs. Brently ordered warmer capes, gloves, boots, underwear and dresses from Paris, and requisitioned another stove from the Red Cross.

After a week, the sun returned, but the warmth stayed at bay. On a bright, windless day, Kathleen stocked the shelves of the canteen, while Hank and Helen worked at the hospital. The Red Cross had delivered a new shipment of chocolate bars, cookies, and tobacco. The Graves Family Foundation Relief Society had also received a slew of newspapers from the United States: the *New York Times*, the *Baltimore Sun*, the *Philadelphia Enquirer*, the *Chicago Tribune*, even the *Indianapolis News*.

"Gee," Hank had commented as she hunted for a *Denver Post* or *Rocky Mountain News*. "They must not have heard that America goes beyond the Mississippi River."

"Why did we get those?" Helen asked. "We're the only ones here that speak English."

"We'll use them for practice so that we won't forget how to speak English ourselves." Hank began to read in a stilted French accent. "Zee pah-RAHD ah-long Feezh Ah-vay-NOO een Noo Yohrk Cee-TAY—"

Kathleen and Helen had laughed until their amusement turned to hiccups.

Now, Kathleen heard someone come through the front flaps of the tent. A blast of icy air swirled around her ankles. "*Je regrette, nous sommes fermés!*" she called. "*Revenez ce soir, s'il vous plaît!*"

"*Je ne suis pas ici pour le chocolat chaud.*"

She swung around. Behind her stood a man with green-gray eyes and a welcoming smile. He wore a dark military-like uniform, and on his arm was a white band with a red cross.

"You're the *ambulancier*!" she said.

"Over here, we're called *Monsieur le Conducteur Américain*."

"*Monsieur le . . .* what?"

"Never mind." He laughed. "My name is Paul Reston. And you?"

"I'm Kathleen O'Doherty."

"Nice to meet you, Miss O'Doherty." He offered a hand to shake. "It's nice to hear an American accent."

"I'm glad you recognize it. The Brits sometimes think I'm Irish."

"I hear American," he said. "Then, again, I already knew you were American, so I'd probably hear American no matter what. It's a bit of a cheat."

She laughed. "I'm sorry I don't have coffee or cocoa yet. We don't make it until—"

"As I said, I'm not here for cocoa."

"Oh, so that's what you said. I didn't catch it." She stopped in sudden realization. "Your gloves! That's why you're here. They're at the hotel—"

"That isn't why I'm here, either, but I'll take them all the same. You have your own now?"

"Yes, I have two pairs."

The conversation lapsed, and Kathleen noticed how hard her heart was beating. She started to speak. "I can make some coffee now—"

At the same time, Paul asked, "Would you join me for a cup of coffee at the hotel? I know you're busy—"

She laughed, and he said, "Well, it looks like coffee one way or the other."

"I'm nearly finished here," she said. "Just let me close up."

"I'll wait outside."

She finished her work and drew a tarp over the shelves to protect the supplies and equipment. Her fingers fumbled as she untied the knot of her apron, and she scolded herself. Why was she so excited? Why was she acting like a little girl about to receive a present?

Once she stepped outside, though, she knew the answer. Paul Reston was the most beautiful man she had ever seen. His eyes were clear and calm, and his hair and eyebrows were dark and smooth. He had strong cheekbones, an even jaw, and a smile that was all the more charming in that it was slightly crooked. He leaned against a sturdy Packard that had the words "Harjes Formation" and a red cross on its side, his hands behind him on the hood, his shoulders broad and strong.

"So this is your ambulance," she said.

"This is it. It can take six *couchés*, which are—"

"Those who cannot sit up—"

He smiled. "And four *assis*, who can sit, in one trip."

"We've heard the Packards aren't as quick as the Model Ts."

"They aren't," he admitted. "But we can carry more men. It comes out even." He offered her his arm. "Where are you from, Miss O'Doherty?"

She laid her hand on his arm, and they started down the street. "I'm from Denver, Colorado."

"Denver! My aunt lives there—Julia Reston, do you know her?"

"No, I'm sorry, I've never met her."

"She used to live in Paris, and I think she might return someday—after the war, that is. France suits her better. So, how have you come to be in Montdidier?"

Kathleen told him of working at Graves Oil and of the Graves Family Foundation Relief Society. "We write letters every week to, um, Mr. Graves, telling him what we're experiencing, and he puts them in the newspapers at home so everyone can know what it's like. I send sketches, too, when I can."

"Is that so?" Paul said. "My aunt is an artist. She paints—mostly with oils."

"Someday I want to do that."

"Tell me what you draw."

"Whatever I can, whatever I remember from the day." Kathleen's words were quick and happy. "I try to capture expressions on faces, and to . . . well, I'd love to be able to draw it exactly as I see it."

"So what would you sketch right now? On this street, at this moment?"

You, she thought. Your hands, the cowlick of your hair, the grace in your eyes. Quickly, she looked down the street, where the colorful awnings of the shops bent in the breeze. Most of the buildings were three or four stories, with mansard rooves and delicate wrought-iron balconies along the windows of the upper stories.

"I've already done some of it," Kathleen said. "The bakery over there, the *butcherie*, and the soldiers who march through town."

"Surely you've done l'Hôtel-de-Ville? And Saint-Sepulchre?"

"I've tried." They paused in front of the marvelous edifice, with its two-story arched windows, rounded dome, and ornate decorations. "Mostly it comes out as a bunch of swirls. The church was easier—more vertical lines."

"You'll have to visit my aunt sometime," Paul said. "She delights in meeting young talents. Julia believes the apprentice, not the master, brings passion and vision to art."

Something came to her. "You know, I think I've seen your aunt. Is she connected with the National Woman's Party?"

"Are those the women who chain themselves to public monuments in order to get arrested?"

"I think so."

"Then I have no doubt that Julia would be among that crowd. When did you see her?"

"At a rally before the war." Kathleen told him of seeing Miss Crawley talking with an older woman. "I noticed her eyes. They were so beautiful."

"Our eyes."

"Yes." Kathleen looked away, afraid he would read her thoughts in her face. "She's lovely."

They came to the hotel, and Kathleen looked mournfully at the little café where the girls ate in the evenings.

"I suppose a cup of coffee isn't very appealing to you," Paul said.

"I don't mind, as long as it isn't powder and water mixed in a forty-gallon can."

Paul laughed. "Do you want to walk for a while, instead? Will you be warm enough?"

"Let's do that," she said. "We've barely had time to exercise, and, well, I'm a tea drinker anyway."

He laughed. "I'm glad you told me. I know where to get the best Irish tea you'll ever taste. Straight from the source—an Irish lad from County Clare. So strong you can stand your spoon up in it, as he likes to say. I'll bring you some the next time I come."

Kathleen flushed with happiness. It wasn't until they were nearing the edge of Montdidier that she remembered the gloves. Just as she was about to remind Paul, the houses fell away, and the street opened up into country lane. Rolling, fallow fields stretched on either side of the road, gradually rising up to wooded hills. Great trees lined the road, their branches bare, but majestic and ancient. A haze of fog hung just at the horizon, and a herd of dairy cattle grazed peacefully in the meadow.

"This is beautiful," Kathleen said. "We've been so busy since we arrived, I haven't had time to walk through the town, much less out here. I wish I had my sketchbook."

"You can come again. It's not that far."

"We're spending fourteen hour days in the canteen. We're hard-pressed to find enough time to sleep."

Paul looked out across the fields. "We put in twenty-four hour shifts," he said. "Or more, sometimes, when things are going strong. But then, there are long stretches when we have nothing to do, and that's when I find myself seeking out places like this. Ten miles in that direction are fields of wheat and little villages filled with people who don't even know there is a war. They farm, they go to church, they get married and eat and sleep without a thought as to what is happening up north. Someday, I'll take you out there and show you."

Kathleen glanced at him, but his gaze was still on the horizon.

"I didn't know what to expect from France," she confided. "I still don't. The first night we were here"—she shivered at the memory—"was so terrible that one of our Society members left. But since then, it seems—and please don't misunderstand me—it's been an adventure—"

"I know," he said. "But it won't last. Just now, both sides are lying down until the American army arrives in full in the spring."

"Oh." Worry wrenched through her. "My cousin is with them."

"The AEF?"

"Yes, and he's here, in France. I don't know where."

"Probably in the quiet zone." When she glanced up with a question, he said, "That's what the training area near Verdun is called. Thousands of Americans are there—probably tens of thousands by now. General Pershing won't let them fight until they are fully trained."

"Verdun," Kathleen said. "Isn't that where—?"

"Yes," Paul said. "Some of the worst fighting of the war happened there. But it has been stable for some time now."

"I'm thankful for that," she said. "How long have you been here?"

"Since the summer of 1916, just before the Battle of the Somme. I came after I graduated from college." He laughed. "At least, I think I graduated. Julia says she received the diploma in the mail, but I have yet to see it. It's a strange world when Yale Law School becomes a correspondence school. "

"You're a lawyer?"

"Someday, perhaps," he said. "I had a job offer from a law firm in Boston before I left."

Confused, she asked, "So, you don't live in Denver?"

"I've never been to Denver," he said. "I'm originally from Vermont, but my parents died when I was young. Julia took over my care—she was already living in France—and we lived in Paris until I went to college. That's when she moved first to New York, then to Denver."

"Why did she leave New York? I was just there for the first time, and it is wonderful."

"A better question is, why did she leave Paris?"

Kathleen smiled. "That, too."

"She left Paris because she wanted to be near me while I was in Connecticut," he said. "She left New York because her dear companion, Francine, suffered from tuberculosis, and they sought the drier climate of the West."

"I've heard of that. There's a hospital in Denver for it alone. The people who go there are mostly, well, they're Jewish."

"As was Francine," Paul said. "She died about two years ago."

"I'm sorry." She gathered her cape around her. "Why didn't you wait until America joined the war to come over here?"

"I didn't know if we would," he said. "There was so much resistance in America. I hear it's very different now."

"It is." Thinking of Jim and his push for Preparedness, she told Paul about the parades and speeches and rallies. "Before we left, we attended two or three events each day. People turned out in huge numbers to them."

"It's about time, too. The French soldiers mutinied in April—perhaps you heard about that—and the army is still in disarray. The British have been trying to fight the war on their own, but they haven't enough men left. America's soldiers are our only hope. We're losing."

They had stopped walking at the crest of a rolling hill, and the wind blew a thick squall of snow around them. The hood of Kathleen's cape slipped, and she shivered, the war again a terrible reality.

"I'm sorry," Paul said. "I shouldn't have said that."

"I think I knew." She told him of the silent, ghost-like soldiers coming back to Montdidier from the Front. "I hope Seaney—my cousin—is never that way."

"He won't be," Paul assured her. "One thing I have learned in the past year and a half is that we are different. De Tocqueville's exceptionalism, Manifest Destiny, and all that. It's true."

"I'm not sure what any of that is."

"It's you," he said. "Coming over here to help, even though you stand to gain nothing. And caring on your very first night here about whether a certain ambulance driver had his gas mask."

Warmth rushed into Kathleen's face as she took up the flirtation. "But he had kindly lent me his gloves."

"He did, didn't he? And it was probably the best bit of luck he's had in his life, because he had to reclaim them and, in doing so, was able to see you again."

She laughed, and Paul reached for the hood of her cape and lifted it back on her head. His fingers brushed her cheek. For a moment, she imagined that he might kiss her.

Her resolve to wait for it failed her, and she spoke. "You've come over here with nothing to gain."

"Oh, but I'm paid the same as any French soldier. Five sous a day."

"Five sous! Isn't that about the same as a nickel in America?"

"What do you think the mutiny was about?"

A gust of wind and snow in her face took her laughter from her. They turned so that the wind was at their backs, but Kathleen could feel the cold in her fingers and toes.

"We should go," Paul said. "And on the way back to town, you can tell me about yourself."

As they walked, Kathleen told Paul about Redlands and how she had come to work at Graves Oil. She mentioned Mary Jane, who had arrived, according to Mrs. Brently, safely in Denver. "I'm sorry she didn't stay," Kathleen said. "We've been friends since the day I started working at Graves Oil."

"Is someone coming to take her place?"

"Not yet," Kathleen said. "Mrs. Brently says that she can't ask Mr. Graves"—she stumbled over the name—"that she can't ask her brother to send another group until we've proven that our mission is a good investment, as she calls it. We haven't even spoken to, much less helped, any American soldiers yet."

"You will," he said. "Soon enough, I'm sure. We've had a few deserters in our ranks, too."

"Deserters? But you said you came of your own free will."

"I did, but we're still part of the French Army, even though we don't wear the same uniform," he said. "Or we were. Now we're under U.S. command and only assigned to the French, but things haven't changed much yet. They will this spring. Then—who knows?"

At the hotel, Kathleen ran upstairs to her room to retrieve the gloves. When she handed them to Paul, who waited for her in the lobby, he said, "*Merci, Mademoiselle.*"

"*De rien, Monsieur le . . .*"

"*Monsieur le Conducteur Américain.*"

She fumbled through the phrase, then said, "That was awful, wasn't it?" Her face was hot and flushed. "The French laugh at my pronunciation."

"I'll let you in on a secret." He stepped near enough that she could smell a faint odor of soap on his skin. "Paul is pronounced the same in French and English. I'll never know which language you're trying to speak."

She laughed. I have never felt this way, she thought as they walked toward the canteen. As if nothing I do is wrong as long as I believe in what I'm doing. She considered telling Paul how she felt, but her nerves overtook her.

When they reached the tent, she said, "I want to thank you for helping me through the first night we were here. I was . . . scared, I wanted to be somewhere else—anywhere else but here."

He smiled. "That's a thought that doesn't go away. Every time is as hard as the time before."

"But you keep doing it."

"And you will, too," he said. "I'd like to see you again—that is, if I'm not sent somewhere else."

"I'd like that."

"If I am sent away, I'll try to let you know. You'll do the same, won't you? I'm with Norton-Harjes Section 17."

"I will," she said. "Oh, yes, I will."

He reached out and touched her arm, and she caught his hand as it dropped, her fingers threading through his. He smiled, and brought her hand up to his lips, then stepped away and climbed into his ambulance. She watched until the Packard disappeared around the curve along the main street of town. Inside the canteen, Hank and Helen were readying their wares for the busy evening hours. Kathleen grabbed her apron. She felt giddy, too flighty and happy to work.

"Ooh-la-la!" Hank said. "Who's the Yankee Doodle Dandy?"

Kathleen laughed, and Helen said, "It's against the rules."

"What?" Kathleen and Hank asked together.

"Fraternizing with the soldiers."

"I had his gloves," Kathleen protested. "He gave them to me on our first night—"

"He's not a soldier," Hank said at the same time.

"He's a man," Helen snipped. "We aren't supposed to have any contact." Then, accusingly, "We could all be sent home, and it would be your fault. You shouldn't even be here."

"I'm doing my part," Kathleen said fiercely. "I'm working as hard as you—"

"What did you do to convince Mr. Graves to let you come?"

Kathleen took a stuttering breath. "I did exactly the same as you. I applied and passed the interview!"

"You're too young! But in New York, you were always with him—"

"Only on Sunday, when he took me to Mass while you went to—"

"Well, we're all here now," Hank interrupted. "And, anyway, Kathleen was just returning the ambulance driver's gloves. Isn't that so?"

"Yes," Kathleen said. "That's all."

Helen turned away, busying herself with the coffee can, and Hank sent Kathleen a wink before she went back to slotting packages of cigarettes in a display box. Kathleen said nothing more. She already knew that she would break every rule to see Paul Reston again.

NINETEEN

Paul leaned back against the hood of his Packard, one boot up on the fender. The ambulance was parked beside a *poste de secours*, a dressing station. This one was a hole dug into a hillside, with a couple of timbers at the entrance and sandbags piled on its corrugated tin roof. Beside Paul, the orderly, Jean Latour, smoked a cigarette. Paul himself breathed out steam into the frost of the afternoon.

"*Quand? Quand?*" Latour lamented.

Paul did not reply. Latour was not much of a worrier—he had already been through three years of war in the French army and had the cool, unflappable sense of fatalism that nearly every living Frenchman possessed. Yet the question—When?—resonated in Paul's head as well. The fighting must be fierce today, because so far, no *brancardiers* or stretcher bearers had wound their way through the labyrinthine trench system to reach the *poste*. They were probably holed up somewhere—in an *abri* or shelter somewhere—with their wounded patients, waiting for the shelling to stop.

From the *poste*, the entire valley was visible. The trenches, one after another, were long scars in the land, punctuated by craters left by shells. Concertina wire rolled daintily across No Man's Land, buffeted here and there by the wind and the blasts of mortars and artillery fire, ready to slice up human flesh. Everywhere, there were piles of—what? Discarded or lost weapons, mangled bodies, broken-down vehicles? Paul could see an abandoned British tank that had plummeted nose first into a trench, and a pile of tangled horseflesh—once a supply wagon and team of four—at the edge of the field. One horse was still alive, and struggling, trying to break free of the traces, blood streaming from its mouth.

A shell hit the hillside behind them, and Latour dropped to the ground. Chunks of dirt and *éclats*—metal shards—thudded against Paul's tin hat. The earth beneath his feet vibrated, and he stumbled forward.

"Inside!" Latour shouted in English.

He rushed toward the timbered entrance, and Paul crowded in behind him. The passageway was dark, with three or four crudely carved steps that led downward. In the cave, a single carbide lamp threw off an eerie white sheen. Dust swirled around an operating table, a tray of surgical equipment, and a white-coated surgeon, who sat on the packed dirt floor with his back against the wall.

"*Rien?*" the surgeon asked, taking a drag on his cigarette.

"*Pas encore,*" Paul replied. Not yet.

"Have some coffee." Latour helped himself to the pot that was on the makeshift stove. Waving at the doctor, he asked, "*Monsieur?*"

The doctor shook his head.

Paul took the coffee that Latour poured for him and studied the map that was nailed on a wooden slab. It showed the Front from Ypres to Verdun, where the roads were named according to the peril they offered: Dip of Death, Hell's Half Acre, Dead Man's Turn. Several of the roads were hatched-marked with thick black lines, meaning that they had been shelled into oblivion. Areas circled in green showed the presence of gas in the river valleys of the Meuse and Ypres. The map was two days old.

With one finger, he traced the road to Montdidier. He had not stopped thinking of Kathleen O'Doherty since he had first seen her, during that terrible night of *triage*. Images of her were clear in his mind—the way she had tried to help the wounded, even though her face showed how afraid she was; the way she had picked up on saying "God bless you" to every wounded man; the way that life and laughter had come to her when they had walked in the country and she talked of her home and her art.

Why was it that he had never met someone like her during his college years in Connecticut? Why was it only in France, when they could be pulled apart by distance and circumstance in a matter of minutes, that he had found her?

A call came from the entrance at the top of the steps. "*Médecin! Ambulancier!*"

Paul and Latour rushed forward, the doctor close behind them. Outside, the *brancardiers* were swarming, a long line now winding up the communication trench to the *poste de sécours*. Already, other ambulances were arriving.

Latour flung open the doors on the rear of the ambulance, and the doctor quickly chose those who could travel. The stretcher bearers began to load the Packard, sliding the stretchers on rails affixed to the floor. Paul cranked the motor and climbed up under the canopy that covered the driver's and passenger's seats. Slipping on his goggles, he called to Latour, "*Qu'est que c'est?*"

"*Cinq couchés, trois assis.*"

Latour crawled up beside him, and Paul urged the car forward. The Packard lurched in the mud, its wheels churning up a spray of muck as it edged onto the road. It would be a slow, agonizing crawl to Attichy, ten miles away.

"How badly are they wounded?" Paul asked. "How much time do we have?"

Latour twisted in his seat to peer at the patients through the open rear window. Shrugging, he said, "*Éternité.*"

It was true, Paul had to admit. They had forever. If these men died, there would be more—more Frenchmen, more Brits, and now, Americans—to take their places.

One of the soldiers began to moan, his cries growing louder with each jounce of the Packard. Paul slowed down, hoping to relieve the man's pain.

"*Qui fait que le son?*" he asked.

"*Un assis.*" Latour lit a cigarette, then passed it through the rear window. "*Voilà,* he won't be nosy now."

"Noisy," Paul corrected. "He won't be noisy now."

"*N'est pas ce que j'ai dit?*" Latour said. "Isn't that what I said?"

Paul laughed. "*Non, pas du tout.*"

It took nearly two hours to travel to Attichy, the Packard creeping along roads that had the consistency of mechanic's grease. Once, the engine stalled, and Paul had to slog through the mire to crank it, only to drive a few feet forward before it stalled again. At last, he delivered his *blessés* to the hospital and returned to the *poste* for his next assignment.

This time, there was no waiting. The *poste de sécours* swarmed with *brancardiers* piling stretchers nearly atop one another. The ambulances waited in line, the drivers and orderlies poised to jump from the seats and load the wounded aboard. Paul hunched forward, trying to keep the Packard idling. Now and then, shrapnel from an artillery burst would plunk against the sides of the automobile. Latour leaned out of the ambulance, then quickly pulled his head and shoulders back under the protective awning.

"*Zut alors, ils viennent pour nous,*" he said.

They're coming for us. Paul ventured a look out his window just as a battery of French guns along the roadside responded to the artillery burst. He covered his ears against the thunder of the shells being shot from the cannon, but the sound penetrated his entire body, jarring his organs. Under his tin hat, his forehead dripped with sweat, and he knew that the carnage would be bad.

As he nosed the Packard forward, Latour jumped from the car and ran toward the *poste*. He disappeared inside, but soon came back.

"*Ce qui se passe?*" Paul asked, sliding from the driver's seat.

"It is bad," he reported in English. "Very bad."

"Why are so many out in the open?" Paul asked.

"The doctor is too slow. Too many soldiers hurt. They say that in twenty minutes, more than two hundred are killed and one thousand wounded."

Paul looked at the men lying on the ground at his feet. Many had chests or abdomens that were torn apart, leaving a slippery trail of viscous membrane and blood. Some had shrapnel lodged in their eyes or heads, others had bits of metal and debris piercing their skulls. Paul looked away. He knew that that once the shrapnel was removed, the bleeding would start, and the men would die. The terrible irony— they were better off with metal lodged in their brains.

Already, the place smelled—of blood, of vomit and excrement, of the fruity rot of gangrene, and of men dying and dead, and still the number of wounded grew as more stretcher-bearers pushed their way through the communications trench. The situation had become desperate—there was nowhere left for the wounded and no more stretchers, and so they were dumped on the ground.

"*Monsieur Reston!*" Latour called. "*Maintenant!*"

Paul ran back to the ambulance and pulled it forward toward the *poste*. From inside the hovel, the stretcher bearers brought six heavily bandaged *couchés* in various states of consciousness. As they loaded the injured, the artillery guns started firing again. Paul slammed the back doors of the ambulance and ran for the driver's seat.

The mud under the tires had started to freeze, and the road was not as slick as it had been earlier. Paul accelerated, bound this time for the hospital at Compiègne. The route was fairly direct—that is, if the road was still there.

Daylight was starting to fade, and the landscape took on a haunted quality. A light gray mist rose from the muddy, pockmarked fields that stretched on either side of the road, and the branchless stumps of trees were dark and jagged. This was the worst time of the day, the time when the horror was magnified by the twilight. Nothing recognizable remained on the landscape or in the towns—not a house, not a tree, not a horse or buggy or man. Paul felt his lungs constrict, as if someone had punched him. This was when doubt and exhaustion and fear took their toll. He focused on the road ahead.

At last, the buildings near Compiègne appeared, along with the traffic of *camions,* wagons, horses and troops that clogged the streets. Even though special consideration was given to ambulances, it was up to the driver to determine the quickest route to the hospital.

As Paul dodged in and out of the tangle, a team of horses pulling a wagon reared and thrust the wagon into his path. Deftly, he steered around it, jostling his patients.

"Check on them," he ordered Latour.

Latour twisted around. "Alive, dead, who knows? They are mommies."

"*Pardon*?"

"Mommies, those who walk with *les bandages* wrapped all around—"

"Mummies."

"Isn't that what I just said?"

The traffic did not abate near the hospital, and Paul pulled up behind a long line of ambulances. Once again, Latour swung from his perch. He reappeared a few minutes later and climbed back into his seat.

"What's going on?" Paul asked.

"The bookkeepers are behind on their paperwork," Latour reported. "They will take no new cases until they are caught up."

"*Mon Dieu*," Paul said, looking over his shoulder at the wounded behind him.

"*Il n'est pas Dieu qui tient les régistres*," Latour grumbled.

Paul started to laugh.

It is not God who keeps the books.

At four in the morning, more than twenty-four hours after he had started his shift, Paul staggers into the barracks at Jaulzy. The Packard is parked outside, idle now, although Paul has not yet washed the blood and slime from its interior. After the wait at Compiègne, he had been called out for one more trip to the *poste de sécours*. Another six *couchés*, and three *assis*, and this time, a walking case who clung to the running board of the Packard, braving the bitter wind.

But the trip had not gone smoothly. It was dark by then, and Paul had had to drive without headlamps, the route lit only by the exploding star shells at the Front and the moon, which hung in the sky, feeble and spent amid the streaming fireworks. Worse, still, the traffic—which usually moved in the darkness when the roads were hidden from the Germans—was thick and slow, forcing the ambulance to crawl with it.

As Paul navigated the rubble-filled roads, trying not to add to the agony of his wounded cargo, a stray shell caught the *camion* that was traveling in front of him. The truck was loaded with ammunition, and the whole thing went up in pops and flames. When Paul twisted the wheel to avoid the conflagration, the car had slid off the road and ended up in a ditch, one wheel off the ground.

Cries echoed forth from the back of the ambulance, but Paul and Latour—who had to crawl out of the driver's side—had had to work their way slowly and carefully through the tangle of *blessés*. By then, the wounds that had been so hastily dressed at the *triage* station had begun to bleed. One soldier died before Paul could reach him, jumbled as he was among the others. He was buried along the side of the road, his bayonet with a tag attached to the rifle's trigger stuck into the pile of dirt. The others were extracted from the Packard and loaded onto another ambulance, which arrived over an hour later.

The walking case—who never spoke a word—wandered off, bleeding shoulder and all. Paul had no idea if he had been further injured when the Packard veered off the road, or if he had found another conveyance to Attichy, or if he had left the French Army completely. He was, simply, gone.

At last, a group of *sapeurs,* the men who planted land mines, stopped and pulled the Packard onto the road with their *camion.* The engine started—thankfully—and Paul had driven back to Jaulzy, while Latour snored beside him. As the night turned to morning, he wrestled with the terrible feeling that plagued him sometimes: the sense that nothing he did mattered, that no matter how many men he helped, there were hundreds who lay dying on the ground outside some poorly-staffed *poste de sécours* or who perished in the back of an ambulance because of a snag in paperwork.

And what was the reason for all of this—the carnage, the waste, the destruction—anyway?

He stumbles toward his bed and sits on it to take off his boots. Something squirms beneath him, and a voice rumbles, "Get off."

He slides to the floor, too tired to challenge the man who has taken his bed. Grabbing his sleeping roll, he lies down on the cold tile and pulls it over his shoulders. Within seconds, he is asleep.

All in all, it had been just an ordinary day.

TWENTY

At Victoria and Arthur Graves' mansion in Cheesman Park, an elegant Friday night dinner was served for the usual guests: Jim, Uncle Donald and Aunt Minerva, Samuel and Gladys Fallows, the Crawfords. They occupied the same chairs as they always did, their clothes were just as stylish, and to Jim, their conversation was just as dull. The only addition was of a young woman to fill the spot at the dinner table left by Eleanora's absence, and who, of course, was also meant as a partner for Jim. Tonight, it was a Marie Grissom, whom Jim had last seen in New York, and who was visiting an elderly aunt.

He was hardly in the mood for conversation. Only last week, another spell of darkness had overtaken him, costing him three days, which he had spent locked in his study, drinking. Now, everything felt off-kilter. Lights appeared brighter, more chaotic, and objects took on strange shapes or incongruent features. Worse, the talk had turned political—a topic on which he was always expected to have an opinion.

"With Wilson's new taxation plans, we'll all soon be paupers," Samuel said. "Sixty-seven percent of one's income. My God, it's dangerous being a capitalist!"

"It's better than the alternative, isn't it, darling?" Marie nudged Jim.

"I hope that the money our government collects from its citizens is used in taking better care of our soldiers than the British and the French have of theirs."

Jim's father had entered the debate, speaking from the shadows of the corner, where he had retreated soon after the guests had settled into the parlor after dinner. He was a gray man, so thin that sometimes Jim imagined that he had no substance. His father had been more of a stranger than a parent since he lost his children in the lake in the mountains.

"Have you heard about the young man here in Denver who is refusing conscription?" Mrs. Crawford asked. "He says his faith prevents him, but he is Roman Catholic, not a Quaker or one of those other odd religions—"

"He is a coward and nothing more," Jim's father said. "As I understand it, he's a union agitator and socialist."

"One of Eleanora's girls is Roman Catholic," his mother said. "Evidently, she caused quite a fuss in New York City, having to attend her Masses and all."

"She went once to St. Patrick's," Jim said edgily. "At the same time as the others attended Fifth Avenue Presbyterian."

"I met her," Marie said. "She seemed quite proper and dull, everything one would expect in a girl raised not only in the hinterlands of the West, but also in a church that has no sense of humor."

Everyone laughed, except Jim, whose fingers tightened around his glass of brandy.

"How are Ellie and her girls?" Mrs. Crawford asked.

"I believe they are doing quite well," he said.

"I suppose they're scurrying around France like characters in the *The Outdoor Girls* series, solving mysteries and catching spies," Marie said. "Far better than staying at home and knitting scarves and socks with the rest of us."

Mrs. Crawford spoke. "What has become of the one who returned?"

Jim groaned inwardly. It had taken some effort to bring Mary Jane Grayson back to the United States. Ellie had had to arrange for her passage back to Paris with a female chaperone who would not desert her on some war-torn road in France, and another to take her to Bordeaux. Luck was with them on the voyage to America, and Mary Jane had sailed under the care of Mrs. Laughton, who was a friend of the Graves family. For the final leg of the journey, Jim sent a trustworthy female employee from Graves Oil to accompany Mary Jane home on the train.

"Miss Grayson has taken up her position in the typing pool again," he said.

"That's rather presumptuous of her, isn't it?" Mr. Crawford asked. "After all the time and expense you put into her travel to France, she shouldn't expect to be welcomed back into the fold."

"All the young ladies are guaranteed their jobs whenever they return," Jim said. "I have no malice toward her for coming home."

"Why did she come back?" Marie asked.

"I suspect homesickness," Jim said. "According to Ellie's cable, they were put into a trying situation almost immediately."

"What situation isn't trying during wartime?"

"I so hope that Eleanora and the girls will be working with American soldiers," his mother said. "The Red Cross has assigned them to the French."

"Be thankful it wasn't the Germans," Samuel said. "The Red Cross was still maintaining its neutrality and selling ambulances to the Germans until President Wilson ordered it to stop."

Marie leaned toward Jim. "I knew the kinds of girls who joined Relief Societies in college," she said, softly enough that only he could hear. "They live together now as respectable spinster aunties, with a myriad of excuses as to why they've never married."

"Surely you don't mean Ellie."

"Oh, of course, not darling Eleanora—"

Mr. Crawford boozily hailed him. "Tell us a story, Jim." To Marie, he added, "He tells the wildest tales about the oil fields."

"I'm quite aware of that," Marie snipped.

Glad to move on from the subject of the Relief Society, Jim rose to the occasion. "The last time I was in Texas," he said, "I met one Jefferson Davis Jackson. He's a good American, a better Texan, and all Confederate rebel. He's been traveling around France since the beginning of the war, selling mules to the French and British governments."

Mr. Crawford laughed. "Don't they have mules in France?"

"Not enough, it seems, to keep the British and French supplied," Jim said. "Anyway, Jackson doesn't speak a word of French, and quite frankly, he doesn't care to. But he also refuses to eat French cooking, saying it is the worst in the world. So while he's in France, he carries around *The Ladies' Home Journal* to show the cooks what he wants for breakfast."

Samuel asked, "So the Frogs don't know how to cook ham and eggs?"

"Evidently not in the American style."

Jim waited for the laughter to subside. "Now that America is in the war, Mr. Jackson has started working with the Veterinary Department of the U.S. Army to keep the Allied effort supplied with mules. He's actually been given the rank of Major, too. But the best part"—Jim paused before he offered his punchline—"is that he proudly goes by the name of Jackass Jackson."

"Jackass!" Mr. Crawford yelped.

A maid came into the room to replenish the coffee, and Jim was no longer aware of the laughter around him. The maid had honey-colored hair tucked beneath her white cap and a silken sheen to her skin. She busied herself with rearranging the dainty china cups and refilling the sugar bowl, yet Jim imagined that she felt his presence in the room in the same way that he felt hers—like movement through water, toward sunlight, toward warmth. She darted a glance at him, meeting his gaze with blue eyes that were as clear and bright as his. Almost at once, her attention shifted to Marie, who sat at his side.

"What do you think Jim?" His mother's razor-sharp, insidiously sweet voice called him back to the conversation.

He glanced away from the girl. "I'm sorry, I lost myself for a moment."

"Do you think that President Wilson will nationalize the oil fields before the end of this year?"

"I really don't know," he said shortly. "President Wilson doesn't keep me in his confidence."

Jim's mother watched hawkishly as the maid left the room, then eyed him, her expression adamant. Almost imperceptibly, she shook her head.

"I'd be worried, if I were you, Jim," Mr. Crawford said. "The railroads, the telegraph and telephone, the steel mills, even Smith and Wesson—all under government control. President Wilson is acting like the Kaiser himself."

"Most of the oil operators I know are doing all they can to increase production," Jim said. "The government would gain nothing by nationalizing the industry."

"Except its sticky fingers in your pockets," Samuel said. "The farmers have already seen that, now that the Lever Act regulates food—"

Jim went to the window and looked out on the garden. The darkness seemed desperately sweet and compelling. Striking a match, he lit a cigarette. The first snow of the season had fallen, fresh and white, dusting the lawn and the graceful statuettes around the fountain. In the back of the house, the servants would be finishing the bulk of their tasks and would only need to wait out the guests' departure before leaving for their own homes.

Marie joined him, her fingers light on his arm. "Teddy Landry has asked some of his friends to meet us at the Brown Palace later this evening. Come with us."

"What do you intend to do there?"

"We intend to drink and dance. That's why we need you with us. We're just poor out-of-towners who don't know a thing about Prohibition. They might make us follow the law if you aren't along to ease our way."

"You mean to pay the maître'd."

"If you insist, darling," She walked her fingers up his arm to his shoulder. "And I don't want to dance with anyone but you."

Jim glanced behind him at the others. "I have some business to attend to first."

"Heavens, do you ever stop?" She stood on tiptoe to kiss his cheek. "Don't let me down."

As the guests bid their goodbyes, Jim stayed next to the window, leaving them to be escorted to the door by his father and mother. As soon as the chauffeured automobiles rolled out of the elegant circle drive in front of the home, he felt it—the haunted silence that filled his parents' house whenever company left. He had long wondered why his parents stayed here—one could almost hear the echoes of the grief and sorrow that had accompanied the loss of their children. Then, again, he understood their attachment to the place where their children had once breathed and slept and laughed. Bidding farewell to ghosts was not easy.

Soon enough, his mother bustled into the room, followed by his father.

"The roads are looking slick," she said. "You might want to go."

"I live three blocks away," Jim said sourly. "If nothing else, I'll skate."

"How was your trip to Texas?" his father asked.

Jim abandoned the window to pour another brandy. "It went well. I sold thirty-million barrels for a dollar-fifty a barrel to the refinery."

"How much of that is profit?"

"My take, you mean? About thirty cents a barrel once all the expenses are paid."

His father nodded as he did the math.

"Do you want to look at the charitable funds now or tomorrow?" his mother asked.

"Let's do it now."

Jim followed his mother into the study, where she took a seat behind a polished mahogany desk. The charitable funds were little more than a ruse; to avoid being bled to death by income taxes, fifteen percent of his income must go for the common good. With Mr. Hobart's aid, his mother managed the accounts for him. Jim sat in the chair opposite her.

"Here is what Mr. Hobart sent me," she said.

He took the portfolio and glanced at the pages, filing through receipts to the Charity Organization Society, the Children's Hospital, the W.C.T.U. Mission, the Denver Rescue Mission. Poverty, misery, debauchery—such things bored him.

"I'm sure it's all in order," he said, closing the binding.

"You might at least pretend to take an interest."

He reopened the portfolio, the tension in his jaw building as he tried to focus on the numbers. Across the desk, his mother seemed to be holding herself in a far too rigid pose for this time of night. Without looking up, he asked, "Why was Anneka here tonight?"

His mother shuffled papers on her desk. "We've had some change-overs recently. Girls marrying or eloping or that sort of thing as their beaus leave for war. We're already short-handed, and then Gretel was ill tonight. I had no choice but to ask Mrs. Lindstrom to step in."

He laid down the portfolio. His mother's use of Anneka's surname was as much an insult as it was a courtesy.

"I would like to promise you that it won't happen again, but I can't," his mother said tightly. "I'd rather you not have any association with that woman."

That woman. Memories rushed in—the softness of skin, the way she murmured his name with her heavy accent—*Yeem*, the "j" so foreign for her, how he'd teased her for that—and her eyes that reflected his own in color and desire. He had been twenty-three, about to begin his last year at Princeton, home on summer break.

"You don't yet trust me?" he asked.

His mother laid a hand on the desk, as if reaching out to him, although she had not touched him since he was a child. Her blue eyes met his, and he could have sworn that tears swarmed there. How rarely his mother revealed her gentler side—he could hardly believe it.

"Your father and I so want you to be happy, Jim," she said. "You really must think of marrying. This celibacy has gone on long enough."

"Celibacy?" He laughed. "I recently proposed to a young woman and was decidedly turned down. I don't have the stomach for another rejection."

"Who?" his mother asked. "Certainly not Marie."

"Don't worry. Marie's charms don't appeal to me."

"Then, who is she? If it's Emily Curtis, I can speak to—"

"Since she said no, does it matter who she is?"

"I have only your interests at heart—"

He rose and dipped down to kiss his mother on the cheek. "I will talk to you tomorrow."

She sniffed, but did not deign to reply.

****

At home, Jim finds a letter in the silver tray on the credenza. It is from Ellie, the first communication from her that he has received since the Society's arrival in France, other than the desperate cables about Mary Jane. In his study, he slices the envelope with a heavy, silver opener and sits at his desk to read it.

September 19, 1917

My darling brother,

We have settled happily into the canteen that the Red Cross has set up in a town not so far from the Front. It's a bare little thing—just a tent with some tables and a few amenities. We've heard that the soldiers prefer the more luxurious offerings from the YMCA, but we make do with our bare-bones stove and fryer, our giant cans in which we mix powdered cocoa and coffee (yes, they have invented a powder that becomes coffee when mixed with water called, as one might expect, "instant coffee"), and our limited reading and writing materials.

We came into quite a mess. The canteen has not been in service for some time, and everything was filthy. Dr. Thibault, the médecin en chef *of the evacuation hospital that is a few miles away, told us that he had requested fourteen canteeners from the Red Cross because of the increased activity in this area. He received only the five of us, now reduced to four by Mary Jane's departure. The three girls who stayed on are hard-working and manage to keep in good spirits, even though we are rarely off our feet.*

I don't believe that Grand Central Station could be any busier than our tiny train station and platform. We are at an embarkation point for the French and British armies, with troops continually going to or coming from the Front. The town is also along the LOC, or lines of communication, so we endure activity almost twenty-four hours a day. Almost no civilian travel is allowed on the roads or the trains, and military truck convoys rumble through at all hours of the day. We can hear the shells and bombardments falling at the Front, and, at times, the earth shakes when the big guns fire.

The sky is almost never dark, but lit up with rockets and flares. I did not imagine that we would encounter such a complete immersion in war as we have from our first day here.

We spent the first night at the "Salle de Triage," which is a railway station that has been converted into a place to sort out the mess of combats wounds that the mostly American ambulance drivers (who come, in large part, from Yale) deliver to our station. The French give very little medical care at the dressing stations near the Front, believing that it is better to move the men away from danger and then see to their wounds. So they bring them to the train station in our town, where the most severe cases are taken off to expert care at the evacuation hospital and the others on a train bound for hospitals farther behind the lines. I don't know if this is the best system—many arrive in dire circumstances.

We have yet to see our first American soldier. I have heard that a few American troops are at the Front now, and I suppose it is only a matter of time before we will be ministering to them. I dread the day that I see the first badly wounded American boy.

Much love to Mother and Father.

All my love to you.

Ellie

P.S. An orange costs $.25 and a pear $.30 in the small town in which we are billeted. Therefore, I doubt you will fuss at my request for another lettre de crédit *at the Paris bank.*

Jim refolds the letter, relieved that Ellie sounds well and, for the most part, safe. Her absence weighs on him more than he thought it would. They have been close-knit allies and rivals throughout so much of their lives, and now, he has to settle for the likes of Marie for conversation and wit. He glances out the window at the end of the study. Snow falls in big flakes that balance delicately on the branches of the trees in Cheesman Park and make the stark, white amphitheater a winter palace. He leaves his study and puts on his greatcoat. Outside, his Marmon is parked in front of the house, as he requested.

He drives to an unremarkable neighborhood west of the state Capitol building, near Broadway. The streets are deserted, the residents tucked in for the night. Parking in a darkened alley, he walks to a neat cottage that has a picket fence around its narrow, front yard. He lets himself in through the gate and knocks at the door.

Anneka answers almost immediately.

"I thought I might see you tonight," she says. "Come in."

He smiles at the way she pronounces "th" as "t." She speaks slowly, pronouncing each word as if it were made of china, in an effort to be correct.

"How are you?" he asks.

She has changed from her maid's uniform into a peach-colored dressing gown, and her hair flows in rich waves to her shoulders. Her cheeks glow a blushing pink, and her blue eyes gleam under long, delicate lashes.

As she closes the door behind him, she says, "I am good. Your mother is always good to me. The money is good."

De money ees go-de.

She leads him into the living room. The cottage is no less beautiful than the woman, with its fashionable wood furnishings and plush fabrics that are far better than a housemaid can afford. On the floor is a colorful carpeting, and a healthy fire burns in the grate.

Jim sheds his coat, hat, scarf, and gloves and tosses them over the back of an armchair.

"May I see her?" he asks.

"Of course."

He follows the hallway to a bedroom at the back of the house. Mina is sleeping on her side, the blankets pulled up around her shoulders, a teddy bear tucked under her chin. Her white-blond hair curls around her chin, and her skin is pristinely pale in the dim light from the hallway. If her eyes were to open, they would burn blue. She is five, no, six, years old now.

He resists the urge to reach for her, to smooth back a strand of hair, or to sit on the bed and simply watch her sleep. Who is she? He barely knows this child—his child—who is kept so carefully concealed and whom he sees only on her birthday and holidays and other special occasions. Mina shifts, and he steps back into the shadows, in case she wakes. After some time, he becomes aware of Anneka standing in the doorway behind him.

"Who keeps her when you're out at night?" he whispers.

"The neighbor, Mrs. Stroop."

After a last look, he lets Anneka lead him back to the living room.

"Do you have anything to drink?" he asks.

Anneka fetches a bottle of amber liquid from the sideboard. "This is all."

He pours a glass and takes a sip. The whiskey is homemade, most likely brewed by a neighbor in a backyard still. "This is terrible," he says. "I'll have something sent over from my private reserve."

"Do you intend to stop by again?" she asks. "If not, it would be a waste. I don't drink."

He weighs her rebuke. "Why do you have this, then?"

"What do you want, Jim?" Anneka sits on the divan, her legs under her, her slender feet peeking out from beneath her robe. He notices a newspaper spread open beside her, its words incomprehensible to him, its masthead announcing the *Svensk-Americkanska Western.*

Vat do you vant, Yeem?

He takes another drink. He isn't able to answer her. He doesn't know.

"I would think you'd want me to check up on Mina now and then," he says.

"Yes, yes," Anneka says. "But your mother must tell you what you need to know about her." She pauses, then adds, "And about me, I'd think, too."

His mother—the architect of all this. When she had learned that Anneka was expecting Jim's child, she had forced an agreement on Anneka that was as heartless as it was generous: Anneka will be well-paid, clothed, and housed as long as she continues to be employed in the home of Arthur and Victoria Graves, does not marry, and, most importantly, never reveals the identity of the child's father. It's an elaborate ruse. A Mr. Lindstrom, who died tragically young in Sweden, has been invented to satisfy the curious of the household staff, and Anneka's temporary absence from the house was explained away by the need to tend to ailing parents. In return for Anneka's complicity, Mina will have the best of everything throughout her life.

"She doesn't tell me as much as you'd think," he says.

"And you think of us only when something reminds you."

"That isn't true," he says, although it is dangerously close. "How is Mina doing in school?"

Anneka opens her mouth as if to challenge him, then answers, "She likes it, I think. She learns so much so fast. She's very smart."

"She should be." The fire crackles as a log shifts, and Jim takes another drink. "I heard from my sister today."

"How is Miss Eleanora? She's very brave to go to France."

"She and the girls are somewhat too close to the Front for my liking. But I believe this may be the greatest achievement of her life."

The fear that he has missed out on greatness creeps once more into his mind. Anneka shifts, and he remembers the day he had taken her to his family's castle in Turkey Creek Canyon, mostly because she would not believe that it existed. She played the game well—her obstinate skepticism vying with his increasingly outrageous boasts until the structure no longer resembled Inglesfield, but some baronial castle in Europe. Once there, she had counted off its deficiencies—no moat, no suits of armor, no family crest with crossed swords hung on the wall—while he kissed her neck and shoulders.

Teasing, she had run from him, and he had chased her up the stone staircase at one end of the Great Hall and along the balustrades of the hallways of the second floor. Scampering ahead of him, she had found the staircase that spiraled through the turret and run down to the first level again. When he caught up to her, she stood before the yawing fireplace in the Great Hall, claiming victory. As he knelt at her feet, she knighted him with a poker, and he said, *You are my queen.*

"Do you remember the day we went to the mountains?" he asks.

Anneka plays with the drawstring at the neck of her gown. "I remember all the days," she says. "And the days after, too."

He takes a drink, and the whiskey burns with the flavor of turpentine all the way to his stomach. He had been old enough to make a choice when Anneka found out about Mina. Yet it hadn't mattered back then. He was like so many others whose fathers had carved their fortunes from the vast raw resources of the American West and who had favored their sons with riches and opportunity. He could have whatever he wanted. He had left for college that fall without a thought for the seventeen-year-old housemaid who'd been his lover throughout the summer, and he had not learned of her situation until he was home for Christmas. By then, his mother had arranged it all, and he had not protested.

Anneka picks up the decanter from the table. "Would you like more to drink?"

"You don't need to serve me."

"I am being polite, that's all."

"Anneka—"

"No," she says simply. "No, Jim."

Jim sets the empty whiskey glass on the sideboard. "I should go."

"Yes, I think so."

He gathers his coat and things from the armchair. "What does Mina want for Christmas?"

"We have all we need."

"Surely she wants something."

"A pony the color of the rainbow, a fairy's magic wand, a diamond crown for a princess," Anneka says impatiently. "Can you—or your mother—buy those for her? She is a little girl, she does not care for things. She wants . . . dreams."

"I'll send something over."

Outside, he walks to his car in the silence of the night. The snow has covered the Marmon with a film of white. He cranks the car, then drives toward downtown and the Brown Palace.

TWENTY-ONE

Seven months and ten days after Sean joins the American Expeditionary Force, he sits, not in a trench or a pillbox or machine gun nest, but in a drafty barracks outside Neufchateau, more than forty miles from the Front, and nearly two hundred miles from Kathleen.

Just now, the men are quarantined after an outbreak of scarlet fever. No contact is allowed with those outside, for fear that the ailment—along with measles, chicken pox, tuberculosis, ameobic dysentery, influenza, and pneumonia—will drag down the entire American Expeditionary Force. Although a smoking area has been set up outdoors, they aren't allowed to go to the nearby YMCA canteen, where there are electric lights, newspapers, books, a piano, and, most of all, the companionship and conversation of women.

"The best thing we've done so far is get sick," Kevin complains.

"That's the only thing we've done," Sean corrects glumly.

He lies in his bunk, wishing the whole business would hurry up and get over. So far it has been a game of waiting for nothing. Five months at Fort Riley, another month traveling to and training at a camp in New York. After the voyage across the ocean, there were the days lost in marching from Southampton to Dover. Then came the *"8 cheveux, 40 hommes"* French military train—already a joke among the Americans in France—that transported eight horses and forty men across the country to this muddy hole south of Verdun.

He's grown so bored that he has started a diary in a beautifully scrolled, leather-bound book that Brendan gave him before he left. Now, he flicks it open and starts to write:

No letters from home yet. I think the mail ships must be coming around by the other ocean. They may have landed in Hong Kong for all we know, and are being carted to us by camel and Chinaman. So I just have to make do with re-reading the letters that I got at Fort Riley. The news is a little stale by now, but at least I can see Ma's and Mag's handwriting.

Day after day, it's the same thing here. We train under the eyes of some British officer who thinks Americans are as helpless as kittens. We march to the practice trenches that we dug ourselves and that are now filled with icy rain water and mud that can suck the life right out of you. After firing a couple of clips of cartridges at our "enemy," we go over the top, moving across the field toward the dummies at the far end. We're told to walk slowly, with every muscle tensed, our eyes on the enemy ahead, our rifles held at guard position. A few paces from the dummies, the officer yells, "Give it to him! Right through him! Give him hell!" And we plunge our bayonets into them. Once the dummies are only rags and straw, we advance to another trench with dummies lying in its bottom. The order is then, "Jump on him! Kill him! Tear him up!" We keep going, trench after trench, hearing "Pull out his kidneys! Pull out his lungs! Pull out his liver!" and splashing and shivering, until we've reached the final one. That's when we shoot straight down, destroying our enemies with bullets.

By then the water in our canteens is frozen solid, and our clothes are drenched, never to be dry again. Our feet are blistered and purple, and our ears are stuck by frozen rain to our tin hats.

Sean stops, something aching within him. Homesickness, again—for the church and confession and the sacred rites and always-drunk Father Devlin and Brendan and Liam, with his quick wit, and Ma and Maggie and Kathleen. And even for Pa. Just to hear them talk about the price of sugar or the hail that damaged the garden—things he used to think were a stupid waste of time. Or to lie on his bed and read a book by Zane Grey or some other dime novelist that Kathleen, with her love of horses and adventure, has given him. To hear Ma rattling around in the kitchen, pots and pans steaming away, and to eat her food—

Across the wide aisle, beyond where the potbellied stove puffs anemically, sending out only a paltry heat, are six men who were transferred in to take the places of some of those who've been stricken by diarrhea and pneumonia, or who shot themselves through their own stupidity, or who went "trench mad" before they even saw the trenches. The new fellows are Italian and from the east coast of America, poorly suited for a Wild West division such as this one. Tony Necchi and Michael Giordano speak English with heavy accents, but the others rely on a hatchet job of English and Italian. The men stick together, but Danhour, Sean's foe from Fort Riley, has dubbed the six Italians as "dirty wops." To that, he adds his new moniker for Kevin and Sean, "the Irish sops." Sometimes, Sean hears the singsong rhyme murmured behind him as he walks through the barracks to the privies or stands in line in the mess hall. He has never caught anyone as they were saying it, but when he does, he'll teach them a lesson or two.

Right now, the Italians play cards, speaking only their mother tongue.

Sean catches Tony's eye and quickly looks away. He does not want to be lumped in with them, with their dark skin and eyes and their thick-as-mud accents. They don't look American, and they don't act it. Whenever he sees them praying together—a couple of them pray, anyway—with their rosaries and prayer books, he winces. It's as if he's viewing them through Danhour's eyes: they are foreign, backward, strange.

Picking up his diary, he writes:

I've heard that the French are given half a liter of whiskey pour la courage *before they go over the top and the British have rum, but some of our boys are already getting sloppy with liquor. The other day, a few of them went to Toul and came back with pockets full of dirty pictures and stories of their adventures in town. Toul sounds like it is quite the place for sin.*

Around the camp, rumors fly. They say the French are lying down, waiting it out until the American troops are here. But Blackjack Pershing won't let us be absorbed into the French and British ranks and used as cannon fodder. He wants us to be our own Army, and I say, good for him. We heard from a British Louie that the Italians have gone over to fight with Germany now, because they think that the Allies are losing. We've heard from our own officers that ten thousand Americans are pouring into France each day, and a hospital with 50,000 beds is being built in Marseilles for the expected American casualties. Sounds like an awful lot of us are going to end up there.

There's even a story that the U.S. is negotiating for peace right now with Germany, even before we see a single battle, and if Germany doesn't agree, the U.S. won't recognize it as a country for fifty years. I think that's the best—we wouldn't have to give Germany a thought until 1967, when we're all old and gray and—

"Sullivan! Private Sean Sullivan!"

The call echoes down the long aisle of the barracks. "Looking for Sullivan, Sean Sullivan!"

The Italians look up from their game, and Kevin hangs over the bunk. "What have you done now, Sean?"

Sean stands and steps into the aisle. "Yes, sir. Here, sir."

A corporal comes toward him. "Mail," he says flatly, handing Sean an envelope.

Around him, a cacophony erupts—"There's mail," "Hey, somebody's gettin' mail," "Mail's finally here!"—and the corporal barks, "There's no mail. This is from a French address, sent in France."

"From France?" Kevin asks, hanging over the edge of the bunk. "Who the hell do you know in France?" He gawks at the letter. "It's from a girl!"

The aisle fills with those longing for mail from home. "A girl!" "How do you know a French girl, Sullivan?" "You been stepping out to Toul?"

The letter has been forwarded from the Red Cross office in Langres. Sean's eyes tear when he sees the handwriting.

"It's from my cousin," he says thickly. "She's with a Relief Society here."

He opens the letter with fumbling fingers, aware that the crowd in the aisle has grown, the curious and desperate flooding toward him, as if the envelope might contain letters for all of them.

A photograph falls from the folds of the letter. In front of a white tent stand four women—Kathleen and two others with elbows linked, and an older woman standing slightly apart. Each wears a heavy cape and white wimple. The girls smile widely and playfully, while the woman showers a more practiced smile on the photographer. Scribbled on the back of the photograph is the note: "The Graves Family Foundation Relief Society in front of our canteen. Kathleen O'Doherty, Harriet Mills, Helen Parsons, and Mrs. Eleanora Brently."

Sean places the photograph behind the letter, eager to read. Kathleen's frantic handwriting greets him from stationery marked with the prominent heading in gold print, "The Graves Family Foundation Relief Society, Dedicated to the Aid and Succor of the American Soldier in France."

Dear Seaney,

I am praying that this letter finds you! I've had to send it through the Red Cross because I could not convince anyone to tell me where you are stationed. At last, Mrs. Brently stepped in and helped me out. She went all the way to Paris to mail it. So, I hope very much that if someone is reading this, it's you!

I hope you are well, I hope you are safe, and I hope you are not as busy as we are! We work all hours of the day and night, serving coffee and donuts to the troops and helping whenever we can at the hospital. One of the other girls, Hank, says she hasn't had time to wash her hair since we arrived in France, and I believe it. Her hair is a fright, all stiff and smelly. She calls it her helmet, and says it would stop a bullet better than the tin hats the soldiers wear. She gets away with it, too, because we wear our wimples when we work.

Our canteen is the busiest place in a town that is always busy. Day and night, trains, troops and cavalry march along the Rue *right beneath the windows of our bedroom. We've learned to sleep through it all, which isn't as hard as you think, because we are exhausted by the end of the day and have to make the most of it. Mostly we see French soldiers, although the British stop by in fair numbers, too. They sing and make so much noise that we have to shout at each other to be heard. We have a wooden stage at one end of the tent where we do dramatic poetry readings and performances (even though the French laugh at our pronunciation), and a library at the other end where there are books, board games, decks of cards, and notepaper and pens for writing letters.*

Two days a week, we travel to the base hospital in Amiens, which is about 50 kilometers or 30 miles away. It is run by the British, and Mrs. Brently has worked it out so that we can volunteer there because we are more helpful there than we would be at the French hospitals. We do whatever is needed there. We gargle throats and clean and make beds or move mattresses, and we apply carbolic ointment to burns and scrapes and lips that bleed from the dryness of the wind. There's more, but it would take too long to write about all of it.

One of the first patients that I was assigned to at Amiens was an Irish lad who came in dirty as a stray dog and covered with cooties. His nurse and I gave him a sulfur bath, washed and combed his hair, and gave him a clean suit. By the very next morning, he was scratching again. So we did the same thing— bath, hair, clothes—a second time. The next day, it was the same thing all over again. Finally, I figured it out! I asked him to take off his rosary, and when he did, I dropped it into a basin of soapy water. The water turned black with cooties, all of them fighting for their miserable little lives. Every bead of the rosary was crawling with lice! We laughed so hard that we howled.

So, beware, young Sean Murphy Patrick Sullivan. If you find yourself counting more beads than you think you should be, check to make sure none of them have legs!

Stay safe, Seaney, please stay safe, and don't become run down, either. Some of the British nurses we've met are catching some kind of stomach sickness (they call it "campitis") because they're so beat.

All my love,

Kathleen

Sean reads the letter too quickly, then reads it again. Refolding it, he lays it in his lap, although he keeps the photograph in his hands. Giving poetry readings in French, gargling throats, bathing soldiers fresh from the Front? How is it that she barely finds time to sleep when he, a trained soldier of the American Expeditionary Force, idles away hours and hours?

"What did she say?" Kevin asks eagerly, as if he, too, has been waiting for a letter from her. "Is she really your cousin? Did she send a picture?"

Sean hands him the photograph. "That's her, on the end."

"Man, she's swell—"

A voice interrupts. "She probably had to join up with the convent because she's too ugly to get a husband."

It's Danhour. He stands in the aisle, where the mob that gathered to witness the arrival of the letter still gawks and murmurs.

"Get out of here, Danhour," Kevin says.

Sean bounces onto his feet, adrenaline rushing through him. He's out of the slot between the bunks and into the aisle, his fists up, already jabbing, before Danhour has a chance to take a step back. The Italians' deck of cards scatters as Danhour twists backward into the space between their bunks. Tony Necchi jumps up, and all at once, the Italians are in the fray.

Sean tracks down Danhour, landing another punch to his jaw. Danhour comes back, hitting Sean squarely in the stomach. As Sean folds forward, Danhour jumps on him and wrestles him to the floor. They roll into the pot belly stove, and the chimney squeals as the stove slides a few inches. Smoke pours from the ruptured seams.

Sean pulls Danhour up and slams him against the steel frame of a bunk. "Don't you ever talk about her again!"

Danhour slides away by crawling over the straw mattress and through the bunk. Hefting the mattress, he tosses it at Sean.

Sean fends off the mattress, but Danhour escapes. Others have joined in the fight now. It's a melee, the aisle roiling with men. Mattresses and foot lockers fall to the floor, as the battles rage in and out of the bunks themselves. Sean launches himself back into the mess, grabbing at shoulders, elbowing and charging, trying to find his way back to Danhour.

He finds Danhour a few bunks down and tackles him, which sends the bunk screeching across the floor a few inches. Danhour brings his hands up to shield his head, and Sean plants one in his gut. He hears the whistles of the M.P.s, the shouted orders of the officers, but this feels too good. To let it out, to spill it, to forget that Kathleen's letter has made him aware of just how pointless his existence is. He slugs Danhour again and again, dancing on his feet.

"My church taught me to fight, you son of a bitch," he rasps. "What did yours teach you?"

Whistles pierce the air. "Stop it! Attention! Stop!"

Sean pays no heed, but batters Danhour, who has doubled over into a crouch. He keeps going even as Danhour falls on the floor. He feels others plucking at him, trying to trap his arms, and finally, someone manages to drag him to his feet and twist his arm violently backward.

"Hey, stop it now," a voice says in his ear. "You're gonna kill him."

"Let me go."

Sean jerks away and finds Tony, whose lower lip is bleeding, behind him. Tony's chest is heaving, and he cradles one fist in the other. "Look what you done," he says.

Sean looks toward Danhour, who huddles on the floor, his face and the front of his shirt collar a bloody mess. An M.P. bends over him, then straightens and says, "Call the doctor."

"No." Danhour sits up, his back against a bunk. "I'm all right."

Tony points his chin at Danhour. "*Testa di cazzo*," he says in Sean's ear. "Dumb ass."

Sean laughs, even though his head feels as if it will burst from the rush of blood and excitement. He'd never laugh, if he were home. He'd frown at the language, or scold, or shush. But who cares? Home is thousands of miles away, and he isn't going to see it any time soon.

Lieutenant Morgan winds his way through the bleeding, aching hulks of his soldiers and into the middle of the aisle. Waving away the smoke, he commands, "Shove that stove back under the pipe. Straighten up those bunks."

A couple of men rush forward to reposition the stove and beds. As they do, Lieutenant Morgan spies Sean on one side of the aisle and Danhour on the floor. "Get up, Private Danhour," he says.

Danhour drags himself up by holding onto the rails of the bunk. He struggles to stand completely upright, his left elbow pressed against his side as if he is in pain. His right eye is swelling, already closing, his nose still pouring blood. Lieutenant Morgan looks at him with disdain.

"Which one of you started it this time?" he asks. "Let's ask the lucky Irish, why don't we? Private Sullivan?"

Sean clamps his jaw, refusing to answer.

Lieutenant Morgan growls, "I heard you received a letter."

"Yes, sir. From my cousin who is in France with the American Red Cross, sir."

"Well, hallelujah! The Sullivans have come to save the day."

"Her name is not—"

Lieutenant Morgan silences Sean with a vicious look. Turning toward the rest of the men, he snarls, "So, you all think you're ready to fight? Ready to get at it, huh?"

No one speaks, although a few men chuckle nervously.

"I asked you a question," he says. "If you're tough enough to bust up the barracks, then you better be tough enough to kill some Huns! Answer me!"

"Yes, sir!" someone shouts. Others follow, a roar that echoes through the barracks.

Lieutenant Morgan lets the noise fill the tunnel-like room before he holds up his hand for silence.

"That's better," he says. "Good news has come our way—and not from Private Sullivan's cousin, either." He lets the laughter die down. "You are to pack immediately. We're to move within forty-eight hours into the battle zone. We'll be attached to the French, but in our own intact units."

The barracks explodes in cheers. Men who minutes before were beating the tar out of each other shake hands and pat each other's backs. Some even hug in joy. Sean and Tony bump shoulders as they shake the hands of those around them. One of the Italians crosses himself again and again with glee.

"Company dismissed." Turning, Lieutenant Morgan says, "Private Sullivan, Private Danhour, save it for the Germans."

Danhour snivels. "Yes, sir."

Lieutenant Morgan eyes Sean until he reluctantly salutes.

"Yes, sir," Sean concedes.

The men scramble for their bunks, running down the aisles, pulling out their packs, and cramming their things into them. Someone starts to sing, "Over There," and soon there is a full male chorus: "*So prepare, Say a prayer, Send the word, Send the word to beware, We'll be over, we're coming over. And we won't be back till it's over over there!*" The chorus builds into a rough chant: "We WON'T come BACK till it's OVER OVER *HERE!*"

"No more Brit officers!" Kevin gloats. "Finally, they're giving us a chance to finish off the Heines! I bet we'll be home within a month!"

Sean finds the letter from Kathleen still on his bunk. He puts it back in the envelope and sticks it into a pocket on his pack, ashamed of himself. What has he been acting like but the hooligan that his mother has always accused him of being? But now, here is his chance: to be a man, to be the soldier and American and patriot he should be.

As he folds his clothes, he becomes aware of the Italians across the aisle. They talk among themselves, casting looks over at him every so often. He knows they are talking about him in their incomprehensible tongue. Sweat prickles on his back as new anger surges through him—why can't they just be Americans like everybody else?

One of them approaches and hands him the photograph of Kathleen and the other girls. It's creased in the center, with a muddy boot print nearly obscuring the girls' faces. Sean runs a hand over to smooth it out, suddenly embarrassed. He should have taken better care of it.

The Italian spouts his own language indignantly, ending with, "Sees-ter."

"What?" Sean asks. "She's my cousin, not my sister."

From across the aisle, Tony translates. "Nicola says, she's a nun."

"No, she's not," Sean says. "She has to wear a Red Cross uniform, that's all. She's just a normal American girl."

Tony assures Nicola in Italian, then laughs at his friend's reply. "He says, that's good, because who would want to beat somebody's brains out over a nun?"

TWENTY-TWO

In early November, Paul caught a ride to Montdidier on a supply *camion*. Along the route between the towns, the driver dropped passengers off at their destinations, which made him antsy. He wanted to reach the town as quickly as possible—if nothing else, to test whether the anguish he had felt for two weeks had been worth it. His desire to see Kathleen had kept him awake, made him gulp down his food so that he had heartburn after, and made him avoid the conversation of his peers. Thoughts of her dictated his every move, it seemed, from morning to night. When the *camion* at last came to a halt near the rail station in Montdidier, Paul jumped from the back, calling "*Je serai à la Maison St. Denis.*"

"*Une heure,*" the driver responded.

One hour. Only one hour to see her again. He went to the canteen tent. One flap was open, and he ducked inside. Two girls were tending the counter, neither of them Kathleen.

"Good morning, ladies," he called. "Can you tell me where Miss O'Doherty is?"

One of the girls pinned him with an unpleasant stare, but the other answered, "She went to the market. It's"—she waved—"that way. She left about half an hour ago."

"*Merci, mademoiselles!*"

As he strode down the street, he glimpsed Kathleen coming from the other direction, carrying two woven bags and picking her way around the mud holes and refuse strewn along the street. She wore a wool coat and dark skirt, and her hair, covered by a simple scarf knotted at the nape of her neck, streamed over her shoulders.

It was the first time that Paul had seen her in clothing other than her uniform, and for a moment, he simply watched her, his breath taken from him, his heart aching at her beauty.

She met a group of soldiers who were sauntering down the street. They swept their hats from their heads as she passed, and one gave a chivalric bow. Kathleen dipped in a curtsey, and the soldiers began to howl and tease. She kept walking, but someone must have asked her a question, for she turned and called back, *"Oui, à cinq heures et demie."*

One of the soldiers blew a cocky kiss in her direction. *"Merci, Mademoiselle, je t'aime, je t'aime."*

She laughingly waved a dismissive hand.

Paul felt a surge of pride and happiness. This lovely woman, who was admired by others, who showed no trepidation as she walked in this foreign country, who had come here to help as she could—this was the woman he had fallen in love with. As if she felt his gaze on her, Kathleen looked across the street at him. He waved and crossed to her, dodging a *camion* that issued a scolding honk.

Her smile widened. "I'm so glad to see you!"

He gestured toward the bag. "Did you buy tea?"

"I didn't have a *ticket de ravittaillement* for it. Did I say that right?"

"As well as someone who drinks Irish tea should."

She laughed. "Oh, did you bring it?"

He nodded. "And sugar, too."

"Sugar!" she said. "Where did you find that? They're putting lemon in their tea in Paris, now, because there is no sugar, and milk is only for babies and the sick and old."

"One of the ironies of this war is that the food gets better the closer you are to the Front. There's always someone selling or bartering for just about anything you'd ever want."

"Let's see if Madame de Troyes will let us use her kitchen, and we'll have a cup now."

They fought their way through the crowd: masses of loitering soldiers, who were waiting for orders to move up, and the endless streams of *camions* and wagons that followed them, and cavalry, some of their horses as scarred as the men who rode them.

At the hotel, Kathleen tapped on the kitchen door. When the *hôtelier* answered, Kathleen held up the tin of tea and asked, "*S'il vous plaît, Madame*, may I make . . . *du thé?*"

The *hôtelier* beckoned to her. "*Oui, oui, servez-vous.*"

"*Bonjour, Madame*," Paul said, his cap in his hands. "*Je suis Paul Reston.*"

The landlady's face brightened. "*Enfin, un américain qui parle bien le Français.*"

"*Oui, Madame. J'ai vécu à Paris jusqu'à ce que j'ai été dix-sept ans.*"

Kathleen turned toward Paul. "What are you saying?"

"She said she has finally met an American who speaks French well, and I told her that I lived in Paris until I was seventeen."

Madame de Troyes beckoned him, and he leaned toward her, as if they were sharing a confidence. "*Enseigner le français à cette fille*," the landlady said. "*Elle est désespérée.*"

Teach this girl to speak French. She is hopeless.

Paul tossed her a knowing smile. "*Pas du tout, Madame. Elle est adorable.*"

Madame de Troyes burst into laughter. "*Bien sûr, Monsieur, bien sûr!*"

Kathleen glanced at them, a perplexed look on her face. "Did you use the word adorable?"

"Did I?" Paul teased. "Perhaps you misheard."

"I tend to do that."

Kathleen moved about the kitchen, filling the tea ball, heating the water on the stove, and then pouring it into the pot. Paul stood in the doorway to the dining room, talking casually with Mme. de Troyes, but never letting his gaze waver from Kathleen: her hands were delicate and sure, her lips pursed as she worked intently at making the tea, and her green eyes lit with intelligence and grace. In the light from the window, her hair shone, golden streaks in the copper.

Madame de Troyes piled pieces of cake on a plate and presented it to Kathleen. "*Pour vous et Monsieur le Conducteur Américain.*"

"*Oh, merci!*" Kathleen said. "*Voulez-vous*, um, have *du thé* . . . *avec nous?*" Giving up, she added, "Would you like to join us?"

"*Je ne vais pas empiéter sur l'amour.*"

"*Pardon?*"

Mme. de Troyes threw up her hands. "*Allez, allez.*" She nodded toward Paul and said in halting English, "He will tell you."

Paul stepped aside, and Kathleen passed him, carrying the tray brimming with the pot of tea, cups and saucers, the promised sugar, and the cakes into the dining room. Behind her, Mme. de Troyes gave Paul a saucy wink.

"*Merci, Madame!*" he called as the *hôtelier* closed the kitchen door.

"I will not trespass on love," he said, as Kathleen set the tray on the table.

She sat down. "What's that?"

"I will not trespass on love," he repeated. "That's what Mme. de Troyes said."

Kathleen poured the tea, her head slightly bowed. Paul could see that she was pleased as she fussed with the cups and the strainer. When she handed him the cup, she could not hide her smile, and he laughed.

"Tell me about your past two weeks," he said.

"We've been so busy!" she said. "We are doing more and more work at the hospital. I think Mrs. Brently feels that work is better suited to us. It's more serious than canteen work."

"She wants you to be Mademoiselle Misses, eh?"

"What's that?"

"Mademoiselle Miss is an American nurse who wrote a book, just after the war started, about her adventures. She's very proper and dedicated to her work, willing to give all to the cause."

"Maybe that's it." She laughed. "I don't think Mrs. Brently likes us to flirt so much with the soldiers. She wants us to be more high-minded."

"Flirting isn't such a bad thing. When you think about it, it's just another form of kindness."

"I'm not brave enough to tell Mrs. Brently that." She sipped her tea. "This tastes heavenly."

"It's a success, then?"

"It's wonderful." She took another sip. "Tell me about your two weeks."

"Not much changes for us. We wait for the call, and when it comes, we go."

"What do you do as you wait?"

"When we're *en repos*, as it's called? The main events of the day are lunch and dinner."

"You're joking!"

"Not as much as I'd like to be." He sipped his tea. "You see, each ambulance section is attached to a certain French unit. When that unit goes on leave from the Front, we go, too. Even if the fighting is as fierce as it's ever been, there are a number of us sitting idle."

"You mean, you aren't transporting any *blessés* to the hospital?"

"We do what's called jitney work, then, which is transporting soldiers from one hospital to another. Fever cases, pneumonia, and the like. And we fix whatever we've banged up on our cars, which usually takes a lot of wire and a fair amount of genius." He waited while Kathleen laughed. "We're responsible for keeping them running at all times."

"Don't they need everyone who can help and every vehicle?"

"Perhaps." He sipped his tea. "But everyone needs a rest. Some of us would never stop unless we were forced to."

"You mean that you wouldn't stop."

He smiled. "I'm not the only one who feels that way."

"Mrs. Brently makes each of us take a day off every week, although she doesn't ever take one, except Sunday, of course. Today is my turn. We shop or do errands for the others, and it's our time to write letters, too."

"Have you had any time to sketch?"

"Not as much as I'd like."

"May I see your sketches?"

"Oh, yes!" She reached down and pulled up one of the woven bags. "I have my sketching pad with me."

There were a number of sketches in the book. Some were of the other Relief Society members, and others were of the great machine of war—mule teams and wagons, cannons, locomotives, trucks— but most were of soldiers. One struck Paul as especially poignant. Entitled "French Soldier," it was a drawing of a fifteen or sixteen-year-old boy with bandaged stumps for his right arm and right leg, yet with a jaunty lean against a crutch tucked under his left arm and a toothless grin. The drawing was beautifully executed, and Paul imagined the boy, in possession of a man's desire, eagerly posing for a pretty American girl. Moreover, he imagined Kathleen, her attention entirely focused on her subject, determined to draw the most honest and noble depiction of him as she could.

"You have a true talent for capturing human emotion," he said.

"Thank you." She flushed at the compliment. "I really need to bundle these up and send them off."

"Where do you send them?"

"To"—she faltered—"to Mr. Graves. After he sees them, he takes them to my parents. At least, he promised me he would."

"And you don't believe him?" Paul asked. "Why do you hesitate when you mention him? I've noticed that his name always seems to catch in your throat."

"I'm sure he'll deliver them to my parents." Her flush grew darker. "He's been very generous with us all. He's all he's supposed to be."

"What do you mean by that?"

"He's . . . a gentleman, that's all. I don't know him that well."

She closed her mouth, and Paul sensed that she would say no more, although there was obviously more to say. He flipped another page and came across a drawing of a British major mounted on a well-muscled horse. "You like horses, don't you?"

"How did you know?"

"You draw them so well."

She laughed and told him of her horse, Napoli, and how much she loved to ride. Motioning toward the sketch, she explained, "That's Major Lloyd-Elliot. He spent an hour on horseback one afternoon, talking with Mrs. Brently while she stood in front of the canteen. That's why I had time to add so many details."

"He's a nice-enough-looking subject for a sketch. *Et le cheval*—the horse—*est très magnifique.*"

"*Merci, Monsieur.*" She laughed again. "We met Major Lloyd-Elliott on our first night in Montdidier, and he's the one who has arranged for us to work in Amiens. I think he finds Mrs. Brently attractive." Quickly she added, "She's not married. My mother thought, well, we think she's divorced."

"And that is against your beliefs, isn't it?"

"Yes," Kathleen said, then added timidly, "You might have guessed I'm Catholic."

Paul shrugged. "I guessed it, yes. Why do you say it as if it's something to hide?"

"It's . . . it's not popular to be Catholic, I've learned."

"But it isn't anything to be ashamed of, either."

"I'm not ashamed!" Frowning, she added, "What's your religion?"

"My parents were Anglican, but my aunt Julia's lifestyle doesn't fit into a religious belief. There are some who are born to be at odds with every rule of civilized society, as we call it. Julia is one of them."

"What about you? Were you born to be at odds with every rule of civilized society?"

"No," he said. "No, I wouldn't have become a lawyer, if I were." He paused to consider. "Julia has seen how law and rule and convention can be bent and broken in the art world—the bohemian world—for beauty and individual expression. She hasn't seen how law crumbles in the face of human brutality and savagery, as I have in coming here."

"What does she say of your being here?"

"Actually, she approves."

"She does? Why?"

"In driving an ambulance, I have only one duty, and that's to save lives. I don't have to engage in violence or compromise my own moral beliefs, as the soldiers have to, in killing others. I'm not caught in No Man's Land, either literally or in any other sense. I'm in control of my own actions."

Kathleen smiled. "That was . . . write that down for me, so that I can remember it."

"It wasn't that profound," Paul objected.

"Perhaps not to you, but it was to me." She rifled through the bag and handed him a pencil with the words "Graves Oil" glittering in gold near the end. "But please, don't write it in French."

With a laugh, Paul recorded the words as nearly as he could remember them. "There," he said. "My very American wisdom—for what it's worth—is yours. I even signed and dated it."

"'Paul Everett Reston,'" she read. "'November 4, 1917.'"

He flipped back to the sketch of Major Lloyd-Elliot. "You should ask your Major if you can take his horse for a run sometime."

"I wouldn't dare!"

Paul leaned forward. "If he's wooing Mrs. Brently, he'd probably do it just to impress her. The Brits always want to show off—they're all pride and bluster. 'Have a go, old chap' and that sort of thing."

"You're talking about a feminine conspiracy against Major Lloyd-Elliot."

"Anyone with that pretentious of a name deserves a little ridicule."

They laughed together. From outside came the belch of a motor, the screech of brakes, and, a moment later, the honk of a horn. The *camion* that would carry Paul back to Jaulzy had arrived.

"My transportation is here," he said.

"Oh, no! Already?"

He laid his napkin on the table and rose. Together, they walked to the front door of the hotel. Paul turned toward Kathleen and caught her hand in his. "I'll come back as often as I can."

"Soon, I hope."

"Soon, I promise."

As he bent to kiss her cheek, words rushed into his head: *If I could, I would take you away from all this. From war, from men's bodies broken into pieces, from the sorrow of human cruelty. If I could, I would love you and only you until we were old and had only each other for companionship. I would never leave you.*

He straightened, but the expression on her face jolted him. She was radiant and tender. Had he spoken the words aloud? He could have sworn that she had either heard his declaration or that she was thinking the same thoughts.

She spoke. "Paul, I—"

"Yes?"

"I'm so glad you came today. I . . . I've been thinking of you."

"Every day and every night?"

She laughed, shy again. "Yes."

"I think of you always, no matter where I am."

He touched his lips to her forehead, and she rose up on tiptoe. Her hands found their way to his shoulders, and he put his arms around her. Her fingers brushed through his hair at the nape of his neck, and he pulled her closer.

The *camion* driver blasted a long, angry honk on the horn.

Kathleen looked up at him in surprise, as if the noise had come from one of them. From inside the house, Madame de Troyes began to shout: "*Silence! Arrêtez!*" In response, the *camion* driver blasted the horn again.

Both Paul and Kathleen laughed.

"I'd better go before they start another war," Paul said.

"You might be too late!"

After a hurried peck, Paul opened the door and ran toward the *camion*. As he climbed onto the tarped bed, which was crowded with others hitching a ride, he waved at Kathleen, who was framed by the doorway of the hotel, the sunlight on her hair, her face bright and happy.

She blew him a kiss—the one that had been denied by the *camion*'s return—and the other passengers applauded. Smiling, Paul settled back against the sideboard of the *camion*, unperturbed that the others continued to tease him about the kiss—*le baiser*— or that the driver cursed furiously as he navigated the treacherous, pocked road back to Jaulzy.

TWENTY-THREE

Early one morning, Mrs. Brently came to the girls' room in the hotel in Montdidier. Fully dressed in her uniform and wimple, she sat on the empty bed, which had once been Mary Jane's.

"We are being relocated," she said. "We're to report to Cagny, a town that is near Amiens."

Hank sat up groggily. "Why are we moving?"

"The order has come from the Red Cross in Paris," Mrs. Brently said. "We're to be assigned to the British army now at an auxiliary hospital."

"When do we leave?" Helen asked.

"At noon. A truck will be here at that time to collect us."

"So soon!" Kathleen said. She would have no time to send a message to Paul.

"Evidently there is something happening at a place called Cambrai," Mrs. Brently said. "In fact, I received this yesterday." She read from an official-looking letter. "On November 20, the British Expeditionary Force experienced a splendid success in battle at Cambrai. For the first time, ambulatory military tanks have been used in a surprise attack to crush the German Third Army. The Hindenburg line has been broken, and the Germans are all but defeated. Throughout Britain, the bells have been tolling all night and all day in victory."

"So, the war is over?" Kathleen asked.

"Let's not think on that. Let's think about what we need to do now."

The girls packed as quickly as they could, folding their extra uniforms and civilian clothing into their trunks. Though they had kept their room orderly, they had more possessions now than they had brought with them to France: books sent to them from home that they had shared with one another, trinkets from amorous or grateful soldiers, tins that had once held chocolate but were now perfect for collections of hairpins or needles and thread or other trifles. Carefully, Kathleen bundled her letters from home into a neat package and rolled her sketches and tied them with string. As the little room grew bare, the girls looked on it with a newly-blossomed nostalgia.

"Our first French home," Hank said.

"Our first chance to help the soldiers," Helen said. "Oh, I wish they had been American."

"But, isn't it best that America never had to fight?"

"Oh, of course, it is, but—"

Kathleen glanced out the window to where the twin spires of Saint-Sépulcre were visible. *The place where I fell in love,* she thought. In moving to Amiens, she would be farther from the town where Paul was stationed. It was only a distance of fifty-some kilometers—thirty miles or so—but it seemed so much farther in this country where nothing was safe. Yet, if the war were truly over . . .

The girls heaved their trunks down the narrow staircase to the lobby of the hotel in the same way that they had taken them up—by passing them from one to the other over the banister.

"You'd think this would be easier going down," Hank grumbled. "But it's not."

"Let's hope our next home is on the ground floor," Helen said.

At the bottom of the staircase, they found Madame de Troyes, weeping into a handkerchief. "*Je vous aime, mes belles filles.*" She opened her arms, and each of the girls stepped forward to embrace her. When Kathleen hugged her, she said, "*Prenez bien soin de Monsieur le Conducteur Américain. Il vous aime.*"

Kathleen's eyes teared. Madame de Troyes was asking her to take good care of Paul. "*Merci, Madame. Je suis desolé d'aller.*"

"*Enfin! Vous avez appris à parler français.*"

Kathleen laughed. *At last! You have learned to speak French.*

All of France, it seemed, was on its way to Amiens. The lorry that came to fetch the girls snaked and jimmied a path through hundreds of trucks, mule trains, and columns of muddied, marching soldiers in British drab. More than once, it pulled aside as ammunition trucks or ambulances crawled through the traffic, blasting their horns to clear the way. The drivers quarreled, bringing their vehicles within inches of one another. In the ditches along the side of the road, civilians watched the jammed-up vehicles, their eyes blank, their faces gaunt. A few pushed hand carts piled with ragged belongings; others had nothing in their hands or on their backs.

Mrs. Brently sat in the front with the driver, leaving the girls alone in the tarped back. As they were jostled by the swaying truck, Helen asked, "What do you want to do first when you go home?"

"I want to sit in a bathtub full of hot water for six days," Hank said. "I don't care if I'm as shrunken and pruney as an old lady when I get out."

"I want to eat my mother's cooking," Helen said. "I miss it so."

"What about you, Kathleen?" Hank said.

The prospect of returning to the typing pool at Graves Oil flickered through Kathleen's mind. Never again, she vowed. "I'm going to get married," she said boldly.

"Ah," Hank sang. "*À Monsieur Reston?*"

"*Oui, à Monsieur Reston.*"

As Hank laughed, Helen said, "I'm happy for you, Kathleen. I'm sorry if I haven't always been."

"I want to be a bridesmaid," Hank announced.

"You will be, both of you," Kathleen said. "And Mary Jane, too, and my cousin, Maggie, who'll be matron of honor."

"What if you get married here in France?" Helen asked.

"Mrs. Brently will be the matron of honor!" Hank said.

"Oh, no, I can't!" Kathleen said. "She's so much prettier than I am."

At that, they laughed, their high spirits spilling from the truck as it jounced through the ruts toward Amiens.

Upon their arrival in Cagny, they discovered that they were to be housed on an estate that spread over rolling hills. The lawns had been tramped away by the hundreds of parading soldiers billeted in bivouacs near the woods, and the neatly graveled roads ground to dust by passing cavalry and lorries, but the woods in the distance were pristine, with a smoky blue haze barely obscuring them. The entire estate was fortified by a stone wall that looked as if it had stood for centuries.

Yet, inside, the chateau was rapidly transforming into a modern hospital. The ancient, valuable books in the massive library were being concealed behind boards that were nailed onto the shelves, and the graceful furniture, piled on wagons, was being carted away. The many bedrooms and dressing rooms had been tagged with handwritten signs: "Operating Theater, Flesh Wounds," "Operating Theater, Amputation," "Operating Theater, Face Wounds." Around every corner of the massive home, medical personnel bustled: doctors, nurses, orderlies, administrative workers, VADs.

Hank eyed Kathleen with raised eyebrows as they passed room after room designated as recovery wards. "I wonder what they're expecting," she said.

"More than we've seen so far," Helen said. "But . . . if the British have won the war—"

"They'll still have wounded," Kathleen said quietly. "I don't think winning is much different from losing for the soldiers."

The room on the third floor where the girls were to stay had once housed a single maid. Mrs. Brently and the British matron in charge of the nurses would stay in a room down the hall that was twice the size.

Helen looked mournfully at the three iron cots wedged into the room. "Where will our trunks go?"

Kathleen walked to a slotted window. In the distance, a stream cut its way through the lawns, tripped over a demure waterfall, and collected in a serene lake. A footbridge across the lake led to an island that sported a gazebo. The perfect symmetry of a once-tended garden was still visible around the gazebo, although the carefully-sculpted shrubs had long since lost their shapes.

"Look," she said. "It's beautiful."

Hank and Helen gathered around her. Almost at once, Helen said, "Look below."

A string of British ambulances was already traveling up the main road toward the courtyard to the chateau, where the women drivers leaped from their vehicles to oversee the unloading of wounded.

The signs on the rooms of the chateau were prophetic: nearly every type of wound came to the auxiliary hospital at the chateau once the base hospital was full. The ambulances arrived throughout the night, and by morning, the wounded carpeted the floor of the Great Hall, where the stretchers were placed in long rows, only a bare inch or two between them. Walking cases leaned against every available wall, with their arms or legs in splints or with bandages around their heads. Men writhed and moaned in pain, while orderlies squatted near them, cutting the uniforms away from the wounds. Other soldiers were limp and lifeless, their eyes glazed over. Nurses bustled to and fro, checking the tags that were attached to each man and choosing the next to receive care.

On duty by 6:30 in the morning, Hank and Kathleen were assigned to oversee the wounded that were waiting for critical operations to save their lives. The girls' job was to make sure that the men didn't tear off the bandages that had been applied so hastily at the clearing stations. If they did, the bleeding could start again, and the men might die.

"I wish they'd given us rope," Hank said, as she held the right hand and Kathleen clutched the left of a man who was raving and moaning. His entire chest was covered with a seeping bandage, and a bandage looped around his head, covering his left eye. The skin on his face was burned and raw. "We'd just tie their hands down."

Kathleen said nothing. So this was what winning the war looked like. This was what the end looked like. Surely, it was as great a victory as the letter that Mrs. Brently had read made it out to be, but the price paid by these men was far too high. When it was all over, how many of them would be well enough to celebrate? How many of them would never be well again?

Late in the day, Hank and Kathleen found themselves hauling mattresses up a winding, Medieval stone staircase to a gallery that had recently been designated as an overflow patient ward. The gallery was bitterly cold, and the windows were frosted with rime. Kathleen touched one of the iron bed frames that had been set up. The cold of the metal sent a sting up her arm. The careful planning that had gone into the other wards was absent here. The original furniture was piled haphazardly in a corner, without protective sheets to shield it. Two British engineers were poking around the gaping fireplace in the center of the gallery, trying to install a potbellied stove.

"Oh, boy!" Hank eyed the two rows of cots that stretched from one end of the room to the other. "And you thought we were cold in the morning."

She slapped a thin, straw-stuffed mattress on the nearest bed, while Kathleen walked the long, narrow gallery, taking in its beauty. The ceiling was painted a brilliant turquoise, with a delicate cherub peeking out from behind fluffy white clouds at each corner. In the center, a latticed gold star spread outward, its points drawing the eye to the cherubs. Along the interior wall, which was painted a verdant green with gold flourishes, portraits were hung at multiple heights, the more than life-sized faces staring down from golden frames. Dust-laden nameplates were attached at the bottom of each likeness—"Henri Delorme, Comte de Desjardins," "Madame de Charles, Duchesse de Desjardins"—dating back for hundreds of years.

Kathleen drew in a deep breath, marveling at the talent. How did an artist learn to paint with such life-like detail? *Look at the hand here, the eyes there. Look at the ring on this one's finger—it looks as if you could pluck it from the painting and wear it.*

Stepping back, she tried to imagine the scale of the cherubs on the ceiling. This is what Jim had talked about, she realized. The angels, which were probably twenty feet above her head, could not have been created without some sort of guide, such as a grid. She should write to him and tell him about it. Better yet, she would sketch it for him—properly proportioned and all.

"Kathleen!" Hank hissed. "What are you doing? They're looking at you like you're a pint of Guinness."

Kathleen glanced toward the staring engineers, then went to help Hank. Grabbing one end of a mattress, she tried to flatten it against a plank bed. The mattress lay in a lumpy ball. She pounded on it with her fists, to no avail.

"Ugh." Hank scratched at her wrists. "These mattresses have fleas."

Throughout the afternoon, the two girls labored up and down the steps, each of them carrying two mattresses at a time, slung over their shoulders like hunks of meat. When, at last, every bedstead was covered with a mattress, Hank sat down on one, wiping the sweat from her forehead.

She squinted at the portraits along the walls and the cherubs in the corners of the ceiling. "They'd better not put the shell shockers in here," she said. "They'll think they've died and gone to You Know Where—all those eyes watching them!"

"I think it's supposed to be heaven," Kathleen said. "Cherubim and seraphim and all that."

"What-a-fim?" Hank asked.

Kathleen pointed at the ceiling. "Angels."

"Up there, maybe, but look at them." Hank nodded toward the wall of family portraits. "Look at her—she's ugly enough to make milk curdle."

"Hank," Kathleen scolded half-heartedly as she looked upward at the ceiling. "Humans have the ability to create buildings and paintings as beautiful as these, and yet they use their talents to make weapons that kill and maim and hurt men beyond recognition. You have to wonder why."

Hank looked at the cherubs. "I don't want to wonder why," she said. "It would make me too sad." She brightened. "Have you heard from Paul Reston?"

Kathleen did not answer at once. She had sent him the news of their move to Amiens via a *camion* driver who was bound for Croutoy, a few miles from where Paul was stationed.

"Not yet," she said. "I just hope the driver was honest. I paid him two francs."

"Two francs!" Hank said. "That's *true* highway robbery!"

Kathleen laughed. Just then, two stretcher bearers appeared at the top of the winding steps that led to the gallery, twisting and maneuvering, trying to make the last turn. Roughly, they banged the stretcher against the wall. The wounded man on it made no sound, and the stretcher bearers gave no apology as they carried the soldier across to a bed at the end of the gallery.

"Oh, oh," Hank whispered. "It's the 'Rob All My Comrades' boys."

Kathleen put a hand over her mouth to hide her smile. Hank referred to the RAMC, the Royal Army Medical Corps, which had earned the nickname because of the number of wounded who swore that their pockets had been picked before they reached the hospital.

"We'd better go before we're trapped up here," Kathleen said.

Downstairs, in the cluttered Great Hall, the girls inched their way through the stretchers. At one point, Kathleen came across a young man whose uniform had been cut away, and whose blood had soaked the shoulder of his undershirt and dried into a daisy-shaped stain.

"He was here yesterday," Kathleen said to Hank. "I remember the stain."

"How many days do you think it will be before they get to him?"

"Girls!" a sharp voice sounded, and both Hank and Kathleen stopped.

A British VAD had hailed them. "Can you take over water duty?"

"Yes, ma'am," Kathleen said. "We'll need to check in with our supervisor first."

At the canteen, which was located in a side room off the Great Hall, they found Mrs. Brently standing over a boiling pot, her bangs limp in the steam, her starched wimple wilted. Helen sawed wildly at a loaf of bread, cutting it into inch-wide slices. Behind the two women were stacks of crates.

"Our supplies have come," Mrs. Brently called. "Quick, grab a knife and help Helen to make jam sandwiches. I'm making hard-boiled eggs. From what we've heard, some of these men haven't eaten in days."

"We've been asked to help with water duty," Kathleen said.

Mrs. Brently dabbed at her face with a handkerchief. "All right," she said. "But come back in twenty minutes when the eggs and soup are ready."

Kathleen wended her way through the Great Hall, taking the patients near the door, while Hank covered those near the main staircase. The girls carried with them soft cloths to dab the men's foreheads and chins, a sack of jam sandwiches, and the water pitchers. Pouring into a tin cup, Kathleen would offer a drink, swab the lip of the cup, and use it for the next soldier. Anyone who could sit up to chew received a jam sandwich.

But there were so many—too many—and they called out frantically for relief. "Nurse," they said, mistaking her, "Where is the doctor?" or "Can I go home now?" Kathleen soothed them as best she could, deftly avoiding the answers to the questions.

She heard a commotion at the door of the chateau and glanced up. Twenty or so soldiers shuffled along, each with his right hand on the shoulder of the man ahead of him. Gauze was wound around their eyes.

Hank came up beside her, her pitcher empty. "What's all this?"

"They must have been gassed," Kathleen said.

A lieutenant ordered the men to take a seat along the wall. With their hands, they inched their way down the wall and sat, helpless and blind. Then, the Lieutenant left, and the men were on their own to wait for medical help.

"They'll be there for hours," Kathleen said. "If they sweat or spill water on any part of their bodies, they could start the agony again."

"I guess there's not much we can do about it," Hank sighed. "I've heard that the Germans used flamethrowers, too. It melts everything, even their teeth if they're caught straight-on."

Kathleen turned away. *Dear God, don't let any of them come here.* Shamed by her thoughts, she went back to work. She kept her eyes averted from the carnage—it wasn't as easy this time as it had been on her first night in Montdidier. Then, she had reacted without thinking about it. She recalled Paul's words from her first night in Montdidier: *Think of the good you're doing. Don't think about what's happened here.* Today, though, she felt not just revulsion, but anger. How could men do this to each other? What was the point of it all?

Throughout the day, she spooned soup into the mouths of men barely able to lift their heads, or fetched bags of *cotons,* or square bandages, or took the names of the wounded. She tried not to feel the heaviness of exhaustion in her arms and legs, or to count the number of bodies that lay on the floor, or on the lawns outside, or in the outbuildings that had been commandeered for overflow. Still, the casualties kept arriving—everything from a cut hand to men whose limbs or faces were gone, blasted away by a mortar or grenade.

Late in the afternoon, Kathleen went out on water duty again. A number of times, she walked by the young man with the daisy-like blood stain, and still he lay there. Once, when she passed, his eyes were open but uncomprehending. She offered him a sandwich, but he simply stared at her.

Realization dawned on her. "*Wasser*?" she asked.

"*Danke.*"

As he drank from the cup, she wondered: Should she be kind to him? Was she supposed to comfort him? He was the enemy. But he was also a young man far from home, no different from Seaney. But he was German—the cause of all this misery. But she had come to France to offer whatever help she could, and no one—not Mrs. Brently or the American Red Cross—had told her that she should help some and exclude others. And Jim had said that all men were the same, regardless of their loyalties. But . . . but . . .

"God bless you," she said quietly, then moved on.

At the canteen, the eggs had run out, and Helen was now cutting the bread in the thinnest slices she could. Mrs. Brently dabbed a bit of jam on them and handed them to the hungry. Kathleen took over spooning watery soup into tin bowls and serving coffee and hot chocolate with Hank.

Suddenly, Hank let out a whoop. "Mrs. Brently! Look!"

Kathleen followed Hank's pointed finger. Standing in the doorway of the canteen were three men in the khaki colored uniforms of the United States of America.

"This is the day we have been waiting for, ladies," Mrs. Brently said. "Straighten your uniforms. Look your best. These are our boys."

She left the canteen and walked toward the soldiers. They doffed their caps and shook her hand. She led them back to the canteen.

"Girls," she said. "This is Eddie Fairbanks from Portland, Oregon, Johnny Tapp from Brownstown, Indiana, and Davy Beringer from New York City." She introduced the girls before saying to the soldiers, "You are the first American soldiers we've met in our time here."

"We're from the 11th Engineers," Davy said. "We were building roads up near Gouzeaucourt when all of a sudden the Heines came to visit."

"They thought they'd eat breakfast in Paris," Johnny added.

"But we said no." Davy teased with a wink.

Spontaneously, Hank put her hand over her heart and started to sing, *"O-oh, say can you see, By the dawn's early light—"*

Kathleen and Helen joined her, singing as proudly and as loudly as they could. The three soldiers and Mrs. Brently sang as well. Tears welled up in Kathleen's eyes—oh, how she missed home.

After the song ended and cheers were shared all around, Mrs. Brently said, "I suspect you want something to eat."

She and Helen prepared a meal of soup, sandwiches and coffee for the men, while Hank found three chairs for them.

"I want you to sit right here, where I can hear every word you say," she said. "I want to hear English spoken the right way, without any swoops at the ends of the words"—her voice went up—"or without it sounding like the most boring school marm in the world."

"The French and the British, huh?" Davy said.

"That's right."

"You haven't seen many Americans yet?"

"Only the ambulance drivers," Hank said. "They come in now and then."

Davy looked at Eddie. "*Croix de Guerre* hunters, you mean."

"What?" Kathleen asked.

"Everybody in the States knows what they're up to," Eddie said. "College boys, too afraid to fight. So they join up with the French, and they stay behind the Front, pretendin' to be doin' their part, when all they're doin' is tryin' to get a medal pinned on their uniforms without ever seein' a real, live German."

"That's not—"

"Why are you here?" Helen asked. "You aren't wounded."

Davy spoke. "Some of our boys are. We came to visit, but they're out there"—he pointed with his chin—"somewhere. We've heard that we had about seventy casualties."

"Are they the first Americans soldiers to be wounded?"

"I don't know," Davy said. "Must be pretty close."

"Well, when we find them, we'll make sure they get extra special treatment," Hank said.

And so, the day continued into evening and the evening into night. With the arrival of the Americans, the girls forgot that they had been on their feet for hours, and that the air coming into the drafty chateau was cold and damp, and that they would probably have no sleep that night. They chattered with Davy and the others. When Kathleen went out on water duty late in the night, she made it a point to check on the German soldier. The second time she passed, he was gone, his piece of floor taken by a Tommie.

TWENTY-FOUR

Paul picked his way along a road—or what was left of it—in his Packard. In the past, the road had led to Havrincourt, but the Germans had long since overrun that city. Only an hour or two of darkness remained, and he wanted to reach and leave the *poste de sécours* before daylight. Beside him, Latour seemed as stoic as ever, smoking a Sweet Caporal that he had begged off an American lieutenant at Allonville.

He began to sing, *"Quand la guerre est fini, les Tommie soldats partis, Laissez les pauvres Françaises, Un souvenir Bébé."*

Paul laughed. When the war is over, the Tommies will go home, Leaving the poor French women, a souvenir baby.

"Il n'a même pas de sens," he said, complaining about the atrocious grammar of the song.

Latour shrugged. *"Mais c'est vrai."*

But it's true.

Paul made no reply.

The Packard shuddered and leaped forward on the road as a concussion from a mortar round jolted it. Ahead, a black jumble appeared, outlined by the phosphorus rounds that were being sent up near the trenches. Paul braked the car just as the ground rocked beneath them with the explosion of another shell not more than a few hundred feet away. Anxiously, he searched the darkness ahead. The teams of horses that hauled supplies to the Front spooked when the shells fell near them. They became uncontrollable, running over anything that was in their way to get away from the noise. They could trample men to death or jostle cars—even one as heavy as the Packard—into ditches, leaving their drivers and passengers bleeding and dazed.

He could distinguish nothing in the darkness of the road ahead. "What now?" he asked Latour.

"*Je vais voir,*" Latour said, climbing out of the car.

Paul waited. By now, everyone knew that Cambrai was a rout for the British. The Royal Tank Corps had been hopelessly ineffective after the first assault, its tanks stuck or upended or broken down into heaps of metal, and as so often happened in this war, the Germans had somehow known that there was to be an attack. It felt like Ypres all over again, where British men died from the stupidity of their commanders, and the exhausted French troops were left to clean up after them. What was thought to be the end was only another beginning.

Latour returned from his search. Speaking English, he said, "There is much up there that is wrong. The shell hit directly in the *centre* of the road, and it killed who knows what—the drivers, horses, *les bonhommes*—and destroyed the *camions* behind. They are trying to untangle it all."

"Can we get through?"

He shrugged. "*Vous pouvez essayer.*"

You can try.

It was as good as he was going to get, Paul knew. He urged the Packard forward, passing a shattered wagon, the mangled horses scattered across the road, the driver lying dead nearby. The bodies of several soldiers had been recovered from the road and laid out in a long row on one side. A few feet beyond, a group of French soldiers, who had probably been sent to bury them, were sitting in the mud, smoking.

Paul traveled only a little way before the road was once again blocked.

"I'll take a look," he told Latour.

He climbed from the Packard. The ground shook beneath him as shells fell along the trenches. Even from this distance, dirt and *éclats* swirled in the air. Along the Front, the phosphorus bursts kept the sky ablaze with sickly-white light. At a pool of mud, a gang of French soldiers had gathered around others who stood knee-deep in the ooze. Using lengths of board or long rods of metal that they had salvaged from the ruin, the men plied the mud, trying to dislodge something. Paul stepped forward. All that was visible in the mud was a man's back. The rest of his body had sunk into the mess.

"*Un, deux, trois!*"

The soldiers leaned on the makeshift levers and tried to lift the man upward. Nothing happened, even after a second attempt. A soldier near Paul remarked calmly, "*Trop nombreux ont sauté sur lui. Il est coincé indéfiniment.*"

Too many have stepped on him. He is stuck forever.

Evidently the officer in charge agreed, for the order was given to assemble and march. As Paul watched, the column tramped through the mud toward the Front. He stood transfixed, his eyes on the spot where the man had been lost, his stomach and heart knotted, a voice within him still crying, *My God, you cannot leave him, you cannot refuse to rescue him.*

But once the column had passed, Paul could see there was no indication that a man had ever slumped to the ground on that spot. He was gone, all trace of him obliterated in the mud that had glazed over, smooth and icy. What would be told to his mother, his wife or children? That a man's life was worth so little in this world that he could be left behind like a newspaper that had been dropped on the ground? Dazed, Paul walked back to the Packard.

"*Ce qui se passe?*" Latour asked.

Paul slid into the driver's seat. "We can't go farther. *Trop de boue.*"

He swallowed a couple of times. Why should the soldier's death in the mud bother him so? He had seen far worse in the past year and a half. But everything seemed more dire now, now that his love for Kathleen was at stake. It made him both afraid for the two of them and equally determined to do his work to the best of his abilities, all for her.

Out of the darkness, a single rider galloped up on his horse. In the dying light of the phosphorus round, a French lieutenant hailed Paul. The man's uniform was slathered with mud to his knees. His horse was covered up to its shoulder.

Paul leaned out. *"Qu'est que c'est, Monsieur?"*

"Vous ne pouvez pas aller dans cette direction," the Lieutenant answered. *"Les routes sont fermées. Vous devez retourner."*

"The roads are closed," Latour remarked unnecessarily. "We must go back."

"Oui, Monsieur, nous allons retourner," Paul replied to the Lieutenant.

The Lieutenant shouted commands to the loitering soldiers behind them to clear the way. Paul began to back up, trying to stay on course by leaning far out the driver's side, while Latour leaned out the other and shouted directions.

At last, he found a space that was large enough for the Packard to turn around. He reversed, cranked the steering wheel, and pulled forward, trying not to bury the tires in the slop of mud. He had maneuvered the Packard around and started down the road when he caught movement from the corner of his eye. About twenty men had risen from the darkness beyond the road. Some appeared to be crawling through the muddy craters left by shells. Others were clinging to the backs or shoulders of their comrades. Blood-stained bandages trailed from their heads, arms, legs and torsos, unraveling with every step in the mud. Two of them dragged a wounded man behind them. Others bore an unconscious man between them, their arms linked around his shoulders.

"Aidez nous, s'il vous plaît!" one of them called.

"What's happened?" Paul asked in French. "Where did you come from?

"Le poste de sécours a été bombardé. Nous sommes tous cela est laissé."

"Le médicin?"

"Il est mort."

The *poste de secours* must have taken a direct hit in the bombardment, Paul realized, killing the doctor and most of the *blessés*. Those who stood in front of him were all that had survived. Quickly, he nodded toward the unconscious men. "Bring them here," he said. "Let us take them."

With Latour's help, he loaded three into the back of the Packard. As he turned around, one of the soldiers called, *"Moi aussi!"*

Others joined in the commotion. *"Non, non, moi, c'est moi!"*

"Non, non, s'il vous plaît, ne pas nous quitter!"

The *blessés* surged forward, clamoring at Paul. One grabbed Latour by the shoulder, shoving a bloody arm into his face, begging him to let him ride in the ambulance. A man with a stomach wound removed his hand, and blood gushed, dripping on the ground near Paul's feet. Paul took a step backward, flattening himself against the side of the Packard as they pleaded. *Look, look, my leg already stinks with gangrene. But I was lying on the battlefield for three days before they found me. Look, my head is bleeding, a bullet has gone in through my eye. See, I have counted fifty wounds from* les éclats *in my back and sides. I will die—*

Latour jerked away from the soldier who had grabbed his shoulder and called to Paul, *"Monsieur, ils vont nous emporter."*

They will overwhelm us.

Paul's head swam. Latour was right—if too many climbed on or clung to the Packard, it would mire in the mud, and they would all be trapped here. Pointing at the five *blessés* that looked most injured to him, he said, *"Vous, vous, vous, vous, et vous. Personne d'autre."*

"Mais, je vais mourir!"

"Non, personne d'autre," Paul said. No one else.

The chosen ones lurched toward the Packard, tearing open the doors before Paul or Latour could reach them, and climbing aboard. The others tried to follow, shouting and crying now, shoving one another, desperate to reach the ambulance. They grabbed at each other's ragged bodies and beat at each other's wounds. One of the soldiers pummeled the man with the stomach injury until he fell into the ditch. Those already in the ambulance kicked and punched viciously at those who were trying to board.

"*Arrêtez!*" Paul shouted. "*Arrêtez, maintenant!*"

A soldier whose face was wrapped in a filthy bandage hobbled to the front of Packard and laid himself across the hood of the car, his hands clenched around the headlamp. Latour grabbed him by the collar and cast him to the ground. "*Laissez-nous aller!*" he shouted to Paul. "Let's go, now!"

Paul ran for the driver's side of the car and jumped inside. Latour swung aboard as Paul twisted the steering wheel wildly, trying to slide through the mud of the road without bogging down. He drove as quickly as he could, dodging the traffic that had clogged the road farther to the west. His heart pounded, and his stomach was so tight he could hardly breathe. A few miles down the road, hundreds of *camions* filled with rations and ammunition, mules pulling supply wagons and cannons, and masses of soldiers were stalled behind a military blockade. A French soldier waved the ambulance through to the main road to Compiègne.

Paul glanced in the mirror that was attached just outside the driver's side. He could see a conflagration behind him, mostly likely another shell that had set whatever was left behind on fire. Even from here, he imagined he could hear the swell of screams and shouts, the agonies of the dying and deserted.

Just as the French commander had left the man in the mud to die, Paul was certain that he had condemned the *blessés* who were left behind to their deaths.

TWENTY-FIVE

A knock on the door roused Kathleen from sleep. She rose from her bed and immediately stumbled over the leg of Hank's bed, set so close to hers in this room that had once housed a single maid. Opening the door to the narrow corridor, she saw Mrs. Brently, standing beside Major Lloyd-Elliot, who carried a lantern. Shadowy faces crowded in behind them.

"Kathleen," Mrs. Brently said smoothly. "We have been asked to give over our beds for the wounded. I want you and Hank and Helen to gather your sleeping bags and clothing for tomorrow and come downstairs to the canteen with me."

"Yes, ma'am."

Sleepily, the girls gathered what they needed and went into the hallway. Already, the narrow corridor was lined on one side with stretchers. As soon as Helen, who was the last one to leave the room, was clear of the door, a man with a head injury was carried inside. Up and down the hallway, others were being chased from their rooms. Even the nurses, who slept only a few hours each night, were awake and packing.

There were no cots set up for them in the canteen. Kathleen spread her sleeping bag across the marble floor. She was chilled already, just from walking from the top floor of the chateau to the ground floor. In the little room, cold drafts battered a door that led to the courtyard outside. She blew out her candle and pulled the bag up over her head.

Soon, she became aware of movement near her head and around the curves of her sleeping bag. She could hear Hank and

Helen shifting in their bags as well. Finally, Kathleen raised her head and looked out. In the darkness, lit only by the moonlight from outside, she saw a mouse scurrying along the floor.

"Oh!" she said, sitting up. Mice were scavenging on the floor, unafraid of the humans in their midst. Kathleen tried to count them, but soon, it appeared as if the entire floor was swarming with them.

Helen twisted upright. "One's in my bag!" She grabbed the bag by the end and shook it fiercely.

Hank lit her candle. "We swept before we closed up. Why are they here?"

"Let's sweep again," Helen suggested.

Hank swept while Kathleen and Helen wiped down the tables again. Behind the counter, they checked for anything that might attract the vermin. When they all lay down, ready to sleep, they clustered closer together, seeking protection in each other.

But it was no use. Sleep evaded Kathleen through the night. She was cold, the floor was unspeakably hard, and she was afraid the mice would come back and nibble at her or build nests in her hair. She knew that mice must be climbing all over the suffering, wounded men in the Great Hall. With effort, she kept herself from waking Hank and Helen with a plea to go and help the poor souls.

When Mrs. Brently came into the canteen in the morning, she looked as haggard as Kathleen felt. Evidently, she had had no more restful of a night.

"You can use the nurses' dressing area to change your clothes," she said. "Then, it's to work."

The canteen opened at ten, with Hank and Helen working furiously to keep up with the streams of soldiers that came in, cold and hungry. At noon, Kathleen was called to assist in the Gas Ward. Every man in the ward was to receive oxygen for twenty minutes from a massive metal tank that was wheeled from bed to bed. Her job was to hold the mask over the mouths and noses of those who could not do it for themselves. As she moved from man to man, she wondered if she was helping those who had been left to sit in the Great Hall the day before. Or was it the day before? Maybe it was two days ago or a week ago—she had lost track of time. In the afternoon, she helped the nurses give the men alkaline baths. Her job was to gently pour water mixed with baking soda over their blistered and swollen flesh as they sat in a copper tub while the nurse inspected the skin to see that it was not broken and infected.

When she went downstairs to check in with Mrs. Brently, the Great Hall was crowded with more wounded. A steady stream of stretcher-bearers carried the worst cases directly to the operating theaters, moving in and out with the same tedious precision as a colony of ants. Orderlies followed, mopping up blood and mud from the marble floor.

Late in the evening, as Kathleen wearily plodded through another round of water duty, Hank found her in the Great Hall.

"Guess who?" Hank said with delight.

"What?" Kathleen asked, too tired to think.

"He's here! *Monsieur le Conducteur Américain*! Here, I brought your cape. He's outside the garden door. I'll tell Mrs. Brently that you needed a few minutes to rest."

"Thank you, Hank," Kathleen said. Grabbing her cape, she went outside into the darkness. Only a dim light shone from the chateau, where most of the windows were masked. Paul stood near a small, bricked-in courtyard that had quickly become a popular smoking place for the orderlies and other hospital workers.

She rushed to him, and he opened his arms and pulled her into an embrace. He looked as if he had not slept in days, and a dark growth of beard covered his cheeks and chin.

"I only have a moment," he said. "I'm on my way back to Aumale—"

"I'm so glad you got my note—!"

"I'm relieved you weren't sent farther away."

"I thought only the British were in this battle."

"Who do you think takes up the rear when the first troops are worn down?"

"Oh, of course," she said. "I'm just . . . I'm tired, that's all. It's been so much worse this time. I don't know if it's because we were so happily settled in Montdidier or—"

"Kathleen." His voice was desperate. "I had to see you, I needed to talk to you."

"What's wrong?" she cried. "What happened?"

"This morning, at . . . I can't remember where, I was waiting for the *brancardiers* to bring up the wounded. I could see them—a dozen or more—coming up the trench. But when they reached the end, they turned and went the other way. I called to them that I was waiting and one of them said, *'Il n'y a pas de blessés. Tous sont morts.'*"

He spoke quickly, and Kathleen could not catch the words. "What?" she asked. "I didn't understand—"

"There are no wounded," Paul said. "All are dead."

"Oh, Paul." Kathleen ran her fingers down his cheek, and he grabbed her hand, holding it between his own. "Oh, no—"

"Sometimes I don't know why I do this," he said. "I don't know why I stay here. The little that I do means nothing—"

"Oh, don't leave me, please don't leave me."

"That's just it." He kissed her forehead. "I can't leave. Every time I think of it, I think of you, and I can't go. Come away with me, we'll go home together. I have never felt such sweetness and desire as I do with you—"

He kissed her—once, twice, and more. She wanted him, she realized, as much as he wanted her. She wanted him to touch her, to hold her, to lie beside her and . . . How was it that they had fallen in love, so quickly, so fiercely, without any sort of hesitation or doubt?

"Monsieur Reston?" A voice sounded from behind her.

The weariness returned to Paul's face. *"Oui, très bien,"* he said. "I need to go."

"I'll be here, whenever you can come again—"

He kissed her forehead, and then hurried around the corner of the chateau to the street beyond. She followed, watching as he climbed into the driver's side of the Packard, while his French aide took the passenger's seat. As the ambulance rolled out of the courtyard, the Frenchman waved merrily at her.

She pulled her cape around her. From inside the chateau, she could hear the pulsing drone of those who sought to save lives and ease the pain of dying. Outside the chateau, the gravel of the drive crunched as ambulances and wagons and the ever-present *camions* pulled up before the wide doors and unloaded their grievous loads. Suddenly, it all seemed too much—too much sorrow and destruction, too much ugliness. She wanted to call Paul back, to take him up on his offer escape from all this, to be free of worry and grief and exhaustion.

A match was struck nearby, and the flame flared long enough to illuminate the face of Eddie Fairbanks. Kathleen inhaled sharply, afraid.

"That was a pretty scene," Eddie said.

"I didn't know you were—"

"Why are you chasin' that *Croix de Guerre* hunter?"

"I'm not chasing—"

"Cowards is what we call 'em in Oregon, honey," he said. "No better than conscientious objectors. And you know what Uncle Sam is doin' with them? Sendin' 'em to Alcatraz to do hard labor."

"You know nothing about it," she lashed.

She turned to go inside the canteen, but Eddie's voice followed her. "Ask him sometime why he don't join up like the rest of us—"

She ran inside and shut the door behind her, trembling.

At the canteen, Hank was serving hot cocoa. Mrs. Brently and Helen were not in sight. "What happened?" Hank demanded. "What did he do to you?"

For a moment, Kathleen thought that Hank meant Eddie. "Nothing," she said. "It's just—"

"Oh, come on, Kathleen, I'm not Helen. I'm not going to get all prissy on you."

A sob burst from Kathleen's throat. "It wasn't him. He's . . . he's wonderful."

"Well, then, come over here and tell me." Hank embraced her. "And don't cry in the cocoa. It's watery enough. We've run out of powder."

Early in the morning, unable to sleep, Kathleen leaves the canteen, where the girls are still bedding down on the floor. At the end of a long corridor that breaks off from the Great Hall is an arched window that overlooks the courtyard. As she steps up next to the window, she sees the end of a cigarette glowing in the darkness and the faint sheen of a square white collar.

"Mrs. Brently?" Kathleen whispers.

The cigarette tip moves quickly toward the floor, and a foot squelches it.

"You don't need to do that," Kathleen says. "I don't mind."

"It's against our rules." Mrs. Brently gives a silvery laugh. "All the same, would you like one?"

"No, thank you."

Mrs. Brently takes another cigarette from her case. In the light from the full moon, her hair is sleek and shining, her skin flawless. "I don't think I've hated the war as much as I do today," she confesses. "I've seen enough of wounds and torn up flesh. I don't see how these people have borne this for so many years."

Kathleen says nothing, unsure how to respond.

"I'm sorry I exposed such innocent, sweet girls as you and Hank and Helen to this." She inhales, and the glowing end of the cigarette flares. "I was mistaken about our mission here. I was . . . naïve."

"No, you're wrong," Kathleen says, then quickly adds, "I'm sorry, that sounded rude." She swallows. "I wanted to do this . . . I *want* to do it. I, well, I sort of . . . I broke the rules to come, and I don't regret it at all."

"So you did." She laughs weakly. "And I'm glad you did. I like you, Kathleen. You have a good heart. I believe that is what my brother sees in you as well."

"Oh," Kathleen says, surprised and pleased. "Thank you."

Mrs. Brently digs in the pocket of her dress and hands Kathleen an envelope. "I received this a few days ago and haven't had the chance to give it to you when we were alone. It's a letter from Jim."

"For me?"

"For you, alone, not for the others. I suspect part of it is to scold you for not sending sketches. You aren't holding out on us, are you?"

Kathleen panics. In the bottom of her trunk are the sketches of Paul, and of the tea cups, and Mme. de Troyes, and the *camion*—all drawn after the day he visited her in Montdidier. She has neglected everything to work on them—letters to her parents and Aunt Maury and Maggie, and even to Seaney and Jim. In the sketches, she focused on capturing Paul's features—his lovely gray eyes, his polished smile, his even profile—yet none of them show enough grace in his eyes or gentleness in his mouth. Every sketch is of a good-looking man. It isn't of *him*.

"No," she says quickly. "I haven't had time, but I want to sketch some of this place, if we have time before we go."

"Before we go?"

"Didn't you say the war might be over?"

"Oh, no, Kathleen," Mrs. Brently says. "I think that everything that was gained has been lost again."

"Oh," Kathleen says, stunned. "Then our army will have to fight."

"Mostly likely." Mrs. Brently blows out a dainty stream of smoke. "I don't think Jim understands our situation here. In fact, I don't believe anyone could possibly understand it unless they were here. When we go home, there will be a difference between those who've lived through it and those who haven't. I think we will feel . . . grateful, perhaps, to have lived so fully. I think we will continue to live as if it could all end tomorrow."

Her words catch Kathleen's imagination. In dealing with so much death and dying, they must live well and completely, aware of how precious each day is. Not to do so would be a sin.

"May I ask you something?" she asks.

"Of course."

She tells Mrs. Brently of the German soldier that she'd helped. "What was I supposed to do? Was I to treat him the same as the others?"

"What did you do?"

"I gave him water, but I didn't know how to talk to him. So I just said, 'God bless you.' I know he didn't understand."

"He might have. The German word for God isn't all that different. And he would have known from your voice that you carried no ill will toward him."

"So I did what I should have?"

"Do you really need to ask me that? You know the answer."

"Mr. Graves—Jim—told me that the Germans aren't any different from us."

"Did he, now?" Mrs. Brently said. "That certainly wasn't very politic of him. Then again, he rarely does what's expected."

She looks out the window, where an ambulance—without headlamps and guided only by the light of the moon—has just pulled into the courtyard. Kathleen cranes her neck to see if it is Paul, but the car is a G.M.C., a British ambulance, and the driver a woman.

"They're only coming about every fifteen or twenty minutes now," Mrs. Brently remarks. "The battle must be slowing."

Kathleen watches the driver climb from the vehicle to direct the unloading of the wounded. "Do you think they are cowards?" she asks, more fiercely than she intends.

"The Germans?"

"The American ambulance drivers." Kathleen's words spill out. "Eddie said they're cowards who are only trying to win the Craw de—"

"The *Croix de Guerre*?"

"Yes, that's it, from the French Army."

"I've never seen it that way." Mrs. Brently peers down into the courtyard. "Do you?"

"I think they're brave," she huffs. "And what they're doing is right. Some of them have been here for years, and they've left their jobs and families to do this for next to nothing. Who knows how many lives they've saved?"

"If you feel that way, it's odd that you would ask for my opinion."

"I, well . . . I respect you, and I want to know what you think."

Mrs. Brently smiles generously. "I wouldn't be surprised if most of the ambulance drivers have already won the *Croix de Guerre*. They're good men—at least those I've met are. As for their reasons, don't you think they're here for much the same reason as we are?"

"Yes, I do," Kathleen says. "Oh, thank you."

Mrs. Brently laughs. "Go to bed. We'll probably have another long day tomorrow."

Kathleen motions toward the light coming in by the window. "May I, uh, read my letter first?"

"Of course. Goodnight."

Mrs. Brently leaves, and Kathleen opens the envelope and tips the single sheet of paper toward the moonlight. In his smudged and tortured scrawl, Jim writes,

Dear Kathleen,

I recently had the pleasure of meeting your mother and father, and of seeing your beloved home of Redlands. It is, indeed, very pretty in that area, and the red rocks near the foothills were resplendent with a touch of new snow on the day I was there.

Before I left, I asked your mother if there was any news that she might want me to deliver to you. She wanted me to remind you that you are to go to Mass as often as you can—daily, if possible— and to pray for this war to end and for your safe return home. She advises that you should spend less time sketching and more time devoting yourself to praying to God to keep you from sin. She cautions against any conversation with the French soldiers. She wants you to refrain from any nursing or other duties that require you to work closely with the men. She also wants me to tell you to keep your clothing clean, so that your uniforms will last for the duration of your overseas trip.

Your father would like to see more letters and sketches from you. He passes on the sentiment that he is very proud of you and your service to our soldiers.

Your father's wish is one that I would like to repeat. It's disappointing that the only letter I have received from you came in the packet that is shared with the employees of Graves Oil. Do you have any thoughts for me? I want to assure you that my offer to you in New York was not an idle or passing thought. I fell in love with you, Kathleen, with your courage, your sincerity and your beauty, and I have not doubted it for a moment since you left.

I want you to know that there is nothing I would not give or do to have you here beside me. Be safe, my sweet, and come home to me. I have heard that Germany is close to surrender. Let's hope it is very soon.

All my love,

Jim

P.S. I saw your horse, Napoli, while I was visiting Redlands. He is a beautiful and spirited creature, much like you, and seems to miss you as much as I do.

Her heart quavers—Redlands, oh, Redlands, and Napoli! She's so far from home, and all at once, she's tired of all of this. She lied to Mrs. Brently: she does regret it, just as Mary Jane did. Yet, as she refolds the letter, her eyes wet with tears, her thoughts are already churning. What had Jim thought of the run-down buildings at Redlands, the poor furnishings in the house? What had he made of Mama in her faded blouse and Papa in his stained bib overalls and manure-coated cowboy boots?

She scolds herself for her lack of generosity, yet her mother's demands embarrass her. Go to Mass, stay away from the French soldiers, keep your clothes clean! They must have sounded ridiculous to Jim, meant for a ten-year-old child.

Which she most certainly is not.

But why does she care so much about what he thinks?

How far in the past that picnic in Central Park seems now! She cannot entirely remember his face, or his voice, or his laugh. She cannot remember why she thought—even for a moment—that she might marry him. Not now, not after meeting Paul.

She goes back to the canteen. Lying on the floor with her face toward the wall, she tries to reach back to the start of the day, but fails, her thoughts clouded by too many emotions and too little sleep.

Only one phrase stands clearly in her mind: *I have never felt such sweetness and desire as I do with you.*

She touches her lips. With the memory of Paul's kisses in her heart, she falls asleep.

TWENTY-SIX

Sean dozes under a canvas tarp in a dugout near Troyon. The mud beneath his legs and back hasn't warmed, and never will, and dirt falls on his head from the sandbags piled atop the timbered roof. The smell of filthy bodies—his own included—has overpowered any hint of fresh air. The makeshift wire bunks are filled with soldiers, some of them two deep. Some snore, and even though he is only half-awake, he thinks how stupid it is to sleep soundly. They've been warned, they've been told, scolded, ordered. Never sleep, never let down your guard. It is too easy to miss something: the creep of a cloud of poison gas, a shell smashing into the dugout, the Germans sneaking up on you while you lie helpless.

Or the rats.

Last night, a rat had scurried through the dugout, seeming to bounce off walls and tear through wood as the men struck at it. Finally, someone stabbed it with a bayonet and hauled it, still squealing and thrashing blood, outside.

"Better save it," someone else called. "It's fresher than what we're getting in our meal kits."

The rats are the one thing Sean cannot bear. Having lived on an endless diet of flesh for the past three years, they are enormous and fearless, and they make no distinction as to whether the flesh is still attached to a living creature. A rat bite can become infected so quickly in the sauce of mud, blood, vomit, and shit that is the trench floor that a man can die of it before he reaches a first-aid station. One night, in an effort to keep them away, someone dumped creosote in the dugout where Sean was sleeping. The men inside nearly died of fumes—and at the hands of some brainless oaf who decided to smoke—but the rats only sneezed a few times before they continued their scavenging in the packs and kits.

When he does sleep, he dreams that he is marching for miles or kilometers—no matter which, it is long—through France. In daylight, he relives those dreams. Half the time, the troops march somewhere, only to find that they have to retrace their paths because they have forgotten something—sheddite bombs or ammunition or rations—or have gotten lost. Most of the time, the marching is done at night, but in the daylight, they pass through towns that are filled with young women by the scores, dressed well, hoping to attract the eye of a doughboy. Sean cannot blame them—the French troops that the Americans are attached to are middle-aged, graying men in stained and torn sky blue uniforms. A Frenchman younger than thirty-five or older than thirteen does not exist.

Sean's division has been at the Front for three weeks now under the watchful eyes of the French commanders, who are overseeing the Americans' introduction to trench warfare. Nothing much has happened yet—only a few skirmishes. Mostly, the Americans have been staring over the tangled barbed wire of No Man's Land toward enemy trenches that don't seem to have anyone in them. They roil with energy: let's bombard them, let's smoke them out, attack when they least expect it, let's finish this damned war. The French just "tsk" at them. Wait, they say. Wait. But after waiting so long to get here, to wait longer seems more hellish than to go into battle.

The French call the Germans here the "Verdun Boche" because of the stranglehold they have kept on this part of France for nearly four years. They refer to No Man's Land itself as "thickened up," because of the mess of old trenches, shell craters, broken-down fortifications, and tangles of wire that are permanently wedged into the earth. The land has been tarred over so many times with the dead that boggy humps of rot and stink rise up like the mounds of prairie dogs in Colorado. It isn't unusual to see a piece—a hand, a foot, the hoof of a horse—protruding from the lumpy earth. Sean has quickly grown numb to it all—he doesn't even smell it any longer—because there is no reason to think about anything that happens here. There isn't enough space for all of them in the dugouts, there isn't enough water to both drink and shave, there isn't enough food for three meals a day, there aren't enough latrines. There isn't enough life here to make living worth it.

The German troops have supposedly built bunkers beyond their front trenches that dip thirty feet into the ground and have all the comforts of home. Electricity, running water, beds, and cooking posts. It's said that there are even beer gardens where the Germans boast of their victories and entertain women.

But they are vicious and calculating foes. One visiting American lieutenant told Lieutenant Morgan and his new-to-the-trenches charges that handpicked German commandos steal over at night and assassinate any soldier who isn't at full alert. "One night," he said, "a German crawled on his belly right up to the parapet of the trench, where two men were posted as sentries with their rifles on the sandbags. He knelt, one knee on each rifle, and shot them point-blank between the eyes."

"They didn't see it?" Tony Necchi had challenged the lieutenant.

"No, the night was pitch black."

"They didn't feel nothing when the German sat down on the rifles? Like how a chair moves when you sit in it? Nothing made a noise?"

The lieutenant hadn't answered, a sour expression on his face, and Tony had remained skeptical, saying later, "So, you don't feel it when a hundred-fifty pound weight comes down on a long thin stick you are holding. You are an idiot."

Since the dust-up in Neufchateau over Kathleen's letter, Sean has watched Tony from the corner of his eye. The terror of war doesn't seem to bother the Italian. He observes, as if from a distance, detached and ready to scoff. He doesn't get the jitters—the "wind up," as they call it—that have convinced the French that the Americans are nothing but babies crying for their mothers, seeing the enemy whenever a rat scurries through No Man's Land. Sean wishes he, too, could stay that calm and skeptical.

A figure swallows up the dim light that filters through the door of the dugout. It is Lieutenant Morgan, followed by a fifty-something dumpling of a Frenchman.

"Attention," Lieutenant Morgan says, and men roll out of bunks, groan as they flop onto the floor and scramble to find their packs and rifles.

Sean rises to his feet and wipes his sleeve across the crust on his face. He hasn't shaved in over a week, and the scraggly reddish growth on his face has started attracting lice. His fingernails are caked with dirt—something that would make his mother scold—but here, there is no shame, no judgment, no censure. Much to everyone's amusement, some of the men have had to cut their socks from their feet with knives. The mud that cakes their clothes is as thick and binding as glue.

"As you were," Lieutenant Morgan commands. "We aren't moving out."

A dimwitted silence takes over. Sean has noticed that if there isn't a clear direction or order, the men are like cattle, with no ability to act on their own.

"This is Sergeant Henri," Lieutenant Morgan says. "He's looking for volunteers for a clipping detail. The engineers who were supposed to take the job have been held up by flooded roads."

Someone scoffs. That's the way it is with this war—the people who are supposed to show up don't, and the people who show up die.

"We need four men to volunteer from this section," Lieutenant Morgan says. "If we don't have enough, I will choose."

No one speaks for a moment as the threat sinks in. At last, someone asks, "What do you have to do?"

Sergeant Henri takes over in heavily-accented English. "You go out and clear the wire away from the German trench so that the infantry will be able to get through tomorrow morning without being caught up."

At Sean's shoulder, Kevin whispers, "Jesus, that sounds like suicide."

Sergeant Henri takes tools from his pack. "You crawl out beyond our fortifications and you take the nippers and cut the wire"—*you tehk zee nee-PEAR zand cut zee wAHr*—"and make the path." He mimes the actions. "Tomorrow, we know to send the soldiers through that place during the fight. *Comprenez vous*? You see?"

No one answers Sergeant Henri.

A red-faced boy timidly raises his hand. "Ain't that what the bombardment is supposed to do? Take out the wire?"

"*Oui*, but there is still too much, *n'est-ce pas*?"

"We still need four volunteers," Lieutenant Morgan reminds them.

Tony steps forward. "I'll go, sir."

At almost the same moment, Sean says, "I'll go."

"Necchi, Sullivan," Lieutenant Morgan acknowledges. "Two more."

Kevin—who usually follows Sean—volunteers, as well as Arnie Green, the boy who posed the question.

"We leave in *une heure*," Sergeant Henri says.

"One hour," Lieutenant Morgan repeats needlessly. "Use this time to check over your weapons and refill your canteens and eat. You'll be out most of the night."

"What about tomorrow?" Arnie asks, at the same time as Kevin grouses, "Eat what?"

It's a good question. No supplies have arrived for three days to replenish the men's depleted rations. Evidently, their food is stuck in the same place as the engineers.

"What about it?" Lieutenant Morgan hears only Arnie's question. "We attack at oh-five-thirty."

"You'd think they'd at least let us sleep some," Arnie grumbles as Lieutenant Morgan leaves the dugout. "We're gonna be dead on our feet."

"Better than dead anywhere else," Tony says.

"I tell you what," Kevin says. "We'll attack on real time, which will be one hour later. That way, we'll get a whole hour of sleep."

Sean snorts, and Arnie laughs. France has implemented something called Daylight Saving Time that sets all the clocks forward an hour in order to conserve energy. Mostly it causes confusion among the American troops, and Sean doesn't know if the Germans have changed their watches as well. It doesn't really matter—a man can be killed as easily on French time as he can on German.

During the hour's wait, Sean packs his belongings into his rucksack. How does a man's life become so small that it fits into a single pack? The only comfort he finds is the letters that have finally arrived from America. Ma's letter went on about Maggie's and Liam's wedding, while Maggie's detailed how happy she is as a *"Young Housewife (note the capital letters, me brother, I am very proud of them)."* From Auntie Eileen, he has received an admonition never to forget that sin is nearer than it ever was in a country as godless as France. All of that is fine—he doesn't even mind that Auntie Eileen has taken it upon herself to save his soul—but from Kathleen, he hears about how much fun the war is. That one rankles him.

He digs into the pack to make sure the bundle of letters is there. His fingers tease the paper, catching at a corner again and again, as if he can touch home. Before his time in the trenches, he always thought of the human body—of his body—as strong, sturdy, reliable. Then he saw the humping, decaying bodies of No Man's Land—black, maggot-choked lumps on the ground, horses with legs stiff and bellies bloated until they split. Now he sometimes touches his arms and legs to reassure himself that his muscle and flesh, resilient and tough, still exists. Every night he prays: *Dear God, if I go, let there be something left of me to bury.* Somehow, he worries less about dying than he does about the possibility that he could, like so many others, die unrecognizable, unknowable, a sack of parts.

When the time comes to head out, Lieutenant Morgan calls for the four volunteers to stand at attention while Sergeant Henri sizes them up with an irritating smugness. Sean has yet to hear a single French *bonhomme* admit that the raw, unseasoned Yankee boys are their only hope for salvation. You only need look at the villages that are piles of chalky rubble and the cemeteries that stretch through prime farmland to know that France is all but lost.

"Here." Lieutenant Morgan hands a metal cup to Tony. "Put this on your faces."

"What is it?" Tony tentatively dips his fingers into the cup, blackening the tips.

"Burnt cork."

Tony rubs the stuff across his nose, cheeks and forehead before handing it to Sean. Sean dumps a dusty bit into his palm, rubs his hands together and then smears his face. He looks at Tony, whose eyes glitter in his darkened face.

"I'm not so white as you," Tony says. "It don't take so much for me."

Sean laughs as Sergeant Henri commands, *"Allez."*

Without the benefit of a lantern or flashlight, he leads Sean, Tony, Kevin and Arnie into a maze of twisting, muddy trenches. They travel one way, then turn and travel another, walking through waist-deep water, crawling over fallen sandbags, and sinking into the yellow slime on the trench bottom. At times, the trenches are no wider than Sean's shoulders, and he has to wiggle sideways through the narrower spots, his sixty-pound pack catching at the walls. At one point, they have to pass the packs over the top of the trench walls, while Sergeant Henri scolds, *"Attention, attention, ne pas être vu."* Don't let them see us. All the same, he makes no effort to help the Americans.

They walk half a mile, or a mile, or two miles—it really doesn't matter. The water seeps into Sean's boots and socks and drenches his calves. Mud falls from the crumbling walls and collects on his shoulders, weighting them down even more. His ears start to freeze—a common occurrence—below his tin hat. At last, Sergeant Henri stops, and Sean and the others come to a halt behind him.

There are no firesteps or parapets here. Sergeant Henri propels himself upward with his back braced against one side of the trench, his feet on the other. With field glasses, he surveys No Man's Land. Scaling down the wall into the trench, he says in heavily accented English, "There is wire both directions. There will be Germans patrol parties everywhere. Do not speak, do not make any noise, if you can help it."

"Okay." Tony looks at the others. "Ready to go?"

"Don't forget, the *barrage* starts at oh-two-thirty."

With a nod, Sean monkey-walks up the trench wall and pulls himself up over the top. Once on solid ground, he lies motionless, face in the mud, clamping his tin hat on his head, as he waits for a bullet or shell to strike him dead. Nothing happens, and he sits up, pulls his gloves and nippers from the pouch that hangs around his neck, and squirms forward toward the concertina wire that lies in waves across No Man's Land, his rifle thudding against his back. He crawls out about twenty feet, slipping under the barbed wire that protects the French trenches. On his right, Tony is doing the same. To his left is Kevin.

It's no trouble to clip the protective fences, which are barbed wire stretched across sticks in haphazard lines, like spider webs that have no symmetry or direction. The concertina wire is another story. It is unwieldy and liable to spring back and lacerate his face or poke out his eye. Reluctantly, Sean pulls himself up on his feet and crouches on his heels, clipping as quickly as he can. Almost at once, a sniper begins to shoot, and he flattens himself against the soggy, half-frozen earth. His heart beats in an uneven rhythm, and he gasps for air. My God, what a fool he is to volunteer to die.

A flare streams upward into the sky, clearly outlining the shattered stumps of the trees in what was once forest and the thorny bramble beneath that seems to be all that can survive this war. Sean's heart clumps in his chest, but nothing more happens. No concentrated gunfire or no mortar round. The sniper fires sporadically, pegging away like a little boy experimenting with a drum—sometimes fast and rhythmic, sometimes slow and reverberating.

Sean catches his breath again. Slowly, he lifts up into a crouch and begins to clip wire again. And something strange happens. He begins to feel safe as he crawls through this wasteland where thousands of men hide from one another, each one trying to live long enough to make it home. He feels at peace, even. This is the first time he has been alone since last May, and it is the first time he can hear the sound of his own breathing and the blood rushing through his body. He can even hear his own *thinking*, something that has not happened in months.

He remembers the barbed wire fences of Redlands. Kathleen could crawl between the strands without a single snag, but he inevitably caught his pants or shirt on a barb and got a fussing-at from Auntie Eileen or Ma. He thinks of the creek where Kathleen and he would wade, of the old wooden swing tied with rotting rope to a massive willow branch that arched over the water. "Drop, drop!" she would call, and he would fall, into the bitterly cold water of the creek.

He surges forward, as if he is cutting a path back to his past or forward to his own freedom. How far are the German trenches from where he squats? How many patrols are scampering through the darkness, trying to catch him, the enemy? It doesn't matter to him anymore. All he wants is to keep clipping, to make some progress in this place where there is only destruction and waste.

"Hey!"

The whisper in the darkness brings him back to himself, and he realizes that he is far from the trenches, deep in No Man's Land.

"Hey!" the whisper sounds again. "Come on."

Sean spies Tony, beckoning to him from a prone position and waves in reply. On his belly again, he elbows his way through the cold mud to the trench.

"Castelnau," whispers a voice from the parapet.

"Castellane."

Sean wraps his tongue around the French, with the hope that it will sound convincing. Some of the American boys have nearly been shot as enemy soldiers because of their butchery of the French language.

"*Entrez.*"

He drops in, feet first, and arms catch him and keep him from falling flat. Tony drops in a moment later, after having given the same password.

"How did you do?" Sergeant Henri asks.

"I cut a good lane," Tony responds.

"Mine joins his right there." Sean points to the map in Sergeant Henri's hands.

Sergeant Henri notes the position of the breaks in the wire, and Sean knows that the same is happening up and down the line, with other details cutting the wire across No Man's Land. The compiled information will determine the path of the infantry attack tomorrow.

Arnie and Kevin are waiting a little down the trench. With shaking hands, Arnie scratches at his stubbly face. "I ain't doing that again," he says.

The men slosh back through the trenches behind Sergeant Henri as the first shells of the bombardment start to whistle through the air. Glancing over the top of the trench, Sean sees the dirt flying up from the German trenches. If there were men there, they are now spattered across No Man's Land.

"Sounds like we woke up the Heines," Tony says.

An eager audience awaits them in the dugout. The men are packed and ready to move at first light.

"So how was it?" someone asks.

"Not half as exciting as fixing a gas leak," Tony says.

Kevin brags. "When the flares went off, I just covered my face. The Huns think they're smart, but they can't shoot beyond their own asses."

Sean says nothing. He wants to ask Kevin or Tony if they had felt a sense of serenity in No Man's Land, too, but he doesn't want them to think he is "trench mad," as they call it. More than that, he's afraid that his words will somehow reach Danhour or Lieutenant Morgan, and he'll be in for another round of ridicule. Lately, he's learned that it's best to keep his own counsel.

As the bombardment picks up, more men crowd into the dugout. The noise from the sky is deafening with the whir of broken air, the lumbering roar of the shells shot from the thirteen-ton howitzers, and the coughing of smaller artillery. One of the big guns that shoots bombs filled with shrapnel begins its monotonous, steady booming, punctuating the mess. It's impossible to stand up straight when there is this much noise, so Sean grabs onto a wall support. In the concussions from above, the wood squeaks at the joints, the nails working their way out.

"What's happening?" a new recruit near him cries. "What is it?"

"Calm down," Kevin says. "It's only the beginning."

Sean looks at the kid and then at Kevin, who raises his eyebrows and shrugs. Some of the newly-arrived soldiers haven't been as well trained as those who enlisted at the beginning—the French and British are always pressuring the Americans to move faster—and they come to the trenches with their nerves already shot. The men of the Regular Army, who have been in this game for nearly a year now, call them "jumpers."

"What's your name?" Sean asks the kid.

"Oscar Marsh."

"Where are you from?" Tony offers a cigarette, and the boy shakes his head.

"Slocomb, Alabama. It's a town near Dothan—"

"Yeah?" Tony says. "I don't know nothing beyond Brooklyn."

Sean takes a swig from his canteen. Poor kid—stuck into the fray with a bunch who no longer feel fear or care much about kindness.

"I'm only sixteen," Marsh confides. "But I lied about my age to come over."

"Why would you do that?" Sean asks.

"I didn't want to miss it. They say it'll be over any time now."

"Miss what?"

"The Great Adventure. That's what they're callin' it back home."

"The Great Adventure," Tony muses. "You ever been over the top?"

Marsh quivers. "No, but maybe today?"

"You just might get lucky."

Everyone laughs. Innocence is always fair game for ridicule.

They wait. One hour. Two. Through the small hours of the dawn. The sky pounds with the fury of the onslaught; the earth shakes. The noise, so loud that some men pass out, roots in Sean's innards. He feels as if he's been physically shaken, everything inside him unlatched and displaced. His stomach floats upward, his heart sinks somewhere, his bowels feel distended and sore. The clanging sirens blare, signaling the creep of poison gas, and the men strap on their gas masks so that they look like a cross between a beetle and a human. Sean checks through his training: If the sky is greenish and smells of pineapple—which he isn't sure he's ever smelled—it is chlorine gas. If it is brownish and smells of garlic, it is mustard. Phosgene smells of burned cabbage. In other words, if it stinks of anything other than death, it's probably poisonous.

After the din of the barrage has nearly deafened them, the first light of day lifts the gloom outside the dugout. Lieutenant Morgan consults the mimeographed battle plan that he was given last night and calls, "Stand by to move out!"

It's another slog through dimly-lit trenches. These are wider than the ones they traveled through last night, and meant for infantry. At the firestep, Sean climbs up next to Kevin, whose presence beside him reassures him.

"What do you think will happen today?" Kevin asks, and Sean laughs. It's a joke they share, a pact against the death that is coming across No Man's Land for them.

At once, a guttural cry breaks the din—who makes it, that animal sound? It seems always to come at the first of the battle, from their own throats—whether German, American, or French—unwanted, unplanned. Around Sean, men fall—one, two, too many. Shells drop in front of the trench, crumpling the parapet and spewing shrapnel over their heads. He focuses on the hellish landscape in front of him. Shattered trees, scorched ground, every shadow gray against gray, indistinguishable from everything else.

Lieutenant Morgan shouts something. The order is echoed by sergeants up and down the line: "We're going over! Second wave whistle."

A minute later, the whistles screech and the first wave of Americans pours over the tops of the trenches in front of them, moving directly toward the Germans. In the trench, the cry persists—what in the hell is that? Then Sean realizes it is Marsh, supine on the ground. The boy never took his place on the firestep. Sean kicks at him, barking furiously, "Get up! Get up!"

A shell falls directly behind him, and he curses himself for not hearing it. The walls of the trench crumble, and Sean stuffs sandbags into the holes. The next shell rocks the ground to the right of Sean. He is catapulted forward, over the parapet, atop the sandbags. He flails on the uneven surface as the sandbags sink, sliding downward, dropping on those in the trench. Sean rips off the gas mask—he can't see out of the blasted thing—and claws his way forward, to keep from being swallowed by the mud, shredded wire, and debris.

No Man's Land is thick with dark, putrid smoke. He can't spot the Americans who went over in the first wave—surely some of them gained their objective, surely not all were cut down. To his right, he sees a foot, bare, the boot blown clear off. The foot is attached to a leg, but whether there is any more to the body, he cannot determine. Sean looks one way, then the other. My God, he has lost all sense of direction! He doesn't know which trenches are Allied and which are German. His head spins with the rush of blood and panic—if he crawls to the wrong one, he will be dead. Yet he can't stay here, where he is as likely to be cut down by American bullets as by German.

To his right, a whirlwind of dirt spews into the air as a bomb falls far short of the trenches. Desperate, Sean rolls toward the nearest crater in the gray earth, and falls downward into it.

At once, a soldier scrambles out of his way. "*Verschwinde!*"

Sean fumbles for his service pistol in the holster at his side, as the German turns on him, a short ax in his hands. Without aiming, Sean cocks and pulls the trigger, and the soldier drops the ax and grabs his throat. Sean sees his face—dark eyes, light brown hair, lips that are red and boyish and that open and close, as if he were trying to speak. Blood pours from the wound, dousing his field gray uniform. He crumples against the muddy floor of the crater, and brackish water washes over him. Blood swirls into the water.

His breath coming in harsh gasps, Sean falls back in the mud of the crater. Blind terror overtakes him, and he tries to will himself back to ten minutes ago. *Take me away, don't let this happen, my God, did it really happen? Did I kill him?* The body of the dead German settles, and Sean realizes that no one will come looking for him here. This will be his grave, his body another rotten, brownish lump on the gut-strewn earth. Sean vomits once, twice, but nothing comes up. When he lifts his head, he realizes that he is not done.

Carefully, he pulls the body toward him until he can cut the insignia from the soldier's uniform with his clippers. The man's gun is still over his shoulder, and Sean takes that as well. The ax lies just under the body. They would tell me to take souvenirs, he thinks. The watch, the buttons, the helmet—everything. But he cannot. He cannot desecrate the boy—for he is younger than Sean—more than he already has.

He lies in the mud until the light starts to fail. Then, squirming through mud and tangled knots of wire, he lifts his head from the shell hole and chooses a direction. Making his way toward the nearest trench, he lunges in headfirst over the parapet. God grant that this is the right trench. He finds bodies and mats of flesh and blood everywhere. Timber and sandbags have fallen from the trench wall into a slanted pile. An American Springfield gun is propped against one wall.

"Kevin," Sean says. "Lieutenant Morgan." He murmurs other names, but no one answers. He stays low, for the walls are barely two feet high in parts. He repeats the names, then stops. Somewhere, a whimper. "Kevin?" he asks. "Lieutenant?"

"Here."

It is Marsh, the kid from Alabama, his body nearly covered by mud. His head droops forward, his chin against his chest. "Where does it hurt?" Sean whispers.

"I can't breathe."

"You must be able to. You're alive. Where are the others?"

Marsh coughs. "I can't breathe."

Sean glances around, but he sees no motion. "Why haven't the stretcher-bearers come for you?"

"Hurry," Marsh whispers.

"Be quiet."

Sean begins to dig, plunging into the sand and mud with his hands. After some time, he thinks to take his shovel from his pack. He scrapes away the dirt that covers Marsh's chest.

"Can you breathe now?" he asks.

Marsh doesn't answer. His head lolls forward, and blood soaks his uniform. Sean scampers back, his stomach churning. The dirt clumped on Marsh's chest was keeping his stomach wound from bleeding out.

He closes his eyes and presses his face against the muddy back wall of the trench. Marsh has been with the unit for less than a month, and here he is, killed in his first battle, almost the first hour of battle. There isn't a heroic story to tell Lieutenant Morgan or the kid's parents in Alabama or anyone else. It isn't even tragedy. It is pointless and stupid.

He hears a rustle, a slight scratching, and quickly smears the tears on his face with his sleeve. Raising his rifle with bayonet poised, he prays, *Not rats, please, not rats.* They become ravenous at the smell of blood, and he is covered in it.

"Hey, come on."

It's Kevin, reaching over the parapet of the trench—or what is left of the trench—from behind. "Anybody else here?"

"No," Sean says. "I don't think so."

"We're back in the communication trench," Kevin says. "The tunnels are destroyed. You have to come into the open."

Sean scales the parapet, sinks to his knees, then to his stomach. Kevin crawls with him, moving inch by inch across the ground. Clods of muck strike Sean's side, the mud grows slicker, harder to muddle through as his elbows grow raw and his knees start to hurt.

At last, Kevin rolls over the side of a trench, and Sean follows. About ten members of the unit are there—Lieutenant Morgan, Tony, Michael, Arnie, Danhour, others. They are filthy and hurting—mud and tar covering their helmets and uniforms, scratches or gashes on their faces and hands, items lost from their clothing and gear. One man rocks back and forth, one arm cradled in the other. Most of them huddle against the wall, knees squeezed against their chests, as if they are trying to keep their innards from sliding to the ground and mixing into the mud.

"We got caught in a trench full of wire and came back to wait it out," Kevin says.

Lieutenant Morgan steps forward, his face haggard. "Where have you been? Did you see anyone else?"

"I was blown out into the open," Sean says. "The only one I found was Private Marsh. He was hurt."

"We need to send the stretcher-bearers—"

"He's not with us anymore."

"We took you for dead, too." Lieutenant Morgan lowers his voice. "We've had quite a few casualties."

Tears sting in Sean's eyes again, and his throat closes. He pulls the insignia from his pack. In his hand, the patch crumples, as dead as its owner.

"What's this?" Lieutenant Morgan says. "You killed a man?"

"Yes, sir."

Everyone crowds around—"You got a Hun?" "How close were you?" "Did you use the bayonet?" "Can I hold it?"

Lieutenant Morgan turns the insignia over and over in his hand. At last, he says, "Congratulations, Private Sullivan. As far as I know, you are the first of our unit to kill an enemy soldier."

Nausea swells over Sean. My God, my God, he has killed—and not just in from a distance, destroying a nameless, faceless target. The uniform patch was once warm, a source of pride to the boy's mother, or sister, or wife. Now it and the wicked ax and the pack and gun, which he left behind in the trench, will be used to tally the company's kill. They are the spoils of victory, to be bragged about. He moves away, ignoring the pats on the back from his fellows, who grab at his limp hands in an attempt to shake them. At last, he comes to rest against the trench wall, about ten feet away from the others, who still fondle the insignia. He slides down into a crouch.

A voice sounds from above. "Wanna cigarette?"

It's Tony. With trembling hands, Sean takes a cigarette and lets Tony light it for him. The smoke burns in his throat, stings his eyes.

"Look at them." Tony nods toward Lieutenant Morgan and the others. "All day, they've been scared and sad, and now, they think they can be the bravest soldiers on earth."

I wasn't brave, Sean thinks. I was scared. I was more of a coward than I've ever been. I killed him, I took his life, but when I cut off the insignia, I didn't look at his face. I couldn't look at his face. I couldn't stand to see his eyes again.

As if he has read Sean's thoughts, Tony says, "You done what you shoulda done. Now come on, we move out at next whistle."

TWENTY-SEVEN

December 10, 1917

My darling brother,

I am taking only a few minutes of my time to write to you. We are desperately busy here. The latest British effort near the beginning of this month did not go as planned, and we have been overrun with wounded. Just know that we are all well at this time.

The girls have been taking turns between working in the canteen and helping the British nurses, which leaves little time for rest or writing. We have seen the most dreadful things. The mutilés— those whose faces have been lost—are the worst, and I have much trouble tending to them, although Helen is quite willing to do it. Every wound is terrible, though. There is a method of care known as the Carrel-Dakin treatment, which requires a soldier's wound to be left open to allow for the infection to drain via rubber tubes planted deep into it. The pain (and the smell) is excruciating, but it supposedly allows for a much quicker and more complete recovery. Still, it is awful to see the suffering these men have to bear.

We do whatever comes to us at the hospital, no matter how menial. I laugh now to think that I believed we would be doing "social" work— writing letters home, reading Dickens classics to the convalescents, planning poetry readings and evening song festivals, and generally being sweet and charming. I thought we would never dirty our hands. But we're more likely to be scrubbing floors, unloading supplies, or "pot slinging," as the British nurses call it (you can imagine what that is).

Only yesterday (quite late, I know), we celebrated Thanksgiving with the American engineers stationed near here. Once we decided to have a feast, it became a "big deal" for all involved (as everything American does). The captain in charge requisitioned decorations, plates, and flatware from the army. He asked for a piano and other instruments as well, but was turned down, so in the end, some of the boys stole a piano in the dead of night from the YMCA canteen that is nearby, simply loading it up on a truck and bringing it here. (No one has come looking for it yet.) In the meantime, the girls and I filched supplies for a fine, if unusual, Thanksgiving dinner. Turkeys have long since disappeared, so we had sausage meat, some funny little clams that greatly upset the stomach, boiled vegetables, bread, and an apple for dessert.

After the meal, Helen recited a poem called "The Story of the Pilgrims" that she had learned in High School, and Hank, whose voice is quite lyrical, sang a lovely rendition of "Hush-a-Bye My Baby." One of the engineers played the piano while another young man joined her for a waltz across the stage, which was, I must admit, accompanied by much hooting and whistling from the audience. Kathleen followed with a presentation that turned out to be almost magical. She set up a drawing station and claimed she was going to create "An American Picture Study." She then asked for the soldiers to call out their home states and to describe whatever was special about that place, such as the woods of the Pacific Northwest, the city streets of New York, or the plains of Texas. She sketched the place right there and then, with a remarkable degree of success, and gave the picture to the young man. As for me, I sang a duet of "Till the Clouds Roll By" with a young fellow from Boston who belongs to a vaudeville troupe.

For a finale, the girls sang their favorite, "I'd Like to Be a Monkey in the Zoo," which they had heard in New York. Shortly after, the boys took over the piano, and we were treated to a medley of songs that are popular in the States—some of which were appropriate for our girls' ears and some of which I had to ban from the festivities.

Now that we have been attached to both French and British, I should so like for us to be at the service of the Americans before we *leave here. Our Thanksgiving festival made me so long for America and everything that is American and speaks of "home." I don't dare imagine how I will feel at Christmas.*

Much love to you and to Mother and Father,
Ellie

Jim sat at the desk in his office, the arched windows behind him looking down onto a snowy 17th Street below. Ellie's letter had arrived in a carefully wrapped packet only two days before Christmas. Digging inside the packet again, he removed the weekly letters that the members of the Graves Family Foundation Relief Society were required to write for the edification of the employees at Graves Oil and for publication in the *Denver Post*. Unfolding the first letter, he found that it was written by Harriet Mills: *The French winter is very cold. The only way we can stay warm is to keep moving, and so I have instituted an exercise regimen. We do calisthenics in the garden of the chateau every morning. We do ten jumping jacks with the collars of our uniforms and our wimples flying, and then twelve . . .*

Without finishing it, he moved to the letter from Helen Parsons: *We see a number of German prisoners around. They are supposed to be working loading trains, building outhouses, or other jobs, but I have yet to see one lift a finger and do a thing. The French are much too good to them, and they are as well-fed and healthy as any of the soldiers, but quite stupid looking. I believe they should be punished for their part in this war by . . .*

He refolded the letter and picked up Kathleen's: *The British recruit women for their ambulance drivers, but there are a number of American ambulance drivers attached to the French. Many of them are from the eastern colleges such as Yale. Some criticize them for not serving their country, but the French say that the American ambulance drivers are winning the war for them. The drivers are extremely brave and go into situations very near the Front to save the lives of wounded soldiers. They are paid the same as the French soldiers, which is only a few cents a day, and not . . .*

Jim flipped through it. It spanned three pages, all of it drivel about the valor of the ambulance drivers. He laid it down and peered into the packet. One more envelope remained. Pulling it out, he unfolded a sketch of a cherub, its face, neck and upper torso visible, but the rest of its body hidden behind a frothy cloud. The cherub's arms, with pudgy hands, were crossed in front of it.

A carefully-written note accompanied the sketch:

Dear Jim,

I understand now what you were talking about when you said that the ceilings of the great cathedrals of the world were painted by using grids. The ceilings of the chateau where we are living also have grand scenes of Greek mythology, according to Mrs. Brently. I've sketched the angel that I like the best for you. I don't know how big the painting is, for the ceilings are twenty feet high, but its head must be larger than that of a human being. Mrs. Brently says this is Eros.

Sincerely,

Kathleen

P.S. Please keep this sketch for yourself. Merry Christmas!

With a laugh, Jim looked again at the sketch. He wondered if Kathleen had realized that Eros was the god of love or if she had drawn the sprite simply by coincidence. He could just imagine how she'd blush at being told that she had sent him what amounted to an illustrated love letter.

He leaned back in his chair. He was disappointed that she had said nothing personal. No protestations of love, no indication of homesickness or of missing anything—or anyone—in Colorado. He recalled the day he had delivered her first series of sketches to her parents at Redlands. After taking tea with both Mr. and Mrs. O'Doherty, Jim and her father—who insisted upon being called Irish—had walked out to the corral where Kathleen's horse, a beautiful sorrel, neighed impatiently.

"Poor creature," Irish had said. "He doesn't understand where she's gone. She rode him nearly every day before she moved to Denver for her job. Rode him like a wild Indian, both of them one stumble away from breaking their necks."

"You didn't object to that?"

"It wouldn't matter if I had." Irish shrugged. "Not much stops that girl." Then he had turned to Jim and said bitterly, "When we married, I thought we would have a true Catholic family. Seven children, twelve— that was the size family that I came from. But here we are, past the years when we can reasonably hope to have children, with only one. And a daughter at that. Not even a son to take over the ranch for me."

"But Kathleen is an exceptional and beautiful young woman."

"Yes, she is," Irish had said. "She is our one and only."

At that, Jim had felt a terrible longing for something that didn't exist for him—not in his world of offices and business deals, not in his own palatial home, not in the dazzling world in which he lived. It was something elemental, brought on by the image of a young woman, in sunshine, riding a horse through open countryside, nothing but air and speed and blood in her head. How long had he been a stranger to that sort of visceral, primal joy? In fact, had he ever been a part of it?

The door of Jim's office opened, and his secretary, Joel Spratt, looked in. "Mr. Graves?" he said. "Professor Norlin from the University of Colorado is here to see you."

Jim rose from his chair to greet the thin, light-eyed man who entered the room. George Norlin had sparse, graying hair and wore a stern black suit with black tie and white shirt.

"Professor Norlin," Jim said. "How nice to see you. I believe we met last January at the Inaugural Ball for Governor Gunter at the Denver Auditorium."

Professor Norlin reached for Jim's outstretched hand. "You were in the company of a most beautiful woman that evening."

"That was my sister, Mrs. Eleanora Brently. She's currently in France."

"Ah, yes." Professor Norlin took the seat that Jim offered him. "I read the letters from the young women that are published in the newspaper. They seem an impressive lot."

"They were chosen from the most outstanding female employees of my company." Jim returned to his desk and sat down. Opening a cigarette case, he offered it to his guest. "Professor?"

"No, thank you." Professor Norlin spoke with just the slightest accent, as if some words stuck on his tongue. "But please go ahead."

As Jim lit a cigarette, Professor Norlin continued. "I've come here today to talk to you about a new campaign in our state called Americanize Colorado. In doing research requested by Governor Gunter, I've discovered that about fifty-six thousand of Colorado's eight hundred thousand residents are of German parentage or born in Germany. If we add in those of Austrian birth or heritage, the figure is closer to ten percent of our state's population."

"I wasn't aware that the number was so high," Jim said. "I have heard that there are a number of Russian Germans living on the northeastern plains of our state."

"Yes, there are," Professor Norlin agreed. "In the 1700s, Catherine the Great of Russia asked Germans to come and live in Russia to increase the population. But Tsar Alexander II wasn't so welcoming. He took away many of the benefits the Germans had from living in Russia. As a result, entire communities fled to the United States. Because they were skilled in farming, most eventually ended up in the Midwest or West." The professor paused. "I apologize for the history lesson."

Jim laughed. "I've heard that your literature classes at the university are not to be missed."

"Thank you."

Jim caught the stick in Professor Norlin's speech again, on the "th" of thank.

The professor continued. "As part of his State Council of Defense, Governor Gunter has asked me to head a Committee to educate the German born population in American ways. We hope to eradicate the threat that German aliens pose to our way of life. As someone who has brought so much prosperity and industry to our state, I felt that you would be a fine addition to the Committee."

"I'm honored to be considered," Jim said. "Who else has been asked?"

Professor Norlin named a number of professionals and other professors from the University of Colorado. "Senator Shafroth has also shown his support. And, of course, the Governor himself."

He cleared his throat. "But to be fair, we are choosing members from both political parties. We would be quite pleased to have a Republican on board."

Jim laughed. "How does the Committee intend to achieve its purpose?"

"We've determined that the foreign born worker living in Colorado, who is unable to read or speak English, is shut off from the influences that would make him a loyal citizen in our country. We hope to reach him and bring him to American citizenship. It's a program of education and welcoming into our culture."

"From what I've seen in my time on the eastern plains, some of the small towns aren't particularly welcoming to the foreign born," Jim said. "Perhaps we need to offer education on both sides."

Professor Norlin frowned. "A high level of caution is necessary for those living in our small towns and cities. Many of the enemy aliens listen to agitators who try to engage them in a war of one class against another."

"Socialists?"

"Yes, labor agitators and the like. The coal mines in the southern part of the state near Trinidad are especially rife with union representatives who stir up strife and dissatisfaction against the operators of the mines."

"That has always been a cauldron of dissatisfaction, especially after the tragedy a few years ago—"

"Ah, yes," Professor Norlin said. "What they now call the Ludlow Massacre."

"You can rely on me to do whatever I can to help you," Jim said. "Do you need financial support?"

"The state has given us some funds, but certainly we will need more to accomplish this. Any help is appreciated."

Jim took his checkbook from the drawer and wrote a generous check. "There you are. I'm sure this will be a pleasant partnership."

"Thank you." Professor Norlin stood and walked to the wall where Jim's framed diploma hung. "I see you're a college man, Mr. Graves."

"Yes, sir, I am." Jim joined him. "Princeton. Class of 1910."

"When you have a son, send him to the University of Colorado. By that time, I guarantee that it will be as academically rigorous and sound as any school on the East Coast."

Jim laughed as he shook Professor Norlin's hand. "I will keep that in mind."

"Thank you, Mr. Graves. I'll be in touch after the New Year. Merry Christmas."

After the professor left, Jim went to the window. To be asked to serve on the governor's committee would certainly increase his political connections and power. It was a solid first step toward elected office. More importantly, it would please his mother.

A tap at the door alerted him. Once again, Joel stepped into the room. "I've had the packages loaded into your car."

"Thank you."

Still in a buoyant mood, Jim donned his greatcoat and drove to the cottage near the State Capitol. The winter sun had broken through the clouds in the west, tinging them a deep pinkish-orange. From the car, he took a full-sized wardrobe trunk and a smaller package wrapped in sturdy, elegant paper embossed with flowing bows. Leaving both on the porch, he knocked and waited.

Anneka opened it. "Jim!" she said in surprise. "Why are you here?" She glimpsed his car behind him. "And you are parked just outside—"

"Merry Christmas."

"But shouldn't you move your car—?"

"It's all right." He picked up the wardrobe trunk and hauled it into the house. "I told you I would bring Mina something for Christmas."

"What is it? That is the largest trunk I've ever seen! The one I brought with me from Sweden isn't nearly as big."

He laughed as he set the trunk on its end before the fireplace. "She's here, isn't she?"

"Of course." Anneka called toward the back of the house, "Mina! Mr. Jim is here!"

Mina ran from the back of the house. She was dressed simply in her school clothes and pinafore, with white lisle stockings and sturdy black shoes on her feet. Upon seeing him, she curtseyed. "Hello, Mr. Yeem."

Jim chuckled at her pronunciation, learned from her mother. "Come here and give me a hug."

The child skipped over to him and hugged his thighs. He lifted her up and kissed her cheek. "I have something for you, Mina," he said. "A Christmas present—"

"We should wait until Christmas to open it," Anneka said.

"There's no need." Jim set Mina down and took off his coat and hat. Tossing them over the back of the chair, he said, "It isn't wrapped. Come and see it."

Mina glanced at her mother for permission. After Anneka nodded, she inspected the trunk, which was nearly as tall as she was. Her face was serious, almost studious, with the same gravity and grace that made her mother so lovely.

"Open it," Jim said. "Here, I'll help."

He undid the latches of the trunk and spread it open, and Mina gasped. On one side was a doll with whitish-blond hair and blue eyes that stood a little over three feet tall. Her exquisitely-painted china face had a blush of rose on her cheeks and tenderly red lips, and her lashes lifted delicately on china eyelids that opened and closed. Her torso was of cloth, but her arms and legs were china from the shoulders and knees. She had tiny grooves in her fingers to resemble knuckles and dainty depressions where her fingernails would be.

"She is beautiful," Mina said.

"Who do you think she looks like?" Jim teased.

Mina considered. "My mother."

He laughed. "She looks like you, Mina. She was made to look like you, to be your twin."

"Me?" The little girl shrieked in joy. "Oh, Mother, may I keep her?"

"That isn't all," Jim said. "Look over here, on the other side of the trunk." He ran his hand across a row of dresses that were hung inside the trunk. "There is a dress for you here, and a matching one for your doll. All in all, five dresses for each of you."

He dislodged the doll from the trunk and handed it to Mina. She held it tenderly, stroking the soft, human hair. She cooed a few words that Jim didn't catch to the doll; perhaps they were in Swedish.

"Which dress do you want?" he asked. "Let's try the blue, to match your eyes. Go on, put it on."

Mina took the matching dresses and started to dance from the room. Anneka spoke sharply to her in Swedish, and Mina turned. "Thank you, Mr. Yeem," she said.

"You are welcome, Mina."

As Mina flew down the hallway, she carried on a conversation with the doll, telling her about where she had come to live. In the silence left behind, Jim sat on the divan and lit a cigarette.

Anneka took a seat in the armchair. "She is growing so fast, I don't know how long she will be able to wear those dresses."

"I'll have more made for her."

"Jim, I thank you for your kindness, and your mother for hers, but Mina is a little girl, not a . . . thing to be petted and spoiled. This is too much—"

"Every child should be petted and spoiled."

"Every child who has both father and mother should be spoiled," Anneka corrected. "A child such as Mina . . . if you or your mother decide I am no longer needed or wanted, we will be poor, and without a home, and what will she think then?"

"I won't let that happen." He exhaled smoke and balanced the cigarette in a silver ashtray on the table. "I have something for you, too."

He retrieved the second box from the porch and handed it to Anneka. She removed the wrapping paper and lifted the lid. Inside was a full-length beaver coat.

She did not touch it. "I cannot have this."

"Why not?"

"Where would I wear it?"

"Wherever you want," he said, annoyed. "Even if it's just for a walk around the block."

"A maid doesn't have clothes such as these. You are wasting your money, Jim."

He reached for his cigarette, his fine mood souring. "It's my choice."

Anneka ran a hand over the coat, leaving only the sounds of the shifting logs of the fire and Mina's singing in the back of the house. "There is a man I have met," she said at last. "I think he will ask me to marry him."

Jim stopped mid-exhale. "What will you do?"

She lifted her chin. "I will marry him. I will find work somewhere else, and we will raise Mina together. She likes him, and I think he will make her a good father."

"Mina would be losing a great deal. So would you."

"Would we?" Anneka asked. "Yes, the fancy clothes and shoes, the nice toys and things. But she would have a father"—*faudder*—"to love her, and maybe brothers and sisters to play with. She would not have to pretend her doll is her twin."

Jim studied the fire, stung by her words. "What have you told this man about Mina?"

"I told him her father is dead in Sweden. He doesn't ask for more."

"Don't you think he will?"

"I will not tell him about you. You don't need to worry."

"What about me?"

"What do you mean?"

"I want to be able to see Mina."

Anneka shrugged. "All those pretty girls who come to your mother's parties. You will marry one of them, and there will be children. You will not miss Mina."

"You know I would have done this differently if—"

"Would you have?"

Mina ran into the room, dressed in the periwinkle blue dress, the doll in matching outfit in her arms. She twirled around. "Isn't it pretty?"

"It is beautiful," Anneka said.

Spying the coat, Mina went over and touched it. "It's so soft," she said. "Is it yours, Mother?"

Anneka flashed a look toward Jim. "Yes," she said quietly.

"Are you going to wear it?" Mina asked.

"Why not?" Jim prodded. "Put it on.

He rose and gathered the coat from the box, holding it as Anneka slipped her arms into it. When she turned toward him, Jim straightened the collar and arranged her honey-colored curls over the brown fur. She made no effort to stop him.

"You look lovely," he said.

"Marta doesn't have a coat," Mina said.

"Your doll?" Mina nodded. "Well, then, I'll see to it that she has a coat like this one. And I'll see to it that you have one, too."

"Oh, Mr. Yeem—"

"You must tell Mr. Jim that he does not need to buy a coat for your doll," Anneka said firmly. "And you must tell him that you have a good coat and do not need another."

Mina's face closed. "Thank you, Mr. Yeem. Marta does not need a coat. I don't either."

"Won't you ever want Marta to go outside with you?" Jim asked.

The girl looked toward her mother. "Yes, I want her to go with me."

"Then you'll both need coats. Let's see another dress."

Mina started toward the trunk, but Anneka stopped her. "One dress is enough for today. Tomorrow, you and Marta can try on another dress."

"Let her try them all on," Jim said. "What harm is there?"

Without answering, Anneka spoke in Swedish to the little girl. Mina left the room, but by the look on her face, Jim guessed that she had been told she was not to change her clothes.

Once Mina was gone, Anneka slid out of the beaver coat and sat in the chair, the coat on her lap. "When I was seventeen," she said, "I accepted your mother's offer with gratefulness. My family would have abandoned me, and I knew so few in Denver. I had nowhere to go, no one to help me. But now, I need to live in a way that is more . . . true, I think. All this—it is not true, it is a lie."

"And telling the man you're to marry that Mina's father died in Sweden isn't simply trading one lie for another?"

"Yes, but this time I have chosen the lie. I have not had it chosen for me."

Jim said nothing. He had never considered that Anneka might not accept this arrangement for her entire life. Surely, she had everything she needed or wanted.

"I will never shame you, Jim," Anneka said. "And I will never allow Mina to show disrespect for you or your family. You can trust me."

"I've never doubted you."

"But I want to raise Mina as I would have her to be." She stumbled some over the words. "I don't want her to grow up to think that she can be something more than what she is."

Jim thought of Kathleen, with her country girl simplicity. Anneka's mutiny seemed just as bull-headed and chancy as Kathleen's decision to pass up his proposal of marriage. He remembered Ellie's words: the lives of girls such as these were directed and shaped in ways that seemed incomprehensible to those born into privilege.

"If you marry, you can still count on my support for Mina," he offered.

"And how would I explain such a thing to my husband?" Anneka folded the coat and laid it in the box. "It is getting late. Mina has school tomorrow."

Outside, Jim had nearly reached his car when Mina burst from the house, now wearing the rose-colored dress. "Goodbye, Mr. Yeem," she called.

He scooped her up in his arms and lifted her. Her arms wrapped around his neck, and she kissed his cheek.

"What are you doing out here without a coat?" he asked.

Anneka appeared in the doorway of the house. "Come inside, now. It is too cold."

"I'll bring over your fur coat as soon as I can," Jim promised.

"Mina!" Anneka called.

"Go, before your mother skins me for a coat." He set Mina down and gave her a playful swat on the behind. "I'd make a pretty funny looking one, don't you think?"

Laughing, Mina ran inside. Without another glance, Anneka shut the door behind them.

TWENTY-EIGHT

After the battle at Cambrai, the war quieted, and everyone, it seemed, grabbed whatever bit of life they could. Both convalescent and able-bodied British and American soldiers discovered that the grounds of the chateau near Cagny provided scores of secret places. British nurses courted newly-met colonial beaus by the waterfall, and French girls met Tommies on the artificial island, or in the gazebos, or on garden benches hidden behind shrubbery. The weather seemed to approve of it all. The clouds cleared, and the sun promised enough warmth to solidify the ever-present mud.

Given ten days *en repos*, Paul took a room in a boarding house in Amiens so that he could see Kathleen as often as her schedule allowed. On blustery afternoons, they strolled along gravel paths that led in geometrical circles back to the chateau, and they pried open the rusted locks of garden gates to walk through shrubs that were once pruned into ovals or neat squares, but were now wild and bushy. They met on the bridge over the lake and sheltered from the misting rains in the gazebo. When he couldn't be with her, Paul entrusted Latour to carry messages to her. A true Frenchman, Latour was always willing to assist the cause of love—especially when it was carried out in secrecy.

"I don't think I'm the only one," Kathleen told Paul one afternoon as they watched the waterfall. Her hair was bound beneath a scarf, and she wore a white blouse and black wool skirt under her coat.

"Who do you suspect?" Paul asked.

"Everyone. Hank seems to have a soft spot for Davy, one of the American engineers, and I saw Mrs. Brently and Major Lloyd-Elliot walking opposite the parade ground the other day—"

"I think that one's a given."

"And Helen's been spending almost every afternoon with an Anzac named Arlen, who is a patient in the ward. She tells us she's writing letters for him, but he must have written to all of Australia by now."

"Not Helen," Paul teased. "Not she of 'It's against the rules.'"

"It certainly wouldn't bother me if she took up with him."

"Don't you take up with any of the dashing young men in the wards."

"I don't think I will." She laughed. "I think I'll take up with someone who brings me Irish tea, so that I'm always fortified against the cold, and who has an aunt in Denver—so that I'll always know where he is—"

"—and whose aunt is an artist—"

"That's right— whose aunt is an artist, who can teach me how to paint, and someone who interprets for me so that the French don't *garotte* me when I speak *le francais* to them."

"Maybe I'm protecting them."

She elbowed him. "*C'est cruelle.*"

He elbowed back. "*C'est vrai.*"

When she looked at him with a question, he said, "*Vrai* means true." He reached for her, and she wrapped her arms around his waist. "My next gift to you is going to be a French dictionary."

"It wouldn't help. I'd need you to spell the word for me."

He kissed the tip of her nose. "*Pour toujours, Mademoiselle.* Always."

When Kathleen could leave her post, she and Paul explored the small towns that clustered like obedient children near Amiens. Thousands of refugees had fled to Amiens from Belgium and the north, and now they struggled to live in the shadow of the great cathedral. In carefully guarded patches between broken walls of masonry and in the brightly lit corners of alleys, nascent gardens appeared, the tiny rosettes of plants brightly green in the bleakness of gray dust and snow. Clothes were draped over ledges to dry, and women lined the streets, watching their children at play.

In the middle of December, the weather turned unexpectedly glorious. A blue haze hung over the flat, open country near the city, much like in a painting by Corot. Golden green sprouts pushed their way through the soil of the fields.

On a day that promised warm sun and little rain, Paul invited Kathleen to walk with him into the countryside. "I have something to show you," he said. "But wear your gum boots."

"I've learned never to walk outside without them."

They walked along the road that led away from the chateau's heavily wooded forests and miles of lawn. Kathleen carried a picnic basket, filled with food filched from the chateau's kitchens, and her sketchbook, and Paul carried a thick, woolen blanket in his rucksack. In the distance, high on a hill, a small, broken-down tower rose into the air. Vines had tangled around most of the exterior and poked through narrow, slit-like windows to the inside. A low-lying door of rotted wood allowed entrance into the base.

"What is that?" Kathleen asked.

"Our destination," Paul said. "It's a Medieval lookout. Come on."

They scampered up the hill, sliding backwards at times in the mud. They looked ridiculous, Paul realized, with their arms cast out and their bodies pitched forward, trying to keep their balance. It didn't help that they both laughed as they struggled upward. Once they reached the top, they puffed as they tried to catch their breaths.

"This is much better than Hank's calisthenics," Kathleen said. "All we need to do is climb this once a day."

"Let's see what's inside." He opened the creaking door and stooped to enter. "Watch your head."

Inside, a lashed-together wooden ladder led up through a center hole to the first *étage* or story. The picnic basket in one hand and the rucksack on his back, Paul climbed it, then called down to Kathleen. "It's sturdy enough, come up!"

She followed him upward, making for one of the windows as soon as she stepped onto the stone floor.

"These slits are for archers, I think." Paul told her. "They can rain arrows down on their enemies. They can pull up the ladders behind them, too, for defense."

"Is everything in this country about war?"

"It seems that way, doesn't it?" He gestured toward another ladder that rose to a second landing. "Shall we, milady?"

"Why, yes, kind sir."

The second ladder was followed by a third, which came out onto the roof of the tower. Stone walls surrounded the landing, allowing for a clear view of the plains through stout crenellations.

Kathleen ran her hand along the walls, stopping at a gap to look around. "It looks like a chess piece."

"So it does," Paul agreed. "The rook. Or the castle."

"The castle." She turned to look at him as she repeated the word. "What is it?"

"Someone told me I would see castles in France," she said. "But apart from the chateau—which isn't what I imagined a castle would be—I haven't seen any."

"Most are to the south, I think." Paul moved to one of the lookouts. "Come over here."

The French countryside lay beyond them—the fields draped in the yellow of last year's wheat chaff, the rolling hills of pine, the azure sky. A flock of birds twisted and turned beneath the high clouds, as if winding a net. The breeze sang between the stones, whining softly.

Paul dug in his rucksack. "Here." He handed her a set of field glasses. "Let's see what's out there."

She held the glasses up to her eyes, and Paul helped her adjust them. Standing just behind and beside her, he watched her as she leaned out, the glasses clapped to her eyes.

"Oh, there's the cathedral," she said. "From here, it looks as if it stands alone on the plain."

"Can you see the chateau?"

"Not that I can . . . maybe." She lowered the glasses and handed them to him. "See if you can."

He took the glasses. "I think we need to shift a bit." He pointed at another gap in the wall. "Let's go over there."

He searched for the chateau, but to no avail. Handing the glasses back to her, he said, "Look again."

She scanned the horizon, stopping about midway. "Everything ends," she said. "It turns gray, and . . . it looks as if the land is gone, there. What is it?"

Paul took the glasses. In the distance, he could see ugly crosshatchings in the earth, with blackened stumps and debris scattered about it. "It's the trenches," he said. "Probably from a while ago. Last summer, maybe, or longer."

"The trenches?" she said. "It looks as if they've killed the land, too."

Paul lowered the glasses. "That's exactly what they've done. There are no trees, no grass or plants, no birds or other animals where the fighting has been. It's all dirt, mud, coughed up by the earth and poisoned with gas, and spent shells, and what's left behind after battle."

"Oh," she said quietly. "My father and I used to play a game where we'd say, 'The same sky hangs over' and we'd name the wildest places we could. It was a joke to see who could come up with the strangest name." Her voice grew tender. "The same sky hangs over Amiens, Papa."

"Come over here, and you'll see how beautiful that sky is."

She followed him to a vantage point that overlooked the land to the south.

"See," he said. "The same sky hangs over your Redlands."

She laughed weakly, and he asked, "What are you thinking?"

"The Colorado sky is so much bluer. And bigger, too."

He kissed her forehead. "Don't make yourself homesick."

"Too late."

He spread the blanket on the stone floor of the tower. As they ate, they talked lazily, discussing the gossip from the chateau and the news from home. The war, for a moment, seemed far away.

After they had packed up the picnic, Paul dug into his rucksack. "I have something for you. Close your eyes and hold out your hands."

She did so, then squinted one eye open and asked, "It isn't a frog, is it?"

"A frog? Why would you think that?"

"It's something Seaney would do."

He laughed as he laid a shallow, rectangular tin in her hands. The bottom of it was red, and the top of it carried an image of the Alps. "Merry Early Christmas," he said.

She opened her eyes. "Oh, I don't have your present finished yet—"

"Don't worry. I couldn't wait to give you these."

"What is it?" She lifted the lid from the tin, and Paul leaned forward, as curious as she was about the contents. "They're pencils," she said.

"They're more than pencils. Look and see."

She drew one from the box and studied it. "It has colored lead— or, not lead, something softer. I didn't know such a thing existed!"

"I didn't either," Paul said. "I don't think they really do, unless you know who to ask."

"Your Aunt Julia?" Kathleen touched her finger against the point of a yellow pencil. "Oh, they're beautiful!"

"A friend of hers in Switzerland makes these for artists," he said. "Now, you can capture the colors that you see. They're much easier to carry than oil paints and easel."

"These came all the way from Switzerland?"

"It's not as far as you think."

"Oh, Paul!" She threw her arms around his neck. "Thank you, oh, thank you!"

"You'll have to thank Julia," he said. "I sent her a letter explaining that you wanted to learn to paint, but that it wasn't practical here. This was her reply."

Kathleen lifted a yellow pencil from the box. "You'll have to give me her address."

"I will. But for now, you can draw whatever you like."

She dug in the picnic basket for her sketchpad. Quickly, she drew a rainbow that arced from one edge of the paper to the other. "Look," she said. "That's the first rainbow I've ever drawn. What's the use if it's black lead?"

"That's the loveliest rainbow I've ever seen."

"Don't tease." Flipping to a fresh page, she said, "Talk to me as I sketch. Tell me everything about you, from your first memory to this moment."

"Are you that curious about me?"

"No, I mean, yes!" She laughed at the gaffe. "It makes me less nervous when I'm sketching if I'm not watched."

"I want to watch you," he said. "You're beautiful, with the color up in your cheeks and your eyes so bright. I don't want to take my eyes off you."

She smiled, a coy upturn of her lips. "Well, you'll have to, at least for a while."

He took up a post at one of the lookouts. Occasionally, he glanced back at her as she sketched. She had a habit of playing with the hair at the nape of her neck as she brooded over her work, but she never let her concentration wane. He scanned the countryside again, guessing at the features she would include in the drawing.

"Oh," she said. "The orange doesn't work."

He turned and went to her. "What?"

She rubbed at the tip of the pencil. "The lead—or whatever it is—of the orange doesn't work."

"Here, let me sharpen it."

He dug in his pocket for his knife, but the pencil did not work even with a fresh point. "It's a dud. I'm sorry."

"It doesn't matter," she said. "I'll make my own orange from yellow and red. Now, shoo, so I can finish."

He retreated until she called him back to her. The sketch she handed to him took him by surprise. She had drawn him as he stood near the stolid moss-flecked wall of the tower, his back to her, with only a sliver of the landscape—hazy blue of sky and hill, the splashes of snow against the dull green field, shadows of black and gray—beyond. It was all neatly proportioned and detailed, yet somehow unsettling. It seemed to Paul that the man in the portrait—that he—was longing for something he could never have.

"It's for you," she said.

"I will send it to Julia for Christmas. She will love it. But now, it's my turn."

"Your turn?"

"I'll sketch you." He flipped back to the page on which she had drawn the rainbow. Using a green pencil, he drew a circle directly below the rainbow's arc. A blue line served as her body, and yellow twigs were her arms and legs. With the red pencil, he scribbled a generous head of hair on the stick figure.

"*Voilà*," he said.

Kathleen laughed. "*C'est terrible!*"

He lay the sketchbook aside and reached for her. "For once, you got it right."

He is in love with her, but it isn't until they visit the great cathedral in Amiens that he understands how much he loves her. The cathedral, one of the largest in France, is visible from miles away, rising above the flat plain. As they approach it, she stops to study it all—the nearly-unimaginable intricacies of western facade that show Christ sitting in judgment with an array of saints—one standing above another's head—up the tympanum, the jutting gargoyles, the gallery of kings beneath the rose window, the grandeur and glory of the cool stone.

Inside, they walk in silence along the black and white geometrical floor, while they gawk at the vaulted ceiling more than twelve stories above their heads. Delicately-wrought stained glass windows allow light to radiate through the cathedral in a bounty of color and brilliance. Some of the individual pieces are only inches long, making each window a compilation of thousands of tiny, glittering shards.

"See that chain?" Paul whispers, pointing upward to an iron bar chain that circles the wall just above the arches. "After the cathedral was built, the walls started to heave under the weight of the ceiling. See the cracks where the stones have shifted? To stop it, the Medieval builders installed that chain while the metal was still red hot. As it cooled, the metal shrank some and reinforced the walls."

"That chain must weigh hundreds—no, thousands—of pounds," she whispers. "How did they lift it, especially when it was hot?"

"I don't know, but it worked. The building hasn't fallen."

As they move up the narrow, center aisle of the nave and through the transept, a wall of sandbags appears at the base of the soaring central columns. They tower above Paul's head, probably twenty feet high, enclosed in brackets. A tarp covers the elegant floor, hiding the dizzying design.

Kathleen studies the sandbags, then sends a questioning look to Paul.

He whispers, "They might save the cathedral if it's bombed."

"Oh," she says, as if the information hurts her somehow.

They continue up the aisle, flanked on either side by the sandbag walls. Ahead, the French flag flies on either side of the altar. At the sight of the rose window, where the light falls with brilliant clarity into the church, Kathleen brings her hand to her throat, as if her heart has lifted up into it.

"Look at the colors," she whispers. "Do you mind if I—?"

She motions toward the wooden chairs at either side of the aisle.

"Sketch?" he whispers.

"No," she says, as if the thought had not crossed her mind. "I'd like to pray."

He retreats as she genuflects, crosses herself, and slides into an aisle. Rather than sitting down, she kneels and rests her hands in an attitude of prayer on the crossbar. She lowers her head, and Paul can no longer see her face, only the graceful curve of her neck beneath the shawl that covers her hair and falls over her shoulders. How does she still have faith, he wonders, after all she has seen? Why does she think that God has any thought of man, when men seem to have no other purpose just now but to tear each other apart?

He hears a commotion near the back of the church. Five soldiers have come into the church, obviously sightseers, and from their uniforms, Australian. They talk in street voices, discussing the size of the church and the amount of stone that went into it. A priest rushes along behind them, saying, *"S'il vous plaît, s'il vous plaît, c'est un lieu de prière."*

The soldiers eye the priest, and the meaning of the words dawns on one of them. "I think he wants us to be quiet," he says, without lowering his voice.

"*D'accord, d'accord,*" one of the other soldiers says. They come up the aisle, quieter but no more respectful, and Paul steps out of their way and into the shadows of a column. He glances at Kathleen, but she has not moved. Something rushes up inside him. It is admiration for her ability to see this place as sacred yet, even as its towering stone walls are shored up by dirt against the petty squabbles of men, and even as it is breached by strangers—himself included—who either don't understand God or don't believe in Him or who cannot reconcile the idea of a caring deity with what they have seen at Ypres, or the Somme, or Cambrai. In this moment, he knows how much he wants her, not only in the most earthly of ways, but as a light for his soul.

TWENTY-NINE

Sean sits in an abandoned house in a town whose name he isn't quite sure of. Six of them have been billeted here—Sean, Kevin, Arnie, Tony, Nicola and Michael—and Sean is thankful that there is at least some semblance of the structure left. Although the windows are blown away and half of the northern wall of the house is missing, there is still a ragged roof.

They fought for a week to retake this small town that has been in German hands for over three years. It was only a matter of capturing a few hundred yards—with at least one American soldier killed for every yard—but the euphoria was contagious. Americans can fight as well as the French and British! They are heroes after all!

Now, they'll stay here, possibly until after Christmas, unless they're called upon to kick the tripe out of the Germans again. But it's said that the Germans are starving to death in the north, much to the glee of the American troops, and won't be able to fight until the crops come in next summer.

Kevin, who is reading a newspaper, says, "There's something going on in Russia."

"What is it?"

"They've upended the Tsar and started fighting each other instead of the Germans. So now the Germans who were on the Eastern Front will be coming here." He riffles the paper as he turns the pages. "Bloody Bolsheviks. Just when we were about to end it."

Sean laughs. In his diary, he writes:

Our trip through No Man's Land was an interesting one this time. We had hardly left the trench when the Boche started raking us with machine gun fire. We crawled through the underbrush, trying not to show ourselves, and trying to shoot as many of the buggers as we could. My sleeve caught on a wire fence, and I got peppered in fine style until I ripped the blasted thing loose. Some of those who dropped down beside me found blackberries in the brambles and started picking them and popping them in their mouths. It's just one of those strange things that happens in war— in the middle of a hot fusillade, we're eating our way across No Man's Land, fingers stained purple by berries.

Most of us made it to where the Germans had been. They had a strong position there—deep trenches and a dozen or so concrete pillboxes. But they'd been pretty well smashed up by our artillery, and they'd turned tail and run by the time we joined up with them.

Some of the boys had a fine time looting the German dugouts. They'd left behind beer, salmon sardines, sour bread and these delicate yellow cakes that tasted like heaven. There were other souvenirs, too—wristwatches, quite a few helmets, and some pipes and tobacco. I'm not one for digging through the bodies—I guess I'm still too tender or something—so I came away with very little treasure.

He looks up at the glassless window frame that has been plastered over with an oilcloth for protection against the wind and snow. He still has not forgotten—he will never forget—the German in the shell hole. Although he is a Corporal now, with a medal for bravery on his uniform, he considers himself a fraud. Others in the unit have killed, but their feats haven't been so dramatic, and no one except Sean has had the honor of claiming insignia. He hasn't confided his thoughts to anyone. He just stews in it, as he does in the stench and filth of the trenches.

He writes again:

As we marched forward, we saw how completely a village can be destroyed—buildings in shambles, blasted to rubble, fields filled with great craters, dead animals all around. That's what we'd fought for—a pile of junk. Yet, where the Germans had buried their dead, they had built bordered walks and flower gardens. There were even permanent stone monuments with names written in German. They must have thought they would never leave. Some of the Americans took hammers to the German names and defiled the gravestones with urine or shit. They were quickly disciplined, but still, it bothers me. I can't help but think that the dead are sacred, no matter who they are—

"Hey, Sean." Kevin waves the newspaper at him. "You seen this?"

He passes the paper to Sean. It's the company paper—thank heavens, Sean won't have to try to piece together what it says with his primitive French. The paper is put out by the soldiers themselves to keep up morale and record the history of the company. In it are reports of progress on improvements to the food—which never happen—and announcements of concerts by the company band. The front page features photographs of American soldiers parading for French civilians—women, children and old men lining streets with blank eyes, gaunt cheeks, and their mouths gaping open in what's known as "bread starvation."

Sean reads an article about the Hanging Virgin of Albert. Caught in the bombardment between the German Third Army and the British during the battle of the Somme, the basilica of the Catholic Church in Albert was shelled. Even though the town was reduced to rubble, the basilica did not fall. One side of it, however, was torn apart, and a golden statue of the Virgin Mary that stood atop it was dislodged. To this day, the Virgin, who holds her baby Jesus in her outstretched arms, is suspended at a precarious ninety degree angle to the basilica.

A picture of the basilica and the leaning Virgin accompanies the article. It appears as if Mary is offering her precious baby to the men below on earth.

"They say whoever brings the Virgin down will lose the war," Kevin says. "Right now, the Brits are using the basilica as a machine gun nest. My bet's on the Germans bringing it down."

"Good news for us," Sean says.

He frowns at his words. What is he doing, wishing for the desecration of something sacred? Has he become so godless, so lost, that he can't separate good from evil? He doesn't know himself anymore, doesn't know anything.

He certainly isn't the same boy who came to France.

Les Yeux Bleus—Blue Eyes. The women in the French-sponsored whorehouses marvel at the lightness of his eyes and the paleness of his skin coupled with the ebony of his hair. The houses are off-limits to the American soldiers—Pershing does not believe that his troops require such services—but most of the field officers overlook the infraction. In fact, some even partake of the opportunity.

At first, Sean had refused to go, thinking he would keep himself pure, follow the commands of the Bible, and of Father Devlin and Blackjack. But after that harsh spell in the trenches, he realized that he might not go home again, he might never know what it is to love, to be loved, to make love.

That day, there was a woman at the house named Béatrice. After Sean paid, she had held up one finger and asked, *"Est-ce votre première fois?* One?"

"Pardon?" Sean had said.

"Il n'y a pas de femmes en Amérique?" In clipped, laughing English, she had said, "There's no girls in America? All of you Yankees"—*Yahn-keez*—"this is the first time for you."

Béatrice was slim, with dark, snapping eyes, marcelled brown hair, and a *"certificat de santé,"* or health, from the French government that she produced once he'd shown her his delousing papers. She knew how to draw a bath that smelled like lilacs instead of sulfur, how to soothe with a sponge, how to stir the feelings taken for granted by the living. He remembered how warm he had felt after they made love, as if the blood was flowing again in his veins, and how he had not wanted to leave, even after Béatrice told him flatly that it was time to go. It is she who called him Blue Eyes.

He closes his diary and picks up a letter that has come from Kathleen. He has already read it twice, but he can't reconcile what Kathleen has seen in France with what he has experienced:

Think of it, I'm living in a chateau! I will brag about it for the rest of my life because I will never live in a house this big again! There are hundreds of rooms, it seems, and so many winding hallways that we become lost almost once a day. We live in what was once the servants' quarters, at the very top of the house. Our canteen isn't a tent this time, but a room on the lower floor which was probably once a cloak room or powder room or something. We actually have electricity, too—sometimes—rigged up by the British engineers.

One thing I have to say, though, is that the French don't have a good sense of how to heat a place. The fireplaces are all blocked up, so that we nearly die from smoke whenever we light even the feeblest of fires. I've been sleeping with two pairs of bed socks on my feet and the heaviest flannel nightdress that Mrs. Brently has been able to buy, and I still feel like an icicle in the mornings.

There are no bathtubs here, either. We usually depend on a few pitchers of eau chaude *(which isn't "hot" at all) that we heat up on the tiny stove that is in our room. Two of the British nurses have a collapsible rubber bath tub that they lend us—when they are feeling generous, which isn't often, because they work so hard. Whenever I feel like I can't take another step, I look at them. They work for days at a time, without even eating or sitting down. We follow them around with bowls of soup and bread, trying to feed them, but sometimes we're more of a pest than we are a blessing.*

We have fixed up our room by swiping whatever we can find. I know it is breaking a commandment, but everyone steals here—it is comme il faut. *All the furniture in the chateau was taken by the British, so the only things we had in our room are bed frames. So Helen asked the lorry drivers for spare pallets that we used to build a dresser of sorts and a writing desk. For the top of the desk, we "commandeered" a slab from an abandoned tombstone shop—don't tell anyone! We had to bribe five Royal Scots with free chocolate from the canteen so that they would carry it up to the third floor of the chateau for us—*

Now, Tony comes into the room. Since that terrible day in the trenches, he and Sean have stayed close to one another. They are always side by side at the firestep; they spend the time they have at leisure together.

Sean hands the newspaper to Tony. "Did you see this?"

With the same speed and decisiveness that Tony does everything, he skims the article and tosses the newspaper on the table. "Huh," he says. "Must be the last virgin left in France."

Kevin laughs, delighted.

Tony says, "Hey, Sean, come with us."

"Where are you going?" Sean asks.

"They said there's whores set up on the far side of town, where the French are billeted."

"And a wine shop," Kevin adds.

Sean pulls on his boots and coat. Arnie, Michael and Nicola join them at the doorway of the house. Tony offers Sean a flask. "Get up your courage, huh? And whatever else you need."

They wind along the curving main avenue of the town—or what is left of it. Last night's rain has turned the mess of broken stone and brick in the street into a churning yellow slop. A few shops are unmolested, but they have long been closed. In what was once the *Charcuterie*, sausage skins still hang in the window, the meat from them long since stolen. A dressmaker's window flaunts dust-laden folds of fabric and lace. As they round a corner, the blasted hulk of a church appears. A steeple still stands, but at a tilt. Nothing remains of the arched windows of the sanctuary but crumbling, gaping holes. Stone steps lead up to the entrance, where a wooden door has been precariously reattached to the structure.

"Want to go in?"

Without waiting for an answer, Tony bounds up the stone steps and pries open the door. The others crowd into what was once the main aisle of the church. Ten rows of short wooden pews—some of them shattered or shifted—run up to what used to be the apse. Nothing remains there—no altar, no statue of Christ, no stained glass windows.

The men fan out in front of the rows of pews, like the altar boys they all were in the distant past. Sean tries to imagine how the church once looked, but he cannot. Something rises up in him, a great sorrow, the knowledge of great loss. How poorly places of worship have been treated by this war.

"Look," Kevin says.

He points to something anchored in the rubble. It is a silver cross, with only the top and one arm protruding from a pile of rocks and dust.

"I wonder why they didn't take that with them," he says.

"So we could have it," Tony says.

He leaps over what is left of the altar rail and moves toward the cross. As he reaches for it, a voice rings out in the back of the church: "*Non! Non! Arrêtez!*"

Sean turns to see French soldiers filing into the church. The one who shouted—who looks to be an officer of some sort—moves forward. "Do not touch!" he says in English.

"Okay." Tony lifts his hands like a surrendering criminal.

"The Germans," the Frenchman says in English. "They leave this all over where they have been. It is not safe. *C'est une bombe.*"

Speaking in French again, he orders two men forward. As Sean and the others watch, the two Frenchmen carefully loop a rope around the cross' visible arm.

"*Sortez!*" the lieutenant calls to his own men. He waits for the men to exit the church before he addresses the Americans, "Go, get behind the . . . hide yourselves. Keep your heads down."

Sean and Kevin take cover behind an undamaged pew. The French soldiers at the front of the church disappear behind a pile of stone.

"Now, watch!" the lieutenant calls, once they are all positioned. "*Regardez!*"

Lying on his belly, one of the French soldiers jerks the rope and easily yanks the cross out of the rubble. At the same time, an explosion sends bits of stone and wood scattering. Sean covers his head, crouching down onto the rough tiled floor. When he looks up again, a fine dust floats over the apse and through the last rays of sun that stream from the west.

"Jesus Christ, it's a booby-trap!" Kevin exclaims.

Some of the French edge forward toward the smoking rubble. One soldier kicks at it, while others flatten themselves along the opposite wall, as if afraid the pile will explode again.

"You Americans, you must think!" The lieutenant points to his head. "*Pensez! Pensez!*"

Outside, others are coming, alerted by the bang, running toward the church, guns in their hands. An officer on horseback gallops up the avenue, and a number of soldiers drag a water wagon into place, prepared for a fire. In the chaos, the Americans leave without anyone taking notice. Kevin and Tony forge ahead, while Sean and the others follow. Tony stops, shielding his mouth with cupped hands as he lights a cigarette.

"There's a million ways to die in this country," he says.

Kevin and the others laugh, but Sean's stomach twists.

"I think I'll go back," he says.

Tony looks up. "You okay?"

"I'm just . . . yeah, I'm okay."

He turns away, heading back to the billet in the house. He can feel the explosion yet in his gut—even when you know it's coming, it churns up everything that you have inside—and his eyes and nostrils sting, still, with the smoke from the blast. He thinks only in fragments: *If Tony had grabbed the cross, if the French lieutenant hadn't come in, if Marsh had stood up and fought, if that German had chosen another hole to hide in, if he'd seen me first . . .*

He walks down the main thoroughfare of the town, dodging horses and wagons and the *camions* of the French and the trucks of the Americans. The town hums with activity—newly arrived troops set to move forward from this position, the engineers who will prepare the next battlefield, an excavating crew picking up supplies and equipment abandoned by the Germans, the spent troops—like himself—loitering in packs along the street, observers only.

At the edge of the town, he comes to a small hillock that rolls upward just before the French military blockade. It might even be the hill that they had fought so hard to take back from the Germans—

he is no longer sure. Hiking upward, he sits on a rock that hasn't yet been blasted to pebbles. From here, he can look down on the town. He sees the bustle still around the church, and he can even hear orders and exclamations in both French and English. He sees, too, the defiled cemetery, now closely guarded by American MPs.

A cold wind blows from the west, and he pulls his collar around his neck. What is this all about? Why is he here? What is he trying to be, to do, to become in this place where the monuments of the dead are hacked at and defaced, where a sacred statue is the object of a callous bet, where a silver cross is a path to death?

A million ways to die.

He lowers his head, studying the ground between his knees. *Dear God,* he thinks, then stops.

He has forgotten how to pray.

THIRTY

Maggie stood in the kitchen of her house, steam coming from the pots on the stove, and the oven bristling with heat. She wiped her hands on her apron, nervous. She had begged Ma to let her fix the dinner for Christmas Day, even though her mother had not wanted her to work that hard. As she lifted a lid on the stove to check the boiling potatoes, the baby moved. Maggie put her hand on her stomach, comforted by the tiny life inside.

In the living room, where the dining table was set with the best that she and Liam had, conversation buzzed between Liam, Brendan, and Ma and Pa. A swoosh of cold air from outside announced that Auntie Eileen and Uncle Irish had just arrived from Redlands. Maggie wiped her hands on her apron and went to the doorway between the two rooms.

Uncle Irish shook Liam's hand, but Auntie Eileen sniffed as Liam kissed her cheek. Without a word to him, she moved toward Ma, and the two came into the kitchen.

"Look at you," Auntie Eileen said to Maggie. "The baby's kickin' now, is it?"

"He started to move right after Thanksgiving."

"He? You think it's a boy."

"I think it's a healthy, happy boy."

"We'll see in time, I suppose." Auntie Eileen turned her attention to her sister. "How was the Mass this mornin', Maureen?"

"As beautiful as ever, of course, and—"

Maggie turned back to the stove to stir the gravy, piqued by her aunt's snub of Liam. Since his expulsion from the Knights of

Columbus, she hadn't been able to take a single breath without releasing a stream of bitter bile into her blood and mind. Attending Mass had become a miserable burden, even though Liam insisted that they go daily. Rather than praying, Maggie spent her time in the sanctuary trying to discern who was a friend and who thought poorly of them.

Tomorrow, Liam would appear in court on the charge of distributing propaganda. The People's Council of America for Democracy and Peace had provided him with a young lawyer by the name of Judah Rapp, who believed as strongly as Liam did that the war was for the benefit of the rich. A short, slender man with a thick, black beard, Judah had promised Maggie that he would do his best for Liam.

But today, Maggie was determined that it would be the happiest holiday her family had ever celebrated—no matter that Seaney and Kathleen were missing, no matter the dark clouds of war, no matter what happened tomorrow.

"I'm ready to take everything into the dining room, Ma," she said over her shoulder. "Let's eat."

Once the food was on the table and everyone was seated, Brendan said the grace. As the dishes were passed around, Maggie waited anxiously for someone to say something about the food. After a few bites, Brendan said, "This is delicious," and the others joined in with compliments.

"It's better than what Seaney's probably havin'," Ma said. "They say the food's terrible in France."

"Were you able to send a Christmas package to him?" Brendan asked.

"Aye, we have," Ma said. "But we've since gotten a postcard from him that is all he's allowed from the Front—"

"'Tis a series of boxes that he can check," Pa said. "I am well, I am not well, and the sort. Doesn't tell us anything."

"Well, it's good to know that the army is protecting its men from the eyes of spies," Brendan offered. "What about your daughter, Mrs. O'Doherty? What have you heard from her?"

"She tells some wild tales," Auntie Eileen said. "I don't know what they're doin' over there. She told a story of drivin' a truck to pick up some supplies from another village."

"Which side of the road do they drive on over there?" Brendan asked. "Is it the right?"

"I don't know," Auntie Eileen admitted. "Anyway, Kathleen and Hank were sent out together—"

"Hank is Miss Mills, isn't she?" Ma asked. "Her letters in the *Post* are so funny."

"Yes, Harriet Mills." Uncle Irish took over the story. "Well, the truck became stuck in the mud along the road, which Kathleen says are not so much roads as obstacle courses. They were unable to get out on their own, but fortunately, a French division was passing by, and a number of the young men stopped and helped to push them out—"

"I want to know why they were on their own," Auntie Eileen said. "Without a male companion or guide."

Uncle Irish shrugged. "It seems to be the way it's done over there."

"But that isn't all," Auntie Eileen said. "Kathleen said that at about ten o'clock that night, long after the canteen was shut tight, the division arrived in the town. The French soldiers threw rocks at the window of the hotel where the girls were stayin' until they roused them to come make cocoa and doughnuts for them. It was nearly three in the mornin' before they were able to go back to bed."

Uncle Irish laughed. "From the sounds of it, the girls had a ball—"

"That's seems pretty chancy, doesn't it?" Ma asked. "Rousin' young girls out of bed and keepin' them up until dawn? Exposin' them to every sort of soldier that comes along? What do you think, Father?"

"I doubt there is any way to weed out the undesirable soldiers from the more gentlemanly ones," Brendan said. "Perhaps a male protector would be a—"

"Those girls should have a proper chaperone," Auntie Eileen said. "The sister doesn't seem to do much of anything. From what Kathleen's written us, it sounds like they've been on the loose since New York, seein' Broadway shows and the like. I never wanted my daughter involved in this foolishness, and I don't want her runnin' wild in a country as godless and dangerous as France—"

"I will pray for her safety, then," Brendan said.

"And I don't think they've done a single bit of war work," Auntie Eileen said. "Kathleen never writes about helpin' soldiers or prayin' for the wounded men. It's all shenanigans and foolishness."

"Perhaps she doesn't want to burden you with the more troubling parts of war," Brendan suggested. "Or, perhaps, she can't tell you because of the censors."

"Oh, the censors," Ma started. "Seaney's letters have so many holes that—"

"Kathleen and Seaney are both doin' what they should," Pa growled. "Doin' their best for our country."

Silence fell. Maggie glanced toward Liam, but he made no effort to defend himself. He simply sipped from his glass of water and took another bite of corn.

She lifted her chin and said defiantly, "I've had some good news this week."

Auntie Eileen squinted a frown toward her, and Ma laid down her fork. Liam looked up curiously, while Uncle Irish kept his habitually bemused look. It was Brendan who spoke. "What is it, Maggie?" he asked.

"I sent a story I wrote called 'Evelyn's Joy' to *The Ladies' Home Journal,* and they've decided to publish it," she said. "Yesterday, I got a letter and a check for twenty-five dollars from the magazine's editor. The story will be published in the March magazine."

No one spoke for a moment. At last, Uncle Irish said, "Well, that's something to crow about, Muffin. Where's the letter? Read it to us."

Delighted, Maggie jumped up and opened the drawer of the sideboard. She had hidden the letter there last night with the hope that someone would want to see it. Sitting down again, she unfolded it as if it were made of spun glass and read, "Dear Mrs. James, We are proud to accept 'Evelyn's Joy' for publication. The story shows a true understanding of the nature of marriage and offers a moral tale that many of our readers, young housewives, appreciate—"

"Who's Mrs. James?" Liam asked.

"I am!" Maggie said. "I wrote it under the name of Margaret James because I didn't think anyone would publish a story by Margaret Mary Sullivan Keohane—"

Liam leaned back in his chair, his face clouded.

"James is the American translation for Pa's name." Maggie pressed on. "I thought it was a clever clue as to who I am. Don't you think it's clever, Ma?"

Her mother's gaze shifted. "What made you send your writin' to a magazine?"

"Well, Kathleen does it," Maggie said hotly. "Her letters and sketches are in the newspapers now, and—"

"What's the story about?" Brendan asked.

"It's about a young woman named Evelyn who finds that being married is the best thing that's ever happened to her," Maggie purred. "And the magazine has asked me to submit another story about Evelyn. So I've been writing one called 'Evelyn's Hope,' in which the heroine finds that she's carrying George's child."

"Sounds familiar," Uncle Irish said. "Well, congratulations. You've done well, Muffin."

"Do people want to read such things?" Liam asked.

"It's *The Ladies' Home Journal*!" Maggie protested. "Hundreds, probably thousands, of women read it."

Liam looked away, but Brendan said, "You'll have to show it to us in March."

The rest of the meal passed in pleasant conversation—more stories about Kathleen's adventures and Seaney's complaining—but Maggie said nothing more. Why was it that only their exploits were noteworthy? Liam was silent, too. Maggie worried: his dour face reminded her of when he had risen from the swimming pool without his glasses. It was as if he could not see outside of his own thoughts and feelings.

That night, she stood by the window of the bedroom. Outside, the night was quiet and dark, the festivities of Christmas already forgotten in the snowfall that was covering the streets. When Liam came in from washing up, he stood behind her and put his arms around her, his hands resting on the baby. She covered his hands with hers and leaned back against him.

"It was a lovely meal," he said.

"But now we have to face tomorrow." She turned so that her cheek lay against his neck, and she could breathe in his scent of musk and salt. "What will happen to the baby and me if you go to jail?"

"Brendan will take care of you," Liam said. "We've talked about it. Judah, too. He has promised to look out for your wellbeing, whatever you need. Money, legal help—"

"Brendan? Judah? That isn't what I mean. Who is going to be"—she waves toward the bed—"*here* for me? Who is going to wake up with me or talk to me or hold me?"

He moved away from her and sat on the bed. "Maggie, you have to be strong—"

"Strong?" She laughed mockingly. "I am strong. I can roll forty pound kegs on and off a delivery truck and wrestle down a slab of beef for Pa. But I need you here, to help me with our baby, to love him as I do—"

"I do love it as you do." Liam reached out and touched her arm. "I have to know that you will be—if I am . . . taken away, I have to know that you will always care for our baby and stay true to our love."

"Of course, I will! How could you think differently of me?"

"You've changed your name."

"That's because my own name is so Irish!" she said wildly. "All the well-known authors have simple, Protestant names. Elinor H. Porter and Grace Livingston Hill and—"

"Is that the only reason?" Liam asked. "You aren't ashamed to be married to me?"

"Never!" she swore. "But what about you? Why did you ask whether people want to read stories like mine?"

"With all the sorrow and evil in the world, why would people read about things that are so unimportant?"

"It lets them forget all the bad things." Her throat tightened, and she confessed, "It lets me forget the bad things when I write them."

He smiled sadly. "That's what prayer is for. Promise me you'll go to Mass every day."

She hedged. To tell Liam that she no longer prayed, but railed against God as she sat in the sanctuary, would waste precious time. "I'll go every day that I can," she said. "But I don't know what will happen after the baby is born."

He seemed unwilling to challenge her. "Let's go to bed," he said. "Tomorrow will be a long day."

It was, indeed, a long day. Sitting with Brendan in a high-ceilinged, ornate courtroom at the monolithic Denver County Courthouse, Maggie perspired, even though the snow continued to fall outside on Tremont Street. Ma and Pa had declined to come with her, saying that they needed to tend the store. She knew they were ashamed.

Liam's case came up late in the afternoon. He was sentenced to nine months in the Denver County Jail, that cold, stinking bastion of darkness. He did not look back at Maggie or Brendan as he was taken from the courtroom, but kept his head down, his gaze on the floor. *Nine months,* Maggie thought, a handkerchief against her mouth to silence her sobs. The same number that it took to bring a child into the world. By the time Liam had served his nine months, though, their baby would be cooing and crawling.

"Are you all right?" Brendan asked her as they left the Courthouse.

"Yes," she answered. "I just want to go home."

But home was nothing without him. A house, carefully-polished furniture, a prettily-made bed with fluffy throw pillows. Lying alone that night, she stared at the ceiling. The baby moved as she stretched out her body, then settled, it seemed, into peaceful slumber. Was this what her life would be? Alone, her child without its father, like some poor woman who had married a dishonest or cruel man, or who had been left pregnant and penniless at the altar, or who, like Liam's mother, had been deserted by her husband when he found out they were to have another child he could not afford to feed?

Unable to sleep, she went to the vanity. Taking a page from the drawer, she read: *In the kitchen, Evelyn decided that for this very special dinner she would fix the things she liked to eat. She looked around as she tied on a frilled apron. The old black stove glowed with a well-stoked fire, and the modern gas stove was just waiting for her command. She made a wild search through the cupboards for a can of corn and—*

Who would want to read this? Special dinner? Can of corn? She crumpled the page and threw it across the room. Liam was right—it was foolishness, rot, in a world where everything was bitter and wrong. Lying down in bed again, she cried herself to sleep.

Yet, once again, Liam came home two days later. This time, he had not been beaten or starved or left to sit in his own foul stench. This time, he wore the suit, still fairly clean and unwrinkled, that he had appeared in at the trial. Maggie ran to the door just as he was murmuring a prayer and crossing himself with holy water. Brendan and Judah were with him.

"What happened?" She threw her arms around his neck. "Oh, Liam, did they let you go?"

Judah replied. "I entered an appeal that Mr. Keohane was exercising his freedom of religion. He's been released for now."

"Freedom of religion!" Maggie laughed. "Of course, that's what it is!"

"It isn't final," Brendan warned. "There will be another trial."

"Why didn't you tell me you were planning this?" she asked Judah.

"I didn't know if it would work," he said. "I didn't want you to have false hopes, Mrs. Keohane."

Maggie let go of Liam to shake Judah's hand. "Thank you, oh, thank you."

Liam rounded the corner to sit down on the couch in the parlor, and Brendan and Judah took their leave. Maggie headed for the kitchen. "What do you want to eat?" she asked. "Do you want tea? Do you want a bath?"

He didn't respond, and Maggie came back into the parlor. His face was closed and set, his shoulders and spine rigid and unyielding, as if he could not relax. At last, he said, "Maggie, sit down."

She sat on the edge of the couch, fear coursing through her again.

"I don't know if I am brave enough for this," he said.

"What do you mean? Brave enough for what?"

"To do what I need to for my God."

"Then, don't try to be." She laid her hand on his thigh. "You've done all you can to fight the war. Now, it's time to think about our lives together. Our marriage was in the Church, in the eyes of God, according to His law. We've followed the rules of the Church. We go to Mass, we pray, we go to confession, we live the way it tells us to. Why doesn't that count?"

"Count?" he asked. "This isn't some sort of race or game. It's not some foolish competition. This is about the eternal soul of all men."

She rubbed her forehead, the words too painful to speak. Finally, she said, "You keep saying that it's about God, yet they keep accusing you of being too cowardly to serve. It isn't about that, is it? Not even a little? The fear of serving?"

Liam's words were just as slow coming back to her. "I don't see how you can ask me that," he said stiffly. "I will not fight for a country that values wealth and imperialism over the lives of its people. I won't fight for a country that bends God's laws to justify its own system of greed and oppression—"

"We aren't at a meeting of the People's Council," she snapped. "You're talking to me, Liam, to *me*. How can this fight that you've made for yourself be more important than our marriage?"

"Made for myself? Is that what you think it is? That I've made this up?"

"No one else is this stubborn!" she cried. "Frank has registered and gone, and he didn't want to go any more than you do, and Donnell, and Seaney—"

"It isn't a question of whether I want to go. It's a question of my moral duty to God's law."

"We're back to where we started, aren't we?" Maggie asked bitterly. "You said you wouldn't let the war change you, but it has. It's made you into someone I don't . . ."

She stopped, afraid of what she might say.

"Someone you don't like?"

"That I don't know," she said. "Come back to me. We'll be who we were—remember? We used to walk around the lake, and talk about whatever came into our heads, and we read books together and argued about who our favorite author was, and we'd laugh and tease—"

He lowered his chin to his chest, and his body shook, and Maggie realized that he had begun to cry. She reached for him, and he fell sideways, his head in her lap, his clenched fists wadding the fabric of her skirt. His sobs wrenched from his lungs in great violent breaths. Desperate to comfort him, Maggie let her own tears spill unchecked as she bent to wrap her arms around him. "Oh, Liam, I love you so," she whispered. "Oh, I love you so."

THIRTY-ONE

Three days after Christmas, packages wrapped in brown paper arrived for each of the girls of the Graves Family Foundation Relief Society. The girls gathered around one of the lop-legged tables in the canteen to open them. Mrs. Brently presided over the activity, watching with pleasure.

Inside, under a raft of colored tissue paper, were collars and muffs made from the fur of the American fox. Both pieces were lined with a rust-colored satin. Helen stroked hers gently without removing it from the box, while Hank said, "Fur! I've never had anything made out of fur! Here, help me put it on."

Kathleen arranged the collar around Hank's neck. "You look beautiful," she said.

At once, Hank reached up to pet the fur. "I can hear it purr."

"It's you who's purring, not the fur," Kathleen said.

As Helen and Hank laughed, Mrs. Brently said, "The collars should fit the exact measurements of our capes. According to our rules, they can be worn only when we are at special occasions, not for every day."

"Oh, thank you, Mrs. Brently!" Helen said. "They are so nice!"

"They have come from Mr. Graves," Mrs. Brently said. "He asked if there was something we needed. Since warmth is scarce, I thought of these for when we are at nighttime or outdoor events."

"We'll write to thank him right away," Hank said.

Kathleen's own fur piece lay just over her collarbones, warming them immediately. She slipped her hands inside the muff and brought it up to her face, tickling her cheeks and lips with the soft fur.

"Look, Kathleen." Helen offered a hand mirror. "It almost matches your hair."

She looked at her reflection. Helen was right—her hair was only a few shades darker than the fox. Turning, she caught Mrs. Brently's expression, which was both troubled and knowing. Instantly, Kathleen realized that the choice of fox had not been casual, but wholly intentional. Jim must have imagined how the color would complement her coloring.

The first opportunity that the girls had to wear the furs came on New Year's Day. The British command at Amiens—led by Major Lloyd-Elliot—had invited the members of the Graves Family Foundation Relief Society to a celebratory meal and musical performance. The girls wore their wimples and uniforms, which had been scrubbed with ether to remove as many of the stains as possible, and their capes, adorned with the brooches of the American flag that Jim had given them when they left New York and the fur collars. Their hands were tucked into the muffs. As they journeyed to the barn, they chattered among themselves, while Mrs. Brently walked ahead of them in the company of Major Lloyd-Elliott. She, too, wore a fox collar and carried a muff.

"You'll have to sketch us while we're all dolled up," Hank said to Kathleen. "Especially now that you can do it in color."

Kathleen laughed. Both Hank and Helen had been as excited about the pencils as she had been, and Helen had even asked to borrow the pencils to draw a flowery heart in a letter to her younger brothers and sisters.

"Who will sketch you?" Helen asked.

Kathleen thought of the sketch that Paul had made of her—the stick figure beneath the rainbow. She had kept that etching—silly as it was—and hidden it in her trunk. Every time she looked at it, her love for Paul arose in a bubbly, dancing joy.

"Maybe I'll draw myself," she said, thinking that she would give him the portrait as a belated Christmas present. "I've never tried it."

She had given Paul his present a few days before Christmas, which was the last time she had seen him. From yarn that she had requested from Aunt Maury, she had knitted a scarf with large blocks of blue, white and red—or red, white and blue, depending on the way it was viewed—in honor of his service to both the French and the Americans. It didn't match the perfection of his gift to her, but he had loved it— at least, he said he had. Wrapping it around his own neck first, then looping it around hers, he had drawn her closer and closer to him, until he could kiss her, both of them warmed by the knitted scarf.

She smiled as she remembered it.

"I love this muff so much," Hank said. "I'm going to be sad when it warms up."

"I won't," Helen said. "I'll be happy enough when it's spring."

"They say that this is already the coldest, snowiest winter that France has ever had," Kathleen said. "And it's just started!"

The New Year's Day festivities were held in a barn north of Cagny that had been bombed early in the war. Through gaping holes in the roof, the sun cast a patchwork of light and shadow across the tamped dirt floor. At once, Kathleen's fingers started to twitch as she yearned to pull her sketchbook from her bag and record the scene.

A large oaken table—undoubtedly filched from some abandoned home—was positioned under the least damaged part of the roof and set with the finest of china and silver. Throughout the rest of the barn, the other tables were not so grand in nature, but a hodgepodge of what was available—saw horses with boards laid across them, kegs and drum barrels with stools surrounding them, chairs of various sizes and conditions set here and there for those unfortunate enough not to secure a table. A platform had been erected at the far end of the barn, under open sky, as a stage for the performances. Positioned near the tables were pot-bellied stoves that puffed a steady stream of smoke with only a hint of warmth.

Graciously, Major Lloyd-Elliot directed Mrs. Brently to a chair on his right, as if she were the hostess. The girls were seated next, with Helen and Hank on one side while Kathleen sat two chairs down from Mrs. Brently. A courtly Captain, who had evidently been told to show great interest in her, sat to her right, while an equally charming Lieutenant sat to her left. The makeshift tables in the more exposed end of the barn were given over to groups of non-commissioned officers and regular soldiers.

Halfway through the meal, which was served by privates who had been coached in the niceties of domestic service, snow started to fall. At first, the flakes disappeared without notice, but the squalls rapidly picked up, with large, wet flakes falling through the holes in the roof. Snow began to stick on the cheesecloth-covered baskets of bread and on the shoulders of the diners. Kathleen reached up and adjusted her wimple, thankful for the fur collar that kept the snow from slipping down the back of her neck.

Around her, the conversation continued, although the voices of the men at the exposed tables grew into good-natured complaining as the snow gusted through in the barn in whirling dervishes. Kathleen tried to memorize it all for later—the pert young officers with their shoulders covered with what looked like a year's worth of dandruff, Hank and Helen with snow sprinkling the fur of their collars and their cheeks blazing red with cold, Mrs. Brently and Major Lloyd-Elliott acting as if nothing was amiss, decidedly determined to ignore the storm, finish the meal, and proceed with the musical entertainment. Neither mentioned the weather, but kept talking about the Major's estate in Surrey and the mountains of Colorado. Mrs. Brently went as far as to shake snow from the napkin in her lap.

Kathleen looked over at Hank and Helen, who had long since given up their attempts to maintain sober and dignified expressions. The young Lieutenant next to Hank was catching snowflakes in his hand and then pretending to transfer them to his other hand in a mock-up of the shell game. Hank laughed aloud as she chose a hand only to have him open it and say in pretend amazement, "By Jove, it's gone!"

The wind gusted again, and heavy snow swirled downward. The Captain seated next to Kathleen started to shiver. Still, he kept up a conversation with her in the most polite of tones, asking about the books she had read. Major Lloyd-Elliot signaled to the "maître d'," a sergeant charged with keeping the servers in check. The privates shoved more coal into the pot-bellied stoves, but the heat simply escaped in the draftiness of the barn.

At last, the hilarity—and the grumbling—could not be ignored, and Major Lloyd-Elliott threw down his napkin in resignation. "I will have mutiny if I don't do something," he said.

Beside him, Mrs. Brently trilled her silvery laugh, then looked toward the girls. "Are you warm enough?" she asked.

"I am," Helen said, while Kathleen nodded.

"We owe it all to our foxes," Hank said.

Standing, Major Lloyd-Elliott announced, "I believe that we shall have to postpone our musical revue for today. Our performers run the risk of transforming into snow men before our eyes."

His announcement was met with a mixture of jeers and laughter. Most of the soldiers seemed relieved that the bitter weather had finally been acknowledged.

"Yet, if you will give me a moment," the Major said, "I think it would be proper to end this New Year's gathering with a summation of the year past and a look toward the days to come."

He paused until he had the attention of the men. "We have arrived at the end of this year of His Majesty George the Fifth Nineteen-Hundred and Seventeen at a critical hour in this terrible conflict. As we look toward the continuation of this struggle, we must remember that the people of our great nation are behind the efforts of our troops to achieve a righteous end to this war."

Kathleen looked toward Mrs. Brently, who was gazing at the Major with admiring eyes. The officers seated at the long table were also watching him. They were the lucky ones, Kathleen knew, who had lived to see the start of another year.

"But many among us now are tired and worn," the Major said. "And some have let the spirit that sustains our cause flag in their weariness. To those I would say that we must remember that we are fighting for a just and lasting peace, and that our noble belief in our democratic cause must carry each and every one of us to fight on to the end of this conflict. The safety of our homes and the Freedom of all men alike depend upon it."

The men cheered, and Kathleen's eyes filled with unexpected tears. Even in the short time she had been here, so many had died. She looked toward Helen and Hank. Helen touched a handkerchief to her eye.

"We owe—" Major Lloyd-Elliott's voice faltered. "We owe our situation today to the determined fighting and self-sacrifice of our troops. I cannot find the words to express the admiration I feel for the splendid bravery and camaraderie offered by all ranks of our Army in these most trying and difficult times. Men such as you"—he choked up again—"who persevere and struggle against the greatest evil we have yet known stand head and shoulders beyond their peers in this world. Yet we must also honor the memory of those who have gone before us. As the poet Laurence Binyon has written—"

He raised his wine glass, and all the young men at the tables stood and lifted theirs. Kathleen stood as well, her glass in her hand, as Major Lloyd-Elliott continued:

"They shall grow not old, as we that are left grow old:
Age shall not weary them, nor the years condemn.
At the going down of the sun and in the morning,
We will remember them."

Throughout the barn, the toast rang out as a single call. "We will remember them."

"We will remember them," the Major said again.

Kathleen touched her glass against the glasses of the Lieutenant and Captain who sat beside her, memories running through her mind. The men who feared they were blind because their eyelids were swollen shut by poison gas, and the men who came into the hospital with more shrapnel wounds than could be counted or closed up, and those who choked on their own breath because their lungs were burned raw by mustard gas, and those with holes in their backs, foreheads, chests, and shoulders who waited hours for care because their wounds were not "bad" enough, and those whose legs, feet, arms, and hands had been lost to bullets and bombs. And those without faces—oh, the terrible loss of what made them human beings.

She joined in with the others. "We will remember them."

Then, in a rush of love, she held her glass over the center of the table. She wanted so badly to tell Hank and Helen what they meant to her. She wanted to assure them that all would be well, that the war would end, and the world would be right again, and that they would be forever blessed in having come through it together.

As if the same thought had come to them, Hank and Helen held their glasses forward. A tear rolled from Kathleen's eye, and she dashed it from her cheek with a knuckle, while Helen gave a sob-like sigh. Mrs. Brently joined them, holding her glass near theirs.

"We will remember them," Major Lloyd-Elliott intoned for a final time.

The women touched their glasses together and promised, "We will remember them."

The adventure has only begun!
Follow Kathleen, Sean, and Maggie as the *White Winter Trilogy* continues.

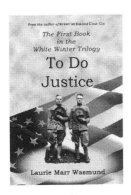

To Do Justice
Three young Irish-Americans encounter the turmoil of a world at war and embark on a journey that will forever change their lives, their country, and the world.

To Love Kindness
In spring, 1918, the Americans mount their greatest battles against the Germans. For Kathleen, Sean, and Maggie, each passing day threatens to take from them the things they love most.

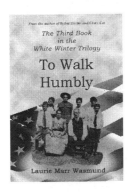

To Walk Humbly
The war is over, yet in Colorado, a more daunting foe has awakened: the Ku Klux Klan. A new battle begins for Kathleen, Sean, and Maggie—one in which the stakes are even higher.

If you enjoyed *To Do Justice,* read *To Love Kindness* and *To Walk Humbly,* the final books of the White Winter Trilogy!

Contact me at **lost.ranch.books@gmail.com**.

Help others enjoy this book, too!

Share it with others!
Pass on your copy to friends and acquaintances.

Recommend it!
Please help other readers find this book by recommending it to your friends, book groups, libraries, and discussion boards. If your book group or library is in the Rocky Mountain region, contact me at **lost.ranch.books@gmail.com** to discuss the possibility of an author visit!

Review it!
Please tell other readers why you liked this book by reviewing it at Amazon or Goodreads. If you write a review, please send me an email at **lost.ranch.books@gmail.com** so that I can thank you with a personal reply.

Visit lostranchbooks.com for more information.

AUTHOR'S NOTE

Years of research have gone into the writing of the books in the White Winter Trilogy. For *To Do Justice,* my main source was my great uncle Henry Halgate Storm's diary, *A Soldier's Diary of World War One.* Both Henry's and my grandfather John Marr's experiences are detailed there. Other sources include: *American Women in World War I: They Also Served* by Lettie Gavin; *"Out Here at the Front": The World War I Letters of Nora Saltonstall,* edited by Judith S. Graham; *The Long Way Home* by David Laskin; and *Gentleman Volunteers* by Arlen J. Hansen. The Colorado Historic Newspaper Collection, which is available online, supplied a snapshot of events and attitudes in Colorado during the war years. I also found most of the information for Liam's story online by researching the incredible life of Ben Salmon. See my website, lostranchbooks.com, for a full list of resources used to write this book and the others in the trilogy.

Countless readers have given me advice and help in writing this book. I wish to thank all of them for their encouragement. I would especially like to thank the following: C.J. Prince, Karen Steinberg, Mark Putch, Jesse Kuiken, Jordana Pilmanis, and Tom Reeves. My sincerest appreciation goes to Linda Burnside and Cynthia Norrgran, who read early drafts of the full manuscript for me. My daughter, Julie Newlin, offered fine editorial advice that helped me to shape the characters.

I must also thank my two advisors on the project: Sue Gaffigan, who helped me to present the Catholic Church and faith in a realistic way, and Nick Cresanta, whose knowledge of military history is extensive and impressive. Their patience and willingness to answer questions were invaluable. The French dialogue in the book derives from my own knowledge of French and from translations found on the web. Any errors in theology, military history, or the language are mine alone.

Once again, my deepest indebtedness is to my husband, Bill, whose generous and constant support allows me to write. Thank you, my love.

Made in the USA
Lexington, KY
13 November 2019